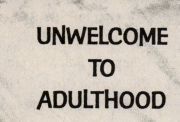

UNWELCOME
TO
ADULTHOOD

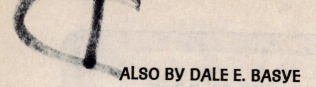

ALSO BY DALE E. BASYE

PRECOCIA

THE SIXTH CIRCLE OF
~ HECK ~

DALE E. BASYE

ILLUSTRATIONS BY **BOB DOB**

A YEARLING BOOK

THIS BOOK IS DEDICATED TO MY SON'S TEACHER, MR. KIM LE BAS. KIM IS THE KIND OF TEACHER WHO TREATS HIS STUDENTS AS FELLOW EXPLORERS, GUIDING THEM GENTLY YET FIRMLY THROUGH THE PRICKLY LABYRINTH OF CHILDHOOD SO THAT THEY MAY EMERGE UPSTANDING, OUTSTANDING, AND WITH THE UNDERSTANDING THAT *EVERY* JOURNEY IS AN EDUCATION. THAT EVERY DAY IS A CRAYON OF A NEW COLOR. A MYSTERIOUS PACKAGE ON THE DOORSTEP STAMPED WITH FOREIGN POSTAGE. AN ICE CREAM TRUCK ON FIRE, CAREENING AROUND THE CORNER. OR SOMETHING LIKE THAT . . .

• • •

Text copyright © 2013 by Dale E. Basye
Cover art and interior illustrations copyright © 2013 by Bob Dob

All rights reserved. Published in the United States by Yearling, an imprint of Random House Children's Books, a division of Random House LLC, New York, a Penguin Random House Company. Originally published in hardcover in the United States by Random House Children's Books, New York, in 2013.

Yearling and the jumping horse design are registered trademarks of Random House LLC.

Visit us on the Web! randomhouse.com/kids

Educators and librarians, for a variety of teaching tools, visit us at RHTeachersLibrarians.com

wherethebadkidsgo.com

The Library of Congress has cataloged the hardcover edition of this work as follows:
Basye, Dale E.
Precocia : the sixth circle of Heck / by Dale E. Basye ; illustrations by Bob Dob. — 1st ed.
p. cm.
Summary: Following sentencing in the court of Judge Judas, eleven-year-old Milton and his older sister Marlo find themselves in Precocia, the circle of Heck for kids that grow up too fast.
ISBN 978-0-375-86835-1 (trade) — ISBN 978-0-375-96835-8 (lib. bdg.) —
ISBN 978-0-375-89885-3 (ebook)
[1. Future life—Fiction. 2. Reformatories—Fiction. 3. Schools—Fiction.
4. Brothers and sisters—Fiction. 5. Humorous stories.] I. Dob, Bob, ill. II. Title.
PZ7.B2938Pre 2013 [Fic]—dc23 2012002296

ISBN 978-0-375-86807-8 (pbk.)

Printed in the United States of America

10 9 8 7 6 5 4 3 2 1

First Yearling Edition 2013

Random House Children's Books supports the First Amendment and celebrates the right to read.

★ CONTENTS ★

FOREWORD

As many believe, there is a place above and a place below. But there are also places in between. Some not quite awfully perfect and others not quite perfectly awful.

One of these places is crowded with children who, in their attempt to grow up way too fast, went down way before their time. It's a place where every day of the week is Freaky Friday; Halloween and Christmas have been permanently canceled because they're just so, you know, immature; and everyone's Salad Days are served with some awful No-Regret-Vinaigrette.

Here children are saddled with bulging backpacks and schedules packed tighter than a tin of fat sardines in spandex and forced to rush frantically toward some kind of finish line. But the only things truly finished once that line is crossed are the exhausted,

1

overburdened runners. Seriously: these kids are all stressed up with no place to grow.

And, really, what's so great about being grown up? When you get right down to it, being fully grown is a big groan. Sure, you get to stay up all night, but if you do, you're exhausted for work the next day and risk losing a regular paycheck that, oddly, you don't get to squander on candy but instead is almost entirely gobbled up by your monthly rent. Playing dress-up becomes something you do for work, every day, first thing in the morning when you're half asleep. Instead of hours of make-believe, it's hours of itchy discomfort and aching feet. Good news, though: there are no more nasty monsters under your bed. Bad news: that's where you keep your tax returns.

The mysterious Powers That Be (and any of its associated or subsidiary enterprises, including—but not limited to—the Powers That Be Evil) have stitched this and countless other subjective realities together into a sprawling quilt of space and time.

Some of these quantum patches may not even seem like places. But they are all around you and go by many names. Some feel like eternity. And some of them actually are eternity, at least for a little while.

But be warned: In this place—where the bad kids who don't think they're kids go—there's no kidding around. Ever.

1 · iN THROUGH THE OUT DOOR

THE ONLY THOUGHT in Milton Fauster's baffled head that seemed to make any sense at all was that nothing around him made any sense at all. He had a sinking feeling that he was floating . . . or a floating feeling that he was sinking . . . and that something terrible had just happened, something that he couldn't prevent but had *tried* to prevent, right up to the very end until it had proved unpreventable.

Milton—eleven years old at the time of his untimely death—was dizzy, nauseous, and utterly confused.

He also happened to be drowning.

Milton found himself thoroughly submerged in thick, shimmering liquid that made him tingle and itch all over. It was as if he were swimming in a gurgling aurora borealis filled with dozens of blurry, vaguely familiar faces . . . living memories that he couldn't remember living.

Milton fought against the flow of flickering liquid, looking for a way out.

Spangled lights fluttered softly overhead. Kicking out in vigorous spasms, Milton shot to the surface of the glimmering pool, a preteen cork gasping for breath. He paddled to the shore against the surging undertow that fought to reclaim him.

Milton coughed up the weird, twinkling water and looked around, dazed and exhausted. He was inside a spacious underground grotto—at least a half mile across—filled with surging, radiant liquid. It trickled from dozens of burrows dug into the rock, feeding the massive, churning pool. The surface danced with fleeting images, squirming, darting, and flickering in mesmerizing ripples and eddies.

The kerchief pouch tied to Milton's belt wriggled and hissed. Milton tried to untie the pouch but noticed that his hands were rigid, with the tip of his right hand pressed firmly into the palm of his left. The gesture was distantly familiar to Milton.

"Sign language for 'again'?" he murmured, his lips numb from the water. "Again, *what*?"

Out through the loosened kerchief popped the fuzzy white head of Lucky, Milton's ironically named pet ferret. Lucky always seemed to be at the epicenter of utter calamity, having died at least twice; for a cat, with its surfeit of lives, this might not be that big of a deal, but for a ferret used to sleeping at least fifteen hours a day, passing back and forth through death's pet door was a hassle. Lucky yawned and glanced around the grotto with an expression of mild surprise before sneezing. Milton chuckled.

"Lucky!" he cried as he scritched the twitchy ferret's head with his odd, stiff hands. "Finally something familiar!" The feeling was slowly coming back to his hands as he smoothed Lucky's nappy fur.

A splash grabbed Milton's attention. A mop of damp blue hair struggled in a Technicolor whirlpool a hundred feet away.

"Marlo!" Milton yelped as he set Lucky down and dove into the pool to save his thirteen-year-old sister from dying a second death.

Marlo was floating on her stomach like a Goth rag doll. Milton hooked his arm around her and towed her to the rocky shore.

Her eyes fluttered like moths drunk on the glow of a porch light. Milton pumped the center of Marlo's chest with his palms. A gush of thick, iridescent water spilled out of her mouth like liquid velvet. He tilted Marlo's head back, lifted her chin, and—after pinching her nose—did pretty much the most repulsive thing a brother could do to his sister: apply mouth-to-mouth resuscitation.

After a few forced breaths, Marlo's eyes shot open. She bolted upright, regaining sudden, furious consciousness.

"*Back off, bro-fish!*" she sputtered, wiping her lips with the back of her hand.

Milton went red.

"I was giving you mouth-to-mouth," he said with unease. "The kiss of life."

Marlo spat onto the black volcanic rock.

"If you give me the kiss of life again, it'll be the fist of *death* for you," she said, clenching her small yet not-to-be-trifled-with fist. "Or double-death . . . *what-ev* . . ." Marlo gazed out across the luminous pool. Slivers of flashing color reflected in her wide, haunted eyes. "Were we able to do it?" she murmured.

"Do what?" Milton replied.

The two Fauster siblings stared dumbfounded at each other.

"I'm not sure," Marlo said with a hollow sadness. "All I remember is that I forgot something. And that some-thing is . . ." She sighed. "*Everything.*"

"I feel the same way," Milton added. "Like I showed up to school and forgot to study for a big test."

"Me too," Marlo replied. "Only for me it's like I stole a Victorian corset dress from a thrift shop and forgot to nab the matching black ankle boots."

"Yeah, just like that . . . ," Milton said with a roll of his eyes. He rubbed his stiff hands. "When I came out of this weird pool, my hands were frozen like *this*," he said, pressing his right hand into his left palm. "The sign for—"

"Again."

"How do *you* know sign language?" Milton asked.

"Aubrey Fitzmallow and I learned some signs to help us communicate when we'd 'borrow' stuff indefinitely from department stores," Marlo explained. "But most of the time security thought we were flashing gang signs and kicked us out anyway."

Lucky's twitching pink nose peeked out of the sopping-wet kerchief, taking in the scent of his master's sister, an odor that was reassuringly familiar yet often smelled like trouble.

"Lucky!" Marlo yelped as she reached over to scratch Lucky's magic spot at the back of his neck. "Lucky *fou fou.*"

"Fou fou?" Milton asked as he lay down, exhausted.

"*Fou* is French for 'crazy,'" Marlo replied. Lucky arched up and rubbed his head against Marlo's hand to attain the perfect scratch.

"Since when do you know *French*?"

Marlo shrugged.

"*Je ne sais pas.* I guess there are things about me you don't know that even *I* don't know."

Milton sighed. "The hand sign must mean something. . . ."

"Like how we need to do something *again*?" Marlo said next to him.

"Yeah," Milton muttered. "Like we failed at something but have to give it another try. Whatever 'it' is."

"It's pretty," Marlo said, staring up at the roof of the

subterranean grotto. The rocky ceiling was covered in a gently glowing phosphorescent moss. The cool green light mingled with the varicolored glimmer thrown onto the ceiling by the swirling pool. "It's like a laser light show, only without all the hippy-dippy music," Marlo added. "Maybe we're not in Heck anymore."

"Then where *are* we?"

"Someplace else. *Anyplace* else. What does it matter?" Marlo sighed. "It's so peaceful. I could spend the rest of my afterlife here. I *never* want to leave. . . ."

Suddenly, the serene quietude was shattered by a squealing scrape and a colossal splash. The pool was ruffled by something, a something the size of a killer whale, swimming fast just beneath the surface. Milton noticed an odd white light speeding toward them.

"I'm out of here," Marlo said, rising quickly to her booted feet.

The beam of light blinked off and on as three barbed tentacles lashed out of the pool. Milton stepped back, feeling something squish underneath his foot. A fat greenish white worm was twitching at the end of a long spiral groove etched into the rock floor.

"*Eww,*" Marlo said, glaring at Milton's shoulder. "You've got a maggoty thing on you." A stalk of corkscrew-shaped asparagus with a tiny mouth at one end and feathery tendrils at the other crawled up Milton's arm.

"No eating my brother just 'cause he's dead," Marlo said before swatting it away.

A horrific yowl exploded from one of the burrows, making the downy hair on Milton's arms go stiff and bristly. Light glimmered from the mouth of the tunnel, growing brighter and brighter, until out shot a twenty-foot-long corkscrew squid with a great, blinking floodlight for an eye, pocked skin like a cheese grater, and flailing sawtooth tentacles waving behind it.

If Milton's pants hadn't been wet already, they surely would be now. He backed away from the pool and scooped up Lucky and his kerchief.

Marlo noticed hundreds of the tiny glowworms writhing on the ground, each of them scratching spirals into the rock with their rough, metallic skin.

"I think mommy maggot is back home from wriggling her errands," Marlo said, "and doesn't like the babysitters that sat on her babies. . . . *C'mon.*"

Milton and Marlo trotted across the glittering gravel floor.

"We got *in* here somehow . . . so there must be a way out," Milton said.

Marlo dared a quick, fearful peek at the glimmering kaleidoscopic pond. Three of the squid creatures were slicing through the water, only moments from reaching the shore nearest the Fausters. The farther they strayed from the glowing pool, the darker it became.

"What if that *curieux* pool is how we got in here?" Marlo asked in the ever-dimming light.

"There's got to be another way," Milton replied, feeling his way across the rock wall. "And stop using French. It's unnerving."

"*Bien,*" Marlo murmured. "Hey . . . over there. There's a crack in the ceiling."

Above a cascade of luminous limestone that resembled a petrified waterfall was a wide crack. Weak yellow-orange light throbbed through. Beneath the crack were footprints, a dusty dance of sneakers and Goth boots.

"We were here before," Milton whispered.

"At least our shoes were," Marlo said.

A wet, furious yowl exploded throughout the grotto. The teeth-gritting sound of grinding, squealing stone and frantic splashing soon followed.

"Going up," Milton muttered as he grasped a lump of limestone and scaled the ceiling.

"*Next floor* . . . hopefully something better than being ripped apart by angry squids," Marlo grunted as she clambered up the wall behind her brother.

2 · CLIMB DOESN'T PAY

THE CLEFT IN the rock was too smooth to grab on to, yet narrow enough that Milton and Marlo could wedge themselves through and—using their backs and feet to press against the vertical walls—climb up to the open fissure forty feet above.

Milton's back ached and sweat poured down his forehead, stinging his eyes. One of the creatures bellowed, its roar so thick with fury that Milton and Marlo could feel it whooshing past them in the crevice. Its breath smelled strangely pleasant, like dust and clocks and people.

"Hey, we're . . . kind of like . . . a wedgie," Marlo huffed, her face shiny with sweat, as she scrabbled up the rock face. "You know: halfway up . . . the crack."

Below, the headlamp eye of a corkscrew squid blinked angrily at the two Fausters.

"What do you remember last?" Milton grunted, trying to take his mind off the clicking of the creature's eyelids.

"I remember us . . . on the way to Precocia. We were . . . in the back of a stagecoach. It stopped. And . . . and I think . . . we bolted."

"Yeah," Milton puffed as he worked his way closer to the top, like a human inchworm with broken glasses. "That's what I . . . remember, too."

A tentacle—barbed and dangerous—wriggled up through the rock cleft.

"Hurry!" Milton yelped, scuttling up the crack as the creature's limb strained upward, just out of reach.

After frenzied yards of grunting heaves and stretches, Milton cleared the crack, reaching down to grab Marlo's wrist and hoist her up to the floor of a shallow cave. They rolled onto their backs, panting with exhaustion. A greasy brown-orange light spilled in from the mouth of the small rock hollow. They could hear the faint murmur of voices. Marlo put her finger to her lips and grabbed Milton by the hand. They peered cautiously out of the cave. Milton's stomach dropped.

Several hundred feet outside the small cave was a motley throng of creatures. There were nappy, molelike demons with massive claws and flashlights duct-taped around their heads; squat, tortoise demons with hardened humps on their backs and owlish, sparsely feathered heads; and—literally swarming about—salami-shaped demons with delicate blade-shaped wings and tiny, grotesquely human faces.

"We're still stuck in Heck . . . ," Milton lamented.

"Yeah, in some new scarylarious place," Marlo whispered.

A tanned man with a clipped gray beard, dressed in a tight padded doublet, tights, and boots paced just thirty feet away.

"Still no sign of the fountain?" the man grumbled with a Spanish accent.

"No, Mr. Ponce de León." A mole demon shook his head, wincing in the light.

"*Señor,*" the man corrected.

"Yes, sir, I know you're senior to me, sir, but—"

"Just keep looking!" Señor Ponce de León spat. "And don't forget those buckets of water and *repugnante* worms for Dr. Skinner."

"Dr. *who?*" Milton said from the mouth of the cave. Marlo covered her brother's mouth with her hand.

A team of hefty creatures with mismatched eyes and coiling tusks heaved a cart stacked with massive fragments of stone.

"How are we supposed to get all of these back to Precocia?" one of the tortoise demons complained, pointing to a pile of rubble and blinking his large round owl eyes.

"Heckifino," replied his moleish cohort.

"Look, if you don't know, just say so. You don't have to be rude."

"No . . . the beasts with the carts. *Heckifinos*. When this team unloads the broken disks, they'll come back for this junk."

The disjointed, spindly-legged creatures—the Heckifinos—were familiar to Milton and Marlo. Milton had seen Bea "Elsa" Bubb—Heck's malevolent, thoroughly detestable Principal of Darkness—riding one when he had escaped from Blimpo, and later, after Milton and Marlo had switched bodies in h-e-double-hockey-sticks, the siblings had been strapped to the back of the beast. A Heckifino raised its feathery turkey tail and discharged a fresh mound of steaming, speckled dung. The smell—a hot tang of methane and pepper—made Milton sneeze. One of the tortoise demons swiveled his owl head.

"There! By the cave!" the demon screeched.

Marlo seized Milton by the hand.

"Let's skedaddle," Marlo said. She tugged Milton out of the cave. They raced away from the startled demons through the barren landscape of volcanic rock and sparkling black dust.

"This is, like, the closest we've come to freedom . . . in a long time," Marlo said as they ran along the edge of a massive outcropping of rock. "Maybe we're off the grid here, wherever 'here' is. . . ."

A tall, scabby demon popped out from behind a nearby boulder.

"Here they are!" the demon shouted, his festering

skin peeling off his raw red body like black bark. "Asmodeus! I've found them!"

Milton and Marlo skidded to a stop, birthing a thick cloud of dark brown dust.

The demon was joined by a slender blue creature holding a rope net.

"Nice work, Jehu!" the demon said as a stale wind ruffled his fringe of indigo feathers. "We'll teach those two to hop out of our stagecoach!"

Milton's heart was beating so hard that it rattled his rib cage like an angry zoo animal.

"We've got to make our way across that desert," Marlo panted, pointing out to miles and miles of dusty nothing in the distance. "Run as fast as we can."

"No," Milton said, swallowing hard. "This way. The field with all the boulders."

"Why?"

"It's like the asteroid scene in *The Empire Strikes Back,* where the Millennium Falcon eludes capture by—"

"Whatever, Nerdy McNerdmonson," Marlo replied. "It's all geek to me. Let's do it."

Milton ran for all he was worth into the field of boulders, with his sister close behind. The long-legged demons began to close the gap.

"They're . . . too . . . fast," Marlo panted. "I think I'm gonna . . . toss my Girl Scout cookies."

Asmodeus and Jehu hurtled toward Milton and Marlo with their net spread between them.

"Zigzag," Milton gasped. "When I say—"

"We've got them!" Asmodeus yelled as he and Jehu held the net high over their heads.

"Now!" Milton yelled. He and his sister broke apart, swerving around either side of a large boulder. A loud thud boomed behind them. Marlo glanced over her shoulder. Asmodeus and Jehu lay groaning on the ground.

"If they meant bruises, then, yeah, they definitely 'got them,'" Marlo snickered.

The slender demons quickly sprang to their scaly feet.

The stitch in Milton's side felt like a bleeding gash.

"We can't . . . do this . . . forever," he wheezed. "They're too fast."

Marlo saw, beyond the field of boulders in the distance, the demons' stagecoach. Two black Night Mares snorted and pawed the ground in agitation.

"Their stagecoach!" Marlo yelped. "C'mon! If we run faster than we've ever run, we can take it!"

Asmodeus and Jehu barreled across the tundra toward them.

"The only thing *you* two are going to take," the raw, red, decomposing demon hissed as he and his partner tossed their net into the air, "is time to heal!"

The rope net spilled across Milton and Marlo just as they tried to sprint away. They fell to the ground in a jumble of rope, limbs, dust, and dashed hopes.

3 · INSPECT THE
UNEXPECTED

BEA "ELSA" BUBB, Heck's reigning Principal of Darkness, knew perhaps better than anyone that eternity is a very long time. And one of the lingering side effects of eternity is a nagging feeling that you've seen it all before. Yet here in Limbo—where every day is just like the last because it is indeed the same day, only recycled— Principal Bubb was seeing things that she never before thought possible.

Demon guards clutched not freshly sharpened pitchsporks poised to tenderize newly dead bottoms, but brooms. *And mops.* Bea "Elsa" Bubb was so furious that an overproduction of stomach bile threatened to digest her loathsome body whole. *Limbo was actually being cleaned.* And Principal Bubb—instead of flaying her subjects and screaming, "Repent! Repent!" in the classic, old-school way—was telling her staff, "Repaint! Repaint!"

Why was the great down under being made over? Because of the new, acting Prince of Darkness—the archangel Michael, of all creatures. Satan and the archangel had switched roles, like foreign exchange students studying abroad. One previously immaculate angel plummeted all the way down to h-e-double-hockey-sticks, while the afterlife's most notorious fallen angel suddenly took the invisible escalator up, if not to the very top, then to a suite so high that it would give a mountain goat a nosebleed.

All because of two frustrating children: Milton Fauster—a career goody-goody, which down here in the underworld makes him a notorious baddy-baddy—and his sassy, brassy, far-from-classy sister. Their combined testimony at the Trial of the Millennium was the nail in the coffin.

Satan had been accused of attempting to bring about the apocalypse through television, sending all of humanity to a miserably dull ball of rock in the Sirius Lelayme system so that he could sell the very Earth beneath them to an extraterrestrial race. While not completely guilty, he was found to be an accessory to the crime nonetheless. The archangel Michael, meanwhile, turned out to be the *real* mastermind behind the sinister surreal-estate scheme. The verdict had not only doused Principal Bubb's burning hopes of assuming Satan's vacated throne but also had turned the afterlife into some kind of perplexing pineapple upside-down cake.

As her demon hordes punished the walls with soap and elbow grease, the principal snapped her talons at a leathery pink demon with tiny ram horns, fledgling bat wings, and a budding mace tail.

"Cato," Principal Bubb called out. "I have some bidding I need done."

The creature hobbled toward her, his face almost naked in his "humanness" and resembling a sort of bearded, blue-eyed baby. Principal Bubb, despite having laid eyes on most every sort of forsaken creature conceived by devolution's twisted sense of humor, was always unsettled by guards undergoing the awkward demonization process.

"Cato, I need you to interrupt me—"

"Now, ma'am?"

"*No, let me finish.* When Michael is here for, say, a half hour—"

"A half hour."

"I want you to interrupt us . . . say that the toilets aren't backed up enough and you need my assistance, immediately. Okay?"

Cato bowed with a weak flap of his new wings.

"Yes, ma'am," he replied in an adenoidal squeak.

The principal sighed. "What a mess," she moaned.

"What is, ma'am?"

"*This,*" the principal replied with grim fatality as she

waved her claws in the air. *"Everything.* Satan up there and Michael down here, getting in our business."

"Maybe Mr. Satan, sir, will appeal Judge Judas's verdict," Cato offered, his bearded baby face wide with misguided hope.

"Satan's boneheaded lawyer already tried," Principal Bubb replied, "but the idea of an appeal didn't appeal to Judge Judas. I could pull a few chains and *force* a second trial, though. But Judas would only call the same witnesses, resulting in the same terrible verdict."

Principal Bubb glanced down at her Pseiko-Path watch: 13:13. The exact same time it always was in Limbo. She stormed toward the Gates of Heck.

Her hooves clacked to a halt in front of an ornate iron gate decorated with sugared spikes, candied skulls, and barbed licorice. With a great gush of steam, the gates creaked open. Out from the whorls of mist stepped the archangel Michael and his entourage: a small flock of assorted once-heavenly beings and those too lowly to even lift their eyes skyward.

Bea "Elsa" Bubb offered her claw in greeting. Michael rested his unnervingly clear blue eyes upon them for a fitful moment before arching his perfect brow to the man on his right.

The man—olive skinned and dressed in a glaringly white Nehru jacket—nodded and gave the principal's claw a few fleeting shakes instead.

"Bless you, Malik," Michael said.

Malik gave another quick, deferent nod, his dark eyes glittering beneath his black bangs. The principal noticed the faint ruffle of wings from behind the man's jacket.

Angel, Bea "Elsa" Bubb thought with contempt. *Of course. It's like an aviary down here now.*

Behind them, beneath the ABANDON ALL HOPE, YE WHO ENTER HERE (AS WELL AS ALL CAMERAS AND ELECTRONIC RECORDING DEVICES) sign, a group of lizards in gold lamé suits crawled over broken toy pianos, horns, and guitars.

"If you've lived a life so bad, that you drove your parents and teachers mad," sang one lizard into a tiny microphone against a jazzy beat.

Principal Bubb quickly swiped her foreclaw in front of her throat, silencing the band.

"I don't haveth much time," Michael said in his cool-as-marble voice. "I must tour Purgatory-While-U-Wait this afternoon, and that will taketh me forever."

"Yes, Mr. Michael," Bea "Elsa" Bubb replied. "Or do you prefer Prince of Darkness?"

"I believe Michael would prefer that we get along with the tour," Malik interjected.

"Of course," Principal Bubb replied through clenched fangs, eggplant-colored splotches of rage seeping through her industrial-strength mortuary-grade foundation. "Come with me . . . *sir.*"

★　★　★

Bea "Elsa" Bubb led the group of angels and demons through Heck's Foul Playground, stepping over the warped hula hoops, two-wheeled tricycles, and deflated basketballs scattered across the ammonia-reeking floor. Principal Bubb examined Michael from the corners of her goatish eyes. Angels, in general, gave Bea "Elsa" Bubb the willies. But Michael was *creepy* perfect, as if chiseled from the finest marble. His gleaming white teeth had never known gingivitis or unsightly tartar buildup. Michael's perfection was almost grotesque, like someone at a Hollywood gym.

"That will haveth to go," Michael said to Malik, waving his hand at a demotivational flyer tacked to the wall: THINK TODAY WILL BE YOUR LUCKY DAY? THINK AGAIN: DUE TO CIRCUMSTANCES BEYOND YOUR CONTROL, YOUR LUCKY DAY HAS BEEN INDEFINITELY POSTPONED.

Malik nodded and tore the flyer down in one swift, efficient stroke.

"Michael, sir," the principal said. "May I ask—"

"Limbo needeth not be a sad place with children sitting in stuffy rooms wasting time watching broken clocks," the archangel said as he strode past clumps of children wincing at his painful angel light.

"Well, actually, sir, that's rather the point," Principal Bubb replied. "See, historically, Limbo is an uncertain, unendurable period of—"

"Sir, what if we put a suggestion box right here?" Malik interjected as the entourage passed the KinderScare:

Where Little Kids Get Big Nightmares facility for the younger unfortunates condemned to Limbo.

"A suggestion box?" Principal Bubb spat, her horrified expression causing a little girl being put down for a nap to scream in her gingerbread coffin. "Is this a joke? You mean, like a booby trap to weed out the insolent?"

"A most excellent idea, Malik!" Michael replied, radiating a blaze of light as some kind of reward. "Alloweth the children to share in the architecture of their rehabilitation!"

"Really, Michael," the principal said. "Suggestions are simply complaints with whipped cream and chocolate jimmies on top."

Michael stopped abruptly in the howlway, his majestic white wings spreading out behind him. "Good principal—"

"You needn't be insulting—"

"Hereth in the underworld, I have thusly discovered that there are many, many screws badly in need of tightening. . . ."

The group shuffled along the howlway toward Limbo's dreary Cafeterium. Michael and Malik whispered to each other.

"Malik haveth another divine suggestion," Michael said. "About updating Heck's image."

The Principal of Darkness glared from beneath her scraggly centipede of an eyebrow.

"*Update its image?* Now look—"

"Down here, just like up *there,* appearances are everything," Malik said, his black eyes peering intently from beneath his dark, sugar bowl haircut. "And if Heck exuded an air of refinement and civility, then its under-age denizens would, more than likely, follow suit. And as the 'face' of Heck, Principal Bubb—"

Malik's eyes skittered across Principal Bubb's features like a mosquito on a stagnant pond.

"Hmm . . . ," Malik mumbled, "maybe there's a way to frame your face where your hair isn't necessarily involved. Or perhaps congeniality lessons—"

"I DON'T NEED CONGENIALITY LESSONS!" the she-demon shrieked, sparks shooting out of her snout, black flecks of bile spraying out of her maw.

Michael's blue eyes blazed like ice-cold fire. He turned, a sweep of pristine robes and vestments, and strutted back toward the gates.

"With all due appearances of respect, Heck is a place of punishment," the principal called out as she clacked behind Michael in his beatific wake. "*A deterrent.* If we make it an Equal Opportunity Destroyer, with every snot-nosed, still-warm tyke who passes through those gates having some kind of say in their eternal retribution, it misses the whole point of—"

"I'm not suggesting we forgoeth punishment," Michael said, his feathers visibly ruffled. "Just that we punish heretofore with more *finesse.*" He stopped suddenly, causing the less graceful members of his troupe to collide into one another like bumbling bumper cars.

"Though the afterlife is infinite, resources sadly areth not," Michael lectured, his body stiff with righteousness. "Keeping the accursed submerged in boiling filth, for instance, is fine in the short-term, but the energy expenditure required to thusly sustain that punishment alone for all eternity is significant. Even resorting to merely lukewarm filth would thus result in an energy savings of nearly—"

Just then, the newly demonic Cato came rushing down the howlway.

"P-Principal, ma'am," he sputtered, his human face as raw as a freshly scraped knee. "I came to spontaneously interrupt you, just like you asked. To tell you the toilets aren't backed up enough . . . or something . . . I forget what exactly you told me to say, exactly."

Bea "Elsa" Bubb sighed, collapsing inside like a wet taco.

Michael shook his head in disgust, each strand of his lustrous, golden-brown hair falling back into perfect alignment after having taken flight.

"We musteth be going as well," the archangel said as he stormed across the Foul Playground.

A gush of brilliant white steam settled into the shape of an elevator, preparing to ferry Michael and his entourage away.

"Heck hath become flabby about the midsection," Michael continued, his piercing blue eyes darting, almost imperceptibly, to the middle of Principal Bubb's body, where a waist may well have been buried. "I haveth come in the nick of time to sweep away what clearly does not serve the underaged underworld and institute what—and *who*—does. I shalt be in touch with ye when ye are less . . . *touchy*."

The elevator of steam gently rose from the ground.

Principal Bubb caught a glimpse of Malik through the whorls of luminous fog. The angel's face was smudgy and indistinct—like a charcoal drawing of a face left out in the rain—but Malik's intentions were all too clear: he wanted Principal Bubb's job.

"That sandal-licking suck-up," the principal muttered between clenched fangs. "What a display of holier-than-thou crackpottery! If it weren't for that twerp Milton Fauster and his damaging testimony . . ." She flexed her claws as if strangling an invisible foe. "If only there was some way he could just . . . *disappear*," Principal Bubb muttered, a quiet fire burning behind her snot-green goat eyes.

"Maybe I can help, ma'am," Cato squeaked. Startled, the principal nearly leapt out of her loathsome skin.

"Do I need to tie a bell around your neck?" she gasped.

"Why, ma'am?"

"So I don't wring it . . . What do you want?"

"What *you* want, ma'am," the leathery pink demon said with a wag of his mace tail. "For things to be as they were. This might help. . . ."

Cato handed Principal Bubb a business card. It was black and round with a large hole in the middle.

"What's this?"

Cato shrugged, causing his tiny bat wings to flop like wilted lettuce.

"I have friends in low places," he said with a squeak.

"I find that hard to believe," the principal murmured as she noticed something embossed on the pitch-black ring.

"That I know people in low places, ma'am?" Cato asked.

"No, that you have friends."

Principal Bubb shifted the card in the blaze of a nearby torch. She could make out a phone number.

(777) REVENGE

Hmm . . . , Principal Bubb thought, picking her fangs with the tip of her talon. *Instead of just waiting for the other sandal to drop and having my job taken away from me by an ambitious angel, perhaps I can turn this whole thing around.*

4 · STUCK IN THE RIDDLE

THE SNARLING BLACK demon horse nipped the neck of the festering filly bridled next to it as the two steeds galloped madly across the dusty flatlands.

"Jehu," the blue demon stagecoach driver scolded, smoothing back his purple Mohawk of feathers. "Your haste is making Cocoa Puff nervous."

"Haste?" Jehu replied with supreme irritation, his raw red skin flushing purple as he held tight the reins. "Who's got time for haste, Asmodeus?"

Milton and Marlo stewed in the back of the gleaming black coach, their wrists bound tight with rope.

"I don't know what's worse," Marlo grumbled. "Bruised, battered, and on our way to Precocia, or listening to Big Red and the Blue Bird of Testiness go at it the whole way."

The carriage slowed, ultimately stopping with a

smattering of confused hoof clops, whinnies, and the squeak of wooden wheels.

Milton rubbed the grime off the window with his forehead and peered through the smeary streak.

Outside the stagecoach was a huge stone Egyptian sphinx, like the Great Sphinx of Giza, only this one was wearing a tie and reading glasses. Asmodeus leapt off the driver's box and yanked open the carriage door. He grabbed Milton by the collar.

"Your stop, sir," he said, his angry flesh throbbing beneath his peeling, barklike skin. Asmodeus threw Milton to the ground. Marlo scooted away along the wooden bench, her boots raised like hard leather fists.

"Just *try* it, Scabby McEyesore," she seethed.

Asmodeus laughed, a wet, explosive sound like an old car backfiring at the bottom of a swamp.

"I know I shouldn't play with the sphinx's food, but you've got so much spirit!"

Jehu threw open the door behind Marlo. She tumbled out onto the gritty ground.

"I'm sure it wouldn't mind us tenderizing its meal first, though," the plumed demon cackled as he hoisted Marlo to her feet.

"Hands off, Smurfin' Bird," she snarled as the big blue demon pitched her forward next to Milton.

The two stared at the imposing stone statue, featuring the face of a man, the body of a lion, and the wings of a bird.

"This is an Egypt thing, right?" Marlo asked her brother. "Like Cleopatra? King Tutti-Frutti . . ."

"Tut*ankhamen*," Milton corrected.

The demons shoved Milton and Marlo toward the gaping stone mouth of the sphinx. They stepped over the statue's limestone incisors and onto its smooth, sanded tongue.

"The sphinx is both a benevolent guardian and merciless monster, depending . . . ," Asmodeus said as the stale wind ruffled his purple Mohawk.

"Depending on what?" Milton asked, pushing his broken glasses up the bridge of his nose.

"Depending on whether you answer its riddle," Jehu interjected.

"What if we *don't* answer its dumb riddle?" Marlo asked.

"Then you've just given the sphinx something to chew on," Asmodeus replied.

"Yes, *you*," Jehu added.

Two round portals opened at the back of the statue's throat. The heavy doors scraped against the limestone.

"Ladies first," Asmodeus cackled as he pushed Milton into the nearest portal.

"Actually, I'm a—" Milton said as he tumbled inside the statue. The door slid closed.

"I'll just wait till he's through, then," Marlo said, sitting down on one of the statue's sculpted molars.

"No need," said Jehu, the peeling, unappealing demon, grabbing Marlo by the scruff of the neck. "To the sphinx, children are like dessert: *there's always room for more. . . .*"

Jehu tossed Marlo inside the other portal and the stone door closed behind her.

Milton was trapped inside the dark, cramped compartment. It reminded him of when Marlo had put him through "astronaut training" one summer when he was four, basically an excuse to lock him in her "flight simulator" in the laundry room and set it on air fluff for fifteen minutes.

Another door slid open on the far side of the stale chamber. Brilliant white light poured out. Milton crawled through the opening, creeping toward the light on all fours.

Marlo hugged her knees in the narrow space, rocking back and forth in the dark. A door opened and white light spilled into the chamber. Marlo crawled toward it.

Milton scrabbled down the tunnel on all fours. The walls were smeared with finger paintings: abstract streaks and swirls of bright expressive colors, clotting together into murky confusion. Farther along the shaft were crude, childlike crayon drawings of mutant animals, smiling families of irregular proportion, and unicorns pooping bouquets of hearts. With each yard or so, the drawings became more refined and realistic, with the content maturing: glamorous princesses and fashion models, ninjas and heavily muscled warriors, wizards, astronauts, superheroes, and rock stars. The tunnel grew taller, allowing Milton to at first shuffle along like a monkey, then eventually becoming high enough for him to walk normally.

What possible riddle could this be? Milton thought as the stone portal slid closed behind him, echoing through the tunnel with all the cheerfulness of a terminal diagnosis.

Marlo stretched, finally able to walk upright.

"Now I know why cavemen evolved—it's murder on your back," she grumbled as she walked along the stone corridor. The tunnel was covered with hundreds of photographs: boys and girls awkwardly holding hands, teens throwing their graduation caps high into the air with looks of grinning triumph, young people biking past European landmarks, twentysomethings stuffed in business suits sitting in front of computers, young, nervous couples at the altar, and exhausted mothers cradling their newborns with looks of intense pride and quiet terror smeared across their bleary faces.

*It's like I'm walking through someone's photo album . . .
through* everyone's *photo album,* Marlo thought as she
took stock of all the faces, all the cultures, all the races.

The tunnel grew slowly steeper as the people in the
photos grew older. Middle-aged men and women holding grandchildren slowly evolved into gray-haired couples driving across the country in Winnebagos.

Even the photographs seemed to get older: becoming yellow, faded, and turned up at the corners. The
incline made it harder and harder for Marlo to walk.
The ground became uneven and the roof of the tunnel
lower until she strained to take a single step forward.

"What am I supposed to do?" Marlo shouted in
frustration.

Milton noticed a wooden cane lying on the floor of the
cramped, steep, uneven shaft. With a grunt, he hobbled forward, using the cane to gain traction and balance. The ceiling gradually lowered, forcing Milton
to stoop. The photographs covering the walls became
faded and somber: senior citizens waiting in doctor's
offices, sterile convalescent hospitals, a procession of
funerals . . . The images grew blurry and dim until
the only things they conveyed with any clarity were
feelings of profound loss and loneliness. Finally, after
a dozen yards, the tunnel became pitch-black. Milton
panted in the dark, exhausted from hobbling uphill.

Suddenly, another brilliant white light appeared ahead. Silhouettes came into view, beckoning Milton forward.

"Nanna Fauster?" Marlo exclaimed as she tottered unsteadily on her cane. "Crazy Uncle Claudius?" She lurched forward into the light, wrapping her arms around what she thought was her favorite uncle.

The man was cold and rigid in her arms.

"Uncle?" Marlo cried, stepping back and realizing that her supposed relatives were merely just robotic cutouts bathed in a blinding klieg light. Marlo walked toward the light, noticing another small doorway.

"Milton?" she called out.

"I'm in here," Milton replied. "But be—"

Marlo fell through the doorway, tumbling down a steep shaft for a dozen yards before slamming headfirst into her brother.

"*Careful,*" Milton groaned, rubbing his head.

The two Fausters were in a small, dimly lit compartment sitting on top of what appeared to be bones. In front of them was a door with a question mark painted on it in red.

"I think we're supposed to answer the riddle," Milton said, "but I have no idea—"

"Oh, *man,*" Marlo complained, rubbing the goose egg hatching on her head. Immediately, the door in front of them slid open, with the stone floor tilting suddenly forward, flinging them to the ground.

The exit portal beneath the statue's tail slid shut.

"Guess that was its sphinxter," Marlo grumbled as she stood up. "How did we get out? It didn't even give us a riddle to answer."

"*Man*," Milton said as he rose from the sandy ground. "That was the answer. You know: that old riddle of 'what has four legs in the morning, two legs in the afternoon, and three legs in the evening?' "

"I always thought the answer to that dumb riddle was 'a Cootie game,' because you start out with all of the legs, then lose some, then always find one hiding under the couch. Anyway, the answer should be *person*, not"—Marlo turned and gaped at the Gates of Precocia—"*man*."

The gate was a towering thirteen-foot-tall digital touch screen, displaying the crisp image of a sleek wrought-platinum entrance, French in style with a pair of large Egyptian Eyes of Horus handles that—to Milton—seemed exhausted, with dark purple amethyst-encrusted circles under each. Tiny analog pocket watches, their hands spinning wildly, and little hourglasses whose sand was sifting swiftly were festooned upon the slender, meticulously buffed platinum bars. The gate's elegant look was, however, marred by hundreds of Post-its stuck fast to most every available surface, flapping in the wind despite being nothing more than digital renderings. Each note listed some unenviable task (*Take out garbage, Do laundry, Have family pet put to sleep*), meeting (*Job review with boss, Marriage counseling, IRS audit*), or obligation (*Get root canal, Night school, Take out second mortgage to somehow pay for ungrateful child's college tuition*).

Marlo examined the gate's touch-screen surface. "Well, since we can't crawl back out through the sphinx's butt, we might as well go inside. This thing is like a giant iSlab, so maybe we just do *this*. . . ."

Marlo pressed her hands against the digital handles and swiped the virtual gate open with a swift flick of her arms. After a couple of seconds, the screen vibrated and clicked before breaking in two and opening with a steady, electric hum.

"Whoa," Milton and Marlo murmured together. Beyond the gates was a path winding through a subdivision of empty, dreary model homes and leading to a prodigious, ninety-nine-story-tall upside-down pyramid. The grim, physics-defying building was an ugly wedge of concrete and steel that cast a dark, menacing shadow over the abandoned neighborhood.

How can something be so tall without a proper foundation? Milton thought as he gaped at the building, which looked like a humongous stake driven brutally into the ground. *It shouldn't be able to stand at all. . . .*

"Looks like King Tutti-Frutti drew his blueprint while standing on his head," Marlo said.

"It's not King . . . *never mind.*"

As Milton passed through the gates, he saw that they were notched at the edges like a growth chart. He and Marlo walked by an electric sign declaring WELCOME TO ADULTHOOD in glaring-red, unwelcoming letters.

Milton looked up at the sky. It was a smudge of deep orange and brown, like a large, upturned plate of egg yolks and cigar butts.

Smog, Milton thought. *As if the skies over Los Angeles and Mexico City had a big, fat, toxic smog baby.*

The capsized pyramid was a skyscraper that *literally* scraped the sky: jagged, crownlike spires adorning the roof scraped raw red gashes in the smog.

The gate shut behind them, its digital surface displaying a large padlock icon.

"Guess that's that," Marlo said as she walked down the path. "We're committed."

The Fausters walked toward Precocia, swallowed up by the building's shadow. In the distance, Milton could see a cul-de-sac past a shaky rope bridge. The dead end was barricaded with a gate of cheerful, primary-colored bars wrapped tight with chains and a padlock.

"Does that say—" Milton said, rubbing the grit from his glasses with his thumb.

" 'Welcome to Childhood,' " Marlo finished, reading the merry sign with her keen shoplifter's eyes. The colorful letters were composed in glowing Lite-Brite pegs.

Milton and Marlo stepped up to the immense and

improbable inverted pyramid, the base of which was about the size of a small garage.

"This place is just *asking* to be toppled," Marlo said as she pressed a button next to a plain, brushed metal door. The door opened with a ding, revealing a drab, beige-carpeted elevator. Marlo stared at the controls—eighty-one buttons, beginning at eighteen and ending at ninety-nine. There was also an electronic card-swipe reader on the side.

"Weirdness," she said, stepping up to the panel. "Well, I guess I'll just—"

Milton wedged himself in front of his sister. "Do not press all of the buttons," he ordered.

Marlo sighed. "I liked it back in the grotto where I had secrets," she said. "Fine. *You choose the stupid button.* Let me guess, See-No-Evil Knievel, you'll pick . . ."

"The first button," Milton said, jabbing the eighteen.

Suddenly, the elevator lurched upward, scary fast. Milton and Marlo collapsed to the floor. Milton's stomach defected from his torso, seeking asylum in his legs.

"Uh-oh!" Marlo said, barely able to open her mouth under the tremendous g-force of acceleration. "Looks like we're *growing* up!"

5 · THE PRICE
OF ADMISSIONS

MILTON AND MARLO tumbled out of the elevator and onto a steel-gray carpet. They were hoisted up by their under-aged underarms and set against the wall. A teenaged boy and girl, silent and gently swaying like drooling zombies after a brain buffet, gaped mutely at the Fausters. The boy was skinny and pale, with thick curly black hair and dark fuzz on his upper lip. The girl had coffee-colored skin and honey-gold hair. She would have been pretty if it weren't for the pimples on her forehead and her slack fish-out-of-water expression.

Marlo groaned and messed up her hair, which had gotten accidentally neatened in the ascent.

"Not much for conversation, are you?" she said. The teenagers were wearing matching mustard-colored suits with tight trousers and huge shoulder pads. Marlo sighed. *"Please* don't have those be our new uniforms," she muttered. "A girl can only take so much."

Marlo surveyed the eighteenth floor of Precocia with her tired, dark-violet eyes. It was a drab, noisy office building by the looks of it, with boardrooms and rows of workstations in the distance. Everything had a ghoulish, greenish cast to it due to the sickly fluorescent lights clustered in flickering clots on the low ceiling in between broken air ducts and patches of dark mold.

A long vehicle rattled toward them down the curving hallway. It was like a motorized scooter merged with a stretched-out, open-aired trolley. Standing at the head of the vehicle, two of her four arms wrapped around the handlebars, was a large blue woman with a riot of thick black hair flowing behind her.

"Hello, Junior Executives!" the woman called out with an Indian accent, her long red tongue lolling out of her mouth.

Milton's eyes were drawn to the woman's grisly clothing: a skirt made of human arms and a garland of anguished human heads draped strategically across her bare blue chest.

"Excuse me, um, miss, are those—"

"It's *Myth.*"

"What?"

"*Myth,*" the seven-foot-tall woman replied, her third hand drumming its fingers with impatience along the handlebars. "*Indian* myth, to be specific. I am Kali, the goddess of time and change, also doing business as She Who Destroys. . . ."

"I sort of got that from your outfit," Marlo said. "It's nice to see clothing that's literally handmade."

"The only thing I'm *not* known to have killed," Kali said, her eyes wide, dark, and red-rimmed against her blue face, "is time. We've got to hurry. We're almost running late."

"*Almost* running late?" Milton replied. "For what?"

Kali drew in a deep, settling breath. "First, we've got to punch you in," she said, two of her arms stretching out to Milton and Marlo, each hand clutching a time card.

Milton grabbed one of the cards: it was a rectangle of heavy cardboard punched with tiny holes.

"Now slip it into the Time Trapper," Kali urged. "*Quickly*. It's how TIC-TOK—the Time Institute of Chronometry, Tabulation, and Order Know-how— tracks the punctuality of all students."

There was a wooden box on the wall with a clock mounted on top and a tiny slot inset beneath. Milton pushed his card into the slot, and after a mighty metallic thump, he pulled it out and returned it to Kali. He noticed that the clock had multiple hands, rather like the blue goddess breathing down his neck with impatience. In addition to the usual second, minute, and hour hands, there were day, week, month, year, century, and even *eon* hands: so many hands, in fact, that it was almost impossible to tell what time it was.

"What if I *don't* punch the clock?" Marlo said, staring at her card with suspicion. The Time Trapper chimed. Suddenly, a bright red boxing glove thrust out of the box, slugging Marlo in the chin.

"Then the clock punches *you*," Kali said with a wicked smirk. "Hurry, get on. I've got to get you to Bad-missions, where you'll meet Precocia's human resources manager, Mr. Grundy."

Milton and Marlo sat in one of three empty passenger cars pulled by Kali's stand-up scooter. The multiarmed goddess had two hands gripping the handlebars, while the other two were busy updating her schedule on a PDA and making a phone call on a bulky, first-generation cell phone.

A small horde of flying demons swarmed in front of the scooter train, fighting, biting, and scratching each other. Kali grunted and waved them away with three of her arms.

"Shoo!" she shouted. "They're so rowdy and undisciplined before noon."

"What do you mean?" Milton asked as the throng of small, winged demons scattered.

"The mayfly demons," Kali explained as she scooted around three buzzing drones tearing their antennae over a jammed printer. "Mayflies, in life, have one of the shortest life spans of any creature, living generally for just one day. In death it's the same. The guards are hatched first thing in the morning, reach middle age by lunch, and then drop off by midnight. There's a lot of turnover with demon guards anyway, but here in Precocia, we're always ahead of the curve."

Kali turned the corner and pulled up to an office door. Painted on its frosted glass was the word BADMISSIONS. The door creaked open. Out walked a woman with frizzy gray-and-black hair corralled into a bun, cradling a baby in her arms.

"Out," Kali ordered. "I must make up for lost time."

Milton and Marlo hopped out of the scooter train, with Kali quickly accelerating, leaning into a hard right turn, and speeding away.

"Namaste!" she called out behind her, giving a brisk three-handed wave.

The woman stepped up to the Fausters as the baby fussed in her arms. She wore a plain black dress that buttoned down from her neck to the ankles of her worn leather granny boots. The woman's skin glowed. Not in the "wholesome, healthy complexion" sort of way, but actually radiating a creepy greenish white light.

"My name is Dr. Curie," the woman said with a slight Polish accent.

"I thought we were supposed to see a Mr. Grundy?" Milton inquired. The baby turned in its blue felt swaddling blanket.

"*I'm* Mr. Grundy," the baby said in a deeper-than-expected voice. Basically, *any* voice defied Milton's and Marlo's expectations. "Solomon Grundy . . . please come in and sit down. We're running—"

"Let me guess," Marlo said as she and her brother followed Dr. Curie into the office. *"Late."*

As Milton walked through the doorway, he felt a weird, invasive tingle, as if he had been bombarded by a blast of intense radiation.

"Exactly," the baby cooed before motioning toward two metal chairs with his shaky, balled-up fist. The baby and Dr. Curie shared a furtive, knowing look.

Milton and Marlo sat down as Dr. Curie placed the baby in his high chair on the other side of the desk. By the left wall was a crib, and next to that was a tall water basin. At the center of the room was an altar with flowers and a cot beside it. Toward the right side of the room was a hospital bed, a coffin, and—piled next to the right-hand wall—a mound of dirt.

"Wait a second," Milton said with sudden realization. *"Solomon Grundy.* Like in the nursery rhyme."

"I don't remember nursery rhymes," Marlo muttered. "Maybe because we never had a nursery, and Dad liked that weird kind of poetry that didn't rhyme. . . ."

Milton recited:

"Solomon Grundy
Born on a Monday,

Christened on Tuesday,
Married on Wednesday,
Took ill on Thursday,
Grew worse on Friday,
Died on Saturday,
Buried on Sunday.
This is the end
Of Solomon Grundy."

The baby burped and nodded. "Yes, my tiresome weekly planner was somehow leaked up to the Surface," Solomon Grundy said. He opened one of the files on his high chair as Dr. Curie spooned strained yams into his little mouth.

"Hmm . . . Marlo Fauster," Solomon Grundy gurgled around his baby spoon. "Destroyed your vice principal in Rapacia . . . irreparably upset Madame Pompadour's Girl Friday the Thirteenth program . . . became the devil's Infern, then production assistant to his Televised Hereafter Evangelistic Entertainment Network Division—"

"That was actually me," Milton interjected before being shushed by a baby.

"Helped to destroy Fibble . . . then Snivel, it seems," Solomon Grundy continued, closing the file and opening another. "And Milton Fauster . . . *the* Milton Fauster . . ."

Marlo rolled her eyes.

"Escaped from Limbo . . . thwarted the Grabbit . . .

led an uprising in Blimpo . . . helped to destroy Fibble, then Snivel . . ."

Solomon Grundy spat up globs of strained yams. The yellow-orange mess dribbled down the front of his pale blue onesie.

"Dr. Curie, if you wouldn't mind?"

The glowing green woman nodded and wiped at the baby's face in that overly efficient, motherly way. Solomon Grundy waved his little arms in the air.

"That's goo-goo," he said, a spit bubble forming on his pouting lips. "I mean, *good.* Anyway, there's one thing that you *haven't* done while here in Heck."

"And what's that, you whiddle snuggle puss, you?" Marlo asked.

"It's *Mr. Grundy,*" the baby clarified with a scowl.

"Sorry, it's those chubby cheeks," Marlo replied. "I just want to . . . *pinch them.*"

"Yes, they *do* have that effect on people," Solomon Grundy said, rolling his tiny eyes. "Lucky for me, people don't feel much like pinching them after midweek."

Lucky stirred awake in Milton's kerchief pouch at the sound of his name. Milton untied the pouch from his belt and surreptitiously set it at his feet.

"As I was saying," Mr. Grundy continued, "you've both done a great deal here in the underworld, but the one thing you *haven't* done is prepare for your SATs."

"Our SATs?" Marlo replied.

"Your *Soul Aptitude Tests,*" Solomon Grundy continued,

grabbing a pen with a rattle on the end. "Where—when your souls turn eighteen—you will be thoroughly assessed, examined, and judged. The results of this grueling, comprehensive, and rigorously standardized test will decide, ultimately, where you will graduate to."

"Meaning?" Marlo asked, hugging her knees.

"You go all the way *up,* or all the way *down.*"

If synchronized gulping were a sporting event, Milton and Marlo would have walked away with matching medals.

"You've got a lot stacked against you," the baby gurgled, "so, with that in mind, I would strongly suggest enrolling in Precocia's accelerated twenty-five-eight learning program—"

"What's that?" Milton asked.

"Twenty-five hours a day, eight days a week," Solomon Grundy replied, rubbing his eyes with his balled-up fists. "That way, we always have a jump on the next day or week. Though grueling, the program is your only chance of avoiding the eternal torments of h-e-double-hockey-sticks. . . ."

Lucky poked his head out of the pouch. His ferret nose twitching, he spilled out of the kerchief like a fuzzy white Slinky. Solomon Grundy screamed.

"White ratty hurt baby! White ratty hurt baby!" he shrieked, pounding his fists on his high chair.

Dr. Curie scooped up Solomon Grundy into her arms and tried to soothe him.

"A *wielki szczur!*" she gasped.

As the Badmissions director pitched himself into a full-blown tantrum, Milton quickly gathered Lucky, squirming and rattled, into his arms.

"He's not . . . whatever you said," Milton said, holding his pet close. "He's a ferret, and he's totally harmless."

"He is a pet, and there is a strict no-pets policy in Precocia!" Dr. Curie said.

"*I'm not getting rid of him,*" Milton said, locking eyes with the creepy, glowing woman. "He's the only thing I've got . . . or I'm the only thing *he's* got. It's complicated."

"I will take him to Dr. Skinner. He . . . *loves* animals. Yours will be fine," Dr. Curie said, setting Solomon Grundy back in his crib.

The woman reached for Lucky. The ferret reared back and hissed, his pink eyes glittering with outrage. Milton stroked underneath Lucky's chin.

"It's okay, little guy," Milton said, his eyes wet. "I'll visit you every chance I get. And there's no way I'm leaving without you."

Lucky sniffed at Milton, seemingly smelling his words, and—judging them to be sincere—grudgingly allowed Dr. Curie to pick him up. She walked over to the door and kicked it open. Two teenagers stood just outside, wearing large mustard-colored suits and vacant expressions. One was a bug-eyed, pasty-faced boy and the other was a chunky Asian girl with shiny black hair.

"Mr. Thorndike and Miss Shu will show you to the

Only Fitting rooms," she said curtly as Milton and Marlo rose from their chairs and walked out of the room. Milton gave Lucky, cradled in Dr. Curie's arms, one last scritch.

"You take care of him," Milton said, his eyes dark with concern.

Dr. Curie smiled a sickly, bleary grin.

"Yes, he will be taken care of; you can be sure."

She kicked the door closed behind them and walked over to a small screen inset in the wall. The woman flicked it on. Two brain scans appeared on the screen. Dr. Curie squinted her silvery eyes at the images.

"Hmm . . . the girl won't quite do. Close, but no kielbasa. But the boy . . . his mind is so nice and open. He's an ideal candidate."

Hoisting Lucky over her shoulder like a living mink stole, Dr. Curie switched off the monitor and walked over to the infantile Badmissions director.

"Milton Fauster," Solomon Grundy said sleepily, trying to keep his eyes open. "He could be just what we've been looking for. The final adolescent agent for change . . ." The baby's face flushed deep purple. "Speaking of change, Dr. Curie," he said, his tiny voice strained with exertion. "Would you mind? I've just made a deposit in the Diaper Bank."

6 · THE FACTS OF AFTERLiFE

MILTON AND MARLO were smooshed together in the back of Kali's scooter bus as the blue four-armed Hindu goddess made a hard left. Marlo sighed with fashion defeat as she assessed her ugly uniform in Kali's convex mirror.

She and her brother had been fitted with the same hideous, mustard-colored power suits that the zombie teenagers had worn: with striped yellow-and-black ties, massive shoulder pads, and pants so tight that they felt like they were *inside* her legs.

"These stupid pants should be arrested, because they're *totally* killing me," Marlo grumbled.

"Your Smarty-Pants," Kali explained. "They increase blood flow to the brain."

Milton tried to wriggle his toes in his painful patent-leather shoes.

"Is that why my shoes feel like they're eating my feet?" he complained.

"Yes, that is right. Also to make you feel like you are growing, always."

The burly blue goddess pulled up to the Boys' and Girls' Boardrooms. "Power Suits create enough energy through limited movement to power PDAs, phones, computers—all the things a Junior Executive needs to be productive in the underworld," she explained.

Marlo squinted at the two boardroom doors. One was pale blue and the other bright pink.

"So why do I have to go in one room while my brother goes into the other? I mean, it's not like a bathroom, right?"

Kali laughed . . . or roared. It was hard to tell with a terrifying Hindu goddess.

"You don't have to be Brahma to figure it out," Kali said, adjusting her gruesome necklace of shrunken human heads. "The boys go into the Boys' Boardroom to talk about *girls,* and the girls go into the Girls' Boardroom to talk about *boys.* Please to get off now."

Milton and Marlo clambered off the scooter bus. Kali heaved her brawny blue body forward. The scooter bus shot down the curving hallway with a squabble of clatters and squeaks. Milton and Marlo stared dolefully at the two boardroom doors.

"This blows," Marlo muttered. "What good are the facts of life to a bunch of dead kids anyway?"

She walked over to the pink door and put her hand on the handle. "See you on the flip side, lesser Fauster."

Milton nodded and gave his sister a nervous grin. "Ditto, big sis."

Milton pushed open the door. The Boys' Boardroom was almost shockingly opulent. While the rest of Precocia seemed business as usual, the boardroom was like a cold marble palace. It was a huge, circular room with a domed ceiling supported by square columns, each with a carved Roman statue mounted up against the pillars. The statues were all of the same smug man in various heroic poses. Bands of gold leaf adorned the ceiling, each framing a painting of some ancient battle.

"Bienvenue," said a small man in a military uniform seated upon a green granite pedestal at the center of the room. His voice boomed against the marble surfaces of the room. It was the man, Milton noticed, who was portrayed in the statues, only there his diminutive form was stretched and exaggerated to godlike status. He was surrounded by a group of boys sitting in tiny plastic chairs.

The hat . . . the hand in his coat, Milton thought as he crossed the mosaic floor that illustrated military battles. *My vice principal is Napoléon, the French military genius and emperor who conquered half of Europe in the early nineteenth century!*

Despite the nightmarish sights he had seen in Heck, Milton still found few things more terrifying than arriving late for a new class. The sudden hush and mass scrutiny of strangers was almost unbearable. If only there was even *one* familiar face in the—

"Milton!" a boy called out from the crowd, waving him forward. "It's me!"

Milton squinted through his broken glasses at the boy. A husky, freckled boy who looked a lot like his friend—

"Virgil?" Milton replied as he sat down next to the boy. "Wow . . . you look so, um—"

"Like I lost a lot of weight, I know," Virgil replied, his small eyes glinting with kindness.

"What happened to you back in Blimpo?" Milton asked. "You led the, um—"

"BOWEL movement," Virgil said with an embarrassed grin. "Yeah, in retrospect, not the strongest of names. It was great, though: overthrowing Lady Lactose and the Burgermeister, finding my voice by bringing their blimp kingdom down with my singing—"

"*Silence*, Junior Executives," Vice Principal Napoléon said with irritation, quickly checking his mobile phone, which he kept in his inside breast pocket.

"Now on to zhe boys and zhe girls . . ."

Vice Principal Napoléon snapped his fingers. Two demon foot servants scuttled forward. The gangly, horned creatures were covered in a sort of stitched-together gunnysack, their eyes burning red from beneath the fabric, with a network of crisscrossed chains keeping them painfully stooped.

"Armstrong, Patrick Harris, *s'il vous plaît*," Napoléon said, nodding to a light switch by the wall.

The creatures nodded and scurried away. The lights went out and a picture of a blond girl with a ponytail flickered onto the wall behind the Vee-Pee, cast by a slide projector.

"Oh, cool," whispered Virgil. "I love movie days."

The slide switched with a click. Words appeared on the screen.

Girls: What You Don't Know Can Kill You.

Virgil gulped. "Or maybe not . . ."

"I'm here to talk to you about . . . *girls. Les filles,*" Napoléon said. "Do you know why zhey look pretty, are soft, and smell nice? *Because zhey are trying to destroy you.* Girls are like carnivorous flowers: bright, colorful, fragrant . . . beckoning you closer until . . . *WHAM.* You are stuck fast to zheir sticky wiles and are digested, slowly, from zhe inside out."

"Girls can't be that bad . . . can they?" Virgil whispered to Milton.

Milton shrugged his padded yellow shoulders. "I wouldn't know," he said sadly. "The closest thing I ever got to a date was back in Snivel."

"Really? How did it end?"

Milton thought of Sara Bardo, the conjoined twin he had developed a crush on, and how the last time he had seen her she had been unconscious and covered in blood after being severed from her brother by Edgar Allan Poe's flying pendulum.

"Not great."

"So Marlo's doing all right?" Virgil asked, looking down at his fidgety hands.

"Yeah . . . sure. She's next door in the Girls' Board-room."

"She is?" Virgil yelped.

"*Shhhhhh!*" scolded the vice principal from his throne.

"Why? Are you hung up on my sister or something?" Milton whispered suspiciously.

Virgil shrugged his sloping shoulders, staring at the screen. "Of course not," he lied.

The boardroom was breathtaking. More of a throne room than a boardroom, it was much grander than Marlo had expected, judging from the unassuming door. The walls were patterned with tall papyrus stalks, while the floor was checkered with gold and tan tiles. At the center were mud-brown columns bracing a solid gold canopy that loomed over a divan. Stretched out on the elegant couch was a slender, dark-skinned woman wearing a golden headdress and a sheer linen caftan, her gleaming hair plaited into cornrows.

That cool eye makeup, Marlo thought as she hung in the doorway like a fly caught in a draft. *My vice principal* is . . . Cleopatra, Queen of Egypt! *Whoa . . . the face that launched a thousand Goths! Precocia might actually end up being pretty—*

"Ugh! Look what the cat dragged in before having second thoughts and dragging it back out again!" jeered an obnoxiously familiar voice. Yep, there at the center of a flock of girls at Cleopatra's sandaled feet was Lyon Sheraton, the gritty sand in Marlo's social-emotional bathing suit ever since her arrival in the underworld. Lyon was one of those privileged queen bee types who gave everyone around her hives. And right next to her, feeding off Lyon's alpha status like a spray-tanned leech, was her dippy BFF, Bordeaux Radisson.

"Right, Lyon!" Bordeaux said, her pale blue eyes protruding from their sockets as if her scrawny giraffe neck were being squeezed tight. "Because, like, she's really gross!"

"Sorry, girls, I'm a little busy. Can I ignore you later?" Marlo replied, finding a spot between a nervous-looking Greek girl with crazy curly hair and a round-faced Chinese girl with glasses.

"I didn't know Crayola made makeup, *Thrift Store,*" Lyon sneered.

"That is enough!" Cleopatra ordered in a surprisingly husky voice. "We are running behind schedule. And besides"—the vice principal gave Marlo a sly, cat-like smile—"I rather *like* the new girl's makeup. Crude, but with some refinement and mentorship, she could be a young Nefertiti."

Lyon seemed to fold in on herself like a furious lawn chair, collapsing with rage.

"Now, before the interruption," Vice Principal Cleopatra said while elongating herself on the divan, looking every inch the queen, "we were talking about . . ."

She clapped her hands together. Amplified by the stone tile, the slap sounded like an explosion. The room went dark. A screen descended from the ceiling at the back of Cleopatra's throne. A slide flickered on the wall.

Boys: What You Don't Know Can Kill You.

"Boys," Cleopatra said with a clipped, regal air, gazing down her long nose at the girls. "Boys are strong, brave, spunky, and utterly stupid."

As Vice Principal Cleopatra ranted on about boys— the screen behind her flashing from boyish face to boyish face—Marlo leaned toward Lyon and Bordeaux.

"So, how did you two 'blondes,'" Marlo asked, wielding sarcastic air quotes, "end up here? I thought you both were part of some dumb cheerleading squad or whatevs."

Lyon's bright blue eyes swiveled toward Marlo like the turrets of a battleship.

"It was the *Nyah Nyah Narcissisterhood,* troll," she replied. "And it was beyond *awesome,* until it got squashed by all the fatties in Blimpo and then Madame Pompadour disappeared."

"Yeah, jumping around in a short skirt and shouting rhymes at bored kids seems like a truly fulfilling way for a girl to spend her time," Marlo said.

"*Totally,*" Bordeaux replied. "All those kids wanting to be us but they, of course, *can't,* because—"

Lyon elbowed Bordeaux in the side.

"So Principal Bubb sent us here when we tried to renegotiate."

"Renegotiate?"

"*It's something rich people do,*" Lyon said. "So we made an agreement with Madame Pompadour that would keep us on the road, away from Heck, but Bubb called the contract null and void—"

"That's funny," Marlo said. "That's what I call you two."

Cleopatra glared at the girls. "Is there something you'd like to share with the rest of the class, *new girl*?" she said, coiling the words slowly, then giving them a verbal tug at the end as if she were tightening a leash.

Marlo swallowed. "Um . . . I was just . . . well . . . I mean . . . boys can't be all that bad, right, Vee-Pee-opatra?"

Cleopatra gave a snort. "I suppose that *some* boys can be quite charming. And young romance starts off innocently enough. . . ."

The former Queen of Egypt stared off into space, her eyes as brown and glittering as the surface of the Nile.

"It all seems quite a lark . . . *at first,*" she said softly. "Then all at once, your hormones fight against your reason. Everything gets twisted, until you find yourself drowning in a rush of feelings and emerging on the shore, stricken with cooties."

"Cooties?" Marlo mumbled.

"Whether you've shared a candy cigarette, played house, or were the victim of a seemingly harmless dare, cooties isn't just something that happens to *other* girls. . . ."

"But that's not even a real disease . . . right?" Lyon said with a sneer.

"Don't believe me, little queens?" Cleopatra said forcefully, leaning forward on her throne. "Here are some gruesome photos of girls, just like you, who fell prey to a boy's advances: turning the playground into a hot zone of infection. . . ."

A series of grisly photographs flashed behind the vice principal, a near-senseless parade of grotesque human infirmity.

The girls clutched one another, screaming, as images of cooties victims seared their eyeballs.

"That is so . . . *sick*!" Marlo gasped with horror. "And not like the *good* kind of sick!"

"How did you end up here?" Milton whispered to Virgil as Napoléon warned of the treachery of girls.

"Well, all of us were sort of carted away after Blimpo deflated," Virgil explained. "Principal Bubb said I was too big for my britches—which is funny because, with all the weight I lost, my pants were actually too big for me—and sent me here."

"She said the same thing to us," Milton replied.

Vice Principal Napoléon glared at the boys and snapped his fingers. His two demon foot servants appeared at either side of Milton and Virgil, staring mutely at them in the dark with their glowing red eyes.

"Zhe moral of my talk is zhat girls are complicated and you will never, ever do zhe right thing." The pint-sized Vee-Pee leaned forward on his throne earnestly, his tiny hands clasped together. "Which brings us to zhe sensitive subject of . . . *cooties*," he said gravely.

"Cooties?" muttered Milton.

"Whether you've shared a juice box or were zhe victim of an unhygienic game of spin zhe bottle, cooties isn't just something zhat happens to *other* boys. If you suspect zhat you have cooties, don't just *play* doctor. *See* a doctor. Like Madame Curie."

The boys stared at Napoléon with dubious expressions. The former emperor of France scowled.

"Perhaps these repugnant photographs of little soldiers, just like you, shot down by feminine wiles and stricken with zhe cooties, will convince you!" he spat.

A succession of horrific photographs flashed on the wall behind Napoléon, each featuring some mutilated body part.

The boys gasped with utter shock and disgust as images of cooties victims drilled deep into their optic nerves.

* * *

Shaken and disturbed, the boys stumbled out of the boardroom, shivering, as if they had all survived some mutual trauma.

"That . . . was so . . . gross," Virgil muttered, his freckles as dark as chocolate chips against his blood-drained face. "That part where the boy's nose slid clean off his face . . . or the kid whose back looked like over-microwaved pizza—"

"Yeah, yeah," Milton interrupted, surfing the crest of his foaming nausea. "I get it. But cooties . . . that's just a pretend disease. An excuse for boys and girls to keep their distance from one another until they can, you know . . . deal with it."

The girls spilled out of Cleopatra's boardroom, looking like they had all spent the day making deposits at the blood bank. The boys and girls stared at each other with a mixture of slack-mouthed disgust and bowel-evacuating terror. Dr. Curie walked to the head of the two wary rows.

"Now, young *mężczyzn* and *kobiety*," she said. "You have seen the horrors of cooties firsthand. Luckily, as per usual, science is one step ahead of nature. I have concocted a special vaccine against the most virulent strain of cooties: swine cooties."

"Swine?" a boy with a ginger bowl cut asked, unhinged with fear. "Like pigs? But—"

"Well," Dr. Curie replied, "when a boy pig and a girl pig get married—"

"I get it! I get it!" the boy yelped, clapping his hands over his ears.

"So, to prevent you all from *getting it*," Dr. Curie continued, pulling two hugemongous hypodermic needles from her leather satchel, one normal and the other glowing silvery green, "I will now inoculate you all."

"Why two needles?" a little girl with brown braided pigtails squeaked. "For girls and"—she swallowed with fearful distaste—"*boys?*"

"No, child, one is a stronger vaccine for those who seem more susceptible." Dr. Curie pulled out a piece of paper. "So we will start with them. Will the following individuals please step up? Isabelle Lovejoy, Irving Ellingsworth, Upton Davenport, Eunice Yadgiri . . ."

Milton stared as the nervous children stepped up to Dr. Curie. One by one, the woman administered the glowing vaccine.

"Circle, dot, dot . . . now you've got the cootie shot . . . excellent," she said. "Now Spencer DuBois, Sachi Sanghi . . ."

Poor kids, Milton thought.

"Bordeaux Radisson . . ."

I'd hate *to be one of them . . . super-susceptible to that horrible disease. . . .*

". . . and Milton Fauster."

7 · THE TRAGIC
SCHOOL BUS

THE SIXTY–FOUR BOYS and girls had been lined up against the wall of the main office work area of the eighteenth floor. They were separated—which was just fine with them, considering that they were all still queasy due to their recent, creeptastic initiation into the myriad dangers of cooties.

Dr. Curie, her skin positively glowing, sat on a beige plastic chair with a book resting on her lap. "To mark the last day of your childhood, I shall read to you your last storybook," she said. *"Oh, the Places You'll Plan on Going but Will Never Quite Get To."*

Vice Principals Napoléon and Cleopatra emerged from their boardrooms and whispered to one another, glancing at the children as if evaluating a fresh herd of cattle. After sharing a wicked laugh, they strutted toward them in imperious strides, the petite Napoléon taking two steps for every one of Cleopatra's. Napoléon's hunched foot demons skittered behind.

Dr. Curie cleared her throat and read from the book on her lap.

"Congratulations!
Now put on your tie.
It's time to be practical . . .
And kiss childhood goodbye!
You have brains in your handheld.
You have feet on your ruler.
You can walk upright unlike a toddling drooler.
You're on your own.
With no clue what you know.
With only your boss to decide where you'll go . . ."

Milton swayed slightly as he stood at attention up against the wall. Ever since he had been vaccinated for the swine cooties virus, he felt woozy.

"Are you okay?" Virgil asked, his shoulder pressed against Milton's.

Milton nodded. Beads of sweat formed above his upper lip. "Just a little dizzy."

"Oh, the Places You'll Plan on Going but Will Never Quite Get To!" Dr. Curie continued, her eyes covered with a silvery film.

"With your eye on the prize!
There's no time to waste!
All thoughts that are fun must be quickly erased.
No time to relax.
No time for vacation.
Right out of the gate you must choose your vocation."

The girl next to Marlo—olive-skinned with brown curly hair and an overbite—rested her head on Marlo's shoulder.

"Just because I have bed-head doesn't mean you can sleep on me," Marlo said, jabbing the girl with her elbow. The girl collapsed to the ground. Another girl farther down the row—thick-nosed with thick black eyebrows and thick black glasses—fainted just as a boy with a pixie haircut and rectangular glasses fell over in the boys' row.

Napoléon, smirking, walked over to two zombie teens loitering by a copy machine.

"Mr. Tinkham and Miss Escobedo," the Vee-Pee said, "take the children to the infirmary, *s'il vous plaît.*"

The teenagers trudged toward the fallen children and dragged them away.

"And will you succeed?
Growing up like a weed?
Our lawyers advise we make no guarantee.
Kid, you'll move mountains . . . of paperwork!"

With that, three more children fainted. The remaining boys and girls backed away from their fellow students lying prone on the dull gray carpeting. Cleopatra slunk over to another pair of zombie teenagers.

"Miss Engelhart and Mr. Endo," she said in her silky husk, waving her hand, "take them away."

Marlo stepped out of line with her hands on her hips. "Um . . . kids are falling faster than IQ points at a pep rally," she said. "What gives? Is it pig cooties or whatever?"

Dr. Curie closed her book and rose from her chair.

"It's nothing to be concerned about," the doctor said unconvincingly. "With the swine cooties vaccine, sometimes you feel a little worse before you feel better. And I trust that our esteemed vice principals will do everything necessary to contain this potentially devastating epidemic."

Napoléon nodded and tucked his smartphone back into his breast pocket.

"*Merci*, Dr. Curie, for zhe glowing recommendation . . . not zhat you could give any other kind," he snorted, wiping a fleck of foam from his thin, pink lips with the back of his hand.

Milton was suddenly sick to his stomach.

"Wait . . . all the kids who . . . who fainted," he said, fighting the urge to purge all over his patent-leather shoes, "got the big glowing shot."

Dr. Curie exchanged a worried glance with the vice principals.

Napoléon marched toward the row of boys. "Dr. Curie assured us all zhat feeling abnormal is a perfectly normal side effect to zhe vaccine," he said, examining the group of tense, geeky boys as he made his way to Milton. "And, unless you are Monsieur Doogie Howser, I think zhat she is zhe most qualified person here to comment on such matters, Mr. . . ."

"Fauster," Milton replied, roughly eye to eye with the former emperor of France.

Vice Principal Napoléon arched his eyebrow with distaste. *Monsieur Fauster,*" he said, his breath smelling of heavy cream, roast chicken, and dental decay, "today you leave all silly, childish things behind in zhe sandbox of memory and march to zhe military drums of adulthood!"

With a clatter and squeak, Kali's scooter bus pulled up in front of the boys and girls.

"All aboard the Sylla-Bus!" Kali said, her voice booming like a jet engine.

"Sylla-Bus?" a tall girl with fuchsia hair asked as she boarded the open trolley.

"A play on the word 'syllabus,' meaning a course of study, and also our current mode of transportation," the four-armed goddess replied with a wag of her bright red tongue.

Marlo grabbed the pole and hoisted herself onboard as Milton staggered up the steps. "Are you okay, li'l bro? You seem even sicklier than usual."

"I'm just . . . woozy," Milton said as he slid onto a bench on the boys' side of the bus. "Probably from the shot."

Kali hopped off the scooter and handed the boys and girls special pens and paper.

Marlo examined the odd pen. It was silver with a small circular band like a ring.

"Cool," she said as she and the other boys and girls slipped on their pen-rings. Suddenly, the pens contracted tightly around the children's fingers.

"Oww!" Lyon complained. "What's this thing doing to my finger?"

"The pen clamps onto your hand, you silly girl with the orange tan," Cleopatra purred like a baritone cat. "A tiny gyroscope inside helps prevent carpal tunnel from prolonged writing sessions, while a tiny electric generator—"

"Oww!" an African boy with a mole on his nose yelped as he stared, wide-eyed, at his pen.

"—gives you zhe electric shock," Napoléon said, finishing his fellow Vee-Pee's sentence. "To keep you taking notes if you pause for more than a few seconds."

Milton glanced down at his pad of paper. The paper was stretched on two tiny rollers and framed within a metal clipboard. It reminded him of those disgusting hand towel rollers in public restrooms, where the same filthy piece of cloth just seems to go on for infinity. Safety bars lowered over the children's shoulders and locked with a click around their waists. The Sylla-Bus lurched forward.

I wonder where our first class is, Milton thought as a boy next to him—a Korean kid with a spiky shock of hair and an overdeveloped right shoulder muscle—shot his arm in the air.

"Where is our first class?" the boy asked.

Kali smirked. "Right here," she replied mysteriously, waving two long blue arms. "Rushing from class to class is a waste of precious time. Which is why, here in Precocia, the classes are held all at once, and I simply drive you students around and around, through them all."

That doesn't make any sense, Milton thought. *How can we learn all at—*

The boy next to Milton raised his hand, his arm shooting up like a spring-loaded trap. "That doesn't make any sense," the boy said. "How can we learn all at once?"

"Here you don't learn . . . you *memorize,*" the Hindu goddess replied. "That way it doesn't *need* to make sense. Plus you don't muddle your education by imposing your own thoughts on the subjects."

Milton looked down at the row of boys and girls. Most of them were permanently hunched forward from hours of computer work, had reddish marks on their stiff necks from violin lessons, thick glasses from eyestrain, and pasty complexions from lack of sunlight.

It's like looking at a hall of Miltons, Milton thought, his mind growing numb, like how his hand felt in the morning when he'd slept on it all night. *A hall of* me.

Milton sighed. He had spent so many years feeling like a freak for being smart—for being mature and always looking toward the future—and now that he was surrounded by kids who were actually like him, he didn't like it. Being the class brain, the geek, the nerd was who Milton *was* . . . or at least how he had always defined himself. But what did it mean to be a brain in a school of brains? Milton was now just another lump of adolescent gray matter. Another obedient mind to fill. And for what? To become just another cog in a corrupt machine? What good is being clever if everything you think up is exploited by those in power?

The Sylla-Bus turned the corner. Ten yards away was a man with an explosion of white hair, wearing an ill-fitting sweatshirt, battered tennis shoes, and an air of profound distraction.

"Is that—" muttered Milton before the boy next to him raised his hand.

"Dr. Albert Einstein, the theoretical physicist who developed the theory of general relativity and started a revolution in physics," the boy recited in an emotionless monotone. "He is often regarded as one of the most profound intellects in human history."

But why would Einstein be here in Precocia? Milton thought, just as the boy next to him somehow reraised his already raised arm.

"But why would Einstein be here in Precocia?" he asked as the Sylla-Bus slowed down, cruising slowly past Dr. Einstein at a quarter mile an hour.

"Good question . . . vun that I hear all too often," the old man replied wearily.

Milton noticed that Dr. Einstein wore a pair of small platinum blinders embedded with tiny blinking red, blue, and yellow lights. "Vun of my greatest regrets is signing a letter to President Roosevelt in 1939, stressing the urgent need for scientific studies in atomic energy, stimulating America's interest in the weapons potential of nuclear fission. Though my concern vuz in beating the Nazis, my actions led to the use of the atomic bomb against civilians . . . something that has veighed heavily on my conscience ever since."

Milton tried to raise his hand, but between his cooties vaccine sluggishness and the lightning-quick brain-to-arm speed of the boy next to him, he barely managed to lift his hand off his lap before the Korean boy again voiced the question currently reverberating in Milton's head.

"But why are you here in Precocia, specifically?" the boy asked.

The scientist's bushy mustache rustled as he smiled sadly. "I have been found guilty of helping humanity to grow up vay too fast . . . a verdict that even *I* can't completely disagree vith . . ."

The Sylla-Bus was now slowly passing Dr. Einstein at about the speed of an old dog trotting.

I wonder—

"Will you be teaching us your theory of relativity?" the boy next to Milton asked, his hand held high.

"Theory of relativity?" Bordeaux muttered, her bulging blue eyes glassy. "Like, when you think you're related to someone really cool and famous but you . . . you can't really prove it?"

Lyon jabbed Bordeaux silent with her pointy elbow.

"No," the Korean boy with the spiky black hair replied, "the theory of relativity encapsulated by Einstein's famous *E* equals *MC* squared equation, which implied that matter and energy were equivalent and, specifically, that a single particle of matter could be converted into a massive quantity of energy. Are we going to learn about that?"

Dr. Einstein's sad, crumpled face was briefly lightened by a quick smile.

"It sounds like ve already have!" the old man said with a dry chuckle. "Vell, if you must know, my vork began by discarding the notion of absolute space and absolute time. Vat is time, anyway?"

The boy's arm shot up.

"I vas speaking rhetorically," Dr. Einstein said as

he paced alongside the Sylla-Bus. "Our sense of time is entirely subjective. . . ."

At the edge of Milton's blurry vision, he could see Vice Principal Napoléon storming toward the scooter bus.

"Imagine that someone in New York at noon is talking to someone on the phone in Paris, vhere it is nine o'clock at night," Dr. Einstein continued, his eyes seeming to sparkle with every word. "Now, are they talking at the same time?"

Vice Principal Napoléon pulled out a small, sleek device from his inside pocket.

"And the stars above that person in Paris, they are light-years away, meaning that they are but ghosts from the past that left their source many years—"

Napoléon pressed the touch screen on his handheld. Instantly, the lights on Einstein's blinders started to flash.

". . . ago," the wild-haired man continued weakly, his pupils dilating into tiny, dull points.

Bordeaux began to sway in her seat. "Feeling . . . dizzy," she murmured.

"That's probably just because you're awake," Lyon replied. "It'll go away when you go to sleep."

Bordeaux collapsed over her restraint, flopping like an understuffed rag doll.

Lyon recoiled in disgust. "She's got cooties! Get her away from me!" she screamed.

Vice Principal Napoléon strode toward Dr. Einstein as the Sylla-Bus stopped beside them.

"Dr. Einstein," the vice principal ordered. "If you would escort zhis poor mademoiselle to zhe infirmary."

The scientist gave a feeble, obedient nod. He slid Bordeaux out of her restraints and dragged her away.

The scooter bus scooted toward Dr. Curie, who was sitting demurely on her chair a dozen yards away.

"Hello, Junior Executives!" she said, rising to her feet. "Now let's get started!" Dr. Curie walked over to a bulky gray machine on rollers. She flipped a switch on its side, the machine waking with a tremendous hum, and a large rectangular black-and-white screen blinked to life at the front. The woman walked behind the machine. On the screen appeared a skeleton, some shadowy internal organs, and the words "Radiology 101."

"I swallowed lead letters to show you the wonders of modern X-ray technology!" Dr. Curie gushed.

Radiation, Milton thought. *Maybe that's why she . . .*

The boy next to Milton raised his hand.

"Is all that radiation why you glow?" the boy asked.

Dr. Curie smiled a mouth full of incandescent teeth. "*Tak,* that is correct!" she replied. "And, young ladies, let me tell you that high doses of electromagnetic waves are the key to a radiant complexion!" Dr. Curie walked over to a dry-erase board on an easel, becoming winded. "Phew . . . for some reason I get so tired. . . . In any case, *ra-di-a-tion,*" she said, writing the word on the board.

"You hear the most outrageous lies about it. Pernicious nonsense!"

Milton suddenly grew weak and slumped over in his seat. The whole office seemed to spin around him, as if he were at the center of the most boring carnival ride imaginable.

"Milton?" three Virgils asked, just before Milton passed out.

One of the zombie teenagers swiped the card hanging from his neck through the slot beneath the elevator buttons. The elevator dropped fast like a concrete hang glider and stopped abruptly at an unmarked floor. The zombie teens hooked their arms underneath Milton's armpits just as his knees buckled. The doors slid open and the teenagers dragged Milton down a concrete hall, his tight leather shoes scraping against the floor. They turned a corner, walked a few dozen steps, then butted Milton's head against a pair of swinging brushed aluminum doors. The room was sterile, cold, and silent.

Milton felt as if there were a sinkhole inside him, with his consciousness slowly spilling away into the yawning abyss spreading out from his middle. "Is . . . this . . . the infirmary?" he mumbled.

The teenagers lugged Milton past a row of beds, his forehead smacking open another pair of double doors.

His eyesight went gray around the edges as he was dragged down another hall.

"The girl," said a man in a crumpled German accent.

Dr. Einstein?

"Such an open mind. Almost *too* open. Like a hand with no fingers."

"Get that . . . hoodie thing . . . off me," Bordeaux muttered from down the hallway. "It'll mess up . . . my hair."

"What's . . . going . . . on?" Milton croaked, his head hanging down, staring at the concrete floor. Suddenly, he stopped at a pair of old slippers. Milton forced his head up. Staring down at him was Dr. Einstein, his electric blinders flashing, his gaze unblinking. Through his smudgy vision, Milton could see that Einstein's blinders were actually surgically attached to his temples. He held a device to the crown of Milton's head: a small palm-sized black box with a looping coil sticking out the end like a wand.

"Just ripe," Dr. Einstein mumbled. "And beginning to flower."

The old man's eyes, so wide and curious in life, now appeared troubled. His gaze seemed to be desperately fighting to break free of the blinders, as if his mind and spirit were confined as well.

Dr. Einstein nodded weakly to the teenage boy at Milton's side. The boy grabbed a leather helmet from an overflowing bin by the door and thrust it over Milton's head, shrouding him in a smothering darkness.

"Hey," Milton said weakly as he was dragged into another room. The room hummed and squeaked, as if occupied by giant machines.

Something pierced the top of Milton's skull.

"Oww!" Milton yelped. The sharp pain punctured his faltering consciousness.

He was suddenly turned upside down. He heard several grunts as something locked onto his ankles.

"What are you doing—"

"Relax, young man," Dr. Einstein said. "You are going on the ultimate field trip."

"Field . . . trip?" Milton murmured, teetering on the edge of consciousness. "Where?"

He could hear a few young voices babbling against the steady whirring of bulky machines. The sounds were echoey and hollow, as if he had megaphones stuck in his ears.

"Back home," Dr. Einstein said softly as Milton felt himself being lowered.

Something bumped the tip of Milton's odd hooded helmet with a resounding thud and his mind went instantly blank.

8 · THERE'S NO PLACE LiKE HOME

A MUFFLED EXPLOSION roused Milton from the deepest sleep he'd ever had. A band of warmth slashed across his face, spreading out like blood from a fresh wound. His eyes flickered open.

"Sunlight?" he murmured, his mouth as dry as fresh cat litter. "In the *underworld?"*

Milton winced at the glaring sunlight streaming through a window. *His* window.

He rose onto his elbows, very much in his bed—complete with periodic-table sheets—back home in Generica, Kansas.

It was his old bedroom—there was no mistaking it—though it was different in strange little ways. It was painted in a kind of miserable beige, not the usual light blue. All of his posters—*Star Wars, Star Trek, Stargate* . . . most every science-fiction phenomenon beginning with the word "Star"—were gone.

"Is this some kind of freaky dream . . . ?" Milton puzzled. "I'm back home . . . only different. I either somehow got to the Surface, or the whole Heck thing—me dying . . . *twice*—was just some terrible nightmare. . . ."

Explosions reverberated from outside Milton's fluttering binary code–print curtains. They sounded like cherry bombs detonating inside a hippo's stomach.

Suddenly, Milton's door flew open. His father, frantic, burst into the room.

"Milton!" the man yelled. He was wearing a white tunic and sandals.

"Dad!" Milton yelped, springing from his tangle of sheets. Milton's father scrunched up his face, folding it suspiciously like a map of a secret army base.

"It's Mr. Fauster," he replied. "*Blake* Fauster. You haven't called me . . . that word . . . in a long, long—"

Another explosion, a thunderous puff in the distance, shook Milton's Most Least Imaginative trophy from his bookshelf.

"It's time!" Milton's father said earnestly.

"Time for what?"

"*Time for what?*" Blake Fauster repeated with exasperation. "Only what we've been preparing for since you came back!"

"Came back? But I only just—"

"Seen and not heard!" Milton's father shouted as he grabbed Milton by the wrist. "We've got to get to the shelter!" He tugged Milton from his bed and dragged him out of the bedroom. Milton tripped on his somehow-bigger feet, attached to somehow-longer legs.

Weird, Milton thought as his father pulled him down the hallway, now decorated with frilly French furniture. *Maybe I was in a coma and my body grew. . . .*

They entered the kitchen, with Milton squeaking across the gold-flecked linoleum floor in his bare feet. His father yanked open the back door. In the yard was a grim concrete fallout shelter.

"Since when do we have a shelter?" Milton asked as the screen door shut behind them. His father turned, a look of urgency etched deep into his usually lighthearted face. Milton noticed that his father's laugh lines, normally crinkled around his once-sparkling eyes, were gone.

"While you were missing . . . right after the reports came about—" Blake Fauster glanced up with apprehension. Sooty trails of black streaked out behind dozens of sizzling, white-hot dots. The air screamed as meteors shredded the blue sky, like an invisible cat clawing its way through the heavens.

"This is more than a meteor shower," Milton murmured. "It's a meteor *deluge.*"

The ground shook as Milton and his father trotted toward the shed.

"And none of them are burning up," Milton reflected,

the sky slashed with hundreds of black smoke trails. A trio of explosive thuds shook the ground. "It feels like each one is impacting. How did all this happen?"

Milton's father unlocked the steel door to the fallout shelter and shook his head. "You ask so many questions. It's almost like you're, you're . . . *curious,*" he said, the last word dusty and foreign on his tongue, dredged from his vocabulary like an ancient relic. The man scratched at his salt-and-pepper goatee, giving one last look at the sky. *"C'est la vie,"* he said with a shrug. "Maybe it's the stress of what you've gone through. Plus it must be hard to live in your sister's shadow."

They stepped inside. The air was hot and stale. Milton's father yanked the string of a dangling lightbulb. The fallout shelter was filled with shelves of canned food and bottled water.

My sister's shadow? Milton thought as, only just now in the surreal confusion of the morning, he noted the absence of Marlo. Milton's father secured the door, sealing the two of them inside the concrete structure as if it were a tomb.

"Where *is* Marlo?" Milton asked as his father unfolded a drab olive lawn chair. "Is she . . . um . . . back home, too?"

Heavy thuds boomed in the distance, shaking mortar dust from the ceiling.

"Marlo, I'm sure, is safe and sound at the ministry," Blake Fauster replied in a sort of robotic voice. "She was on the METEOR committee . . . you know: Make Everyone Totally Equipped, Obedient, and Ready."

Milton snickered as he gazed out a small window set into the door, reinforced with chicken wire. "Marlo heading a *committee*?" he said with disbelief. "Don't make me laugh."

Milton's father gasped. "I would never do such a thing!" he said, his eyes darting nervously around the shelter as if he were under surveillance.

"Sorry, um . . . *Mr. Fauster,*" Milton replied cautiously, treating his addled father as if he were wearing a vest of dynamite. "What about Mom? Is she with Marlo?"

Milton's father scratched his graying, close-cropped hair. "Your experience must have been so traumatic that it pushed out all of your old memories. That's probably for the best."

"Where is my mom?" Milton repeated, his hands balled into frustrated fists.

The man licked his thin lips nervously and leaned in close to Milton. "I shouldn't really be talking about it. B-but she disappeared right after you were . . . *taken from us,*" he said in a paranoid hush. "Went looking for you."

"*Looking for me?*" Milton said with a gasp. "As in, after I left she—"

Milton's father nodded gravely. "She's not the only biological host . . . um . . . *mom* to react this way. There were others, too. But, of course, we never hear from them again. . . ."

Milton couldn't believe it. He sat down on a sack of instant-croissant mix, weak and overwhelmed. His heart was so suddenly sick that it felt like it was going to vomit in his chest.

Mom . . . killed herself? he thought miserably. *So overcome with grief that she . . . went looking for me . . . in the afterlife? The pain she must have gone through when Marlo and I died. And now that I'm back, nothing makes any sense. Maybe I have brain damage from being dead. . . .*

His red-rimmed eyes blurry with tears, Milton stared at his father. The crumpled, middle-aged man seemed like a total stranger.

Maybe my so-called death affected him more than I thought, Milton speculated as dull thuds shook the concrete shack. *And the loss of his wife . . . his family . . . that would probably be enough to send any man over the edge.*

Milton's father twitched back from his stupor. He offered Milton a small tube plucked from a carton.

"Would you like some escargot-gurt?" he said, brandishing a squeezable container featuring a snail in a beret skiing down a frosty slope of fermented milk.

"Um . . . no thanks," Milton said with a grimace. "I don't think I'll ever be *that* hungry."

Blake Fauster arched his eyebrow. "I thought this was your favorite," he said, staring at his son intently before giving a quick shrug, as if confusion was far too taxing a state to maintain for more than a few seconds. "I suppose you had to get used to new foods where you were."

"Yeah," Milton muttered as he peered out the small window, the sky dark with smudgy black streaks and upturned dust. "The food left a lot to be desired. . . ."

Milton couldn't believe that, of all the questions one could have about the afterlife, Milton's father could only muster brief curiosity at the menu. As distant explosions shook the fallout shelter, he was filled with that rarest of feelings: He actually *missed* his sister. Marlo would have viewed this situation—Kansas pelted with hundreds of deadly boulders hurtling from space—not with fear, but with unabashed excitement. Milton could imagine her with her crooked, maniacal smile pressed to the window, interpreting the impending, wide-scale calamity as some kind of dare waged from the heavens.

But Milton was—to put it mildly—wired differently from his sister. He wasn't scared, exactly: He was so overwhelmed by being alive again that there wasn't any room for fear in his baffled brain. So many things didn't add up. Like, for instance, how come none of the dozens of asteroids plummeting to the ground came even *close* to hitting any—

"It's nice that the ministry gave you a furlough so you could be here—thanks to your sister—before you start paying back your youth debt," Blake Fauster murmured from the corner.

Milton turned. His father's face seemed as if it were trying to forge something of a smile, but, due to years of inaction, his muscles just couldn't crinkle his face the right way.

"Even despite the government's assurances, it's comforting to have someone here during all of this. Speaking of which," the middle-aged man said as he leaned to flick on a small radio on the metal shelving next to him, "let's hear the latest governmentally sanctioned updates on MISTER."

"Mister?" Milton replied.

"This is Ministry Information Sent To Everyone Radio," the radio announcer declared in a deep, emotionless voice. "If you are listening to this, then it is to be assumed that you are still alive, obviously having abided the sage words of the glorious ministry. If you *aren't* listening to this, then—as your reckless disobedience has necessitated the inclusion of this extended announcement—you are hereby wasting the government's time and will be taxed accordingly. *C'est la guerre.* Reports from New Paris estimate that the current meteor shower will last into the night, so remain in your shelters until the ministry informs you otherwise."

A meteorite impact shook a hammer from the top of the overstocked utility shelf, sending it plummeting down onto the radio, smashing it to bits.

"That reminds me of Marlo's tenth birthday," Milton said with the weak smile of nostalgia. "At Upchucky Cheese. When she was on that attention-deficit medication and broke the Smack-a-Vole game . . ."

"Upchucky Cheese?" Blake replied. "What's that?"

"Upchucky Cheese's Ye Olde Lasagna-ganza and Fun Bunker?" Milton said, questioning his father's question. "Only that lame sit-down lasagna restaurant we'd go to all the time with all the queasy rides, broken-down arcade games, and life-sized animatronic rats and cows."

The color drained from Blake Fauster's face.

"That sounds . . . *horrible*," he whispered before retreating into some private world.

What is going on? Milton puzzled to himself as muted explosions sounded in the distance.

Night had fallen slowly, like a tranquilized elephant in an inflatable zoo. Blake Fauster unlatched the fallout shelter's door and poked his head outside. "It's over . . . just like the radio said. It's uncanny how the ministry could figure out exactly when the meteors would stop. But I suppose that's why they're in total control. . . ."

Milton stretched, achy from his long day spent cooped up, and emerged from the shelter behind his father. The sky was as black and thick as fresh tar. No stars. No moon. Just a hovering blanket of upturned dust and soot.

"So the ministry is the new government, huh?" Milton asked as he and his father crept across the graveyard-still backyard to the kitchen.

"Yes . . . but, please, no more questions," he replied

as he opened the back door. "You've asked more today than in your entire life. It's . . . *exhausting.*" Milton's father shuffled toward his bedroom.

Milton sighed and poured himself a cup of cold coffee. "Good night, um . . . Mr. Fauster," he said before choking down the bitter sludge. With a full-body shudder of disgust and caffeine, he went to his room.

I've got a lot of research to do, he thought as he plopped onto his bed and booted up his computer. *I'm home . . . but home isn't quite me. Something's off.* Everything's *off. No Marlo, no Mom. Just me and a dad who doesn't seem like my dad at all. Even my computer is different. Not my zippy Zapple laptop, but a Dull Lacklustratron . . .*

Milton yawned, so wide that the corners of his mouth hurt.

Must've been decaf . . . Man, I'm wiped. But I've got to figure things out. It's weird, for most of my life I wanted to be an only child. And now that I am, I miss Marlo more than ever. It doesn't seem like home without her and Mom. Not at . . . all . . .

Milton stared at the clock of his ugly beige computer.
11:59
I don't think I've ever been this . . .
12:00
Milton was bludgeoned by utter fatigue.
. . . tired . . .
Milton's body went limp, as if he were an appliance whose plug had been yanked out of its socket, and fell into deep, uncompromising slumber.

9 · ANGELS WiTH DiRTY HALOS

"CAN I TAKE off this blindfold now?" Principal Bubb asked the demon pilot as he guided a woven carpet of wasps up to its secret destination. "Something to take my mind off this horrid flying turd?"

The tiny yellowish creature—a green leather aviator's cap pulled down to his red snub-nosed snout—nodded.

"A *Turdistanian wasp carpet*," the pilot said in his dry wheeze of a voice. "And, yes, you can take your blind-fold off now. We're just about ready to board."

Bea "Elsa" Bubb untied her blindfold and gasped. Above was a dark, expansive ring of smoke, levitating in the sky. The pilot lifted a hunk of rotten meat hooked in front of the carpet. The tapestry of angry pests followed it with furious hunger.

The blanket hovered inside the ring of thick smoke. An angel wearing an eye patch and tarnished armor tossed the pilot a line from the smoke-shrouded, doughnut-shaped building.

"A black halo," Principal Bubb murmured as the angel tugged them to a small loading dock. "Of course. Where *else* would you find a highly trained team of fallen-angel commandos for hire?"

The one-eyed angel heaved the principal off the carpet with a grunt while the demon pilot calmed the wasps with a blast of smoke from his smoldering metal tank.

"Welcome to Gehanna, Principal Bubb," the dark angel said snidely. "My name is Azkeel. If you'll come with me, please."

The facility reminded Principal Bubb of a submarine in its cramped, militaristic efficiency.

"I've heard rumors of your organization before," Bea "Elsa" Bubb said as the two creatures walked down the dark-gray, gently looping hallway. "But I thought it was some sort of joke. The Fallen Angel Retribution Team. I mean, the acronym of that is—"

"We're not called that anymore," Azkeel said with a scowl. "In fact, our first act of retribution was to exact swift justice upon the angel who came up with our first name."

Explosions sounded from behind a steel door marked CHERUB BOMBS.

"We now do business as the Embedded Faction of

Fallen Angels for Counterattack Endeavors, or EFFACE. You know—*efface*—as in 'to remove and eradicate.'"

"I know what 'efface' means," the principal lied. "What I *don't* know is if you can carry out the job with the utmost discretion."

A sizzling blur of fire snagged the corner of Principal Bubb's eye. Through the smoked-glass porthole of another steel door, marked HALO HURL, the principal could see rings of fire streaking through the air, smashing into a flaming mannequin. The sound of screams rent the air.

Or maybe not *a mannequin,* Principal Bubb thought.

"We are the forsaken *souls* of discretion," Azkeel said, his heavily muscled biceps straining out of his black armored vest.

A clashing of swords resounded from another room off the main corridor. Bea "Elsa" Bubb could see, through the porthole, ribbons of smoke rising in the air as two angels in chain-mail vestments dueled with flaming scimitars.

"EFFACE are former members of a warrior class of celestial beings, devoted to righting wrongs with other wrongs: brutal, *undetectable* wrongs," Azkeel continued as he marched down the curving corridor in confident strides. "We were forged at the beginning of the world out of chains of black and fire of red. Liquid fury runs through our veins, pumped by the ceaseless hammers of our hearts. Plus, we love our work *and it shows.* . . ."

The tall, hulking fallen angel stopped suddenly. "So you want us to . . . remove . . . Milton Fauster. Is that right?" he said, boring his one eye into the principal.

"Yes," Principal Bubb replied nervously. "No mess. No witnesses. Nothing to tie the . . . act . . . back to me."

"Of course," he replied curtly. "Precocia, you said?"

"Yes."

"Hmm . . . for children fixated with the future at the expense of the present. Well, I have a few candidates I'd like to run past you. . . ."

The burly, hardened angel pulled three 8 x 10 photographs from a leather satchel lashed across his chest.

"This is Malaku," Azkeel said, holding a photograph of a fierce, sculpted angel, shirtless, with a shaved head and spikes jutting out from his wrists. His eyes burned with malice. "Cruel, efficient, reliable . . . though a touch overenthusiastic. But a cleanup crew can be added for a nominal charge."

"He seems a little . . . *intense* for Precocia. And big. Like a boy who was held back for ten grades."

"I see what you mean. Here's another one of our angels. Diabolus. Don't let her good looks fool you. She's cunning, stealthy, and very 'hands-on.' "

Azkeel held a photograph of a silver-haired woman with bright green eyes, claws, and faint leopard spots covering her neck, arms, and legs.

"A little conspicuous, don't you think?" Principal Bubb commented.

"Okay, then," Azkeel replied. "I saved the best for last. Feast your eyes on Molloch. . . ."

A dark-skinned boy with brilliant blue eyes glared at Bea "Elsa" Bubb from the photograph, practically daring her to meet his gaze. Silvery wings glinted from over his broad shoulders.

"A fallen angel?" the principal replied. "He seems like only a boy."

"A boy who's several millennia old," Azkeel said. "Not to mention jaded, deadly, and manipulative."

"I'm not sure . . . he's a little too good-looking. . . ."

Azkeel drew glasses on the photograph, downgrading the boy's looks from "hunk" to "happening nerd."

"See? He cleans down nicely," the dark angel said. "By your dazed expression, I assume we have a deal . . . unless you're having a stroke."

"No . . . he'll do. *He's perfect.*"

"Lucky for you he's far from that," Azkeel said. "Now, I assume you want all of this to be classified, correct?"

"Of course!"

"There is a 'classified' surcharge, however."

"How much is that?"

"That's classified."

Principal Bubb passed another steel door, this one marked HARPERY RANGE. Through the porthole, she could see a skinny angel with flaming red hair, pulling back a harp string with her leather-gloved hand.

The angel released, launching a small, platinum arrow through the air. It sliced an angel-food cake in two.

They walked down the curved corridor past a pillar of fire and cloud, arriving—inexplicably to the principal—back at the landing platform.

"What goes around comes around," Azkeel said, noting the principal's confusion. "That's our motto here. And, luckily, that was also our architect's motto when he designed our floating halo fortress." The dark angel glanced down. "Nice ride," he said, eyeing the demon pilot's buzzing blanket of wasps as Principal Bubb stepped aboard.

"This conversation never happened," Bea "Elsa" Bubb told the dark angel as he kicked away the airborne rug.

Azkeel smiled—a cruel, thin-lipped expression that glinted like a switchblade.

"Of course," he replied. "And Milton Fauster won't be happening for much longer, either."

10 · LiTTLE KiDS
iN THE BiG HOUSE

"WARDEN OF THE *State Fauster!"* a gruff voice boomed, dragging Milton from the depths of his thick, swamplike sleep. Milton opened his eyes. Hovering over him was a jowly, sour-faced young man with a bushy mustache and a large policeman's hat screwed tight onto his head. *"Your shift begins in one hundred twenty-seven seconds!"*

"Shift?" Milton replied, sitting up in some kind of bunk bed. "What are you . . . *who* are—" Milton clutched his throat. His voice was an octave deeper.

"Excuses," the man barked. "That's all I'm hearing when what I *should* be hearing is your boots hitting that floor and then taking you—somehow—to your post in exactly one hundred twenty-three seconds."

"I—" Milton started before rubbing his throat. "I must be sick. My voice. I can't remember—"

The man stripped off Milton's scratchy wool sheet. Milton was wearing the same outfit as the lunatic standing over him: a gray guard's uniform with a charcoal sash draped across the chest and gold fringed epaulets on the shoulders.

"Why am I all dressed up?"

The man scratched at his droopy mustache, which, Milton suspected, was glued on. He could hear a loud ticking in the distance.

"What do you think, we'd waste valuable seconds getting in and out of those . . . those *sleeping suits* that the greenies wear?" he replied, snickering, before clapping his hand over his mouth.

"Now to your post, Warden of the State!" he shouted through his fingers.

"My post?" Milton croaked. He hopped off the bunk and stumbled. His legs felt weird. Too long. Maybe they were asleep, Milton thought as the man shoved a warden's hat into his hands. The wide-brimmed hat had an insignia embroidered on the front—a crib with two babies handcuffed together—with the initials "T. I."

The man shook his head. "Sounds like someone had too much Cabernet Cola last night," he said, his eyes crinkled into suspicious slits. "Tier Five. *Now!* I don't know what you're trying to pull, Fauster, but the greenies should be just waking up."

"The greenies?"

"Get a move on!"

The facility was a grim cross between a prison and a dimly lit warehouse—five levels of catwalks winding up cinder-block walls looking out over a courtyard in the middle. Milton trotted down the metal staircase to the Tier Five catwalk. The place was eerily silent save for an incessant ticking.

Set on the ceiling was a massive clock face, so large that it made Big Ben look like a secondhand Swatch. The little hand hovered at IX, while the big hand clicked to XI. It loomed, oppressively, above, its judgmental clock face sneering down at the gleaming linoleum floor of the courtyard, as if admiring itself in the reflection.

Milton trotted down the stairs to the next level and gasped. To his left was a row of thirty tubular tanks, inside each of which floated a child. The children wore tight gray bodysuits and had snorkel masks lashed to their faces. They bobbed fitfully in the fluid: a purplish murk that made the children appear wan and ghastly. The tanks were set upon a long concrete floor, slightly recessed with drains behind each of the fluid-filled vats. Another Warden of the State stood before the row of tanks, fussing with his bushy, handle-bar mustache.

"What are you doing to them?" Milton croaked, his voice still deep and craggy.

The guard emerged from a sort of stupor. "Who, the greenies?" the warden answered in a voice deeper than his youthful appearance.

The greenies are children? Milton thought.

Just then, a chime tolled. Hatches at the back of the tanks slid open. The purplish fluid gushed out onto the floor and swirled down the drains. The smell made Milton's nose curl. It was like a mixture of vinegar, old juice gone bad, and sweaty gym clothes.

"What is that stuff?" Milton murmured as the children dangled from support pegs beneath their armpits like discarded marionettes.

"Huh?"

"That stuff the, um, *greenies* were soaking in."

The warden cocked his eyebrow at Milton. "You're in a funny mood today, Fauster," he commented. "And I don't mean funny ha-ha. *Ever.*" He shrugged. "How should I know what that stuff is? I just work here. And so do you."

Milton looked down at his black boots. They were huge. "I don't know what's going on," he muttered. "Where I am. What I'm supposed to be doing . . ."

Milton noticed a castaway container in the corner of one of the cells. He knelt down and read the label:

Gro-Better™ Maturation Solution: Fermented Elderberry Juice, Distilled Vinegar, Anabolic Steroids, and Gro-Rite™ Growth Hormones

The warden swallowed nervously, his eyes darting back and forth along the catwalk. "Don't talk that way, Fauster. They'll think you're *fou*. Even your sister won't be able to help you."

"My sister? What does she have to do with—"

The children twitched awake in their emptied tanks. A little girl—probably six, with wet blond hair plastered to her face—took in her surroundings with pale blue eyes bulging with fear. She spat out her snorkel.

"I had this wonderful dream," she sobbed to a little boy in the tank next to her, also blond with similar elfin features, probably her brother. "We were . . . *playing*."

The boy spat out his snorkel with a gasp. "Shhh," he scolded. "You'll get us all *whooshed*."

The other warden stormed up to the tank, his hand on a billy club dangling from his belt.

"Seen, not heard!" he shouted.

Milton noticed that he also had a club hanging from his belt. He cradled the baton in his hand. The children flinched as Milton held it out to the other warden. "What's with the billy clubs?"

"*Billy* clubs?" the mannish boy replied with a twitch of his dirty-blond mustache. "I don't know what's wrong with you today, Fauster, but you will observe proper, formal designations for all Tykers's equipment. *William* clubs. Never . . . *billy*. Now help me transfer these inmaturmates."

The warden hoisted the children off their pegs, one by one. A gangly boy with crooked teeth and rust-colored hair rubbed his aching underarms, accidentally producing a wet farty noise. Milton looked at the boy and smiled. The boy's face went pale. He turned away from Milton, trembling.

"It's a trick," a girl with dark, knitted eyebrows whispered to a boy next to her. "To get us *whooshed*."

Milton shrugged and helped the blond girl from off her pegs. She quickly wiped away a tear. Milton, trying to cheer up the miserable girl, gave her a smile.

"Hey," he said as he playfully snatched at the girl's face. "Look." He wiggled the tip of his thumb through his balled fist. "I got your nose!"

The girl looked at Milton's thumb, horrified, and let out a strangled scream. "Why would you *do* something like that you . . . *monster!*" she squealed.

"I . . . look . . . it's just my thumb," Milton replied, wiggling his thumb. *Man, these children must be traumatized,* he thought as the girl patted her nose, calming down. "I was just making a—"

"Joke," a dark-skinned boy who looked about Milton's age—eleven—whispered in awe from the next tank over.

"Hey!" shouted the other warden angrily. "Watch the language!"

He brandished his William club, training it on the boy. The warden's thumb hovered over a red button on the handle.

"Stand down, LeBeau!" a young female warden said, goose-stepping toward them with an air of authority. The woman glared at Milton with bright green eyes twinkling with curiosity, not like the dull stare of the other wardens. "Give the greenies a little time to de-grog before you *whoosh* any of them, understand?"

"Yes, *ma capitaine*," the other warden replied with poorly masked resentment.

"Now get them to the stretchers," she continued. "You're already fifteen seconds late. And no accidentally-on-purpose dropping them, Fauster."

"B-but I would *never* . . . ," Milton sputtered back in his weirdly deep voice.

The young auburn-haired woman crinkled her long nose. Her green eyes stared deep into Milton's, at first suspicious, then—in a flash—startled and a little scared.

"I almost believe you, Warden of the State Fauster," she replied, straightening into a military posture. "You seem somehow . . . *different* today."

She turned on the heel of her jackboots and marched away, calling over her shoulder, "To Tier Two. Now. It's nearly nine-oh-two. We've got to get the greenies to their stretchers before they dry up or else they'll be in a world of pain."

9:02? Milton puzzled as he and the other warden led the dazed, dripping children to the next level. *Wow, it feels much later than that. Time passes slowly in this awful place. At least I can get these kids onto some stretchers so they can recuperate. Maybe if I just play along, I can figure out what's going on.*

"Put them on the stretchers, *s'il vous plaît*," the grim attendant said in his stiff buttoned-up white uniform, motioning to a row of odd beds lined against the wall.

Milton set the young blond girl and her brother on the nearest pair of beds. The stretchers were white and curved inward like a tanning bed, with two cylinders separating the tops and the bottoms, kind of like the shoe trees Milton's father used to stretch out his tight leather oxfords. The boy raised his arms toward a pair of holes at the head of the bed. Suddenly, his hands were sucked inside the holes as his feet were seized by clamps. Milton jumped back, startled, as the boy bit his lower lip and whimpered.

"What is—" Milton managed before the boy's sister darted from the bed and ran toward the catwalk. Warden of the State LeBeau whipped about, drew his William club from its holster, and shot an ear-popping whoosh of compressed air from its tip. The little blond girl was knocked to the ground and quickly subdued by the attendants. Milton, his heart racing, pulled out his William club and waved it at the other warden. The children dove to the ground.

"I thought we were putting these kids on stretchers!" Milton barked.

Warden of the State LeBeau clutched his William club tight in his meaty hands and trained it straight between Milton's eyes.

"You *imbécile,*" the man snorted, his muddy brown eyes brimming with murder. "That's what we are *doing,* Fauster: putting the greenies on their stretchers, just like we do every morning!"

The boy lashed to the bed moaned to himself as the ends of the device were pried apart by the hissing pneumatic cylinders built into the middle.

"Stretchers?" Milton mumbled, utterly confused, his body coursing with adrenaline. "But why?"

"After they soak for the night, they have their morning stretches . . . just like we all had done to us . . . though you, of course—because of your sister—got your sentence reduced. You got to go home. . . ."

Warden of the State LeBeau twitched his thumb over the red button of his pneumatic club. "I don't care *whose* brother you are. You've had this coming for a long, long—"

"Men, lower your weapons *immédiatement!*" the

female warden ordered as she strode in from the catwalk. "What is going on?"

LeBeau grudgingly holstered his club while Milton, shaking, let his fall to the floor.

"Capitaine Bébête," LeBeau grumbled. "Fauster here pulled his William club on me after a greenie tried to escape. It was almost as if he actually . . . *cared* about the prisoners."

The captain's face twitched as she tucked an auburn ringlet beneath her large warden's cap. Hands clasped behind her back, she stepped up to Milton, her aquiline nose almost touching his.

"Is this true, Warden of the State?" she said, her breath smelling of black coffee.

Milton swallowed. He tried to get a handle on his situation. How did he get here? And why? Everyone certainly seemed to know him, and apparently liked him about as much as lemon juice on a paper cut.

"The stretchers," Milton managed. "They actually . . . stretch the children."

The woman suppressed a smirk. "Yes . . . truth in advertising, Fauster."

"But it hurts them . . . ma'am. It's wrong."

The woman's emerald-green eyes darted back and forth across Milton's face, trying to read him, as if they were engaged in a game of poker and she was about to call Milton's bluff.

"Of course it hurts," she replied. "That's why they call them growing pains."

"But why?"

The *capitaine* slitted her eyes.

"They soak at night so that they are more pliable in the morning. You know this as well as any warden here, Fauster. *We help them grow.* So that they can be ripened as fast as humanly possible. So that they may serve the state and pay back their debt. As we all do now."

A bell tolled throughout the prison.

"And if this is all some ruse to test our procedures and further your advancement up the ranks—" Capitaine Bébête said.

"It's not," Milton said, rubbing his throbbing temples. "I just don't like to see the kids suffer. They shouldn't be here. They should be out playing or—"

The attendants gasped. Warden of the State LeBeau clutched his William club. Capitaine Bébête waved the warden away. Her eyes blazed green like Irish fireworks.

"You are acting very strange, Fauster," she said, reaching into her pocket. "I suggest you take a lunch break after escorting the children to their pressurization sessions. Get yourself something to eat." She slipped a coin into Milton's front chest pocket. "You might like the escargot-gurt," she whispered. "It tastes just like candy." Capitaine Bébête stepped away from Milton and coughed. "Now compose yourself and act like an *adult*."

She allowed her last word to linger in the air before turning to leave.

"You heard her, Fauster," LeBeau snarled as he gripped a boy roughly by the wrists. "Do your job and get these miserable greenies onto their stretchers before they dry out. I don't want to get my service agreement extended by breaking any of them. . . ."

Milton knelt before the quivering blond girl. "What's your name?" he asked kindly and calmly.

The girl's wide-set blue eyes trembled nervously in their sockets. "Sh-Shirley," she squeaked.

Milton took her hand. "That's a cool name," he whispered as he gently led her to a stretcher. "Much cooler than mine: *Milton*."

The corners of the girl's mouth twitched into a fleeting smile, before her fear quickly wiped it away, like a teacher erasing a kid's naughty drawing on a chalkboard.

"It's going to be okay," Milton said as he helped her onto the cruel device. "It'll just help you grow up faster. Then you can do what you want, right?"

Shirley obediently raised her arms above her head. "L-like you?" she asked in a barely audible hush.

Milton's eyes teared up. "Yeah," he lied as the girl's hands were sucked into the machine. "Like me."

What is up with this place? Milton puzzled as the squealing greenies were pneumatically lengthened. *It's as if childhood is a crime.*

11 · GROWING UP THE RiVER

MILTON WALKED DOWN the steel-grated treads of the steep staircase. Every step of his black leather commando boots pounded the stairs like Thor's hammer smashing the helmeted skulls of enemy hordes.

The last kiddie torture session was even worse than the stretching. The children had been placed into high-pressure chambers, like the kind used to train deep-sea divers, where they were subjected to a steady compression that simulated being six hundred feet underwater. Warden of the State LeBeau—a grade-A jerk who practically quivered with hatred for Milton—had grudgingly explained that this was to build resistance to the sort of high-pressure situations the greenies would encounter as adults. Milton found the whole experience gruesome, especially after listening to the children squeal like boiled lobsters for what felt like hours but—according to the master clock on the ceiling—had only been fifteen minutes.

Milton arrived at the basement level: a grim vault with low ceilings leaking greenish fluorescent light. He wiped his nose with the back of his gloved hand. The place reeked of citrus-scented antiseptic, as if some obsessive-compulsive custodian had sworn a sacred "lemon pledge" to coat every surface of the basement with industrial-strength cleaning products. To his right was a break room . . . so small it could have been a walk-in break *closet*. There was a candy machine and a couple of rigid metal chairs that practically dared you to sit in them. Milton stepped up to the machine and surveyed its contents.

Everything seemed so disgusting, so . . . *French*. Foie gras pockets, vichyssoise pudding cups, and at the back of the machine, a lone escargot-gurt. The container looked dusty and old, like a snack discovered on an archaeological dig. Milton shrugged, remembering how Capitaine Bébête had said it tasted just like candy, and put the gold franc into the slot.

The escargot-gurt fell to the bottom with an unappetizing plop. He opened the container and nearly barfed: a tiny plastic crypt filled with moldy clots of yogurt and rancid snail bits. He noticed a small piece of paper rolled up in the yogurt. He fished it out with his finger.

Midnight. The courtyard. Beneath the shoes.

Keep your cool. Toe the line. All your questions will be answered. Eat this note immédiatement. :)

Milton studied the writing: stiff, structured, and efficient save for a tiny smiley face at the end. He wadded the note into a tiny ball and popped it to the back of his throat before he could think about it too much.

Milton walked back into the hall in his painful boots. *Is this a joke? Was that note* really *meant for me?*

Milton saw a door marked RECORDS.

I still have a few minutes before I'm due back from lunch, he thought as he cast a quick glance down the empty hall.

"Um . . . *bonjour?*" he said quietly as he stuck his head inside. The records room was empty save for three file cabinets and a small table that stuck out of the far wall. Milton heaved open one of the heavy drawers and grabbed a fat manila folder.

Maybe this will shed some light on this dismal place. . . .

Milton quickly leafed through the files, a cold runnel of nervous sweat dripping down his back. He pulled out a map. It looked like a close-up of the Great Lakes region of the United States, only instead of five lakes there was just one—Lake Inferior—with two rivers feeding into it from the west and east: the Au Reservoir and the Juve Nile.

Milton squinted at a landmass in Lake Inferior at the mouth of the Juve Nile. *Tykers Island,* he thought, the voice in his head still squeaky and preadolescent. *That's where I am . . . but why? How did I even get here?*

The region on the map was divided by a jagged line down the middle: the east labeled "Mesopoterica" and the west labeled "Les Etats-Unis de la France."

"The United States of . . . *France*?" Milton croaked in his newly deepened voice. An old, yellowed data sheet was paper-clipped to the map.

Tykers Island

As the region's oldest PRAM (Preadult Repository for Accelerated Maturation), Tykers Island is located at the confluence of the Juve Nile and Lake Inferior. It houses Level III inmaturmates—the incorrigibly infantile—within a walled perimeter encompassing eight levels devoted to hastened, full-body/mind ripening:

Basement: Administration and employee concessions
Courtyard
Tier One: Nourishment troughs
Tier Two: KRAMS (Knowledge Resonation through Amplified Magnetics Systems)
Tier Three: Pressurization chambers
Tier Four: Elongation stations
Tier Five: Slumber soaking cells
Tier Six: Warden of State bunks

Like most government facilities in major city centers, Tykers Island is powered by an underground precarium plant. Precarium, being the most unstable of materials, provides unpredictably volatile fluctuations, making it perfect for mass energy generation. . . .

Milton noticed dozens of bulging files in the drawer below marked: "T. I. Inmaturmates." He knelt down and flipped quickly through the folders until he found the "F" file. Milton nearly swallowed his Adam's apple.

Subject Name: Milton Fauster

Notes: Level II greenie arrived
well below maturity levels. Initial
resistance, stubborn. Chronic smirk.
Would have been classified Level III if
not for sibling influence. Eventually
ripened and subdued through intensive
pressurization and KRAMS sessions.
Released briefly to home care in
Generiquois at sister's request for the
Unfortunate Shower.

That must be what Dad was talking about, Milton thought as he scanned the file. *I was here, then came back: not from the dead, but from* this *place. Tykers Island. To be at home before becoming a warden. So that means that my mom didn't try to "find me" by killing herself. She tried to find me after I was sent away* here. . . .

Milton continued to read his file.

```
Currently serves as Warden of the State
at Tykers Island to pay back his youth
debt to society for egregious acts of
wanton immaturity—
```

"Excusez-moi!" a stiff female voice exploded from the doorway. Milton jumped, the folder flying out of his hands and splaying out onto the floor.

The woman—a teenager, really—clacked into the room on heels so high that they forced her to walk on her toes like a hobbled ballerina in military dress. "What are you doing here, Warden of the State?" she asked, her dark hair pinned up so tight that it rendered her face taut and expressionless. "This is a restricted room."

Milton scooped up the papers and stuffed the folder back into the file cabinet. "Oh, I didn't know," he said, getting to his feet. "It didn't say anything on the door."

"It *doesn't*," the woman replied in a passionless voice. "It doesn't have to. No one ever shows any *interest* in how things are run. With the ministry taking care of everything so well, why would they?" The woman covered her mouth with her hands in shock. *"Pardonne-moi,"* she said in a near whisper. "That almost sounded like I was questioning the state."

Milton patted her on the shoulder. The woman drew back like an abused dog recoiling at a human's touch.

"It's okay," Milton said as he stepped out of the room. "I won't tell."

The woman seemed to almost smile. Almost. *"Merci,"* she said with relief, before suddenly scowling. "Wait . . . why were you—"

Milton jogged away down the hall.

How come I don't remember being here before? Was I in some kind of functional coma, sleepwalking through my life? But it seemed like only yesterday I was back in Generica. Or Generiquois. Whatever the heck it's called now . . .

Milton pounded up the stairs.

Heck. It seems like some bad dream. But I feel like I've woken into another bad dream. Another Heck. My file said something about "sibling influence." And Dad mentioned me "living in my sister's shadow." Even LeBeau said something about not caring whose brother I was. Maybe if I can get a hold of Marlo, she could help me get a handle on what's happening. . . .

The bell tolled, filling the smooth, harsh surfaces of Tykers Island with a clangorous din.

Already? Milton thought as he clambered up the steps to Tier Three. The master clock on the ceiling showed that it was now one p.m.

That was not an hour, Milton thought as he stepped off the stairwell and onto the grated catwalk running along the entire length of the cell block. *It couldn't have been. Maybe that's the problem: I've got some chronic time sickness or walking amnesia . . .*

Milton swallowed, tasting the faint, mildewy tang of snail, yogurt, and wet paper at the back of his throat. He grimaced.

If I can just keep my head down and follow orders until midnight, maybe I can get some answers. At least I'm not the only one here who thinks this place is nightmarishly nuts. . . .

Milton stole out of the wardens' bunks after feigning sleep for nearly an hour. All day he had felt like his personal clock had been at odds with the passage of time around him. His Warden of the State's shift had felt like it had gone on for eighteen hours. But the master clock on the ceiling said otherwise. And Milton's "personal time"—from five o'clock on—seemed to pass faster than Christmas tinsel through a kitten.

Milton slunk down the stairs to the tier below. He briefly stopped in front of Shirley's slumber soaking cell. She twitched fitfully in her sleep, as if she were having a nightmare. Milton rapped on the glass with his knuckles. Her eyes blinked open through the murky maturation solution. Shirley regarded Milton warily.

Condensation had formed on the outside of her tank. With his finger, Milton drew a little smiley face. Shirley smiled around her snorkel and fell back asleep. Milton looked out above the catwalk at the ceiling clock ticking oppressively above. He had only ten minutes before his mysterious rendezvous in the courtyard.

Milton snuck down the stairway and past the empty KRAMS machines on Tier Two. The contraptions looked like the MRI machines that people lie inside to have full-body magnetic scans. Only instead of seeking information, the KRAMS machines forcibly *implanted* information: math, language, history—a form of schooling more invasive than even summer school.

Finally, Milton stepped off the stairway and into the courtyard. There, dangling from the catwalk above, was a sight so ridiculously out of place that it made Milton laugh out loud. *A pair of red clown shoes.* His laugh echoed back and forth as if the cinder-block walls didn't know what to do with the sound of mirth.

"Shhhh!" a familiar voice scolded in a sharp hiss, like a librarian on the verge of a nervous breakdown. "Laughing is a punishable offense."

The clock above ticked to 11:59. Milton swayed with the onset of swift, debilitating fatigue. The clack of boot heels—precise and insistent against the linoleum floor—approached swiftly from behind.

It's like . . . what happened . . . back at home . . . just before midnight . . . couldn't stay awake . . .

Milton turned, yet just as he was poised to meet the mysterious person who could perhaps explain why he was here, the clock struck midnight and Milton collapsed to the ground, completely and utterly asleep.

12 · LEARNING THEIR KEEP

FOR HER FIRST few moments of consciousness, Marlo was convinced that she had awoken sealed inside her own tomb. It was dark and cramped, and it smelled vaguely of copy machine toner. She could hear stirring outside of her sleeping chamber when recent events began to trickle into her brain.

"Oh yeah," she mumbled, decrusting her eyes with her fist. "I'm dead in Precocia and was put to bed in a . . ."

Suddenly, the large drawer she had been sleeping in was yanked open by three young, buzzing mayfly demons.

". . . filing cabinet," Marlo continued. She winced at the intense fluorescent lights streaming down from the low, asbestos-paneled ceiling and propped herself up on her elbows.

"What time is it?" she grumbled.

"Time to get up." One of the pint-sized flying demons laughed in Marlo's face.

"Yeah, well, we'll see who's laughing tomorrow, Mister Twenty-Four-Hour Life Span," Marlo grumbled.

Someone smacked the bottom of her drawer bed.

"Hey, Sleeping Butt-Ugly!" Lyon yelled from the drawer beneath. "Move it. I need to, like, get out of this thing!"

"And a very good morning to you, too, Peroxide-Frosted Flake," Marlo replied as she took her sweet time descending the chain ladder dangling from her drawer. "Nice to hear that you woke up on the right side of the filing cabinet."

The girls yawned and stretched in the Young Ladies' Room and Boardroom: a big, empty meeting room with rows of massive three-story file cabinets set against the walls, where the precocious girls of Precocia had been "filed away" for the night. The mayfly demons tugged a portable garment steamer from girl to girl, steaming out the wrinkles of their Power Suits.

"I miss pajamas," a girl with a high forehead and bags under her eyes said sleepily.

"Waste of time," one of the demons—about the size of a bristly airborne sausage—replied as it smoothed out her rumpled mustard-yellow suit with scalding-hot steam. After a few fussy minutes, the mayfly demons scooped up their tiny pitchsporks and jabbed the girls out into the main office area to a sad little break room. The boys huddled around a large sparking microwave where several boxes rotated on a carousel.

"Marlo!" Virgil called out, stepping up to Marlo with his arms extended.

"Oh . . . hey," Marlo replied vaguely, screwing up her eyes at Virgil.

The boy's smile dimmed as he downgraded his hug into a handshake.

"Um . . . anyway, I just—"

"*Virgil?*" Marlo said with a smile as she wrapped her arms around him. "Whoa. I didn't recognize you. You lost some . . . you know . . ."

"Blubber?" Lyon said as she walked toward the coffeepot.

Virgil's face went as red as a Martian stop sign. Marlo glared at Lyon over Virgil's shoulder.

"Actually, I didn't lose the weight, exactly," Virgil said, grinning. "I know where it all is: back in Blimpo."

"I thought you seemed familiar yesterday," Marlo said as they continued hugging. "But after that horrible cooties thing, you know, they separated the boys and girls and stuff so we could clean up and . . ."

After an awkward few seconds, Marlo patted Virgil's back. "Okay," she said, breaking free, "hug sequence deactivated. . . . Hey, is that food?"

One of the boys poked at the contents of his just-microwaved box with a pair of chopsticks.

"That's what the box said." The redheaded boy sighed, gesturing toward the yellow-and-black box labeled FOOD at the top of the overflowing garbage. "But my mouth says otherwise."

Kali's Sylla-Bus pulled up outside the break room. She waved the children inside the bus with three of her massive blue arms.

"Come, little adults, come!" she said in her thick Indian accent. "It is the time for starting your classes!"

The children trudged toward the vehicle, with boys breaking to the right, and girls to the left.

Virgil stopped and turned to Marlo. "Sorry about Milton."

"Sorry?" Marlo replied with a roll of her eyes. "Sorry that he's taking it easy in some hospital bed while we have to go to school? The little runt always catches breaks like this. . . ."

The children sat on their benches as the bus pulled away. Up ahead, an old, bald priest with tiny white angel wings sprinkled water on Solomon Grundy's head.

"Hey, go easy on the waterworks, Rev," the baby-man grumbled, cradled in Dr. Curie's arms and dressed in a small white gown.

"What's going on?" Marlo asked the big blue Indian goddess.

"Solomon Grundy, christened on Tuesday," she said over her shoulder as the Sylla-Bus passed the baptism.

"Now put on your pens. Here comes your first class of the day!"

The bus crept across the soiled gray carpet toward a man with fancy white hair sitting before a small piano keyboard.

"*Guten morgen,* Junior Executives," the man said with a faint German accent. "I—as some of you may have been able to discern from the powdered wig and the harpsichord—am Wolfgang Amadeus Mozart."

"Mozart? The Austrian composer widely recognized as one of the greatest in the history of music?" a skinny Asian girl said in awe.

"So I hear, young fräulein, so I hear. A 'genius before my time' who died before *his* time to spend eternity in this grim place for those who have done much too much, much too young. But enough of me . . . let us begin our lesson. . . ."

The Korean boy with the spiky black hair raised his muscular right arm. "Are you going to be teaching us music theory? And if so, will there be a test?"

"No, silly child, no," Mozart said with a dismissive wave of his fragile white hand. "Vhat good is learning the language of music if no one will listen, much less pay for your vork? Vhat good is structure and form if you cannot put food on the table?"

"But your music brought so much joy to the world," said a girl with strawberry-blond hair and buckteeth. "And recitals. *Tons* of recitals!"

The Sylla-Bus slowly passed the famous composer at the speed of maple syrup pouring onto a stack of pancakes.

"But vhere did all of this grand music get me in life?" Mr. Mozart asked. The Korean boy raised his hand, and the teacher ignored him. "I'll tell you vhere: dead at thirty-five, exhausted, half mad, penniless . . . just another indulgent composer decomposing in an unmarked grave."

The children craned their necks as they drove away from their teacher.

"But down here I learned that music, instead of creating ecstasy and madness in the mind, could be made more practical!" he shouted. "More lucrative! Which is why I will be teaching you how to write commercial jingles!"

The Sylla-Bus drove away from Mr. Mozart. Up ahead, a tall, gangly young man swaggered toward the creeping scooter bus. He looked like a boy who had been hastily stretched to adult size, with a crazy gleam in his mismatched eyes as if he had spent way too much time in the sun.

"Howdy, Junior Pardners . . . *ladies,*" he said with a creepy leer, tipping his crumpled black hat to the girls.

Marlo shivered. "Ugh . . . with a face like that, he should be in pictures . . . ," she whispered to the fuchsia-haired girl next to her. "The kind of pictures hanging on a post office wall."

"I'm William the Kid," the young man said as he straightened the holster slung low on his hips.

The Korean boy raised his hand. "Don't you mean Billy the Kid? The Wild West outlaw?"

The teacher fiddled with the phone headset that traced his stubbly jawline. "I left all that silly 'Billy' stuff up on the Surface for the buzzards to peck at," he replied with a smirk. "Folks take me more serious-like with *William*. And William's here to teach y'all about bill collection."

The Sylla-Bus passed close to William the Kid. Marlo could see that he was dressed as a sort of cowboy detective, with spurs and a gray sharkskin suit that oozed blood from a bullet hole just under the lapel.

"You can make a killin' as a bill collector," he explained. "Just fer robbin' those desperate saps who've robbed the credit companies. But they get their money back in the end . . . and *then* some." William the Kid stuck out his chest, causing him to bleed like a stuck pig. "If someone is late with their bills, that's where William comes in," the outlaw explained. "And every moment is a life or *debt* situation. Get it? Companies pay William to collect their bills for 'em, so they don't have to be the bad guy. But William *loves* bein' the bad guy! Always has . . . just ask the twenty-one fellers William killed up on the Surface! They were William's first victims down here, too. They'd run up some bills and William came for 'em again. If you thought life was plenty funny like that, just you wait: *death is a scream!*"

The children drove away as William the Kid cackled his mirthless hyena laugh. The Sylla-Bus cleared the corner, returning to Solomon Grundy's baptism.

The bald, nervous priest read from a Bible. " 'When John baptized Jesus,' " he said in a shaky voice as mayfly demons swarmed around him, " 'the Holy Spirit came down like a dove from Heaven.' "

The old man nodded to Dr. Curie, who, after handing the infant Badmissions director to the priest, knelt down to a canvas sack by her feet. She opened the sack and released a small flock of pigeons.

"Pigeons are all we can get down here," Dr. Curie apologized as the grubby gray birds flapped chaotically about.

One of the pigeons landed on Kali's steering handles.

"*Nahīm!*" the Hindu goddess bellowed, waving away the gnarled, one-eyed bird. "No let the pigeon drive the bus!" Kali leaned forward, pushing her scooter bus faster back to Mr. Mozart.

"We will start with a deconstruction of Chopin's 'The Minute Waltz,' " he said, cracking his knuckles above the keys of his harpsichord.

" 'The Minute Waltz'?" Lyon whined, crossing her bony, bronzed arms. "How long is *that* going to take?"

"Not as long as you think, *kleines mädchen*," Mr. Mozart replied. "See, I have condensed it to its musical essence, stripped it of all adornment, to reveal the virulent *ohrwurm* beneath."

"Ohrwurm?" Virgil asked.

"German for 'earworm,' otherwise known as song stuck syndrome: those tiny pieces of music you can't get out of your head no matter vhat. It all comes down to the hook, to what is catchy. And a catchy jingle can soon become the jingle of coins in the shrewd composer's pocket!"

"Sellout," hissed the skinny Asian girl with disgust.

"All vork and no pay made Mozart a poor boy," Mr. Mozart grumbled, his nose lifted in the air with offense. "Vhat is so wrong with the composer living to cash his royalty check? Do you think Dr. Einstein and I see one penny of Baby Einstein sales? No . . . we were naive. But not anymore. Why not use music's ability to elevate the spirit to help elevate one's bank account?"

The Sylla-Bus turned the corner, returning to William the Kid. Marlo felt light-headed; it was as if she were trapped in a movie that someone kept fast-forwarding through to find the good parts, only there *weren't* any good parts. A small twinge of worry tickled the back of her mind.

I hope Milton's okay, Marlo fretted briefly before brushing the thought away.

"First, you track the suckers down, the ones with delinquent accounts," William the Kid drawled, walking to meet the scooter bus. "That's when you use *this.* . . ."

Quick as a sidewinder struck by lightning, the teacher drew from his holster. The children ducked. In his hand was a cell phone mounted onto the grip of a gun.

"You harass 'em with phone calls," William the Kid said with a sneer. "With a little research, you can find out exactly when they're sittin' down to dinner, entertainin' guests, or even when they're in the outhouse. It's easy pickins', but yer worst enemy is, by far, other debt collectors. Is there any of you who'd like to help—"

The Korean boy raised his arm.

"Wow, that's one long arm. You ain't with the law, are ya, kid?"

"No, sir."

"Okay, well, then, hop on off and let William see yer skills."

Kali flipped a switch beneath her handlebars. The Korean boy's restraint popped open. William the Kid threw the boy a phone outfitted with a gun grip.

"See, bill collection is a game of who gets there first," he sneered.

The boy stepped off the scooter bus, swallowed hard, and tried to control his shaking arm as he held his phone gun at his side.

"Now on the count of three, we draw."

"*Draw?* Like guns?"

"Yeah," William the Kid snickered, his row of crooked teeth peeking out from behind his chapped lips. "And, normally, William don't care to open debt negotiations with a fight, but you've left William no choice: now William'll whip the whole darned bunch of you!"

"Um . . . there's only me and you asked me to

come down and . . . ," the boy replied with nervous confusion.

"*Two!*"

"But you didn't say—"

"*Three!*"

William the Kid yanked the phone out of his holster in the blink of a gnat's eye. The boy's phone rang, still hanging at his side.

"Um . . . hello?" the boy answered into the phone gun.

"William's got yer number on speed dial, kid," William the Kid chuckled into his gun before blowing on the tip and reholstering it.

The boy gave a quick bow. "Um . . . thank you, Mr. the Kid," he said before running back to the Sylla-Bus as it crept once more to Solomon Grundy's baptism.

The full, crushing, nonsensical tedium of Precocia hit Marlo: an eternity spent driving around in circles, having meaningless information crammed into your life-challenged skull. Hour after hour. Day after day. Week after week. And for what? To prepare for a tedious, pointless afterlife?

"Repent, and be baptized in the name of Jesus Christ for the remission of sins, and ye shall receive the gift of the Holy Ghost," the priest said as he patted Solomon Grundy's damp head with a cloth.

"File that under 'too little, too late,'" the fuchsia-haired girl next to Marlo whispered.

Marlo snickered as the Sylla-Bus returned to Mr. Mozart.

"A jingle must be as short, repetitive, and easy to remember as a nursery rhyme, so that vhen a consumer is walking down the supermarket aisle looking for deodorant, they pick the one vith the catchiest jingle," the pale man said, raising his hands above his keyboard, poised to strike a melody. "Like this: *Figa-roll-on! Figa-roll-on! For vhen you wear hot lederhosen! If you're damp down in the pits, and your AC's on the fritz, be sure you have some Figa-roll-on! Figa-roll-on! Figa-roll-on!*"

For a long, awkward moment, the only sound was the squeak and clatter of the Sylla-Bus, passing Mr. Mozart by.

Slowly, the children began humming their teacher's irritating jingle. Virgil cleaned his ear out with his finger.

"Ugh! Is there a cure for earworms?" he asked.

"The only known cure is the Earvorm Scoot: to replace the offending refrain with something even more infectious!" Mr. Mozart said with glee, his hands hovering threateningly above the keys. "Here, try this—"

The Sylla-Bus turned the corner. William the Kid was waiting, spitting into a spittoon.

"Just say no to tales of woe from those who owe . . . that's what William always says," the teacher said, scratching his privates in public. "I've seen many a good man gummed down by some old lady when trying to collect her gold fillings. The suckers give you the HLS—the hard-luck stories. You know . . . losin' their job, a family member gettin' unexpectedly reborn . . . stuff that leaves them with bills. But if you feel pity for these deader-than-deadbeats, then your career is off the hook . . . and not in the good way. William hears that's a phrase now."

The fuchsia-haired girl leaned into Marlo. "What's with the referring-to-yourself-in-the-third-person thing?" she whispered. "That's like basically telling everyone, 'William is absolutely insane.'"

"Like we didn't get that from his chest wound and itchy cell phone finger," Marlo replied with a smirk.

William the Kid frowned at the girls. "Ladies, you best not be talkin' guff about William," he said as the scooter bus gradually passed him. "William's got a lot of good teachin' to teach you. Mainly about killin' and bill collectin' . . ." He spat a thick brown glob into his brass spittoon. "It's like panning for gold. You make a few hundred calls a day, but one chump will make it all worthwhile. And when they're done blubberin', ya squeeze 'em."

Vice Principal Cleopatra stepped in front of the Sylla-Bus, her thin brown arm wrapped possessively around the shoulder of the most beautiful boy Marlo had ever seen.

"Looks like *Cleo's* got a new squeeze," the fuchsia-haired girl muttered with a goofy smile.

The unashamedly smitten vice principal tightened her grip on the dark, muscular boy.

"Ooh." She giggled as the Sylla-Bus slowed to a halt. "Shoulders like boulders."

The girls in the scooter bus strained past their steel bar restraints to steal a peek at the new boy.

He's . . . perfect, Marlo thought, electricity radiating out from her stomach as if she had eaten a car battery. *But not in that boring perfect way.* His skin was like flawless black metal and his eyes burned like blue fire.

"I'd like you all to meet our newest Junior Executive!" Cleopatra purred, playing with a ringlet of the boy's hair protruding from his black stocking cap. She glanced down at the file she held in her other hand. "Fallon, Angelo!"

"Actually," the boy said in a voice as dark, smooth, and sweet as root beer. "The name is *Angelo Fallon.*" He smiled, which seemed to cause the girls audible pain.

"Angelo," Lyon muttered, eyeing the new boy as if he were a fattening dessert that she'd gladly starve herself all day to devour. "The perfect name for an *angel!*"

The boy laughed.

"I'm no angel," he said, taking off his designer glasses. "Not *quite.*"

13 · WHERE THE
SUN DON'T SHINE

A MOSQUITO LANDED on the bridge of Milton's nose. Milton slapped his face hard and—inadvertently—slapped himself awake.

"I don't want to play slap with you, Marlo!" Milton sputtered as he bolted up, his head thick with the sludge of sleep, like an old carburetor in need of an oil change. His voice rattled in his throat, deep as it was yesterday, only a touch raspier. Milton rubbed the crust of sleep from his eyes and studied his surroundings. He wasn't in his bunk at Tykers Island anymore: he was in a darkened tent, lying on the floor in a snug, olive-drab sleeping bag. He wriggled out of the padded sack and rose to his feet. The top of his head throbbed and his mouth tasted like soggy Grape-Nuts.

"Ugh," Milton mumbled as he stumbled to a mirror hanging over a small sink. "I'm not sure if I'm alive or—" He stopped short in front of the grubby mirror. *"Dad?"*

A man in his late thirties stared back at Milton through the mirror, a man who looked an awful lot like Milton's father when he was younger, only with his mother's eyes.

"But *how*? I . . . I must have time-lapsed again. Fallen into some kind of coma like Rip van Winkle—"

A man with stiff, charcoal-colored hair walked into Milton's tent.

"Talking to yourself, Fauster?" the man said, his voice smooth and mocking. "Guess you *are* your own best friend . . . your *only* friend, really. Anyway, you slipped me a few francs to give you *this* today."

The man held a manila envelope in his hands and considered Milton expectantly with his dull brown eyes.

"I asked you to give me an envelope?" Milton said, his voice sounding as if it were somehow dubbed by his father.

The man cocked his eyebrow and pursed his lips. "You said not to give it to you unless you acted like you didn't know what I was talking about," the man said as he held out the envelope.

Milton took it with a faint trepidation. "Um, thanks, uh—"

"Jérôme," the man replied in a huff. "I don't know

what you're up to, Fauster, but if you think you can pretend to be crazy and go back home, you're crazy. I don't
care *who* you're related to."

Jérôme walked out into what appeared to be the dead
of night. Milton squinted at the envelope, addressed to
"Moi." He tore it open. Inside was a note written in Milton's handwriting—if he had written it with his left hand
while riding on a three-legged camel—and what looked
like a deflated whoopee cushion.

To the Dude That's Me,
That sounds crazy but that's what this whole
thing feels like. The first time I noticed it—
The Big Day Off (figures I can only get a
day off by having some weird amnesia)—was
when the meteorites fell. It was like I had
a 24-hour blackout, only Blake said I was up
and around, though I asked a lot of those
"question" things. Where you actually want
to know something, for some reason. I just
chalked it all up to stress, you know: heading
off to Tykers Island to pay off my youth
debt. But then it happened again, a decade later
to the day. You really messed me up that day
in Tykers, ten years ago—

"Ten years ago?" Milton murmured as he read the
letter. "I've been someone else for *ten years*?"

I woke up the next day and was interrogated
by Capitaine Bébête. Something about a clown
shoe. She didn't believe me when I said I didn't
know what she was talking about. That incident
and my, well, unique work ethic brought
me here. Marlo—excusez-moi—Assistant
Chancellor—won't even help me out. She
says, through her assistant, of course, that
this experience out here at the edge of the
French empire will be good for me—straighten
me out and give me some ambition—and that
things are complicated for her because of the
war and that I just have to tough it out.
I can't even tell her about my/our ... spells.
I've got enough stacked against me as it is
without some Ministry Abnormality Inquisition
Medic (MAIM) starting a psych file on me.
That's almost as bad as being a greenie. Almost.
So, if I wake up and I'm not me but you,
s'il vous plaît, dude: don't mess up my life.
It's messed up enough as it is. Vocational
school dropout ... divorced (that Aubrey
Fitzmallow was a piece of work) ... at least
I'm/we're not aging gracefully.

Long Live the Emperor (or, in case the Egyptian
Empire wins, Praise Ra, Almighty Isis, etc....)
                                    Milton Fauster

Milton stood, paralyzed, in the muggy tent.

This is crazy . . . or maybe I'm *what's crazy,* he thought as the letter fell from his shaking hand and floated gently to the dirt floor. *How can I forget ten years? And I don't even sound like myself, or whoever I am now: the same me inside, but old outside. . . .*

Jérôme barged in. "So, Fauster, you thinking of doing some work today?" he asked.

"It looks like it's the middle of the night," Milton said.

Milton stepped past Jérôme and out into what looked like a desert, cast with a gray, muddy light.

"Is that supposed to be one of those 'joke' things?" Jérôme said, clenching his perpetually put-upon face. "Where a statement is made in willful conflict with reality, with the malicious intent of conjuring"—he cringed—"*humor?*"

Milton looked up. The sky was the color of ash and soot. It was as if there were an enormous dented garbage lid—forged of thick leaden dust—pressing down oppressively from horizon to horizon. There was a faint patch of light gray in the black churning soot, hovering over the eastern horizon.

"The sun?" Milton murmured.

"*Oui,*" Jérôme replied. "Thank goodness for the Widow's Veil."

"Widow's Veil?"

"The cloud of upturned dust that covers nearly the entire planet ever since the meteors fell twenty years ago, *imbécile*. In fact, it was twenty years ago *today* . . . the emperor is even going to give a special speech. Without the Widow's Veil, we'd probably all get sunstroke out here in the Senegal desert."

"Senegal as in . . . Africa?"

"*Afrique Française,* to be precise," Jérôme clarified in a way that somehow confused Milton even more.

Milton's eyes adjusted to the muted light that seemed to smother all color out of the savanna around him. The placid veld was filled with scattered baobab trees—their gnarled branches scratching at the low-hanging firmament like claws—wilted palms, the occasional termite mound, and mile after mile of dead grass. In the distance was a small village of bungalows and cottages. Milton noticed dozens of people dressed just like him—in black-and-white-striped overalls and berets perched atop their heads—circling the village, carrying tools.

"So we're here to help the villagers build houses?" Milton asked.

Jérôme scrunched up his snooty butler face at Milton, his pursed lips suppressing a budding grin. "You're serious," he replied, scratching his graying temple. "We're part of a work detail . . . for Habitat for Inhumanity."

"*In*humanity?" Milton replied incredulously as he saw a worker in the distance remove the vinyl siding from a prefabricated shed with his crowbar.

"*Oui* . . . you know: we tear down low-cost, ministry-sanctioned housing when the owners have defaulted."

Milton gazed at weeping West Africans clad in head wraps and shawls milling about as their ramshackle cottages were knocked to the ground.

"So we're a bunch of callous, unfeeling jerks, then, aren't we?" Milton murmured.

A sobbing child screamed as he was dragged away by French workers for blocking the front door of his former home. The door was soon pulverized by sledgehammers.

Jérôme nodded as he picked up his toolbox filled with demolition equipment. "That's one way of looking at it," the man grunted.

"Yeah, the *right* way," Milton replied with disgust.

"It never bothered you before," Jérôme said as he cinched his beret over his bristly, charcoal-colored hair. "In fact, you usually go at those hovels with gusto."

"Well, not today," Milton said as he sat down in the dust, the sky above choked with swirling eddies of ash.

Jérôme gave a weak Gallic shrug as he walked across the grasslands toward the demolition site.

"I want you out there with the rest of us in an hour."

The lanky man slunk through the tall dead grass, singing softly to himself. *"If I had a hammer, I'd demolish a family's home in the morning, I'd demolish a family's home in the evening, all over this land. . . ."*

Milton stared grimly at the churning ceiling of soot hovering above. The way it clasped the Earth, lower than clouds but higher than any building, made him feel claustrophobic. Like a bug in jar. The cloud of ash reminded him of the smog that clung to Precocia: like a coroner's sheet draped over a corpse.

The meteor shower twenty years ago must have been a massive, global catastrophe, Milton thought. *It's odd, though, that it would kick up enough dust to fill the sky but not wipe out humanity outright.*

The sounds of destruction and anguish drifted across the grasslands.

Not that there seems to be much humanity in the world these days. No compassion. No tolerance for anything but working hard to make the world a more miserable place.

Milton sighed, picked up a nearby baobab branch, and started making a spiral in the dirt.

Figuring out who I am was hard enough before. Now I'm someone I don't think I'd even like if I met him. Or me. I sound like a lazy, self-centered jerk for the nine years, eleven months, and twenty-nine days that I'm not me. . . .

Milton had inadvertently scrawled a smiley face in the dirt. A smirk spread across his face, like a flower bud poking through a crack in the concrete.

But at least today I'm me, and I can live the kind of life I please. The kind of life that can maybe make things just a little bit better . . .

14 · MERCi, MERCi ME

"HIDE–AND–SEEK?" the dark-skinned boy repeated back to Milton, his eyes wide with confusion and fear. "Like when the soldiers try to catch us for stealing food?"

"No, no . . . hide-and-seek is a *game*," Milton clarified, glancing nervously past the boy at Jérôme and the other volunteers smashing the windows of a shabby bunga-low a quarter mile away. To Milton it looked like the "Inhumans" were gouging out the glass eyes of a giant decapitated head made of plywood and plaster.

"*Game?*" the small Senegalese boy said with a faint French accent.

"Um . . . *oui*. Something to do for fun."

"Fun?"

"Something you do for no other reason than to make you smile."

The boy's wide mouth twitched into a shy grin.

"Go tell your friends to hide way over there in that clump of trees," Milton said as he got up off his knees, gesturing toward a dense thicket. "Then you count to a thousand. Okay?"

The boy nodded and dashed away toward a sad clot of children huddled together by piles of splintered wood and gnarled sheets of corrugated tin.

As the children stole away to the trees, Milton trotted back to the volunteers' campsite and grabbed a toolbox. He approached a bony woman with odd, gray-streaked hair heading out to the demolition site.

"*Excusez-moi,*" Milton said. "I noticed that there was something odd about the children."

"Children are always odd," she replied flatly. "They're disgusting."

"Yes . . . *oui* . . . but these children were laughing."

"Laughing?" she gasped.

"Yeah . . . *and holding hands.*"

The woman's mouth hung open like a lipsticked door off its hinges.

"You should tell Jérôme," Milton said, suppressing his smile. "I saw them skipping over *there.*" He pointed to a dense patch of long grass located as far away as possible from where the children really *were* hiding.

The woman ran to the demolition site, and after a brief flurry of gesticulation with Jérôme, she and the other mandatory volunteers fled the dismantled homesteads. Milton smiled and stalked across the dead grass, lugging his overstuffed toolbox behind him.

"They say no good deed goes unpunished," Milton mumbled as he approached the nearest half-dismembered home. "Hopefully *this* good deed won't get what's coming to it until tomorrow, when I'm someone who *deserves* to be punished."

Milton wasn't exactly what you, or anyone, might call "handy." The neighborhood kids, for instance, used to call him "No Door" after he had completed his first, and only, clubhouse made notorious and unusable due to one glaring design flaw.

But now, in the humid, stifling gray of what Milton assumed to be afternoon here in Senegal, he was filled with a quiet pride at his handiwork. In the past couple of hours, he had managed to rebuild—if the definition of "rebuild" was downgraded to "loosely reassemble using irreparably damaged parts"—nearly three homes. He simply assessed what had been undone, and undid that. Now all he needed was a sheet of mangled tin to finish the last roof, which was conveniently handed to him as he teetered atop an aluminum ladder.

"Thanks," Milton said automatically.

"Don't mention it," Jérôme replied from below.

Milton gulped.

At the foot of the ladder were Jérôme and a half dozen other Habitat for Inhumanity unworkers. Over the roof of one of his rebuilt houses, Milton could see the group of children herded under a withered palm tree.

"If it's any consolation, I'm doing a terrible job," Milton deadpanned as he was dragged back to the encampment.

"What do you think you're doing, Fauster?" Jérôme grunted as he pushed Milton along the tall dead grass.

"Something I shouldn't *have* to do," Milton replied. "What do these people even have? Without the sun, they can't grow any crops—"

"They could buy full-spectrum hydroponic grow units just like everyone else," Jérôme said stiffly.

"Buy? *With what?* These people have nothing. And how is dismantling their homes going to help anything? It actually *costs* money to send people out here to do this! It's crazy . . . it's . . . *fou!*"

They arrived outside Milton's tent.

"We'll see how 'fou' you think it is once I've filed my report with the ministry," Jérôme said, his face so grave that Milton felt inclined to put flowers on it. "They'll probably send you back to Tykers. Or *worse*. And not even your sister will help you out of this one. She'd have to be a minister to have enough pull to—"

"The emperor!" the bony woman shouted as she fiddled with a large radio. "He's giving his speech now!"

The woman sifted through a sea of white noise until

she dialed into the ministry's official frequency. A stately voice rumbled through the radio's speaker.

"And introducing his eminence, Emperor Napoléon the Ninth—"

"Napoléon the Ninth?" Milton exclaimed, before the large group scowled him silent.

Vice Principal Napoléon . . . Precocia. It was all coming back to Milton. Coming down with swine cooties . . . fainting . . . being dragged to the infirmary, where Mr. Einstein shoved a hood on his head and told him he was going back home. Only he hadn't mentioned that home wouldn't be *his* home.

"Good day, citizens . . . or night, depending on where you are currently stationed—a conundrum I will conquer by zhe end of my speech," the sovereign ruler of the French empire stated. *"To commemorate zhe twentieth anniversary of zhe Unfortunate Shower, I have a series of déclarations to make to you, zhe citizens of zhe soon-to-be-greatest empire zhe Earth has ever known!"*

The Habitat for Inhumanity workers applauded as they sat in a circle around the radio. Milton looked out at the dilapidated village beyond the veld, considering making a break for it, but instead he sat down, hoping to learn more about this disheartening dystopia.

"Nothing will deter us from our endeavor to eradicate youth. We have made great strides such as zhe six-month gestation period, outsourced and institutionalized development— freeing both adult and preadult to live more productive, focused,

and solemn lives—and are on zhe cusp of breakthroughs such as zhe Premature Aging Phenomenon (PAP) pathogen."

Milton shook his head. *This Napoléon is just as crazy as the Napoléon back in Precocia,* he thought. *I guess the fruitcake doesn't fall far from the tree.*

"But zhere is an enemy to our prosperity . . . and, no, I do not mean zhe Egyptians zhat we have been at war with for so long. Zhis enemy is within our own ranks: plotting with pranks set to tickle zhe funny bone of zhe body politic!"

Milton leaned into Jérôme. "What is he talking about?" he whispered.

"The Pièce de Résistance, *imbécile!*" Jérôme hissed back, his breath a blast of espresso and cigarette butts.

"Zhe French and Egyptian empires realize now zhat zhe enemy is not one another, but zhe juvenility zhat infects humanity at its onset! Which is why we have put aside our differences and united our empires into one: joining forces against zhis worldwide threat of foolishness!"

The people huddled around the radio gasped.

"The war . . . it's over?" muttered the bony woman with the streaked white hair.

"To mark zhe end of zhe French and Egyptian hostilities, we wed our empires together in a very literal way," Emperor Napoléon IX continued. "My heir, Napoléon X, and zhe, um . . . ample Egyptian princess Cleopatra XL will be married to inaugurate zhe glorious new Fregyptian world power!"

The Habitat for Inhumanity members bolted to their feet and applauded.

"And, as our dominance now girdles zhe globe, all time zones will be merged into one—Undisputed Not Juvenile Universal Standard Time or UNJUST!"

"One time zone?" Milton murmured to Jérôme. "How is that even possible?"

Jérôme's face fermented into something so curdled that you could have served it with wine and crackers.

"The Widow's Veil," he replied with exasperation. "It thickens and darkens with every passing year. Soon, we will not know night from day. One time zone will make us all—everyone in the entire world—more productive, more efficient, working as one for a common objectif . . . not that you'll be contributing much, wasting away at Tykers Island."

"And, lastly, I have given Assistant Chancellor Fauster the great task of creating zhe new Ministry of Maturation," the emperor continued, "devoted to bringing our world to its ultimate adulthood!"

The group of humorless men and women turned their dour faces toward Milton, eyeing him with a volatile mixture of suspicion and flat-out jealousy.

"Merci, Emperor," peeped a voice from the radio.

Marlo? Milton thought as the crowd returned their attention to the radio. It was weird enough to hear his sister's voice grown older, but her showing respect for an authority figure—without the smirking sheen of sarcasm—was hard for his ears to swallow.

"We are all cogs in a precision machine of blind, absolute productivity," Napoléon IX concluded. *"Citizens rise up! And now sit back down in a grown-up manner, because zhere is nothing but work to be done . . . get to it!"*

As the members of Habitat for Inhumanity heeded the words of their supreme ruler and one by one grabbed their sledgehammers and crowbars to dismantle Milton's handiwork, Jérôme turned to Milton.

"Maybe I can't send you back to Tykers Island—*yet,*" he seethed. "But, minister sister or not, you're officially no longer part of Team Inhumanity. So sit tight in your tent until I can figure out what to do with you—*mon Dieu!*—and if you commit any more acts of flagrant compassion, we'll tear *you* down!"

Milton sat in the stifling heat of his tent and brooded until nightfall, though with the Widow's Veil it was impossible to tell exactly *what* time it was.

Napoléon . . . Cleopatra . . . it's all too much of a coincidence to not be just a coincidence. Surely there's some point to me being here: another *place where Napoléon and Cleopatra rule. It can't just be some kind of a joke.*

Milton spied the deflated whoopee cushion that had fallen from the envelope that morning. He rolled it around in his hands and discovered the other Milton's sloppy handwriting scrawled on one side.

Dude That's Me—I found this stuffed in my pocket when I woke up the day after you took possession of my body or whatever. It's some kind of rubber handkerchief. I don't get it. Maybe you will—Dude That's You.

Who doesn't know what a whoopee cushion is? Milton thought as he inflated the round bladder and, bored, sat on it. Yet instead of an imitation fart, the cushion bleated out a message.

"If you hear this"—pllltttttt!—*"you must be one of us. HAHAHA . . . the Pièce de Résistance. The punch line to this joke of a government. Await further . . ."*

Milton reinflated the whoopee cushion and sat on it again, hearing the same unsurprisingly farty message.

"The Pièce de Résistance," Milton mumbled. "The group that Emperor Napoléon IX was yammering on about. And now somehow I'm wrapped up in all of this."

An idea crept around the edges of Milton's mind. He reached for the note and flipped it over. He grabbed a pen.

Dear—

Milton hesitated.

—Me. I don't know what's going on here any more than you do, other than, yes, something is going

on. But it must be happening for some reason. I was alive in a place that, while not perfect, was at least a world where you could laugh and play and not worry about being arrested just for being a kid. Then I died ... long story. But somehow I came back as you and—between you and me—I think we can make this awful place a little better. Should we overthrow the government? Should we help the children of the world? Should we shed light in this land of darkness? Should we waste our time asking rhetorical questions? That's a joke, sort of. . . .

Milton's mind softened with a sudden rush of fatigue.
Uh-oh . . . I'm losing it. Just like before . . .
Milton's vision went blurry as he struggled to stay awake.

Our sister. Marlo. She's a minister now. Maybe she can help. The Pièce de Résistance. HAHAHA ... whatever that stands for. You, me, myself, I ... <u>whoever</u> needs to make contact. We could help them to deliver the punch line this joke of a place needs. . . .

Milton keeled over, his fervent letter to himself now a pillow as he fell fast asleep, not quite sure where, when, or *who* he would wake up as.

15 · THE HAND THAT WRECKS THE CRADLE RE-RULES THE WORLD

DR. EINSTEIN PACED in the dim green light of the capacious laboratory like a distracted ghost. A chorus of wobbly, grating screeches—an argument between metal and stone—and a persistent scraping sound echoed throughout the room. Atop the maddening din was a tangle of incomprehensible mutterings.

"Vhat is time but the context of our reality?" Dr. Einstein mumbled as he jotted down notes in his notebook.

Vice Principals Napoléon and Cleopatra entered the laboratory, the petite former emperor of France taking loud, aggressive stomps in his leather boots while the former queen of Egypt slinked across the floor like an imperious cat in sandals.

"*Bonsoir,* Dr. Einstein," Napoléon said, sipping an espresso as he approached the disheveled scientist.

"Is the source of time outside of us or *inside*?" Dr. Einstein murmured to himself as he scribbled, his pupils wide.

Cleopatra rolled her dark, indignant eyes. "Dr. Einstein!" she shouted, her lips flecked with latte foam, while Napoléon reached inside his breast-coat pocket. "You insufferable man! Do you know who stands before you?"

"Vhere in time do ve even exist?"

Napoléon jabbed the Mind Control app on his mobile device. The blinders surgically attached to Einstein's temples flickered like angry electric bees.

The old man blinked. His pupils tightened into pinpoints. "Oh . . . hello, Vice Principals. Thank you. My mind vas vandering," Dr. Einstein replied vaguely.

Napoléon sighed as he surveyed the creaking machines, squinting in the dim light. "We demand an update, *immédiatement*! Time is of zhe essence!"

"*Ja* . . . yes . . . *oui* . . . of course," Dr. Einstein replied, puzzling at his notes. "Vell, most of the sleep mutterings are useless. They are either incomprehensible due to veak connections—minds that are not fully open—or they relay accounts of realities that vould not serve your purposes. *This* one—the skinny blond *mädchen*—just goes on and on about some vonderful place where 'fat is the new scary-thin' and you can eat all you vant."

"Zhen *zhat* one over zhere is our only hope?" Napoléon said, nodding his wide military hat toward a figure hanging upside down in the dark like a bat.

"*Ja* . . . I am getting some very interesting sleep chatter from him," Dr. Einstein said as he shuffled toward one of the machines in his slippers. "His alternate reality seems to not only meet your criteria . . . but also perhaps even *exceed* it."

Dr. Einstein shared his notebook with Napoléon and Cleopatra. The vice principals' jaws dropped open. Unfortunately, as they had both just been drinking coffee, splotches of hot brown liquid fell onto the notes. But, despite the stains spreading out across the paper like conquering hordes, the two Vee-Pees had seen enough to kindle the fires of their shared ambition.

"Our golden rule," Cleopatra murmured with spooky delight. "Complete domination . . . lifetime after lifetime after lifetime."

"It is still too early to be completely sure," Dr. Einstein interjected. "Ve must let this particular Kronosgraph play out."

Cleopatra swept about the colossal machines, her diaphanous white gown trailing behind her.

"Just as the sun god Ra was reborn with every new dawn, I, too, shall be reborn."

"I'm afraid there's scant little sun in this particular

place," Dr. Einstein said with his absentminded air. "I suspect that's how both of you are able to—"

"It is no matter," Napoléon replied briskly. He clasped his tiny white hands behind the small of his back and stepped before one of the great machines. "We shall wait until zhis grubby cartridge is all used up," he said, staring at the cloaked figure that dangled above like a writhing chrysalis. "Zhen we will know for sure if it is safe to regain our rightful thrones up above, while we leave zhis demeaning place—and all of zhese disgusting almost-adults—behind."

Napoléon laughed, a disturbing bray of wicked, one-sided amusement at someone else's expense.

"In fact, those filthy *les enfants* can all burn forever in—"

"Language, Emperor!" Cleopatra scolded.

"You're right. How I long to be free of zhis place so zhat my tongue can be unsheathed!" Napoléon said, gritting his teeth. "Let us just say zhat those children— every child, in fact!—will find zhat zhere are places far worse than Heck. *Far* worse!"

16 · A MARRiAGE MADE iN HECK

"**GOOD MORNING, JOUNG** people," the bald, bespectacled man called out in a Swiss accent, biting down on the stem of his pipe as the Sylla-Bus clattered around the corner. "Did any of jou have any interesting dreams last night?"

The girls, restrained by their steel harnesses, all craned their necks slyly toward the handsome new boy, Angelo Fallon, each with the same vague sloppy grin smeared across her face.

The Korean boy raised his hand. "My dream is that I become the president of a Fortune five hundred company before college," he said, scrunching up his nose to push his thick black-rimmed glasses back into place.

"*Before* college?"

"Yes, sir. I thought it would look good on my college applications."

The man's lips twitched into a smirk beneath his patchy white mustache. "I meant dreams as in 'nocturnal reveries' . . . the gateway to the subconscious . . ." The man uncapped a marker from his easel and wrote on the dry-erase board in tight, squeaky cursive: "Dream Overanalysis: Dr. Jung."

"So, joung people," he continued in a voice as crisp as a freshly starched shirt, "today we will be learning—"

The Korean boy again raised his hand.

"Yes, Mr. . . . ?" the doctor asked, his face tightening with irritation.

"Myung-Dae Euclid Finkelstein," the boy replied. "The Third. What will we be learning today, Dr. Jung?"

"I was just getting to that before jou interrupted me!" the teacher replied. "And it's *Jung*—like *Yoong*."

"Are you sure?" Myung-Dae asked.

"Jes, I am sure!" Dr. Jung barked as he wiped the dry-erase board angrily with a rag. "Now, then, dream overanalysis accomplishes two important tasks. One, it allows jou to make productive use of time normally wasted with sleep and pointless fantasy. And two, it helps protect adults against one of the most tiresome questions that can be posed: *Would jou like to hear my dream?*"

Virgil, harnessed next to the new kid on the Sylla-Bus, raised his hefty arm. "But you can't control what you dream about," he said. "I mean, if you eat anchovy pizza with hot fudge and Fresca right before bed, you get some really weird dreams, like the one I had about the giant squirrel dressed as a Canadian Mountie, only it wasn't *really* a squirrel; it was more like my uncle Augie with a fuzzy tail—"

Dr. Jung waved away the question. "See what I mean?" the teacher replied. "*There's* a minute we'll never get back! But jou cannot only *control* dreams, jou can also *eradicate them,*" Dr. Jung continued as he drew a sleeping stick figure, dreaming little bubbles, then crossed out each bubble with a big X. "Then none of us will have to waste our time with boring squirrels and fuzzy Uncle Arties . . ."

Virgil slunk back in his seat. "It's *Augie,*" he mumbled as the Sylla-Bus rounded the corner. Virgil glanced over at Marlo, as he seemed to do every few minutes. She was stifling a laugh—not quite laughing *at* him, but not really *with* him either, as he wasn't laughing. Still, her amusement made him feel somehow better.

"*That's* what you get for interacting with teachers," Angelo said to Virgil, crossing his brawny arms. He looked down into his palm at a small picture of Milton. His disturbingly blue eyes examined the other boys who—while all sharing Milton's geeky attributes— weren't *quite* the boy he was hired to "deal with."

"Yeah," Virgil muttered back, filled with an odd, sudden unease. Whereas the other kids pressed next to him were physically warm, Angelo seemed to exude a frosty, electric chill: like he was literally too cool for school.

A man with a high forehead, tortoiseshell glasses, and slicked-back hair appeared up ahead.

"Good day, Junior Executives!" the man shouted while buttoning his white lab coat. "My name is Dr. B. F. Skinner and you are here to learn behavior modification!"

On the man's desk were three wire cages, one covered with a white sheet. Inside the cages were an assortment of fuzzy white animals and a few of those long creepy worms Marlo had seen down in the grotto. She strained against her restraining bar for a better look.

"Hey!" Marlo yelped. "That ferret is Lucky!"

"I hardly think so," the teacher answered with a shake of his head. "Unless you think it's 'lucky' to be experimented on."

"No, his *name* is Lucky," Marlo replied. "And he belongs to my brother!"

"No, the ferret's name is *Bueller*. At least it is now after an intense session of negative reinforcement."

"W-wait," Marlo sputtered, filled with sharp pangs of worry. "What do you mean, *experimented on*?"

"I hope you're not some crazy animal activist," Dr. Skinner said suspiciously. "I can tell you from firsthand observation that animals feel very little. They simply haven't the capacity for complex psychophysiological and biochemical functionality."

"You mean *emotions*?" Marlo countered.

"*That's what I just said.* Laymen have this irritating knack for transferring human emotions onto animals, characteristics that are beyond an animal's cognitive capabilities."

"Well . . . you'd better not hurt him," Marlo seethed, her arms crossed defiantly.

"Hurt who?"

"Lucky."

"Lucky?"

"Bueller!"

"I hurt these tools . . . *creatures* . . . far less than the violent chaos of the natural world would."

Myung-Dae raised his hand. "Can you tell us what behavioralism—the methods and principles of the science of animal and human behavior—is?" he both asked and explained.

Dr. Skinner smoothed back his greasy silver hair. "Behavioralism is, yes . . . *that* . . . but, as I see it, it's the acceptance that the external world cannot be fundamentally changed, so we must change our behavior. There's no sense beating your head against how things are. It's far more beneficial for society if you just surrender to the facts and become someone you're not. That's what life is. And death even more so. A series of conditioning events."

"So life is like shampoo and death is the conditioner?" Marlo whispered to the girl next to her.

The Sylla-Bus scooted away, leaving Dr. Skinner behind, grumbling to himself. Suddenly, Dr. Curie came running across the room with lunatic glee.

"He asked me!" she squeaked, her voice as high as a

rubber ducky filled with helium. She waved her luminous green hand, now adorned with a diamond ring.

Marlo leaned into Kali, moving aside one of the severed heads on her necklace so that it wasn't staring back at her. "Asked her *what*?"

"Asked her to install a dimmer switch on her forehead?" the fuchsia-haired girl next to Marlo joked.

"Asked her to marry him," Kali interjected. "Solomon Grundy, married on Wednesday . . ."

"Wasn't he just a baby yesterday?" Marlo asked.

"Children grow up very fast here in Precocia!" Kali replied as a heavyset man with an unruly snow-white beard set a large bundle down on the ground ahead. He was dressed all in fur, from his head to his foot, and his clothes were all tarnished with ashes and soot.

"Hey, that guy looks familiar," a boy with big ears and a buzz cut said.

"He gives me the creeps," Angelo said with his smooth, dark rumble.

Lyon turned and gave Angelo her most practiced smile from her arsenal of supermodel expressions. "I know!" she gushed. "Like, totally gross, right?"

"I know I'm Jewish and everything," Virgil said, staring at the man's twinkling eyes, merry dimples, rosy cheeks, and cherrylike nose, "but, really, there's only one guy who can be . . ."

Kali's dark eyes widened in terror. She heaved the

scooter bus forward and sped past the man, her long tongue lolling out of her mouth like a slimy red scarf.

"Ho-ho-hold on!" the man yelled as he ran after the Sylla-Bus.

Marlo folded her pale white arms together and stared at the man suspiciously. "Santa Claus?" she said with amazement. "I don't believe it . . . or in *him*."

The fuchsia-haired girl looked back at the puffing old man. "And *I* can't believe the fat old guy can run like that!" she said as the man tried vainly to keep up with the Sylla-Bus.

Marlo turned to the giant blue Hindu driver. "What's the dealio?"

Kali straightened her grisly girdle of severed arms and sped past a three-copier pileup.

"My job is to protect you children from childhood!"

"*From* childhood?" Marlo asked as Kali slowed the Sylla-Bus down now that they were out of Father Christmas range. "Why?"

"Childhood is an incredibly dangerous time, when you young people are at your most vulnerable! I help rush you through it so that you arrive at the sanctuary of adulthood as soon as possible!"

"But what does Santa Claus have to do with anything?" Marlo asked.

Kali waved two of her hefty blue arms up in the air in frustration. "If there is one person who has perpetuated the myth of childhood as some enchanted, merry fortress against reality, it is *he!*" she bellowed.

"Okay, okay," Marlo said, her hands on her ears. "Let's use our inside voices, please."

"*Ksamā karēm,*" she apologized as she turned the corner. "Not only does he deepen childhood with muddling magic, but why would *any* sensible person stuff candy and toys in their socks, then hang them above the fireplace? That is just an accident waiting to happen!"

The Sylla-Bus clattered and creaked back to Dr. Jung.

"In waking life, too, we continue to dream beneath the threshold of consciousness, especially when under the influence of repressed complexes!" the doctor shouted as the scooter bus drew near. "Dream overanalysis can help us strip away this befuddling gauze, to make us more productive."

"What is a dream?" the little boy with the buzz cut asked. "I mean . . . exactly?"

"Though decorated with silly details," Dr. Jung replied, twirling his marker in the air, "a dream is often symbolic of an actual situation nagging the unconscious. An issue—"

"Gesundheit," the pale little boy replied.

"Thank you . . . something troubling the mind that has been stuffed into jour brain's laundry hamper, only to be aired out at night in hopes of being solved. Through the practice of overanalysis, we can free our consciences of useless feelings such as guilt and resume our selfish undertakings."

"That sounds great!" Lyon beamed.

The Sylla-Bus crept past Dr. Jung.

"There are a variety of ways of doing this—keeping a dream journal, for one. Dream catchers are another. But I find lucid dreaming to be the best technique."

"Lucid dreaming?" Virgil asked.

"*Jes,* taking the reins of jour unconscious mind, Mr. Giant Squirrel!" Dr. Jung replied. "Simply command jourself to become consciously aware of dreaming so that, instead of dreaming of silly things, jou dream of homework, studying, or even taking tests that will very much count on jour school record!"

"But then we're, like, always at school!" Lyon whined. "With no breaks!"

"Exactly! Then jou have successfully turned a good night's sleep into a hard day's work!"

The children sulked as the Sylla-Bus scooted away.

"Behold the operant-conditioning chamber!" Dr. Skinner shouted. He tugged a white sheet off a large cage. In it was a white rat standing upright atop a metal grid, sniffing at a pair of levers.

"This is rat number twelve, who will show us how reinforcement shapes behavior. See what happens when another rat is displayed on the screen."

The rat sniffed a picture of another rat. Suddenly,

the floor of the cage sparked. The rat jumped back, electrified.

"After several sessions of negative reinforcement, I will have conditioned rat number twelve to be terrified of his own kind."

"That's awful!" Marlo yelped with outrage.

"Awful—wait for it!—*ly* interesting!" the doctor replied, his eyes bulging behind his glasses. "Now see what happens when I replace a usually negative stimulus with a reward."

A picture of a cobra flashed on the screen. A food pellet tumbled down a chute into the rat's dish.

"With consistent *positive* reinforcement, I will have conditioned rat number twelve to overcome its instinctual fear of snakes and in fact become drawn to them."

"How does that help the rat at all?" Marlo asked.

"Well, I suppose a fear of snakes—*ophidiophobia*—must be quite stressful for rats when in their native habitat, twitching at the slightest slither. Rat number twelve, however, will be free of this debilitating fear . . . for the few hours until it is consumed by a real snake."

The Sylla-Bus clattered slowly past Dr. Skinner and his cages.

"You young adults are like rat number twelve: you can all be conditioned to respond more favorably to environments beyond your ability to control," the teacher said, smoothing out his lab coat.

Myung-Dae raised his hand. "How?"

"Let me explain," Dr. Skinner said, pacing before the cages full of miserable animals. "A student's actions, both positive and negative, must be reinforced and punished, until the correct response is consistently achieved. In the weeks to come, we'll rely less on education and more on 'shaping children with electrical shocks.'"

"Shocks?" Marlo exclaimed. "But that's *torture!*"

"It will be!" Dr. Skinner replied with a creepy excitement. "But only when your behavior has been controlled to society's liking are you *truly* civilized."

The Sylla-Bus scooted around the corner.

Mind-numbing boredom is one thing, Marlo brooded, *but being electrocuted and turned into somebody you* aren't *is another.* She shifted uncomfortably on the cramped bench. Marlo was, again, filled with a twinge of worry at the mysterious fate of her missing brother. And now Lucky, his beloved pet, was the plaything of some mad doctor.

Up ahead were Dr. Curie and Solomon Grundy—now a gawky young man with sandy brown hair and big teeth—standing before the same preacher who had baptized Grundy only yesterday.

"We are all gathered here today, and *every* Wednesday, to join Mr. Grundy and Miss Curie in holy matrimony . . . or at least *regular* matrimony," the bald preacher said with a nervous flap of his small angel's wings.

Dr. Curie clutched her bouquet of wilted lilies with trembling joy, her green cheeks glowing like a nuclear reactor gone critical.

"Solomon Grundy," the preacher said with a dusty boredom, "do you take Miss Curie to be your lawfully wedded wife for the week?"

Mr. Grundy shrugged. "Sure, I guess," he replied.

"Do you, Miss Curie—"

"Yes!" she squealed like a radioactive pig.

"May I please have the rings . . ."

One of Napoléon's stooped demon foot servants hobbled down the aisle, fighting desperately against its chains. It held a red velvet pillow on which rested a pair of gold bands.

Solomon Grundy and Dr. Curie exchanged rings and awkward giggles.

"Mr. Grundy and Miss Curie, you have agreed to be dead together in matrimony. So by the power vested in me—"

Up ahead was a pile of desks, thrown into a great heap at the center of the office throughway. The fat man in worn red velvet waved his arms.

"Stop!" he bellowed, his round belly shaking like a bowlful of furious jellyfish.

Kali leaned back, bringing the Sylla-Bus to a grinding halt.

"Are you Santa?" the baggy-eyed girl squealed with unhinged delight, her face shiny and bright.

The plump man, looking less like his right jolly old self, sighed. "What's your name, little girl?" he asked.

"Virginia Teasdale—"

"Yes, Virginia, there *is* a Santa Claus—in a way—but I ain't him. I'm Saint Nicholas. Santa's just some commercialized alter ego of mine that took off on its own. Totally co-opted by the Man. The whole spirit of Christmas thing . . . *that* was my bag. Nowadays it's all about getting as much as you can."

"Duh!" Lyon said with a roll of her blue eyes.

"The whole give/get ratio is off," Saint Nicholas continued with frustration. "How can everyone *get* if no one *gives*? The joy of doing something nice for someone without them expecting anything: *that's* Christmas, man! Not this capitalist machine!"

St. Nicholas took off his cap and nodded to Kali. The hulking Hindu goddess sighed and, flicking a switch on the end of her handlebar, popped open the children's restraints.

"Let me tell you my story," St. Nicholas said, sitting down on the ground. He patted the carpet beside him. "Back in the three hundreds, I was a bishop and my folks were pretty well off, so when they died, I gave the money away to kids in need."

Myung-Dae raised his hand. "As a tax write-off?"

"So I could help someone who wasn't as well off as me!" St. Nicholas said with irritation. "After I died, people began giving presents in my name, which is where that whole 'Santa' thing came from."

"Why are you here?" Marlo asked. "Are *we* your charity cases?"

St. Nicholas kicked off his Earth shoes and grinned. "I'm down here from *up there* . . . as part of the Eternal Quality Unification Adherence Law—or EQUAL—to teach you free time."

"But how do you teach free time?"

"Exactly!"

The skinny Asian girl raised her hand tentatively. "Excuse me, Mr. Nicholas, but what's *free* time? Is that like studying in the car between dance and violin lessons?"

St. Nicholas shook his head sadly. "Oh, you poor little dudes. You're all like backpacks with legs, rushing off from one thing to another. And for what? So you can serve a future that you didn't make yourself. The educational system is just a factory, mass-producing wave after wave of *Homo economicus* on assembly lines, dig?"

The children around him not only didn't seem to "dig," but also apparently weren't even equipped with shovels.

Marlo leaned into the fuchsia-haired girl. "I think Santa's been hitting the eggnog."

"Yeah, he's like one of those guys who stands outside of natural food stores, wanting you to sign his petition."

Virgil stared at Marlo. Angelo watched the boy with detached amusement.

"You like her, don't you?" Angelo said in his cool, velvet voice.

Virgil's round cheeks burned.

"I . . . well . . . she's friends with my brother . . . I mean, I'm friends with *her* brother."

"Here's a tip for you, Tubby," the outwardly flawless boy said with a smirk. "The best way to get a girl to like you is to feed her attention, then, without warning, take it away. Your sudden absence is total girl-poison. Then you come back like some kind of antidote."

"I think I'll stick to just being nice," Virgil replied.

Angelo shrugged his broad shoulders. "Suit yourself, Romeo."

Marlo noticed a large sack slumped next to St. Nicholas. She raised her hand. "Will there be toys, Mr. Kringle?" she asked.

St. Nicholas grinned as he reached back for the bulging sack. He poured a pile of wooden blocks, Slinkys, and felt dolls onto the gray carpet.

"What's this junk?" Lyon said with slack-jawed disgust.

"Toys—*real* toys—the kind that depend wholly on your imaginations," the old man explained. "Playtime is supposed to be like *gym* time for your imagination, making it big, strong, and unstoppable. But imaginations are all burning out! And society *likes* it that way because young imaginations are dangerous."

Marlo's hand felt drawn to the blocks. They felt solid in her hands as she arranged them on the floor.

"So, how did you get here . . . um . . . ?" Marlo asked

the fuchsia-haired girl as she made a mini Stonehenge with her blocks.

"Frances," the girl replied. "Well, I was at circus camp—"

"I already know I'm going to like this!"

"And I had been bragging about how I could ride a unicycle on a tightrope while juggling flaming swords. See, I was always one for exaggerating the truth. It just made everything less boring," Frances explained as she drew a cell phone keypad onto a block with a crayon. "It was great, up until the day I was picked to ride a unicycle on a tightrope while juggling flaming swords. I just hope that my folks got their tuition money back. So, next thing I know, I'm in Heck. I was going to be sent to Fibble, but it was swallowed up by liquid truth or something before I could get there—"

"Yeah . . . I heard about that," Marlo whispered as she slyly pocketed a felt gnome that she had developed a liking to.

"—so I ended up here," Frances said.

Myung-Dae raised his hand. "So what are we supposed to do? To rebel against society and all that stuff?"

St. Nicholas smiled a smile that felt like the toasty, reassuring warmth of a fireplace. "That's simple: be a kid. *Play.* Stop rushing through childhood. Daydreaming, actually, is the best way to subvert the system. Because if you're not spacing out, you're not paying attention!"

"I'm confused," Myung-Dae replied.

"Wonderful!" the chubby old man exclaimed, clapping his gloved hands.

Vice Principal Cleopatra stormed around the corner. "Back in the bus!" she shrieked.

Vice Principal Napoléon marched behind her. "As a honeymoon present for zhe young couple," he said, his aquiline nose held high in the air, "we are all going on a little field trip tomorrow!"

The children cheered. A man—the fancy Spanish guy in tights Marlo had seen a few days ago—walked up to Napoléon.

"An archaeological dig!" Napoléon continued with a smirk. "To find a mythical relic that may not be so mythical after all!"

Dr. Curie rushed around the corner, yelping with excitement, and threw her bridal bouquet into the air. A group of girls instinctively rushed for it. The flowers bounced off Lyon's head and into Marlo's arms.

"Vhell, looks like Miss Fauster may not be a 'miss' for too long!" Napoléon cackled.

"*Fauster?*" Angelo said under his breath as he peered at Marlo over the glasses he didn't need. Marlo grimaced at the dead flowers in her arms.

"Nice catch," he said, giving Marlo his most luminous, prescription-strength smile. "Nice catch indeed!"

17 · A NASTY
PIECE OF WORK

THE ALARM SEARED through Milton's unconsciousness like a high-intensity laser. The sleek alarm clock flitted above his tangle of sheets, like an electronic humming-bird with a blinking digital readout for a face: 8:00.

The bedroom was small and spare like the bland, unlived-in-looking bedrooms set up in furniture show-rooms, with sheered drapes, a gingham quilt, and pillows with fussy little tassels on the ends. The only things that seemed out of place were the gold nightstands adorned with carved cobras and hieroglyphics.

Milton staggered into the bathroom, flicked on the light, and gasped. Gaping back at him from the mir-ror was a forty-one-year-old version of himself: his face drawn and his eyes puffy. Milton's sickly complexion made him seem like a test tube baby scientists had forgotten to take out of the lab. At the lower corner of the mirror was the word "Moi" blinking at him in cold blue letters. Milton tapped the word with his finger and an electronic note slid across his reflection, the mirror now a large touch-screen display:

To the Dude That's Me. I couldn't leave a note by the bed because paper is too expensive now, due to all of the trees dying 'cause there ain't no sun . . . well, there *is* a sun, it's just we never see it behind the Widow's Veil.

It's been ten years . . . that's, like, 3,650 days. Now, imagine taking a pair of hedge clippers and cutting off your pinky toe 3,650 times. That's pretty much what it feels like waking up as Milton Fauster, at least when *I'm* Milton Fauster. Kicked out of Habitat for Inhumanity, the only job I really enjoyed, thanks to the subversive *charité* you showed the locals. And you'd think having a minister for a sister would open doors for me, but whenever I hear a knock, it sure as heck ain't opportunity: more like a bill collector. I tried to talk to Marlo about my . . . our *condition.* But she wouldn't have any of it. Said someone in her position needed to get as far away from potential *scandale* as possible. And when I brought up Rosemary—you know, our mother—she went *balistique.* . . .

A stream of words and numbers whizzed past the bottom of the mirror.

FUSE (Fregyptian Universal Stock Exchange) report . . .
08:03 UN.JUST . . . NPMI . . . Napoléonic Precarium
Mines International . . . 19.03 . . . CCI . . . Cleopatra
Chronometry Innovations . . . 42.27 . . . BETTER . . .
Better Engineered Technology and Time Efficiency
Research . . . 92.28 . . .

Like stock market data, Milton thought as he resumed
reading the note.

And I haven't had much luck with the Pièce de Résistance,
or HAHAHA. They're some *fou* terrorist group that stages
random acts of buffoonery to upset the status quo. Like
that one day when they filled up entire Metro cars with Ping-
Pong balls. That stunt made me 17 minutes and 47 seconds
late for work. Needless to say, I lost my job. Military-grade
annoying. A few times I've been stopped on the street by
weirdos. One had the roundest, reddest nose I've ever seen.
They do that thing where they bare their teeth but not like
they're going to eat you. Smiling, I think it's called. One
congratulated me for rebuilding homes in Afrique Française.
Another thanked me for being . . . kind, I think it is, to some
children at Tykers and wanted to meet me by the Red Clown
Shoes one night. Must be some secret restaurant, despite
the Sensible Eating Decree the ministry passed ages ago.
Anyway, we've got a job interview at Better & Better.
It's the number one Mediarketing Agency here in Tres-peka,
Kansaquois—that's in Midwestopotamia. The agency is on

the corner of Rue des Bourgeois and Tutankhamen Avenue. The CEO, Phelps Better, wants to interview me— us—at 9:13 sharp! Don't mess up my life more than you already have. Keep it *réellement*.

Long Live the Emperor and His Queen.

Milton Fauster

The Widow's Veil was so much thicker now that Milton scarcely noticed when the subway train had emerged from the underground tunnel and onto the monorail. An endless procession of skyscrapers whizzed by, a row of majestic gray crayons built of steel and glass that seemed to melt down from the sky.

Milton sighed, fidgeting in the uncomfortable seat, clad in uncomfortable clothes. He read one of the advertisements crowding the train. It featured a smug young man in a gray wig and an obese, olive-skinned woman sipping from glass decanters.

New H2ODD™. The same bottled water you've been instructed to purchase, now with twice the vitamin D. It's what Napoléon X and Cleopatra XL drink.

Next to the advertisement was a short news article, slowly crawling across a digital screen.

BIAS (Better Information and Advertising Syndicate): One unfortunate side effect of the Widow's Veil is a chronic lack of vitamin D, a vital nutrient we used to derive from the sun. "Unless you enjoy softened bones and dental deformity, you would be well advised to seek out vitamin D," says Dr. Pierre Shill, head of the Important Vitamins Division of the University of Baton Rouge.

An alarm beeped. Superimposed over the windows of the train were maps labeling each street and building. "Next stop: Rue des Bourgeois and Tutankhamen Avenue," announced a strict, recorded female voice. "If this is your stop, you'd best detrain *immédiatement* or you will be criminally late for your day's appointments."

Milton stepped through the automatic sliding glass doors and into the spacious Better & Better reception area. Inset on the wall behind the reception desk was an enormous clock like the one that had choreographed every move back at Tykers Island.

"Monsieur Fauster?" the old woman behind the desk asked. As Milton neared, he could tell that the woman was actually younger than she looked. She had gray streaks in her hair and lines drawn onto her pointy face.

"Um, *oui*," Milton replied.

"Monsieur Better will be with you in exactly four minutes and twenty seconds," the woman said, motioning for Milton to wait on a nearby couch.

Milton sat down and perused the assortment of

magazines splayed out on the kidney-shaped table: *Sweet Sixtyteen*, *Geezmopolitan*, *Graybook*, *Old Time*, *Grandmother Jones*, and *Growth Spurts Illustrated*.

He squeezed his eyes shut and fought back tears. *I feel so disconnected from everything . . . I mean, is this even really my life?*

"Monsieur Fauster?" a reedy voice both boomed and hissed. Milton opened his eyes and saw a pale, hawk-faced man looking down on him from the top of the wide wooden staircase.

"Power nap . . . very efficient use of time," the man stated, his voice echoing throughout the building. "Come. I have better things to do with my time. Understand? Because I'm Phelps *Better*. *And that's not a joke*. It's branding."

Milton trotted up the wooden stairs, his sandals flopping embarrassingly against his heels.

"Don't scuff the stairs," Phelps Better scolded, his gray tailcoat swishing against the back of his knee-length breeches. "They're the most expensive thing in this place. Last of the old growth."

The Better & Better offices were a stern, uncompromising grid of cold concrete slabs and stainless-steel mesh. Milton felt like a human ball bearing rolling along an asphalt puzzle.

The man showed Milton to a large, austere room and motioned for him to sit on a concrete chair with steel pipes for armrests.

Milton settled as best he could into the unyielding chair.

Phelps Better eyed him with a derisive sneer.

"That's not how you sit down," he said as he walked behind his slate desk and lowered himself into his chair. "You do it like this. See? The trunk and upper legs form a one hundred degree angle. It's *better*."

"Um, okay," Milton replied, realizing that not only was the interview already under way, but also that it was already going badly. "So . . . Better and Better. Is it called that because you own it with a relative or something?"

Phelps Better glared at Milton, making no effort whatsoever to conceal his disdain. "The agency is named after me—*twice*—because I am that good."

The man's eyes bore into Milton. Milton felt like he was undergoing a full-body radiation scan. Monsieur Better glanced down at his desk, which, Milton could now tell, also functioned as a computer screen. He flicked at a document, scrolling it with fingers so pointy that they looked as if they had been surgically sharpened.

"Your work history doesn't sit well with me. . . ."

And apparently I don't sit well either, thought Milton as the chill of the concrete chair seeped into his body.

"Lots of unsightly gaps. In fact, if your work history was a mouth, it would require orthodontia."

Ironically, Milton noticed, the man's teeth seemed somehow oversized, like twin rows of bleached skulls crowding his mouth.

"What exactly *is* Mediarketing?" Milton asked.

The man snorted before reining back a horsey smile of amused shock. "Turning the tables . . . asking your interviewer a question, how bold," Phelps Better replied, running his hands through his gray, feathered hair, the fingers parting around two stiff nubs at either side of his skull, just above the ears. "You obviously want to know what Mediarketing means to *me*. My unique spin on the practice. Well, I do the same thing as my competitors do, only Better. See, because—"

"Yes, your name."

"Right. Expertly folding traditional marketing techniques with bogus media stories to provide context and urgency around the products we're selling. It's a technique I picked up from the legendary showman P. T. Barnum, only I made it much more . . . well, *me*."

Like the ads on the Metro, Milton recalled. *An advertisement placed alongside a related news story.*

Monsieur Better extended his arm to scrutinize his three watches: one showing the hour, the middle showing the minutes, and the last showing the seconds and milliseconds.

"While I appreciate your initiative, Monsieur Fauster, my time is precious, and I have *Better* things to do with it than waste it on a candidate who clearly isn't Better and Better material," Phelps Better said in a dismissive way that made Milton feel as if he no longer existed.

Milton sighed and rose shakily from the torturous

chair. "Well, thanks for interviewing me about the, uh . . . ," Milton said, the realization that he had no idea what job he was applying for dawning on him slowly.

"*Copywriting* job," Phelps Better interjected with a roll of his beady eyes, as if his face were playing a game of Yahtzee.

Milton stopped suddenly in the doorway, desperate for some way to not disappoint himself—his *other* self— who was depending on a steady job, even if it meant working for someone as despicable as Phelps Better.

"Why don't you just put me through the paces and see if I have what it takes to work here?"

"I really don't—"

"For free, at first . . . like a trial run?"

Phelps Better's sallow face—like an ashtray full of spoiled milk—twitched and tightened. "Maybe you're right, Monsieur Fauster," the man said as he rose from his chair. "You might have . . . *something*. . . ."

Monsieur Better brushed past Milton. In addition to the fact that Phelps Better plucked his hairline to appear prematurely balding, Milton noticed that the man did indeed have what looked like two horns, filed down to nubs, protruding from his scalp.

"You . . . have horns," Milton said, unwittingly mumbling his thought out loud as he followed Monsieur Better into the hall.

The man quickly patted his dyed gray hair over his temples. "A cutaneous growth made of compacted keratin . . . not horns," the smug man said as he strutted down the suddenly quiet aisle of stark cubicles as if he were royalty. "Anyway, here is your cylindrical."

Milton stared at the cramped, rounded workstations. "Cylindricals . . . you mean like cubicles?" he asked.

"The traditional cubicle workstation is inefficient," Monsieur Better replied. "The corners are wasted space. Cylindricals are rounded, so every inch can be used."

Milton sat down in his cold, concrete chair. On the small desk before him stood a pen upright on its stand, its tail end throbbing red like the butt of an electric mandrill.

"Um, I . . . what exactly do you want me to—" Milton asked as Phelps Better impatiently tapped the butt of the pen. A screen was projected upon the wall while a red keyboard was cast just beyond Milton's fingertips.

"Simply come up with problems that nobody has and solve them with Mediarketing," Monsieur Better explained, his breath declaring that the one thing he *wasn't* Better at than everyone else was flossing.

Phelps Better stalked away. As he cleared the corner, the office resumed its usual hum of work-related chatter.

Milton sighed deeply and rubbed his graying temples.

I so don't *want to do this . . . but it seems the only way I can help myself. Maybe if I can get Monsieur Fauster a job, I can help build him—us—some kind of life. Get an even break in this odd place . . .*

18 · MORE OF LES

Feeling sluggish? Do you leave behind a slimy trail of wasted time wherever you go? Then go from snail's pace to first place with Pace Maker: the Caffeinated Clock! Pace Maker is the big upside-down watch you wear on your *chest,* leaving both hands free to be more productive. "Gusts of highly caffeinated vapor give you the Get-Up-and-Go-tivation you need at crucial points during your busy day," says ministry productivity expert Dr. Effie Shent. "Pace Maker is the proven way to quicken your pulse and quicken your pace." So don't just ticktock it . . . become a quick rocket! With Pace Maker, it's time to win the human race!

Milton had spent the first couple of hours wrestling with his conscience. After finally pinning it to the mat, he had devoted the rest of the day and what felt like some of the night (despite the fact that the company clocks all currently read 4:59:03:417) writing a number of morally questionable ad campaigns for imaginary products.

Is your spam folder about ready to explode? Will one more irrelevant ad drive you mad? Then it's time to take a load off your mind with Brain Sell. "Using KRAMS (Knowledge Resonation through Amplified Magnetics Systems) technology, Brain Sell fills your gray matter with only what matters to you," says Dr. Jackson Germane, minister of meaningful marketing. "It's like ESP ASAP, beaming only the most pertinent advertisements straight to your brain." No more incapacitated in-boxes. No more piles of junk mail. No more telemarketers calling you during dinner. Brain Sell delivers what you really want, right when you want it: instantly. It picks your brain and picks what's best for *you,* so you can mind your business. Brain Sell: A Case of Mind Over Chatter.

Milton had tried to come up with products that could actually *help* the frazzled, overworked people he had met in this cheerless world. And, after all, this was only a test. It's not like any of the ridiculous things he came up with would ever be *used.*

Leaving his bruised conscience behind like a crying child, Milton shuffled along the grim maze of Better & Better as exhausted employees, freed from their gated cylindricals, spilled into the aisle. In the reception area,

Milton noticed an odd visor with a blinking eyeshade lying on the floor, left behind by an employee eager to return home. Milton noted that the brim was a sort of screen. Intrigued, he slipped the visor onto his head.

"Bonjour, citizen," a brisk voice intoned as the eyeshade flickered to life. *"Welcome to Ad Visor. If you know the name of the business you wish to frequent, blink once now."*

A digital grid of the streets outside the Better & Better building appeared on the brim. *"To browse a selection of businesses as well as today's hot deals, blink twice now."*

Milton blinked twice.

"You blinked once. Please state the name of the business you wish to frequent, such as Mentally Sound Pierre's Reasonably Priced Provisions Bunker, where perfectly acceptable supplies are always yours in exchange for the currency demanded—"

Milton, his eyes looking up at the brim, accidentally knocked into a woman in an Egyptian headdress and high-waisted gray skirt.

"Pardon."

Milton blinked twice again.

"You blinked once. Please state the name of the business you wish to frequent, such as Mentally Sound Pierre's Reasonably Priced Provisions Bunker, where—"

Milton blinked furiously.

"You either have pink eye or are expressing confusion. Please spell out your destination, such as M-E-N-T for Mentally Sound Pierre's—"

Milton considered where he would possibly want to go, other than his *real* home back in his *real* time. Maybe he had a relative here in Tres-peka, Kansaquois, wherever that was.

"F-A-U-S—"

"*You have selected Faux-Nature, makers of fine furnishings simulating now-extinct natural environments, located conveniently near Mentally Sound Pierre's—*"

"No!" Milton shouted as he staggered down the sidewalk, earning the glares of several passersby donning gray wigs, tunics, and ornamental canes. "Is anything in this stupid era *normal*?"

"*The Paranor Mall,*" the Ad Visor replied, quickly mapping the quickest route from Better & Better to a small blip across town on the underside of Milton's brim.

The Paranor Mall? Milton thought, stunned. *Les Lobe's museum of the supernatural is still around? It used to be in Topeka, Kansas . . . hey,* Tres-peka, Kansaquois. *I'm in what used to be Topeka, and so is Les, apparently! But how? He was already an old hippie when I was just a kid, thirty years ago.*

"*If the Paranor Mall is your preferred destination, blink once for yes, twice for no, and three times to learn more about today's sponsor, Mentally Sound Pierre's—*"

Milton blinked. *Finally, a friend . . .* Les had helped Milton out when he'd first come back from the dead, showing him how to harness the etheric energy he had lost passing through the Transdimensional Power Grid back to the land of the living. Maybe he could help him through this bad dream come true . . .

"Hello? I mean . . . *bonjour*?" Milton asked as he poked his head into the mini-museum of madness, cluttered with fiberglass aliens, blinking flying saucers, a miniature crop circle, and a life-sized Bigfoot wearing a tiara.

Speaking of paranoid, where was the museum's crackpot curator, Lester Lobe?

"Welcome, Seeker of the Strange, Pilgrim of the Peculiar, or anyone who got our Groupon in today's *Tres-peka Télégramme*," wheezed a familiar voice from the back of the museum.

"Les?" Milton called out as he made his way down a corridor of overflowing cardboard boxes and gaudily painted mannequins of Elvis Presley, progressing from leather-clad thin to sequined-caped portly. "Are you here?"

Milton turned the corner. There before him was what looked like a tall, hulking, swollen monster: a semitransparent creature composed of huge, muscular bubbles with something dark and shriveled at the center, as if it were digesting its latest all-too-visible meal.

"*Bonjour, Monsieur-dude,*" the creature said, its voice muffled. "What brings you to my far-out den of utter groovitude?"

Milton squinted at the withered shape in the

monster's chest. It was a little shrunken man wearing a fez.

"Les?" he said as he tentatively stepped toward the nine-foot-tall figure.

"Yep . . . in the flesh. Or in my Puff-Skin, anyway. When you're pushing ninety years old, the old flesh suit isn't what it used to be."

"Puff-Skin?" Milton asked as he examined the clear inflatable suit that Les was encased in.

"A helium-filled electro-response suit. It's what all the cool kids pushing a hundred wear. My body is, like, totally wasted. With my Puff-Skin, I can still get around . . . though sometimes it feels like I'm inside of a big, bouncy blowfish."

Milton peered into the man's wild, bloodshot eyes.

"My name is Milton Fauster. You don't happen to . . . remember me, do you? I met you a long time ago . . . in a reality far, far away."

Les blew the tassel from his eyes. "I can't say I know you, though you *do* seem sort of familiar, in a déjà-vu-of-something-I-haven't-experienced-yet way."

"Look, this is going to sound crazy—" Milton said.

"Crazy is where I live, man," Les Lobe said.

Milton chuckled, his laugh burning in the back of his throat as if the sound of mirth had never passed through Monsieur Fauster's throat before.

"Okay, well, here's my deal," Milton said, the Loch Ness monster clock on the wall clicking to ten: just two hours before Milton slipped back into unconsciousness. "A few days ago I was dead. A kid, too. A dead kid in a place called Heck—"

"Heck?" Les Lobe replied with a shake, tufts of wild gray hair snaking out from beneath his fez.

"Yeah. Then I got sick—"

"I thought you said you were dead?"

"I was dead, *then* sick."

"Double bummer."

"Next thing I know, I wake up and I'm back on Earth, only it's different, with meteors falling down. And my dad seems really weird, and I thought my mom had died after I did because she was so upset."

"Wait . . . you said your name was Fauster?" Les Lobe asked, crinkling his crinkly face. "Your sister is some big *fromage* with the ministry?"

"Yeah, though she doesn't seem to want anything to do with me."

"And your biological host . . . or mom, Rosemary Fauster. She ain't dead. She and a lot of other mothers are, like, fugitives."

"Fugitives?"

"Yeah, it was a big deal. She led this revolt when the government sent its goons to take her son—*you*, I guess—to Tykers Island. But she and the other hundred or so bio-hosts who joined her didn't have much of a chance."

"Where is she?"

"Probably in Dartmoor Prison, in New Paris, where

your sister and the rest of her fascist cronies do their 'subjugating of all humanity' shtick . . . no offense."

"None taken. Why doesn't my sister free her?"

"Your sister isn't exactly the fuzziest bunny slipper in the closet," Les Lobe said, scrutinizing Milton's face. "But you're different. I can tell. You've got 'Not From Around Here' stamped all over your forehead."

"Tell me," Milton said as Les knelt down, using his Puff-Skin as a chair. "How come France and Egypt are so powerful? Where I come from, they're just countries, not empires."

"Well, I suppose it started around the time of the Louisiana Purchase," Les Lobe replied.

"Right," Milton said, recalling his early American history. "Where the United States bought nearly half of America from France."

"Maybe in *your* reality, but here, Napoléon backed out of the deal and took all of America by force: the whole *crêpe Suzette*. As for Egypt, their empire grew like the ultimate pyramid scheme after conquering Rome."

"*Conquering* Rome? In my reality, Egypt was absorbed by Rome when Octavian defeated Marc Antony and Cleopatra. . . ."

"Not here, dude. On *this* slice of cosmic pie, Antony and Cleopatra were a dynamic, power-hungry duo that took big hungry bites out of most of Europe and the Middle East and *still* had room for the Sahara desert."

The Paranor Mall shook with a violent tremor.

"What's that?" Milton asked as a replica of an Easter Island statue wearing bunny ears toppled to the ground.

"Another earthquake," Les said, his breath fogging up the inside of his Puff-Skin. "Those in the conspiracy community say the epicenter of these tremors is miles below the Hekla volcano in Iceland—where the Fregyptian empire has its more-covert-than-usual military base—and that the earthquakes have something to do with secret tests. . . . Are you okay?"

Milton's eyes were drooping with sudden fatigue. He tried to shake the brain fog from his head. The neck and tail of the Loch Ness monster clock neared midnight.

Really? Two hours just went by? That's impossible.

"Is that clock right?" he murmured.

Les cocked his gray eyebrow. "All the clocks are connected to the ministry's time grid," he replied in a "no-duh" sort of way. "So . . . *oui.*"

"With my condition or whatever, I fall dead asleep at midnight. So I better leave while I still can. . . ."

He gave Les Lobe a weary smile.

"It was good to talk to someone about all of this crazy stuff," he said before staggering to the door.

"I know the feeling," Les Lobe replied in his craggy, muffled voice. "Sometimes I feel like I should just put a 'Gone Insane: Be Back Soon' sign on the door . . . but, you know, I can't."

"Because you're devoted to unraveling life's mysteries?"

"No, because of these puffy hands," the man replied.

"But whatever you do, Fauster, keep digging. You never know what you might find . . . probably a whole lot of trouble, but still. Digging your own hole is better than just standing in the one the ministry dug for you."

Milton smiled and headed out into the pitch-black night. After a few blocks, he saw a peculiar silhouette up ahead. It looked like a pair of long shoes draped over a power line.

"Clown shoes," Milton muttered, his mind bleary with exhaustion. A clock on the corner read one minute to midnight. Milton trotted beneath the shoes.

"Hello?" he called out into the night. *"Bonjour?"*

A figure materialized in the mottled shadows spilling across the curfew-barren street. It wore baggy pants, large squeaky shoes, and had a shock of hair sticking out from the sides of its head.

Milton, his consciousness sinking slowly into the swamp of sleep, staggered forward.

"My name is Milton Fauster. Are you . . . with HAHAHA? Part of the Pièce de Résistance?"

The honk of a bicycle horn served as Milton's answer.

"I—" Milton started before the corner clock tolled midnight. His head suddenly felt dizzy, as if he were hanging upside down. The crown of his skull ached.

"I . . . am . . . on your side," Milton said, fighting for each word. "I want to overthrow this grim, humorless place. But . . . I'm not really . . . myself. . . ."

Milton closed his eyes. He heard the grating squeal

of massive machines and the mutterings of children. He pried his eyes open.

"I can be an ally," Milton said as he fell to his knees. "Your mole in the ministry. A double agent."

Milton's palms slapped against the grit of the street. He forced his head up. Standing over him was what looked like a clown, complete with whiteface and red nose. The clown pointed to a flower on its lapel.

"Would you like to smell my flower, Milton?" the clown said in a distinctly feminine voice. It was all Milton could do to nod. Suddenly, water squirted out of the flower. Laughter pealed from the nearby alley.

"Funny," Milton said as everything went dim. "Contact me in ten years. To the day. I want a meeting with . . . you and your group . . . and then . . . the joke will be on . . . the ministry."

Milton fell to the ground, for all appearances dead to the world.

MIDDLEWORD

Youth—it is said—is wasted on the young (whereas old age is merely the act of wasting away). While it is true that the young and restless often don't fully appreciate their time in the sun—nor wear proper sunscreen while they bask in it—this is how it is supposed to be. What fun would youth be if, without warning, one was stricken with the unquenchable need to reflect deeply upon its tragic, fleeting nature whilst at the skate park engaged in kick flips, fakies, and nose grinds?* Not only would this be almost unbearably depressing (like getting-a-cold-sore-the-night-before-school-picture-day depressing), but also it would probably result in a trip to the emergency room.

If hindsight—the imaginary rearview mirror of wisdom—were 20/20 while one was young, then humanity would be constantly looking over its shoulder. Your youth should be spent with eyes fixed forward, stereo blaring (probably that earsplitting bleep-bleep music all the cool kids in the shiny pants at the mall are pretending to listen to), with nothing on your mind but how good the road feels as you speed toward an unreachable horizon.

Youth is like ice cream served on a hot plate. It must be consumed quickly and thoughtlessly before it melts away. If you managed to distill youth down to one characteristic, it would be surprise. And surprise, I don't have to tell you, is simply **BOO!**

You can't force surprise. You can't fake it—not with any conviction, anyway ("Oh, wow . . . a surprise party! I totally didn't figure that out when I saw ten cars in the driveway and caught a whiff of Brandy's perfume from the sidewalk!"). Surprise is what makes every moment seem new. It's what keeps humanity young despite what the mirror, the bathroom scale, the doctor—okay, most everybody—tells us.

Surprise is the "In Case of Maturity, Please Break Glass (or Wind)" when all else fails. And without humor, youth, and surprise, the world would be so full of boredom and misery that it wouldn't even be funny.

*These are either things one can do on a skateboard or in a barroom brawl or procedures offered by a plastic surgeon.

19 · THE MINE BOGGLES

MARLO JOLTED AWAKE. Mayfly demons darted around her, tugging out the filing cabinet beds in the Young Ladies' Room and Boardroom. Marlo's eyes were nearly swollen shut.

"What time is it, besides no-wake-me-thirty?" she grumbled, rolling over.

Mayfly demons swarmed around the cabinet and pitched it forward. Marlo tumbled to the floor. Lyon rubbed her head, sprawled out on the ground with Marlo and the skinny Asian girl.

"Thanks for nothing, Uggo," Lyon complained.

The mayfly demons bumbled in, carrying bright orange jumpsuits. Lyon waved away the demon swishing one in her face.

"I don't do road-crew orange," she said dismissively.

"Put it on *now!*" one of the demons hissed, its tiny

cheeks flushed with anger. "We've got to get you dressed and out to the Undermines!"

"Our field trip," Marlo said as she stepped into her jumpsuit. "Cool. That silly-bus was making me stir-crazy."

Marlo glanced across the yawning, sluggish mass of girls zipping up their bright orange jumpsuits. She noticed that Bordeaux and the other two girls who had fainted the other day still hadn't come back from the infirmary.

"Hey, Blandie," Marlo muttered as she laced up her painfully small leather shoes. "Aren't you worried about your friend? She and my brother have been in the infirmary for a while."

Lyon closed her eyes with disgust as she zipped up her orange jumpsuit. "At least she doesn't have to wear gross clothes in bright safety colors," she said while rolling up the sleeves so that they were fashionably tight around her forearms. "They're probably just faking so they can sleep all day. . . ."

"That's what I figured," Marlo mumbled, disturbed that she and Lyon had actually shared the same thought. "But Bordeaux doesn't seem capable of fooling anyone . . . beyond herself, that is."

"And *why* are you talking to me?" Lyon said with a sneer over her shoulder as a fresh throng of mayfly demons buzzed into the Young Ladies' Room and Boardroom carrying a long length of chain. They swarmed at the girls' feet, clasping iron clamps around their ankles so they were all chained together. Marlo kicked at the chain that had her fastened just two feet behind her least-bestest friend in the underworld.

The boys and girls tumbled out of stagecoaches and onto the dusty excavation site like two large, bright orange centipedes. Marlo watched as the line of a dozen boys was prodded out toward the sparkly black cliffs of hardened lava. Angelo radiated a fuming indignation at being chained and herded. The boy, sensing Marlo's regard, locked his insanely brilliant blue eyes with hers. The raw intensity of his gaze was so powerful that she had to turn away.

"He's dreamy," a horsey Latino girl said from behind.

"Like a succession of images passing through the mind during sleep?" a round-faced girl with a blond pageboy haircut replied.

The Latino girl sighed, her face buried in thick black ringlets. "Yeah . . . like that."

"Where are we?" mumbled the skinny Asian girl behind Marlo, nudging her glasses up her wide nose.

The brown-yellow smog hung low in the sky, looking like a big runny egg that someone had used as an ashtray.

"The Undermines, I guess," Marlo replied. "Me and my brother were caught here. It's full of caves and tunnels and creepy undergroundy stuff."

The nappy mole demons shuffled along in the dust with their squat tortoise-demon counterparts carrying buckets of exhumed rock.

A sleek black stagecoach wheeled around a jagged, volcanic cliff. The driver brought the pair of snorting Night Mares to a halt in front of the children. The driver—a large, rotting scarab beetle—scurried alongside the stagecoach and flung open the doors. Cleopatra extended her long brown leg and descended the carriage steps like a Mesopotamian supermodel. Behind her was Napoléon in his French military regalia. The ex-emperor of France lingered on the last step, which hovered a couple of feet from the ground until Cleopatra, with a put-upon sigh, seized him at the waist and set him on the ground.

Napoléon tugged his military uniform smooth. "*Merci*, Vice Principal," he said with his nose up in the air.

The old Spanish man with the Elizabethan ruff around his neck emerged from one of the caves.

"*Hola*," the man said as he reached the vice principals. "Where is Solomon Grundy? I thought he was to lead the *niños* into the mines. . . ."

Napoléon surveyed the excavation site with the fastidious air of a general. "He took ill. It is *Thursday*, after all," Napoléon replied. "Zhe children will have to go down unescorted." He turned on his polished heels to the children. "*Bonjour, les jeunes adultes*," the vice principal said with distaste at the young faces before him.

"I would like to introduce to you zhe famous Spanish explorer Ponce de León."

Marlo cuffed Lyon on the shoulder.

"*Oww!*" Lyon spat, clutching her shoulder. "Teacher, this freakaholic troll hit me!"

"Oh," Marlo said with mock remorse. "I thought he said *punch the Lyon*."

"I am *Señor* Ponce de León," the man said, scratching his pointy beard. "Today you will be going on an archeological excursion: the search for the *Fountain of Youth!*"

Myung-Dae raised his hand. "You mean the mythical spring that was supposed to spew out water that made you stay young?" he said, scratching his spiky black hair.

"*Sí*," Señor Ponce de León replied. "Eet's a story that's been told for thousands of years by cultures from all over the world. And if a myth is that widespread and enduring, there must be a drop of truth to it, no?"

"Or it's just something that people wanted to believe so bad they made up stories about it," said a little Russian boy. "Like the rumor about how Vasilisa Gredenko, our school's head cheerleader, dug nerdy boys."

Ponce de León shot Napoléon a confused look. "*Sí*, yes, well . . . when I was the first governor of Puerto Rico back in the sixteenth century, I traveled to what is now called Florida, seeking the fountain—"

"Um . . . you went to where all the old people go to look for the Fountain of Youth?" Frances said from the back of the line.

"Well, I had first heard the stories about the fountain from my subjects after conquering Puerto Rico," Ponce de León continued.

"Yeah, those are totally the kinds of stories I'd believe: those told by the people I just conquered," Marlo whispered to the Asian girl, who shyly bit her lip in response.

"So I launched an expedition," Ponce de León said, his eyes sparkling with delusional glory, "searching every river, brook, lagoon, and birdbath along the Florida coast to find the legendary fountain . . . but no cigar."

The ancient Spanish conqueror wilted like a wet sock.

"After my death, though, I began to suspect that a spring promising eternal life would have to exist *beyond* life . . . right here! So I shared my suspicions with Vice Principals Napoléon and Cleopatra, who helped to secure my transfer from Rapacia so that I might devote my death to the obsession that consumed my life!"

Marlo crossed her arms crossly. "But why are *we* here?" she said.

"To explore these dangerous caves and perilous caverns!" Cleopatra yelled, veins bulging on her long, slender neck.

Myung-Dae raised his hand. "Will this be extra credit?" he asked.

"No, but if you resist, you will be tortured," she replied.

"But, like, why us?" Lyon asked with a scowl.

Napoléon gave a smile as cold as the Russian front.

"Who better to go down in zhe mines than a bunch of *minors*?"

Crawling in a cramped tunnel of rough volcanic rock was hard enough, Marlo thought as she scraped her hands and knees along the rough floor of the cavern. But doing it chained to ten other girls in near darkness was *way* worse. She felt like a railcar on a whiny train, chugging along, clueless, in the hot and humid darkness.

The girls wore lights strapped to their foreheads. The sound of rattling chains was beginning to rattle Marlo's nerves.

"Spelunking was one of my extracurriculars," said the Asian girl behind Marlo. "That and fencing . . . and cello . . . and pre-pre-med . . . and scheduling my extracurriculars."

"Well, Little Miss Perfect, *my* extracurriculars were petty theft and spe-*flunking* out of school," Marlo replied.

"*Little Miss Perfect,*" Frances said longingly from the back of the row. "Now *that* was a pageant! And I would have won it, too, if I hadn't dyed my hair a non-pageant-approved shade. . . ."

The lava tunnel ran through a whole series of colors, from reddish brown to pale yellow, like someone had melted a special autumn-themed box of crayons and smeared them all over the walls. The sides of the tunnel were also scratched with intricate spirals, each one subtly different from the last. The patterns reminded Marlo of the spiral etchings carved into the floor of the subterranean grotto she and her brother had emerged from.

"Eww . . . a big gross white worm!" Lyon squealed.

Marlo's headlight caught the corkscrew-shaped white worm as it wriggled along the side of the tunnel wall, slowly carving a spiral into it.

Part of Marlo wanted to tell the other girls about her experience here in the Undermines: the little white worms, their scary-big squid mamas, the underground grotto with the huge Technicolor pool, the tiny cave opening . . . but another part, the tiny *sensible* part, felt that she should keep all of this primo info to herself. After all, why should she help the vice principals find whatever they were looking for? She didn't have money or influence. But Marlo *did* have something—a scrap of secret knowledge—and, until she knew what it was worth, she was going to keep it all to herself.

.

The boys leaned over a volcanic boulder and gazed down into a wide shaft. Virgil's hair stood on end, the threat of plummeting to his doom acting as some kind of electric hair gel.

A ledge of rocky outcroppings looped down the side

of the shaft: a wild and savage staircase without a banister. The ten boys sidled down the ledge, their chains rattling like Victorian ghosts in rehearsal for an under-Broadway version of *A Christmas Carol*.

"So what do you know about that girl Marlo?" Angelo asked suddenly. "You said you were friends with her brother. . . ."

"Yeah," Virgil grunted as he edged his way along the ledge. "I met them both . . . in Limbo. We—the three of us—were going to escape. But Milton was the only one who could."

"In that soul balloon," Angelo said.

Virgil turned and studied the boy's face. Virgil's headlamp made Angelo's eyes flare, like the eyes of an exceptionally handsome Halloween cat.

"How do you—"

"Kids talk, right?" Angelo said with a shrug.

"Right," Virgil replied, not entirely convinced.

Dirt crunched underneath the soles of their painful shoes.

"So then I saw Milton, Marlo's brother, again in Blimpo," Virgil continued, wanting to take his mind off the yawning mine.

"Where is he?" Angelo blurted impatiently.

Out of the corner of Virgil's eye, it seemed that Angelo's stocking cap smoldered with a faint orange glow.

"Why do you want to know so bad?" Virgil asked with suspicion.

"I'm just making conversation," Angelo replied in his smooth, deep voice. "I can tell you're nervous." His perfect nostrils flared, as if tasting the air. "I can practically smell it," the brawny boy replied. "Besides, you keep bringing them up—Milton and his sister. They're obviously important to you. And I don't see the target—I mean, Milton—anywhere around."

"Target?"

"What?"

"You said target," Virgil said as he hugged the side of the lava shaft.

"I mean, he might be the target of . . . of someone who has it out for him. So you . . . *we* . . . should try to find out where he is."

Suddenly, a broken chunk of black stone fell against Angelo's back, causing a fleeting shower of silver sparks. He sidestepped a larger falling rock with a boxer's grace. Virgil gaped at Angelo as he teetered on the edge of the precipice.

"You *sparked*," Virgil said over the noise of falling stones.

"Must be the rocks," Angelo replied vaguely.

Virgil, with a colossal lapse of common sense, peered down. His legs turned to Gummi worms. He reeled.

"I'm going to . . . ," he murmured as he flailed in the dark.

Time seemed to slow. Virgil's headlamp slashed across Angelo's statuelike face. In the boy's fathomless blue eyes, Virgil could see hesitation, as if the boy was weighing his options. Angelo's eyes settled on the shackles that bound all the boys together, and just as Virgil was about to fall headlong into the gaping well, he was drawn back by a firm and powerful hand.

"Y-you," Virgil sputtered as he clung to the wall, "were going to let me fall."

"*You're welcome,*" Angelo replied. "Seriously, if I wasn't here, you'd be toast." He laughed, the sound ricocheting in the dark like gunshots. "I'm like your guardian angel or something."

As Virgil drew in quick, humid breaths, he had a sinking feeling that Angelo was anything *but.*

A blotch of sizzling yellow-orange light blazed up ahead. Marlo scrunched her eyes. It looked like the light was leaking out from some hole in the wall.

"Hey, I see something ahead of us," she said. "Let's take a break and check it out. Besides, I'm thirsty."

The ten girls bunched together in the cramped cave. A gangly girl with a café au lait complexion and honey-colored ringlets passed out juice boxes she pulled from her satchel.

Marlo took a sip and grimaced. She glanced down at the box, trying to read the label in the flickering light.

U-Grow-Girl: It's Like Growth Hormones on Steroids!™

Marlo tossed the juice box to the ground and looked for the source of the light. It was coming from a crack just a few feet away. Marlo crawled toward it and peered inside. On the other side of the wall was a deep cavern the size of a small airplane hangar illuminated by a flickering torch. Carved into the porous lava walls were tens of thousands of small potholes, most every one sporting a glass bottle that fit snugly in its rocky nook.

Just then, Marlo saw someone small move into the torchlight.

"It's Napoléon," Marlo whispered. "Everybody turn off your headlights."

The vice principal examined a row of bottles intently as if inspecting a row of infantrymen standing at attention. After a moment's scrutiny, he selected a bottle, opened it quickly with a corkscrew produced from his sleeve, and took a long drink of its contents. Frances, with a soft jangle of chain, joined Marlo and peered down into the cellar.

"What's Fun-Size drinking over there?" Marlo whispered, squinting at Napoléon as he waddled back and forth, taking deep swigs from the bottle.

"It's wine from the li'l emperor penguin's private reserve," Frances replied as the other girls crowded around the crack in the wall. "I heard one of the demon guards say that he had this huge wine cellar when he was emperor of France and figured out some way of bringing it here when he died."

"Shhhh," Marlo hushed. "Someone else is coming."

The children peered through the fissure. Ponce de León strode into Napoléon's secret chamber.

"Would you like some wine?" Napoléon said mysteriously, his smile not quite stretching up to his cold, calculating eyes.

The conquistador nodded, the poofy flower stuck in his wide, round hat fluttering.

"*Muchas gracias,* Vice Principal," the man answered. "You are too kind."

Napoléon strode to a sizzling torch stuck into the side of the cave.

"I can't say I get zhat a lot," Napoléon said as he grabbed the torch with his delicate hand. "I do believe, *señor,* zhat I possess a rare Rioja wine . . . sixteenth century. Just like *vous.*"

"Ah, *sí,*" the man replied with a sparkle in his sad brown eyes. "It would be like drinking in my homeland . . . how it was. Tasting it, once again, upon my parched lips."

Napoléon tossed Ponce de León the torch.

"You will find it in zhe back," Napoléon said as Ponce de León snatched the torch from the air. "With my most precious vintages."

Ponce de León walked down the near-endless row of wines until he arrived at the back, where a few old bottles were cradled. He kicked at the sandy ground.

"The floor is coated with silvery sand," he said.

"*Oui*," Napoléon said as he marched forward, stopping at the rim of silver dust. "I find it keeps zhe older wines nice and dry."

Ponce de León removed a round-bottom flask from the rack, the sand up to his ankles. He uncorked the wine and tilted his head back. The wine spilled down his neck in dark red rivulets like blood. The grizzled conquistador spat it out, grimacing.

"It is spoiled! It is the *vinegar*!" he grumbled, wiping his mouth on his flouncy sleeve.

Napoléon chuckled. "It is an acquired taste."

The features on Napoléon's face danced in the torch's flickering light, like a victorious jig on the grave of some vanquished enemy.

"And, just as vinegar cannot turn back into zhe wine, zhe dead cannot live again. I thought zhere was no going back. But I thought wrong."

"Even if there was a way . . . to go back," Ponce de León replied, "our contract with Heck is binding. *Physically* binding." He looked down with confusion. He was up to his knees in sand.

"*¿Que?* What is going on? I am sinking!"

"So you are."

"Help me, please!"

Napoléon clasped his hands behind his back and stiffened, as if in a military parade.

"*Merci beaucoup* for all your help leading us to zhe Fountain of Youth. I can sense zhat we are near. But zhere comes a time when one must cover one's tracks. And *you* are my tracks!"

The silver quicksand was now up to Ponce de León's chest, making it hard for him to breathe.

"What use . . . is the fountain . . . to you?" Ponce de León cried, vainly trying to free himself from the pool of swirling, sparkling grit. "It is my obsession, but for you . . . for *anyone* on this side of the veil . . . eternal youth is pointless!"

"No, you silly old *fou!*" Napoléon cackled as Ponce de León was swallowed up by the hungry, shifting sands. "We don't want to find zhe fountain to *attain* eternal youth! We want to *detain* youth eternally. . . ."

All that was left was the torch, poking up from the sand.

"To plug it up!" Napoléon proclaimed. "For good."

The skinny Asian girl next to Marlo gasped. Marlo quickly covered her mouth as the torch sank into the sand and all was dark.

"Forever!"

20 · ARMED AND DANGEROUS

MILTON'S EYES SHOT open. He was suddenly, inexplicably awake. He propped himself up on his elbows. His chest ached and he could hear a persistent ticking coming from . . .

He swallowed hard as he stared down at his chest. There, sprouting from his shirt, was a small clock—faceup—with two dangling pendulums clicking together in perfect, creepy sync with his heartbeat.

"It's . . . attached to me!" he yelped as he tried to remove the ticking clock.

The clock-tie felt like it was prodding Milton's heart to beat faster, like an impatient stagecoach driver lashing at his horse with a bullwhip. The clock read 8:05 . . .

then 8:06. Milton couldn't believe how fast time passed with a timepiece hot-wired to his heart.

Milton eased himself out of his rigid twin bed, his body seemingly held together by vague aches and twinges. He was in a small, drab bedroom with fluorescent tubes casting down an uncompromising glare. He stumbled over to a window covered by tightly drawn curtains, the floor feeling unsteady beneath his feet. Milton opened the curtains, and outside was the dismal skyline of Tres-peka, Kansaquois, shrouded by the dense black pall of the Widow's Veil.

This thing on my chest . . . it seems so familiar, Milton thought as he walked to the bathroom. *Maybe I needed some kind of futuristic pacemaker because I'm getting so—*

Milton saw his gaunt fifty-one-year-old face in the mirror.

"—old," he said in a creaky voice.

A phone rang, shattering Milton's thoughts. He searched his small apartment, but he couldn't locate the source of the shrill, incessant ringing that seemed to come from everywhere.

"Hello?" Milton called out in frustration.

"*Bonjour,*" a stilted female voice answered from hidden speakers.

"What is it?"

"*Your phone.*"

"Yes, I know it's my phone, but who's *on* the phone?"

"*Your phone.*"

"My phone is on the phone?"

"*Oui,*" the voice replied. "*I have a message for you.*"

"From who?"

"*From you.*"

Milton's recorded voice filled the room.

"*Dude That Used to Be Me,*" Milton's other self said.

It's weird, Milton thought, *how he sounds like me because, well, he is me, but he approaches the words differently.*

"*In the last ten years, I've had a lot of time to think about my* fou *situation, and I've come to the conclusion that you're not real. You're just, like, some disassociated personality that I suppress (thankfully, considering how* désastre *my life gets when you show up. How would YOU like waking up in the middle of the street in a sketchy part of town?). My Expectation Therapy software says you appear when I'm stressed out and it's just a coincidence that this terrible nice-or-whatever side of me rears its kindly head every decade. But not anymore, okay? I worked hard for years at Better and Better (helping Monsieur Better with his amazing Pace Taker and ARM innovations) and am now middle chancellor at the Ministry of Persuasion and have a staff and everything. So just in case I'm having a stressful day and you show up, don't be late for work . . . not that we can with Monsieur Better's Pace Taker technology that I apparently helped him develop. Adieu and praise Ra (not that Egyptians ever see their sun god) . . .*"

The room went quiet, leaving Milton alone with his

thoughts and the rapid-fire ticking of his clock-tie that read 8:58.

"Eight fifty-eight?" Milton exclaimed. "Already? There's no way that much time could have—"

"*This is your phone,*" the female voice answered. "*I am not programmed to address non-conversation-related issues. For time-related queries, please consult your Pace Taker.*"

"My Pace Taker?"

"*The ticking clock connected to your heart.*"

That's it! Milton thought. *My dumb idea for a caffeinated clock on your chest. Pace Maker. It's been turned into something out of a nightmare!*

The frantic timepiece on Milton's chest clicked to 9:00. Suddenly, the front door unbolted and slid open with a pneumatic whoosh. Milton stepped through the door and into what seemed like a maximum-security office building. Employees emerged from dozens of open doors lining the inside of the building like cells. The building—the Ministry of Persuasion—was a gigantic concrete and steel hive, brought to sudden, surging life at the stroke of nine.

All the employees actually live *at work,* Milton realized as he walked out onto the dark-gray industrial-carpeted hallway.

The clock embedded in his chest, his Pace Taker, seemed to relax: each click of its twin pendulums growing more gradual, with Milton's heart—in surgical sympathy—slowing, creating the sense that time itself was now unfolding at a less frantic, more focused pace.

"*Bonjour,* Monsieur Fauster," a bug-eyed woman with a gray wig and wrinkles drawn on her face said to Milton with a quick nod of deference.

"*Bonjour,*" Milton replied blearily. The woman stopped and cocked a dyed-gray eyebrow at him.

"Your meeting . . . it's still in the Salle de Conférence, isn't it, monsieur?" she asked.

Milton stared at the woman, dressed in a gray fitted suit with gold epaulets on the shoulders and Egyptian-style sandals on her feet. He was mesmerized by the ticktock of the Pace Taker peeking out over her lapel.

She squinted her dark, steely eyes at Milton. "I get it: *this is one of your tests.*"

"Um . . . *oui,*" Milton said as he turned and walked toward where he assumed he was supposed to be. "And you, uh, *passed.*"

She nodded, walking a few paces behind Milton.

They entered a long, concrete boardroom with a black oval table occupied by seven grim, gray-haired men and women.

"Your new wrinkles look *très magnifique,*" one woman commented to another.

"No matter what I use, I'm still cursed with this awful, supple 'baby face,' " a man said. "So I'm saving up for a surgical face-sag—*Monsieur Fauster!*"

The Ministry of Persuasion employees stood to attention.

Milton was hypnotized by the ticktocking Pace

Takers. All of them, including Milton's, were in perfect sync. His staff stared back at Milton expectantly. The bug-eyed woman Milton had met in the hallway—his assistant, he assumed—chimed in.

"You were going to lay out the new departmental review cycles and quality assurance milestones," she offered.

"Right," Milton replied as every eye in the room seemed to be physically pushing him toward a large dry-erase whiteboard.

I'll just waste as much time as possible, Milton thought as he picked up a marker, *and when I get a break or something, I'll try to find HAHAHA or make contact with Marlo. . . .*

Milton, his back to his employees, drew a large circle onto the board.

"Monsieur," his assistant said. "You forgot to turn on your suit."

"My suit?" Milton replied, noticing a small red button on his cuff. He pressed it and, instantly, his suit seemed to disappear.

Not disappear, exactly, Milton thought as he spotted a tiny camera on his lapel. *It turns my suit into a full-body screen projecting what's in front of me so everyone can see what I'm doing. . . .*

Milton carved his circle drawing into little wedges.

"This, um, is a pie chart of . . . my favorite pies. First there's pumpkin, then cherry, then probably Boston cream . . ."

"Pies, sir?" the bearded, baby-faced man asked.

"Each slice must represent a division's unique roles and responsibilities," Milton's assistant offered. "And their 'flavor' of management style."

"*Oui,*" Milton replied as he drew a big yellow circle with a black mouthlike wedge.

"And this chart represents . . . um . . . Pac-Man," Milton said.

"What's *Pac-Man?*" a dark-skinned man with circles drawn underneath his eyes whispered to a colleague.

"It must stand for *Persuasion Action Committee Management,*" the woman replied under her breath.

Milton had no idea what he was doing, and soon his employees would be able to see right through him— more than they already could with his electric camouflage suit. He quickly erased the whiteboard.

"Change of plans," Milton said, turning to address the baffled employees. "That was a test. But now, I'd like, uh . . . *you,*" he said, pointing to his assistant, "to come up here and tell me all about the . . . Ministry of Persuasion."

The woman, her large gray eyes filled with fearful confusion, stepped up to the whiteboard. Milton handed her a marker.

"Well," the woman started shakily, scrawling the letters "MOP" on the board, "the new Ministry of Persuasion is a bureaucratic entity grown around Monsieur Phelps Better's ground-breaking ARM: the Affective

Reasoning Machine. It's a Better, more direct way to unite the empire. You know, 'Better' like—"

"How does the machine work?" Milton asked. "I mean, *I* know, of course, but I'd like to hear how *you* think it works."

"*Oui,*" the woman replied with a gulp. "By using the Invasi-Net Why-Ask-Why-Fi? grid, the ministry can execute strongARM tactics: broadcasting state-approved messages into citizens while they sleep."

"*Into* citizens?" Milton gasped. His staff stared at him quizzically. "I was hoping for a more . . . specific explanation."

The woman's pale face blanched, accentuating her drawn-in wrinkles and crow's feet. "By updating old KRAMS technology—"

"Like those awful machines back in Tykers Island?" Milton blurted.

Milton's staff narrowed their eyes, apparently questioning their boss's sanity, looking for hairline fractures in his authority to exploit as they scaled the corporate ladder.

"Awful . . . *ly effective* machines," Milton clarified. "I'm familiar with them. . . ."

The Affective Reasoning Machine. I helped to develop this terrible invention, too, with my dumb Brain Sell idea. I tried to make this world better and only made it Better!

"These messages are fed into the apparatus and amplified," the woman at the whiteboard continued.

"Currently, the machine has only a limited range. But with the mother lode of precarium found in Iceland, the ministry is working tirelessly to truly flex the ARM so that it cannot only 'persuade' at a greater range, but also create a two-way connection—"

"Two-way?" Milton asked.

"So that the ministry has a direct link to every citizen's thoughts. To monitor dissent and disloyalty as it occurs so that it can be swiftly corrected, either with a shot of the ARM or by removing those cancerous citizens from the body of the empire. *Permanently.*"

Milton was overwhelmed. *How could these people so willingly accept such a sick and dehumanizing system?*

"Remind me why the citizens would authorize such an . . . intimate connection to the ministry?" Milton asked.

The woman looked to her fellow employees for guidance. When none was offered, she sighed and continued, feeling as if she were being led into a trap.

"The citizens voted against being bothered by such things *years* ago, as part of the Freedom from Information Act. . . ."

The office suddenly trembled. The whiteboard quivered nervously on the wall.

"Earthquake!" Milton shouted, scrambling underneath the table. A round-faced man with a fake beard peered tentatively beneath the conference table.

"The tremors happen at least five times a day,

Monsieur Fauster," he said cautiously. "It's nothing to be alarmed . . . wait: was this another test?"

Milton crawled out from beneath the conference table. "Uh . . . *oui,"* he said, brushing himself off.

Milton looked down at his Pace Taker. Though he felt as if two hours had passed, his surgically implanted timepiece read only 9:17.

"You're all . . . *dismissed.* Except for . . . uh . . . *you,"* he said, pointing at his assistant. "I need you to take, um . . . this." Milton held out a marker. "To my office. It's . . . important."

The woman's chemically crepe-papered face seemed to fight back all sorts of expressions—mainly of the "Why don't you take your own stupid marker back to your dumb office, jerk?" variety—but, after an obedient nod, she rushed down the hall with brisk flops of her leatherwork sandals. Milton followed her until it was clear which office was his. The woman stopped in his doorway, confused.

"I just remembered that I forgot something," Milton said, brushing past her. "Um . . . *merci."*

Milton, after a quick sweep of his far-larger-than-necessary office—with its concrete pylons and chairs, black marble tabletop, and Ministry of Persuasion wall hanging (a brain caught in the crosshairs of a rifle scope)—pressed the blinking red button on his desk.

"Bonjour," a crisply efficient voice boomed from recessed speakers.

"Who is this?" Milton asked, startled.

"*This is your phone.*"

"Oh . . . right. Hello . . . *phone.* I'd like to call Marlo Fauster."

"*I don't think so, monsieur.*"

"You don't *think* so?"

"*Based on an aggregate assessment of previous phone call outcomes, the likelihood of the party—Marlo Fauster—even taking your call, much less that call ending civilly, is far too remote to pursue.*"

"So you, my phone, won't make a call for me?"

"*My calculations have determined that it's not an efficient use of ministry time. Au revoir.*"

Wow, Milton thought, *I've never had a phone refuse to make a call before. But it's probably right: the Fregyptian Marlo is too important to waste "precious ministry time" on her weird—*

Milton spotted a large, pink-and-blue polka-dotted foil envelope stuffed in the trash can underneath the desk. He fished it out. On the back, written in his alter ego's scrawl, was a note:

To the Dude That May or May Not Be Me.
This arrived this morning. No clue what
the junk inside is. I don't need glasses and I
certainly don't need cans of farts, especially
with the ministry-issued dehydrated kelp we

have to eat since all the crops and livestock died. Anyway, I don't believe you exist but just in case you do, here you go.

Milton opened the envelope and inside were a pair of novelty X-Ray Specs and two cans of Fart Spray.

It's got to be from HAHAHA . . . the Pièce de Résistance.

He put on the glasses and peered intently through the tiny holes in the cardboard lenses. The X-Ray Specs made him feel woozy but revealed no secret knowledge.

Milton cradled the pink and green cans of Fart Spray in his age-spotted hands. He sprayed both cans out in front of him, the twin plumes of mist merging. Milton gasped, first from the powerful blast of sour methane and rotten eggs, then from the words that seemed to magically appear in the air in front of him.

Playground zero @ Rue de Bega & Tutankhamen way. 5 o'clock. spin the N-E-W-S.

Milton heard hard-leather sandals flopping toward him. He turned swiftly away from the door.

"Monsieur Fauster?" his assistant called in her tremulous voice. "Are you here?"

Milton looked down at the tiny camera on his lapel.

My weird camouflage suit. I must have left it on.

"He must be at that Thinking Inside the Box middle-management training off-site," another woman commented. "Though I can hear his Pace Taker and—*Sacré bleu and Holy Ra!* What is that terrible *odeur*?"

Milton quickly tossed the X-Ray Specs and Fart Spray into his trash and deactivated his suit.

"Sorry," he said, turning to face his employees. "Too much, uh, dehydrated kelp, I guess."

A woman, clad in the latest support hose threaded with a trendy varicose-vein pattern, waved the air clear.

"Monsieur," Milton's assistant said with a pinched, sour face. "Sorry to intrude, but your phone wouldn't patch me through. It said that you had had a disagreement with it and that there was an eighty-two percent chance that you wouldn't answer it."

Wow, phones here are off-the-hook smart.

"I just heard from New Paris. The emperor and queen have finally had their baby. The new heir to the Global Fregyptian Empire. And the *royale* couple has declared that today is . . . something called a *holiday*."

"A holiday?" Milton said.

"*Oui*, monsieur, sir. I didn't know what it was either. But I looked it up in the ministry-approved dictionary, and it is an archaic word meaning 'a day of festivity or recreation when no work is done.' So the department would like to know, monsieur, what do we do?"

"You take the day off," Milton replied.

"Take the day *where*?"

"You stay at home and relax . . . or go out somewhere and enjoy yourself."

The women gaped at Milton like fish in the throes of water withdrawal.

"*Or,*" Milton continued, "you can get a jump on tomorrow's workload. From your home cell places. That way we can, um, conserve ministry resources by shutting the office down."

Milton's assistant blinked her glassy blue eyes. "Oh . . . *oui* . . . that makes sense. Only, how will I upload today's messages to the Affective Reasoning Machine, monsieur? Usually I get a list at four fifty-nine that's as long as my—"

"I'll do it," Milton said. "Just leave me the instructions before you go home. I'll do it after my, uh, Thinking Inside the Box training thing. I'm sure I can figure it out. I could probably do it with one ARM tied behind my back."

Milton's assistant looked as if Milton had just emptied two more cans of Fart Spray. Her dyed-gray eyebrow arched suspiciously.

"Um . . . dismissed."

This is my chance to break away and meet up with the Pièce de Résistance, Milton thought as the women shuffled out of his office to alert the rest of the ministry of their strange "holiday." *And if I do, maybe I can help undo all that I done did. . . .*

21 · BOY ABOUT CLOWN

*"**BONJOUR OR MERAHBA**, Citizen, and welcome to Life Visor,"* said the computerized cap that Milton had found in the Ministry of Persuasion lobby. *"If you know the name of the business you wish to frequent, say so now. If you would like directions on how to Better live your life, do not say anything. I will draw from my database of life-choice outcomes based on the decisions of your fellow citizens."*

"Playground Zero," Milton said to his hat. "Located on Rue de Bega and—"

"You did not say anything. Perhaps you should turn left and join the Fregyptian military. Just Because We're Not at War Doesn't Mean There Isn't an Enemy—"

"No, I want to go to Playground Zero," Milton corrected as he walked down a nearly barren street, the Widow's Veil—utterly dismal and utterly impenetrable—pressing down overhead. "It's on Rue de Bega and—"

"*You did not say anything. Perhaps you should turn right and join the Better Innovations Bureau, where—*"

"PLAYGROUND ZERO!" Milton shouted as he crossed the street to Tutankhamen Way.

"*There is no such place as Playground Zero and no such word as* Play *in my ministry databank. The word* Ground, *however, is quite common. And, by turning right, you can break new ground at the Better Innovations Bureau, where—*"

Furious and frustrated, Milton threw his Life Visor into a small, abandoned lot. It soared over the chain-link fence and landed with a clang on top of a round, rusted-metal structure. Milton looked back at the street signs on the corner: Rue de Bega and Tutankhamen Way.

Milton pressed his face against the fence. There was a large rusted circle standing about a foot off the ground. It looked like one of the Big Spinner rides at his old playground back home, where Milton would hang on—teeth gritted, cheeks flapping wildly against the wind—until he entered a world of unimaginable dizziness.

Playground Zero, he thought as he stared at the long-abandoned relic of a ride. *A place so forgotten that no one even knows what a playground is anymore.*

He looked carefully around him. The street, though near empty, still had the occasional passerby. Milton turned on his camouflage suit and, facing the fence, scaled it carefully. The chain-link pattern projected onto his back, rendering him next to invisible. He hopped over the fence and into the small lot. Milton quickly glanced down at his Pace Taker: 4:58. The moment the day had been declared a holiday, time seemed to speed up, as the ticking pendulums of Milton's timepiece taunted his heart to beat faster.

Spin the news, he thought. *What could that possibly—Wait. Not the word "news," but the letters N-E-W-S.* He stealthily approached the spinner, grabbing the old rusted support bars. Milton noticed that one of the bars had the letter "N" written on it. He also saw four points marked on the base of the ride.

Like a compass.

Milton spun the ride so that the north support bar aligned to the N on the ground; then he spun it east, west, and finally south. N-E-W-S.

The metal spinner clicked and flipped up a few inches on one side, revealing a small portal with a ladder underneath.

Milton clambered down the metal ladder for ten feet . . . twenty feet . . . a hundred feet. The tunnel glowed warmly beneath him with flickers of light. Suddenly, the tunnel ended and, below, Milton could make out what looked like a slide. He swallowed. The subterranean darkness and unaccountable appearance of a kiddy slide brought back memories of Milton's first miles-long tumble deep into the bowels of Heck.

This better not be one of Bubb's tricks, he thought as he hopped onto the slide. Milton slid hard and fast for a few seconds and then shot out of a wall and landed face-first in a pit of sand. He rubbed the grit from his eyes and gazed at the underground cavern. The chamber was some kind of decommissioned tank, probably originally used for sewage treatment. The walls were painted to resemble a lush, verdant valley crowded with flowers and smiling animals. Above was a faultless blue sky with a radiant sun beaming down upon him.

In the time Milton had spent in this dark, dispiriting no-fun-house-mirror version of his own home, his eyes had forgotten how vivid and cheerful colors were. *Real* colors: not various shades of gray, but sunny yellows, hopeful greens, energetic reds, and peaceful blues.

Flickering candles burned on top of birthday cakes scattered about the cavern. Milton looked back at where he had come out of: a hole emerging from a painted elephant's ample behind, just above a small trampoline.

"If it's not about elephants, it's irr-elephant," a squeaky voice cackled from the far side of the painted cavern. Five figures lumbered toward Milton with odd, wobbly gaits. They were a bunch of clowns. *Literally.* Five baggy-panted clowns with bright orange fright wigs, grease-painted faces, bulbous red noses, and enormous shoes that slapped against the ground like flopping red fish. The figures stopped at the rim of the large sandbox.

Four of the clowns—paired on either side of their three-ringleader—were brandishing cream pies in a menacing fashion, with bottles of seltzer water holstered to their polka-dotted belts.

"Are you the Pièce de Résistance?" Milton asked nervously, rising to his feet. The ground quaked, unsteady beneath him.

"We prefer HAHAHA," the head clown, a foot shorter than the rest, said in its shrill cartoon voice before sipping helium from a balloon. "The 'Hamper Authority through Humorous Adolescent Happenings Alliance.' Would you like some water? You look thirsty."

Milton, his mouth as dry as the sandbox he was standing in, nodded.

Instantly, the four clowns unholstered their seltzer water bottles and doused Milton with foamy wetness until he was thoroughly soaked.

"I suppose I should have seen that coming," Milton said with a smirk.

"Are you hungry?"

"No," Milton said, his arms held out in front of him, staring at the quivering cream pies the other clowns just ached to lob. "I'm good."

The four clowns drooped and took sulky bites out of their pies.

"Actually, you're *Milton Fauster*," the boss clown squeaked. "A riddle baked in an enigma at three hundred fifty degrees for thirty years until completely confounding."

"You know me? Were you the person I saw ten years ago before I passed out?"

The clown took off its wig. From beneath the shock

of bright orange hair spilled a waterfall of blond curls. The clown took off the bright red nose and wiped its face with the back of its glove. The clown was a woman. A familiar-looking woman with wide-set blue eyes. She took one of her cohort's pies, pressed it against the clown's purple polka-dotted chest, and, with her finger, drew a smiley face.

"*Shirley* you know who I am, Milton," the woman said, her voice losing its helium squeak.

"Shirley?" Milton said, his mind melting the years off the woman's face until she looked like a frightened little girl, someone he met thirty years ago, or—to him—just three days ago. "The girl from Tykers Island?"

She squeaked the nose of the green-haired clown at her side.

"Right! Yes, I am Shirley . . . Shirley Eujest. One of many young unfortunates sent to Tykers Island for the crime of being a kid. But instead of graduating to the grim world of grown-ups, I decided to devote my life to something else. Something both ridiculous and sublime. The bravest, noblest thing one can do in this 'all grown up with no place to go' society"—Shirley leaned into Milton's ticking Pace Taker—"and that's to laugh right in its smug clock face."

Milton realized that the clowns didn't have Pace Takers.

"How come you don't have these awful clocks attached to your hearts?"

The largest of the clowns, suspenders holding his tremendous checkered pants and stubble surrounding his chalky mouth, stepped forward. "We're off the grid," he said in a disarmingly high voice. He unbuttoned his purple shirt and revealed an ugly scar on his chest. "A delicate procedure. Not all of us made it. Luckily Tom Fullery here," he said, pointing at a fellow clown smoking a candy cigarette, "was a surgeon before he joined up."

Milton's head was like a Tokyo subway at rush hour, crowded and hectic.

"But . . . why me?"

Shirley smiled. Her eyes sparkled with crazed merriment. "Simple: you were nice to me. Like you really *cared* that I was sad and tried to make me feel better. Come. Let's talk while I show you around."

Milton followed Shirley and the other clowns into a tunnel, which, like the main cavern, was painted to look like a sunny day in the country. Strangely, Milton felt less claustrophobic down here underground than he did up on the surface with the sooty Widow's Veil blotting out the sky. A thought occurred to him.

"Wait, back in Tykers Island, Capitaine Bébête gave me a coin and told me to buy something specific in the vending machine, and out fell a note telling me to meet someone in the courtyard underneath a pair of clown shoes. Was that some kind of trap?"

"No, not a trap," Shirley replied, her blue eyes

misting. "You see, Capitaine Bébête was my mom. You were supposed to meet her."

"Your . . . your mom?" Milton sputtered. "But she was in charge of all the Wardens of the State. The guards who stretched the children, crammed them in KRAMS, submerged them into tanks—"

"Being *capitaine* was the only way she could be close to me and my brother and protect us," Shirley replied in a faraway voice. "But she couldn't make it seem like she was being soft on us. It was very hard for her. If she let down her guard, she would have been taken away with the other mothers. Imprisoned matriarch enemies of the state, like *yours*."

The burly clown, Tom Fullery, stopped suddenly with a squeak of his long, checkered shoes. "How can we trust him?" he asked Shirley. "Everything we know about this guy—from his Minister of Maturation sister to his dealings with Phelps Better to him heading up the emperor's latest horror show, the Ministry of Persuasion—stinks worse than those cans of Fart Spray. How do we know he's not some ministry spy?"

Shirley scrutinized Milton with her far-set blue eyes. "Have you ever taken truth serum?"

Milton shook his head. "To be honest, no."

"That's good enough for me," she said, her grease-painted face crinkling as she grinned. "You had mentioned, ten years ago today, wanting a meeting with us, with the joke being on the ministry. And there's nothing we at HAHAHA like more than a good joke. C'mon. You can walk and talk at the same time, right?"

"Um . . . yeah."

"Can you chew gum and juggle, too?" She handed him a stick of black gum, which he folded into his mouth. Immediately, his mouth felt like an active volcano.

"Need some water?" a clown asked, seltzer water bottle at the ready.

Milton shook his head. Shirley tossed him three red balls. Milton caught them and instinctually—his "Abra-Kid-Abra" summer Munchkin Magician and Tween Tossers Camp skills kicking in—began to juggle in shaky arcs.

"Why?" he managed, his mouth slowly downgrading from five-alarm to four-alarm status.

"With your eyes on the balls, it will be hard for you to eyeball anything you shouldn't," Shirley said as she and her clown posse entered another chamber.

Peripherally, Milton could see a line of clowns lobbing pies at a target, while another mob of clown commandos doused a mannequin dressed as Napoléon with seltzer water.

"Tell us why we should trust you," Tom Fullery asked, his fingertips stained powder-white from his candy cigarettes.

"This will sound crazy," Milton said, keeping the balls in the air. "But ever since I was eleven, I seem . . . to have these . . . spells. Where I'm me for one day—like today—but then have to . . . wait another ten years . . . before I'm me again. All I know is . . . that when I *am* me . . . I can do some good . . . because this world sucks fermented eggs. . . ."

"Look, I don't know if I believe you, but I believe that *you* believe you," Shirley replied. "And, if what you say is true, you could be of use to us: our undercover sleeper agent who wakes up once a decade. In fact, you could be just the ticket we need to pull off the *ultimate* inside job. We'll just need to make the most of those crucial days . . . *starting right now.*"

Shirley pulled a foil scroll from her pocket.

"The Affective Reasoning Machine is mass brainwashing with some *serious* bandwidth," she continued, her voice somber despite a lingering tinge of helium. "A person's individuality literally coming out in the wash."

"So you want me . . . to destroy it?" Milton asked, his arms feeling heavy as he juggled the red balls in increasingly sloppy circles.

"No, I want you to use it. *Abuse* it, actually. Using the ministry's medium to send a *new* message. A message that, hopefully, will cause mass discombobulation."

"Discombobulation? I'm confused."

"Then it's already working," Shirley replied. The clown queen stuffed the foil roll into Milton's inside pocket. "Confusion breeds questions, which is the last thing the ministry wants."

Milton was quickly ushered past a set of steel monkey

bars—occupied by *real* swinging monkeys—and back toward the entrance cavern. A monkey screeched, causing Milton to drop the balls onto the floor.

Tom Fullery scowled at Milton through his stubbly white greasepaint. "Shirley . . . I don't like this," he said. "How do we know he won't turn us all in?"

The curly blond clown shrugged her polka-dotted shoulders. "We don't," she squeaked in her faded helium voice. "But it might not even matter. He helped me once. He can help us now. And even if he somehow betrays us, it might actually help us to strike the final blow against the ministry. From the inside out. We'll just proceed slowly."

"Slowly? But, Shirley—"

The queen of the clowns turned her back to Tom Fullery. "People like us, who crave light and laughter, are basically alone," Shirley Eujest said to Milton as she plucked the plastic, squirting flower from her chest. "For a time, I lived in the same world as other people, but every day it took more and more effort."

She tucked the flower into a buttonhole on Milton's lapel. Milton looked down. Alarmingly, his Pace Taker read 9:57.

"But with your help, I realized that the enemy wasn't my youthful indiscretion: It was the ministry itself," Shirley continued. "It was the stultifying antiadolescent attitude that swept society suddenly, a hundred or so years ago."

A small explosion reverberated throughout HA-HAHA headquarters, birthing a sickening stench.

"Looks like the stink bomb squad are back to square one," Shirley said, waving the air with her bright orange wig. "But we at HAHAHA are, if anything, greater than the sum of our farts."

Milton laughed as the clowns led him across the sandbox to a small trampoline beneath the painted elephant's butt portal.

"See?" Shirley said with a wide grin of imperfect white teeth. "Laughter is hope. And with your help, Milton Fauster, we can get a leg up on this ARM thing for starters . . . *and prevent the mass obsolescence of adolescence.*"

Milton crept back into the darkened Ministry of Persuasion, his camouflage suit on backward so that he projected the walls behind him. He sidled along the hallway and stole into his office. There, on the imposing touch-screen table, was a blinking note and a foil scroll.

Monsieur Fauster, the note read.

Here are the daily ARM messages direct from New Paris. They arrive via the facts machine every day at 4:59. We are to inject them into the ARM at exactly midnight so that they may be disseminated to the masses while they sleep. The ARM's HAND (Hidden Access Node for Data) is located beneath the empty workspace in the break room since no one is allowed to take breaks.

Yours in Productivity Above All Else,

Mademoiselle Isis Fructueux

Milton unfurled the rolled sheet. Scrolling down the foil in a steady, digital cascade was a series of short, easily digested phrases.

Happiness is extravagance. . . . Rest is for the weak. . . . Neptune's Nibbles brand Dehydrated Kelp Pills are delicious and totally worth the sudden and unaccountable price hike. . . . Individuality is loneliness. . . . Caring is creepy. . . . Cleo-Ped Sandals are on sale at all King Tootsie-Uncommon stores. Buy one at twice the normal price and get the second shoe FREE. . . .

No wonder everyone here seems so stooped and broken, Milton thought as he rolled up the foil display and made his way for the break room. *It's like the basic need to play and explore—to have fun and grow—is no longer part of the human equation. Somewhere, somehow, it got all clogged up.*

The break room was a large walk-in closet with a dehydrated kelp machine, a Perrier cooler, and a few cracked concrete chairs surrounding a small drab table. Milton felt around beneath the desk. With a shove, he was able to rotate the desktop until the bottom of the desk was now up top. There was a horizontal slit beneath a small clock face reading 11:50. The slot was closed.

The slot must open at exactly midnight, Milton thought. *Then I just feed what Shirley Eujest gave me into the machine.*

He unfurled the digital foil roll given to him at HAHAHA headquarters. The odd phrases, riddles, jokes, and assorted nonsense scrolled down the wrinkled metal sheet.

Seventy-three percent of all statistics are totally made up. . . . Do imaginary squids squirt invisible ink? . . . Four out of five dentists agree that the fifth dentist is an idiot. . . . Individuality is all we really have. . . . Honk if you are highly suggestible. . . . What did the mayonnaise say to the ketchup? Close the door, I'm dressing. . . . If you put instant coffee in the microwave, it will be ready before you put it in. . . . Curiosity killed the catatonia. . . . Have the last laugh, and the first laugh, and every laugh in between. . . .

Milton glanced down at his Pace Taker: 11:55. His heart was racing, a drum of muscle pounding a rhythm in perfect time with the clock inserted into his chest.

Suddenly, high-beam flashlights sliced through the dark of the building. Ceiling tiles and air-conditioner duct grates exploded. Men in flak vests and silver helmets dropped from the ceiling on lines.

"You are under arrest!" a voice barked. The five men stalked closer to Milton.

I've been found out . . . somehow. My assistant must have turned me in, thinking my curiosity suspicious. . . .

Milton looked down at his chest: 11:58. He had two

minutes until he could feed the data foil into the Affective Reasoning Machine.

"I'm just doing my job. Helping to flex the long ARM of the law."

Two of the men unholstered something from their belts. The long black wands resembled the William clubs Milton had seen back in Tykers Island.

"I'm unarmed!" he yelped.

"You are accused of being an enemy of the state."

The men trained their clubs at Milton.

"Please . . . *s'il vous plaît*!" Milton said.

Milton's Pace Taker clicked to midnight. The slot whooshed open.

"And, as such, you are to be taken . . ."

The man closest to Milton held his thumb over the red button of his pneumatic baton.

"Take me where?" Milton said before frantically feeding the foil roll into the machine.

"Dead . . . or alive."

Milton dropped to his knees. His mind was a riot of extreme fatigue and electric terror. One of the policemen lunged for the data foil but only managed to tear a small corner before it disappeared into the ARM.

Milton fell, face-forward, dragged into unconsciousness. The last thing he heard was a massive whoosh and a faraway scream that sounded a lot like his own.

22 · A GHOST OF A DANCE

You have a little time at the end of your pig Latin class.
You spend it

A. drawing a picture of you drawing a picture.
B. seeing how long you can hold your breath without
   passing out.
C. filling out college applications, going through
   investment options, and generally planning out your
   entire afterlife.

Marlo, who was highly susceptible to any scenario
involving holding her breath, tapped "B" on the touch
screen.

"Oww!" she shrieked as one thousand volts of electricity were rudely introduced to her body through her
left hand, currently trapped in Dr. Skinner's Juice Box.

"The correct answer is C." The screen blinked in admonishment.

Marlo tried to yank her hand out of the small black box, but it was apparently trapped there until she had answered every question on her Snap, Crackle, and Pop Quiz.

"Sounds like some loser got the wrong— OWW!" Lyon said-then-yelped from behind the cubicle wall.

Marlo smirked. Another question popped onto the screen.

You've just been diagnosed with earworms. Do you

A. stick your head in a stream and go ear-fishing?
B. flush your ear canal with scalding-hot oil?
C. dislodge the earworms with a maddeningly catchy jingle?

Milton would totally ace this stuff in his usual geektasti-cally brainiac way, Marlo thought as she arbitrarily jabbed the screen, selecting "C" since the answer to nearly every multiple-choice question is the last one.

A slightly lower voltage of electricity jolted Marlo's system. "Oww!" she cried.

"Correct! The best way to dislodge a musical earworm is with an even catchier jingle!"

"How come I answered the stupid question right and *still* got shocked?" Marlo whined.

"If you get a question wrong, you get a big electrical shock as punishment," explained the long-faced Latino girl from an adjoining cubicle. "If you get it right, then—oww, *¡Ay, dios mío!*—you get a smaller shock as a sort of reward: negative reinforcement and slightly *less* negative reinforcement. . . ."

Marlo leaned back in her cold steel chair and tried to fold her arms in defiance, which is really hard to do with only one arm free.

"Well, I'm not going to answer any of the questions, then, um . . ."

"Paloma," the girl replied.

"Paloma," Marlo said as a new question appeared on the touch screen.

A dream is your brain

A. sleeping on the job and squandering precious time by playing dress-up and acting all, like, "Hey, look at me!"
B. grappling with repressed complexes and working out subconscious issues that are, for the most part, incredibly stupid. I mean, c'mon already . . . showing up at school in your pajamas? Is that really something you're worried about?
C. All of the above.

Marlo sat there, scowling at the screen for three long

seconds, until a massive jolt of electricity—the strongest yet—coursed through her indignant young body.

"OWW! Flippin' ninja burgers!" Marlo squealed. "That hurt more than any of them!"

"The correct answer was 'C.' Maybe you thought this was some kind of a dream, with you merrily, merrily, merrily, merrily rowing your brain boat when you should have been PAYING ATTENTION!"

The skinny Asian girl poked her head over the cubicle wall.

"Knock much, um . . . ?" Marlo replied irritably, her short fuse nearly blown with electricity.

"Midori," the girl replied sheepishly as she straightened her glasses. "It's just that, well, if you *don't* answer, that's the worst answer of all."

"You're telling me," Marlo grumbled, her hair a blue, prickly, static-clinged bush.

"It's how they teach us to make decisions," Midori said. "Because adults have to make them all the time."

"So it doesn't matter if those decisions are even good or bad," Marlo replied.

"Yeah."

"That is so typically . . . *adult*," Marlo said, shaking her head. "And . . . thanks for the info."

Midori smiled and disappeared behind the cubicle wall. The electricity wriggled inside of Marlo like little white-hot wasps, making her extra edgy and anxious.

A pair of zombie teens shambled past Marlo on their

way to the vice principals' offices. Marlo, her lip bloody from biting down on it, stared at them as they staggered down the hallway.

"What's up with Mr. and Mrs. Personality?" Marlo said, hurling her question over the cubicle wall. "It's like they're . . . I don't know . . . *buffering* or something."

"The teachers' aides?" Midori replied. "No one knows for sure. They used to be—oww! *Itai, oya~tsu!*—normal."

"Normal?" Marlo repeated.

"Yeah, but then they came down with cooties," Midori said. "After a week in the infirmary, they returned but were never the same."

"What? OWW!" Marlo yelped, having just ignored another question on her screen.

Like a feral animal caught in a trap, Marlo leaned into the Juice Box and spat on her hand. Then she squirmed her hand around in the box until it was nice and slick. With one last painful tug, Marlo yanked her hand free.

"My brother has been gone *way* too long," she said, "and his big sister is going to find out what's happening before he turns into a walking sack of zombified nothing. . . ."

Marlo opened the door to Solomon Grundy's office. The pale and drawn old man was lying in a hospital bed with Dr. Curie weeping beside him. Dr. Curie held the man's emaciated hand to her glowing green cheek. She glared at Marlo with her tear-swollen eyes.

"What do you want?" Dr. Curie said with a snort.

"What's wrong with him?" Marlo replied from the doorway.

"He grew worse on Friday," she replied.

"Oh . . . right. Look, I wanted to talk to him about my brother. He and the other cooties kids have been in the infirmary a long time."

Dr. Curie straightened up in her chair and wiped her eyes. "They are very sick. So?"

Marlo put her hands on her hips. "I want to see my brother."

Dr. Curie stood up and smoothed her frizzy gray-and-black hair back into a bun.

"The infirmary is under quarantine," she said sternly. "Vice principals' orders."

Marlo turned huffily on her heel. "Then I'll take it up with them," she said as she stormed away.

The pink Girls' Boardroom door was ajar. Marlo stepped inside Cleopatra's grand throne room, her footfalls echoing against the gold-and-tan tiled floor.

Napoléon sat on Cleopatra's divan, his little legs dangling over the edge. Marlo gulped, suddenly nervous. The last time she had seen Napoléon was in the Undermines, laughing as Ponce de León was swallowed up by quicksand. Cleopatra leveled her simmering, kohl-rimmed gaze at Marlo.

"Knock much?" Cleopatra said with hot disdain as she lay on her elegant throne.

Napoléon, with his dark, murderous eyes, motioned for his demon foot servants to "greet" Marlo.

"I . . . I want to see my brother," Marlo said. "He's in the infirmary."

The hunched demon foot servants rattled toward Marlo, their canvas sack–covered bodies crumpled forward from tight chains wrapped up and over them like suspenders.

"We know very well where your brother is and zhe infirmary is restricted!" Napoléon exclaimed.

Virgil and Frances appeared behind Marlo in the doorway.

"I don't want him turning into one of those creepy, slackadaisical teachers' aides," Marlo continued.

Napoléon's demon foot servants, Armstrong and Patrick Harris, considered Marlo with eyes that glowed red beneath their canvas sack skin.

More curious children began to mill around outside of the Girls' Boardroom.

"*Sacré bleu!*" Napoléon shouted. "What is zhis? Mutiny on zhe bouncy castle?"

"I demand to see my brother!" Marlo declared, emboldened by the children behind her. "Like . . . really soon!"

"Yeah," Frances said, stepping into the boardroom. "And we saw what you did to Ponce de León in the Undermines!"

Napoléon's nostrils flared with rage. "I should send

you teeny boppers to zhe guillotine for such willful rabble-rousing!" he shouted, looking like a furious near-life-sized tin soldier.

Cleopatra patted him softly on the shoulder. "I have a better way," she purred. She spilled off her elegant couch and fluttered her gleaming plaited cornrows with her hand. "I am glad you are all here, Junior Executives." Her voice billowed like the intoxicating smoke of her fragrant incense. "For I have a special announcement: tonight there will be a Precocia-sanctioned social gathering . . . *a dance.*"

The children gasped, their attention shattered like a broken mirror, breaking off into dozens of side conversations.

Cleopatra's lips coiled into a self-satisfied smile. "See, *mon petit* emperor," she whispered, "nothing distracts the teeming teen masses like the delicious disorientation of a dance. . . ."

Marlo and Lyon sat cross-legged on the floor of the Boys' Boardroom, dressed in massive pink crinoline gowns with hoop skirts, curling lengths of ribbon with safety scissors. Punch bowls filled with prune juice and Ensure were set on tables pushed to the sides of the room.

"Why are, like, *me* and Thrift Store here the decorating committee?" Lyon complained.

Midori helped Paloma stick gray balloons to an arch just inside the doorway.

"Vice Principal Cleopatra says that when you're grown up, you never get to work with your friends," Midori said. "You have to work with people you either instantly hate or learn to hate over time."

Just then, four lizards in gold lamé suits slithered into the boardroom. They dragged broken toy pianos, horns, and guitars behind them. The tallest lizard—nearly two feet high—leered over the top of his Ray-Bans.

"Where should we, you know, set up?"

Lyon grimaced and pointed to the corner.

"Over there . . . as far as you can be away from me while still being in this room."

The lizard winked his double-lidded eye and crawled away. As the band set up their pseudo-instruments, the boys started filing in wearing ill-fitting pale blue tuxedos.

"HELLO? Is this thing on?" the lead lizard said into his microphone. "It's great to be here in"—he looked down at a slip of paper—"*Precocia*. It's great to be any-where, actually, with the frightening popularity of lizard-skin boots. I kid. Hey, what do you call a lizard that lays down some funky rhymes? A *rap*-tile! Well, I hope you're all ready to *rock out*. We've been practicing our *scales* all week . . . a one, two, three, FOUR!"

The band launched into a loud, guitar-heavy dance number, with the lead lizard swinging his microphone like a windmill.

"The underworld is hopping
So get out of your seat
These mad, bad beats are dropping
So move the toe tags on your feet."

Virgil and Angelo scoped out the room, with the boys and girls on either side as if the room were a giant, socially awkward teeter-totter. Angelo spotted Marlo. She was trying to look cool and not sway to the music, but she couldn't help herself. She caught him staring at her. Angelo smiled. Marlo quickly looked away.

"So, you said her brother is in the infirmary?" Angelo said nonchalantly.

"Yeah," Virgil replied, hooking his finger around the collar of his too-tight tuxedo. He stared at Marlo who, even in her nauseatingly pink and poofy dress, still—to Virgil—looked like a princess, albeit a dead, surly, blue-haired one with a serious shoplifting problem.

"Why don't you ask her to dance?" Angelo said with a smirk, noting Virgil's interest.

"I . . . I don't really know *how*," Virgil replied. "Unless you count line dancing—"

"Which no one does," Angelo interjected. "Here, watch me . . . I'll show you how it's done."

Angelo swaggered toward Marlo. The girls bunched together suddenly like pigeons.

"Hey, um . . . ," Angelo said with a noncommittal nod of his head.

"It's *Marlo*," Marlo replied, trying to look as cool as she could despite her big, pink Hostess Sno Ball dress.

"Right. *Marlo*."

Marlo wrung her sweaty hands. "So . . . um . . . this dance is pretty lame, right?"

"Yeah," Angelo said, staring off into space. *"Lame."*

Marlo, flustered, began to laugh nervously. "It would be, you know, funny, if we danced or something."

"I don't really do the 'dancing' thing," Angelo said coolly before walking away.

Marlo stared at her feet, fuming with embarrassment. "Dances blow," she grumbled as Virgil awkwardly approached.

"Um . . . hey," he said, willing himself to stop sweating and doing a terrible job of it. "I was, you know, wondering if—"

Angelo brushed past, wedging himself in between Virgil and Marlo. He handed Marlo a cup of prune juice. "Did you miss me?" he said, flexing his jaw muscles to produce two perfect dimples.

Marlo smiled, going from mad to sad to glad in about fifteen seconds flat. "Not really," she murmured, sipping her drink.

Myung-Dae shuffled to the dance floor in awkward mechanical jerks. "You know, if we were all really robots and were doing the 'robot,' we'd really just be doing the 'us,'" he explained to Midori.

Midori laughed and began to lurch alongside of him in cyber-rhythmic fits and starts.

The lizards bowed as they finished their first song. They lapped up the tepid applause as if it were sugar water bobbing with dead flies, which lizards really, really like.

"Thank you very much," the lead lizard said, wiping his sweaty forehead with a kerchief. "We'd like to bring things down a bit now. . . ."

The band slumped sullenly over their instruments.

"My heart beat 'Welcome,'
Then you wiped your feet on it.
Cupid's arrow's dipped in venom,
Now I'm bleeding a sonnet . . ."

Virgil sighed as Frances stepped up next to him to stare at Marlo and Angelo, who were chatting quietly.

"What does *he* have that I don't?" Virgil asked grimly.

Frances sipped a cup of prune juice and grimaced. "Do you want a list itemized alphabetically or by priority?" she said.

"Staring contest!" Angelo suddenly blurted. "You and me . . . GO!"

Marlo and Angelo locked eyes for a minute-long ocular wrestling match until finally, Angelo (despite his intense blue gaze) broke free.

"I win!" Marlo said with a crooked smile.

Angelo grinned. His smile was so bright that Marlo literally had to squint.

"Nope, *I* won 'cause I got to stare at you for a full minute without it being creepy," he replied.

Marlo had so many feelings tumbling within her that she had to laugh to relieve some of the pressure.

"What was that?" Angelo said, the faintest flicker of outrage in his eyes.

"Laughter," she replied nervously as she stepped back against the wall. "You know: the second-best medicine."

"Second best? What's the *best* medicine, then?"

Marlo shrugged. "Medicine."

Angelo leaned against the wall next to Marlo, acting like a fence between her and the other kids.

"You put me on the rack,
Then you tortured me with bliss,
My heart's under attack,
So do me in with your kiss . . ."

With that, Angelo brushed his full lips against Marlo's. Marlo closed her eyes. Her heart fluttered weakly to the slow crawl of the chemical candy music. Her veins felt like they were pumping ginger ale, her mind foaming over with tiny bubbles of fizzy paradise.

"I feel . . . good," Marlo murmured. *"And really bad . . ."*

Marlo crumpled. Angelo scooped her up effortlessly in his strong arms.

"What happened?" Virgil exclaimed. "Is she okay?"

Angelo smirked. "She fainted. Can't say this hasn't happened to me before." He brushed past Virgil across the dance floor. Angelo stopped suddenly in front of the band, holding the unconscious Marlo in his arms while leaning into the microphone.

"I need to get this girl to the infirmary!" he said dramatically. *"Stat!"*

Angelo elbowed his way past Dr. Curie. His keen eyes traced the infirmary like blue laser scopes searching for their target.

"You shouldn't be here," Dr. Curie scolded, her radioactive radiance lighting the way. "This is a cooties hot zone."

"Where should I put her?" Angelo asked as he examined the mostly empty beds.

"Set her there," she replied tersely, pointing to a corner bed with "Fauster" scrawled on the headboard.

Angelo dropped Marlo onto the bed like a sack of Mrs. Potato Heads.

"Where am I?" Marlo muttered, her eyes fluttering briefly. "The infirmary . . . ?" she added before passing out again.

"Where is her brother?" Angelo asked, glaring at the woman with intimidating intensity.

Dr. Curie swallowed. "They are having their

treatments, of course," she said nervously, her eyes betraying her thoughts by quickly flicking toward the hall.

Angelo smirked as he reached behind his back. "Well, I'll just pop in and say hello," he said as he strode past her, stealthily plucking a long, silver blade from his back.

"What is zhis boy doing here?" Napoléon shouted as he marched into the infirmary with Cleopatra slinking just behind. "Zhis area is under zhe quarantine!"

Dr. Einstein shuffled in from the hallway, followed by two zombie teenagers dragging Bordeaux behind them. A few old mayfly demons swarmed behind the vice principals.

Angelo sighed and tucked his blade up into his sleeve.

"I was just leaving," he said. "I wanted to make sure Margot was safe."

He walked past the vice principals, giving Cleopatra a wink as he entered the elevator.

"There's something about that boy," Dr. Curie said, her hand around her throat.

"Yes," Cleopatra said with a vague grin. "He's got 'muddle management' written all over him. . . ."

The zombie teenagers plopped Bordeaux onto a bed marked "Radisson" as two more shambled inside.

"Well, everything seems under control now zhat we've had to *personally* come down to maintain order," Napoléon said with his long nose up in the air. "We will leave you all to coordinate zhe changing of zhe guard . . . or Kronosgraph needles, specifically."

Napoléon and Cleopatra left the infirmary while Dr. Curie and Dr. Einstein, both highly distracted, walked out into the hallway. One of the zombie teenagers stared at Marlo's bed with glassy-eyed confusion.

"*Fauster?* Again? Okay . . ." He grunted to himself before hoisting Marlo, bundled in her blanket, up into his arms. A mayfly demon buzzed alongside him and slipped a black leather helmet hood with a long pointy tip on top of Marlo's head.

"What the . . . ?" Marlo muttered vaguely.

The teenage boy passed a zombified girl in the hallway as she dragged Milton along the floor to the bed that, only moments ago, had been occupied by his sister.

23 · FROM KiDDY
TO OLD BiDDY

MARLO OPENED HER eyes and, after rejecting the absurd images her optic nerves were sending to her brain, rubbed the crusty sleep from them. Yet, after a couple of power blinks, her eyes were again trying to convince her that—instead of waking in the Precocia infirmary— she had arisen in a gray palace.

A canopy the dull, velvety color of a moth's wings hung over her bed. Through the gap, Marlo could make out a low-hanging chandelier and a large window with sunlight peeking through the smoke-colored curtains.

Marlo tried kicking off her steel-gray covers, but she was tucked in tight. She wriggled out like a baby kangaroo that had outgrown its mother's pouch and fell onto the floor.

Weird, Marlo thought as she felt the floor with her palms. *It's all wobbly.*

The next thing she noticed was that, well, apparently the booby fairy had visited at some point in the night, because Marlo definitely had a little something extra in the chest department.

"I didn't know they came all at once like—" Marlo croaked before stopping suddenly and clutching her throat. "My voice . . . it's . . . so low."

Where am I? she wondered as she got up off the gently swaying floor and walked toward the window. *I can't be in Heck, because there's sun outside. So I must be . . .*

She pulled open the curtains. Outside her window was a gorgeous spring day: a clear blue sky, rolling hills of swaying green grass, and the sun streaming down like electric caramel.

"Home," Marlo said in her weird, low voice. She pressed her palm against the window, hoping that the warmth of this perfect morning would leach into her body, her very bones . . .

But the window was cold.

This isn't even glass, Marlo thought as she pressed her face against the window, noting thousands of tiny pixels. *It's just a stupid screen broadcasting some fantastically fake day.*

She wiped her eyes before they could send tears of disappointment splashing down her face.

Must be one of Dr. Skinner's dumb behavior experiments,

Marlo thought as she walked across the room toward a small mirror. *He's probably on the other side, watching me.*

"Hey!" she shouted at the mirror before its image strangled the angry words forming in her throat.

"Grandma?"

Marlo touched her face. The old woman in the mirror brushed her hand against her wrinkled cheek.

"I'm, like, *really* old," Marlo muttered. Her crepe-paper skin was so white it practically glowed.

"At least I've got *major* pallor," she said with amazement. "But this hair"—she lifted the gunmetal strands framing her face—"I look like I should be handing out poisoned apples. And what's this mole thing?" She picked at a black spot near her mouth.

A beauty mark tattoo. Makes me look très *French . . . a* très *French old hag, that is.*

Marlo had her mom's vaguely haunted expression, but there was something about her face that she didn't quite recognize: a snooty air of privilege with a touch of cruelty around her eyebrow-penciled eyebrows. This haughty disdain reminded Marlo of—

"Madam Fauster?" a familiar yet creaky voice called from the doorway.

"Lyon?" Marlo gasped as an old woman stood in her doorway holding a tray: a pale prune of a woman with blond-gray hair and bright blue eyes that, though weathered by time, were unmistakably Lyon's. The woman's cheeks flushed red.

"You've never addressed me by my first name before, Madam Fauster," Lyon said, bowing slightly in humility—to Marlo's utter astonishment and, yes, wicked pleasure.

Lyon set the tray on a concrete table draped with burgundy velvet.

"So, you're like my slave or something?" Marlo asked, working hard to suppress a grin.

"Personal assistant," Lyon replied with a flash of anger in her eyes.

Whatever is going on here, it just got more fun, Marlo thought as Lyon—*my personal assistant!*—removed the silver lid from the tray. On the serving dish was a bowl of slimy green seaweed and a glass of cloudy white water.

"Your seaweed and baking soda water, madam."

Marlo scowled. "Yuck . . . what am I, a sea lion?" Marlo said.

"Of course not, madam. Sea lions died out years ago, along with most other mammals, yet you—much to my great personal joy—are still very much alive," Lyon replied through gritted teeth. "Is your iBud not working?"

"My iBud?"

Lyon unwrapped a small white device from the napkin on the tray. It looked like a digital music player, only it had a long cord leading to a little ball at the end. Lyon quickly flipped through a screen of options on the tiny device.

"It seems to be in order," Lyon said. "Maybe you've had it on too high and are temporarily tongue-deaf. Try it now."

Marlo, at the prompting of Lyon's icy blue eyes, plopped the white ball into her mouth. She scrolled through her iBud's "Taste List." *Bouillabaisse* . . . A salty, fish-soup flavor filled Marlo's mouth. The intensity was shocking. Marlo turned the flavor down a few clicks. *Brie cheese* . . . Yuck, like a wet dog with moldy cream poured on top of it. *Escargot* . . .

"Thnails?" Marlo complained. "Dithguthting!"

Foie gras . . . a buttery, meaty flavor that was a little too rich for Marlo's taste. *Fruit crepes* . . . mmm, *this* was more like it. It felt like her tongue was dancing to the latest Pop-Tart music.

"Doeth ewewyone haff theeze?" Marlo asked.

"Excusez-moi?"

Marlo popped the ball out of her tingling mouth. "Does everyone have these?" she asked.

"Only those of privilege and power, madam," Lyon replied.

Marlo noticed that Lyon had a small, ticking clock pinned to her chest.

"What's that?"

Lyon self-consciously patted the puckering material around her clock as if she were suffering a sudden bout of heartburn.

"My Pace Taker, madam? Is it not working properly?"

"Pace *Taker*? What do you . . . ?"

Marlo patted the front of her nightgown. "How come I don't have one?"

Lyon's blue eyes burned like twin pilot lights. "Again, madam, *only those of privilege and power,* like yourself, don't have Pace Takers. But, of course, you know this and are simply making some kind of point. . . ."

Lyon looked down at her Pace Taker.

"Madam, we must *accélérer,*" she said, shuffling toward a wall. Lyon clapped her wrinkled white hands together. The wall whooshed open, and inside were hundreds of clothes.

Whatever is going on, Marlo thought as she walked over to the packed closet, her joints aching, *I can hang around for a bit longer. I mean, just to try on a few things.*

She flipped through the stunning selection of wool frock coats, starched blouses, and high-waisted empire dresses, whizzing the hangers about like beads on an abacus, trying to solve the daily problem of what to wear.

"Would you like me to dress you, madam?" Lyon asked.

"Would you like me to jab these coat hangers into your earlobes?"

"No, madam."

"And stop calling me madam, *Malibu Retirement Home Barbie,*" Marlo said as she selected a pair of tailored gray pants and matching coat.

"Oui, oui, Minister."

"That reminds me . . . where's the bathroom?"

Lyon clapped twice, opening the wall leading to the bathroom.

"Merci," Marlo said as she stepped inside to get dressed. "So, what was that about me being a minister? I'm some kind of priest, then?"

Lyon allowed herself a double eye roll.

"As Minister of Judgment, you are hardly a priest— yet people *do* have a way of confessing things to you. And, madam . . . um, *Minister,* the Gravity Bureau predicts extreme cases of wobble today, so you might want to wear your Steady-Peds. . . ."

Marlo emerged, dressed, looking crisp and professional, though her hair resembled a frightened gray porcupine.

"Excusez-moi, Minister," Lyon said, wincing. "Your hair—"

"So what's next?" Marlo asked.

Lyon tore her cold blue eyes from Marlo's hairstyle and clapped three times. The window-screen wall opened, revealing an elevator. They stepped inside.

A dream, Marlo thought as the elevator descended. *It's got to be. This is all way too elaborate to be some prank or a test. Or maybe it's that swine cooties virus thing. I'm sick back in Precocia and trapped in some trippy fever dream.*

The elevator door opened. Beyond was a grand, imposing marble hall, cold in both appearance and temperature. It was flawlessly symmetrical, as if there were a huge mirror in the middle reflecting back the exact same square columns and statues.

Lyon marched ahead in her clunky boots, each footfall echoing throughout the empty concourse. Marlo walked just behind her with an unsteady gate, as if the floor itself was rolling beneath her feet.

They approached a large black booth.

"What's this?" Marlo asked.

Lyon shut her eyes and took a deep breath.

"Minister, really. This is all most . . . *étrange*. This is your Adjudication Chamber."

"My what?"

"Where you pass judgment," Lyon said, opening the door of the small marble enclosure with irritation.

Marlo stepped inside. It looked like a spacious confession booth—like the kind that Marlo sneaked into once at the Our Lady of Ample Parking and Perpetual Tuesday Night Bingo church, only the chairs were facing each other.

"So I'm a judge," Marlo said.

Lyon gave her sleek hair, tied into a tight bun, a couple of quick, frustrated pats. *"Oui."*

"But where's the jury?"

"Jury?"

"You know, all the grumpy people who are picked to give a verdict in a court case."

Lyon gave a nervous glance down at her Pace Taker.

"I'm afraid I don't know what you mean, madam, but it sounds terribly inefficient. You provide the verdict *yourself*, Minister. Swiftly and systematically."

"But what about sifting through evidence, hearing both sides, and all of that stuff?"

Lyon snickered, then quickly covered her mouth in embarrassment. "It must be time for my review and you are testing me," she replied curtly, regaining her composure. "It is enough that these criminals are brought to you, Minister. Our system is without reproach, so the fact that these miscreants have been arrested and indefinitely detained, then brought before you is testament enough to their guilt. You merely give your official ministry verdict."

Whoa, Marlo thought. *My self-esteem must be at an all-time low if Lyon is the one with all the answers in my own dream.*

"So it's sort of a . . . formality, then," Marlo said, sitting down in her gray velvet-covered throne. On the table in front of her was a gavel, with a worn rubber GUILTY stamp on one end, and NOT GUILTY on the other. The NOT GUILTY stamp looked like it had never been used.

"*Oui*, Minister." The old woman leaned over Marlo. "Your first ruling is a very interesting one," Lyon said with a slight curl of her lined-by-age lips. "A woman up for parole in Dartmoor Prison. She led a revolt many years ago against our government and our way of doing things. Though quickly apprehended, she is still some-thing of a 'symbol' for dissent."

"And she's up for release?"

"*Oui.*"

"If she's some symbol, then her release would be like saying that we approved of what she did, right?"

"*Oui.*"

"Well," Marlo said, cracking her knuckles, "this shouldn't take too long, then. Bring her in."

An old, unkempt woman wearing a black-and-white striped jumpsuit was brought into the chamber across from Marlo.

"Minister Fauster," Lyon declared officiously, "you will now pass your infallible judgment upon your first case of the day. . . ."

Marlo could now see the woman, framed by the thick dividing window in the Adjudication Chamber. Though worn and decrepit, the woman's haunted, old-movie-star appearance was instantly familiar.

"The State versus—"

Marlo swallowed a lump of dread that felt like a barbed wire ice cube in her throat.

"*Mom!*"

24 · RUN-iN THE FAMiLY

MARLO SLAPPED HERSELF across her wrinkled face. Lyon stared at her boss, half in shock and half in envy that it was Marlo's lucky hand, not her own, that got to strike the Minister of Judgment across the chops.

"Wake up . . . ," Marlo muttered. *"Just a dumb dream."*

"Minister?" Lyon asked.

Marlo's mother, Rosemary Fauster, glowered at her daughter through the reinforced window of the Adjudication Chamber.

"Don't have the stomach to sentence your own mother *again*?" Rosemary Fauster said, her voice a weary yet angry rasp, like a bee dying on a windowsill wanting to go out with one last sting. "Only *this* time so that she can die behind bars in that horrible place?"

The guard standing next to Marlo's mother shoved a

stick in the old woman's side. "Silence! If you don't show the minister some respect, I'll whoosh you!"

Marlo looked up at Lyon, terrified. "What do I do?"

"Well, Minister, if I may be frank—"

"Be whoever you want, Sheraton," Marlo replied.

"The prisoner, Rosemary Fauster, organized dozens of biological hosts—"

"Biological hosts?"

Lyon expelled a put-upon breath. *"Mothers,"* she replied, "who had just had their children taken away . . . greenies who had failed their maturity tests and were sentenced to Tykers Island for accelerated maturation."

A cylinder dropped into the chamber through a pneumatic tube. Lyon opened it and pulled out a roll of odd foil paper. She unfurled it and the image of a document appeared—Marlo's mother's case file. Lyon spread the weird electric paper onto Marlo's desk, scrolling through it with the tip of her French-manicured nail.

"The prisoner," Lyon continued, "resisted the state-sanctioned abduction of her youngest child, Milton Fauster. Shortly thereafter, she made contact with other . . . *mothers* in the same situation, ultimately amassing hundreds of coconspirators."

"Who wanted to protect their innocent children," Rosemary Fauster interjected. "Those blessed with spontaneity and exuberance, unaffected by the cynical machinations of the state! I didn't want Milton to end up like *you*."

The guard reached for his club.

"No!" Marlo shouted. "I mean . . . that won't be, um, *nécessaire*." She dropped her head and rubbed her temples, hoping to mask the tears that were streaming out of her eyes. Her mother, for some reason, viewed Marlo as a monster.

"Are you feeling ill, Minister?" Lyon asked with feigned compassion.

"Just a little headache," Marlo lied, wiping her eyes. "Continue."

"*Oui*, Minister. So the insurrection, while quickly subdued, *did* generate a lot of unwanted attention during the barbaric times before the Unfortunate Shower and the French-Egyptian armistice."

Now Marlo's head really *did* ache. With every word Lyon uttered, Marlo understood less and less.

"And with your unprecedented ascension in the ministry, the prisoner caused undue embarrassment for the government—being your relative and all—resulting in her immediate incarceration in the isolation wing of Dartmoor Prison."

Rosemary Fauster glared at her daughter. It was as if the broken old woman was actually *daring* Marlo to do what she seemed convinced Marlo was going to do anyway: condemn her to death in some horrible prison.

Marlo drew a deep breath. "Not guilty." She banged her gavel on the electric paper, leaving a big blinking NOT GUILTY stamp on her mother's case file.

"*Not* guilty?" Lyon repeated, her jaw hanging open. "This is highly irregular."

"Then you should eat more fiber," Marlo said before turning toward her mother.

Rosemary Fauster's eyes, once filled with fury, now rested on her daughter with a sort of pained questioning. "Is this some kind of . . . trick?" the woman muttered, scarcely able to summon enough breath to speak.

"Nope. Look. Nothing up my sleeve," Marlo replied, tugging on the cuffs of her starched light-gray blouse. She smiled, an expression that Rosemary Fauster viewed with openmouthed horror.

"You're free to go, Mom, er, *Madame Fauster*," Marlo said. She fought back tears as she waved her mother away. "Guard, give her a nice meal—the best seaweed and baking soda water you've got. Let her get cleaned up and take her home to Dad, um . . . her husband."

Rosemary Fauster rose, her head darting from side to side as if expecting some kind of ambush.

"*Merci*," she whispered as the guard escorted her out of the chamber.

"*Really*, Minister, *sacré bleu*! I don't know how you're going to justify that ruling," Lyon said, her perfect nostrils flaring with barely subdued outrage.

"Well, what can I say? I rule!" Marlo said, pumping her fist in the air. After a moment of awkward silence, she shrugged. "See, me letting her go will show everybody that the ministry doesn't care."

"Doesn't care?"

"That we aren't threatened by her or those who hold her up as some kind of symbol, right?"

Lyon rubbed her pointy chin. "I suppose there's some logic to that," the woman conceded. "Well, your ruling was uncharacteristically slow, so we need to make up for lost time."

Lyon rolled up Rosemary Fauster's case file and deposited it into the brass capsule, then slipped it inside the pneumatic tube. It was instantly whooshed away: up and out of the chamber. Another case file soon plopped into its place.

"Minister Fauster," Lyon declared, "you will now pass your infallible judgment upon your second case of the day, Case 10-5401. . . ."

Marlo's long day had been spent presiding over a number of cases, most as dull as a beige rubber butter knife, including a dispute involving some guy's sodium bicarbonate mining rights in Iceland. Apparently the ministry had swooped in and laid claim to them after discovering something called "precarium." *I mean, isn't sodium bicarbonate* baking soda?

"*Minister Fauster*," Lyon overarticulated, nearly stretching the name to six syllables, "you will now pass your infallible judgment upon your last case of the day, Case 10-5427. . . ."

Lyon's stately expression melted into a self-satisfied sneer. "The State versus *Milton Fauster.*"

Marlo swallowed as an old man who looked kind of like her father only with her mother's hazel eyes was shoved into the judgment chair.

"Milton?" Marlo muttered as she peered at the man through the reinforced window. "I mean . . . *the accused?*"

"*Oui,* Madam Minister, aka, 'the sister I could never live up to,'" the man seated across from her said. "Now it's time for you to pretend to review my case before you send me to the electric guillotine for treason."

"Treason?"

"*Oui,* Madam Minister," Lyon explained. "He was interrogated for the last ten years but has revealed nothing. So the next logical step is to try him for his obvious treason before sending him to the electric guillotine."

"The guillotine?"

"Where my head is to be separated from my shoulders," the old man interjected.

Marlo stared at her supposed brother.

Sure, it could be Milton, if you heaped half a century of hard living on top of him, then beat him over the head with an old, rolled-up copy of National Geriatric. *But there's something different about him. The eyes. Actually,* behind *the eyes.*

"As you know, Minister," Lyon explained, reading Milton's case file, "ten years ago, the prisoner, Milton Fauster, was suspected of collaborating with terrorists and was ultimately arrested at the Ministry of

Persuasion, where he was caught feeding resistance pro-paganda into the ARM."

"He was feeding an arm?"

Lyon sighed. "The *Affective Reasoning Machine,* Minister. Where the ministry's messages are transmitted directly into the minds of citizens so that we act as one unified society. Anyway, the prisoner's nonsensical messages created a temporary disturbance in the Midwestopotamian region. There was a sharp dive in productivity, a marked increase in dissent, and a great deal of . . . I believe the word is *giggling.*"

The other-Milton rolled his eyes.

"She knows all of this because she sent me to Dartmoor Prison in the first place," he snorted. "If she put Blake in there, too, we could just call it *Fauster* Prison, *grands dieux!*"

"Silence!" the guard said as he pressed his club into Milton's side.

"Let him talk," Marlo said. "I mean, we might as well, right? Last case of the day, then we all break for seaweed and iBuds. My treat!"

The other-Milton crinkled up his already crinkly eyes at Marlo before ultimately shrugging and leaning back in his chair. "Sure, whatever. You're just going to lock me away so I don't cause you any more embarrassment. I get it. Work comes first. Though, for you, it also comes in second, third, last, and everything in between. The ministry is your family, and everything else just gets in the way. Though you've done a *magnifique* job of sweeping away your 'distractions.'"

The old man kneaded his wrinkled face in his hands.

"So, like I told you ten years ago, every decade since the Unfortunate Shower—"

"The Unfortunate Shower? Like at summer camp?"

"*When the meteors fell,* Minister," Lyon said, shaking her head.

"Oh, right," Marlo replied. "Continue."

"Well, every ten years, I'm not myself. I'm this nice guy. And this nice guy does things that get me into trouble."

"Is this nice guy a sort of goody-goody know-it-all?" Marlo asked.

The other-Milton nodded his balding head.

Marlo sighed. "I know the type." She scooted her velvet-covered throne toward Lyon. "What if I let him go?"

"You would be viewed as a compassionate administrator of justice," Lyon whispered in reply.

"And that's good."

"No, compassion is weakness."

"And that's bad."

"Not necessarily. It would confuse the ministry."

"How do you mean?" Marlo asked, confused herself.

"They would know that *you* knew a not guilty verdict would be viewed poorly, so they would assume that you were up to something."

Marlo rubbed the top of her head, which was blossoming with dull pain.

"The guy is obviously bat-shitake-mushroom crazy," she said. "I mean, becoming someone he *isn't* once every ten years? Someone who makes him do weird, nice things? *C'mon.* So here's what I'm going to do—"

Marlo blacked out.

She felt like she was hanging upside down, her breath hot and stale and in her face, as if she were wearing a bag over her head.

"You got the wrong one!" Dr. Einstein scolded, his voice muffled to Marlo's ears.

"But she was in the right bed," a dull voice replied.

"I don't care . . . her mind won't stay open, not like her brother's. She is ruining the time groove!"

The top of Marlo's head hurt like heck. She wriggled around in the dark until, suddenly, with what felt like a bolt of lightning hitting her at the crown, she was back in the Adjudication Chamber.

"Minister?" Lyon asked, leaning into Marlo.

"I was just . . . *deliberating,*" Marlo replied.

I must be waking up. That was Dr. Einstein and a zombie teen arguing, back in Precocia.

"Are we adjourned or what?" the other-Milton asked.

"Silence!" the guard said, wedging his club in the old man's side.

"Order!" Marlo yelled, waving her gavel. "I find the defendant . . . well, kind of creepy. I also find him guilty—because he physically did do all of that stuff—but also *not guilty* because he's a few eggs short of a soufflé."

"So, you are ruling the prisoner—your brother—both guilty and not guilty?" Lyon asked.

"By reason that he's a nut job," Marlo said, giving her increasingly fuzzy head a quick shake to de-lint her thoughts. "So he should serve out the rest of his sentence in a mental institution. A really nice one, right? So he can be rehabilitated."

"*Sucré!*" the other-Milton gasped. "That's the nicest thing you've ever done for me, Madam Sister Minister!"

"I doubt that, at his age, there will be much likelihood of rehabilitation," Lyon said with a shrug. "But obviously it's your call." She allowed a sly smirk to cross her heavily lined face. "Though I'm pretty sure that the ministry might find it *intéressant* that Minister Fauster showed favoritism to not only one Fauster felon but *two* . . . in one day, no less."

"Well, that's my . . . decision," Marlo said, her thoughts going gray around the edges. Her eyes fluttered to the back of her head.

★ ★ ★

"Take her down!" Dr. Einstein yelled. "She's hurting the Kronosgraph . . . and fetch me her brother."

Marlo, her head throbbing with every beat of her heart, felt mayfly demons crawling all over her. She shook them away with a violent shudder.

"And my decision is . . . ," Marlo said, half in the Adjudication Chamber and half back in Precocia. She slammed the gavel down onto her desk.

"*Final!*" she barked before passing out.

Marlo, dizzy and delirious, could feel herself being carried. She was wearing a hood and could smell her hot breath: it still had the faint tang of prune juice from the dance. Her hood was yanked off, and through eyes still cloudy with confusion, she could see that she was in the Precocia infirmary. A zombie teenager with dark fuzz on his upper lip carried a boy who looked like Milton out of the room.

"Milton," Marlo croaked. "Where are you . . . taking him?"

Dr. Curie appeared by her bed, holding a hypodermic needle. "You don't belong here," she said before jabbing the needle into Marlo's arm. "You just had a bad dream . . . now sleep. *And forget.*"

25 · AN INHOSPITABLE HOSPITAL

MILTON AWOKE SWAYING in a stiff canvas hammock.

"Where am I?" he murmured in a voice like a worn gravel road. With a lurch, he pitched himself onto the gleaming linoleum floor.

"Ugh, it's like my body is a haunted house," Milton muttered. "Spooky and full of weird creaks."

He sat up and tried to marshal the hodgepodge of thoughts rattling in his head. The last thing Milton remembered was being arrested by a squad of commandoes after stuffing the Affective Reasoning Machine full of nonsense.

The whole room—which was like a sterile hospital room—seemed to rock back and forth, as if it were floating on a stormy sea. Milton yanked down his weird blue plastic smock: a gown made of slick, unyielding vinyl.

"Must be some kind of prison ship," he said.

A nurse in a crisp white dress walked into his room carrying a tray. "A ship? No, Monsieur Fauster," she said, setting the tray down on a swinging table suspended from the ceiling. "But you'll be *ship*-shape soon enough!" She covered her mouth with her gloved hand. "Oh . . . *excusez-moi* . . . that was almost immature. It must be contagious."

On the tray was a carafe of pitch-black liquid and a plate of cigarette butts.

"Why is everything swaying?" Milton asked.

The woman brushed back the short gray bangs that clung tight to her face.

"*Très fou*," she replied in an overly calm voice. "It is the Wobble, of course!"

"The Wobble?"

"It's nothing to be concerned about . . . just the Earth shaking itself apart. The ministry assures us it's just the planet experiencing some growing pains. Here . . ."

The woman handed Milton two pills: one black, one white. He stared at the pills in his trembling, liver-spotted hands.

"Your Equi-Lib pills," she replied. "To keep you *balanced*. You know: they affect your inner ear to help counteract the disorientation of the Wobble."

Milton reluctantly popped the pills into his mouth, washing them down with the bitterly strong liquid.

"Yuck!" he said with a grimace. "This stuff is awful! It's like drinking tobacco boiled in hot bile!"

The woman shrugged. "Your *Coffaux*. Fake coffee. You've never had a problem with it before. Now eat your cigarettes like a *bon garçon*. . . ."

"*Eat* my cigarettes? Are you crazy?"

"No, *you* are," the woman said with a pout of her surgically wrinkled lips. "Acknowledging this is the first step to recovery . . . that and a diet of serious, retoxifying foods."

"*Retoxifying?*"

The woman sighed. "Your game is growing tiresome, Monsieur Fauster. You know how we frown on fun and games. Remember our motto here at the Hôpital pour les Malades Mentaux Criminels et Enfantin: 'Wipe that grin right off your chin!'"

"Hôpital pour les Malades Mentaux Criminels et Enfantin?" Milton replied. "Doesn't that mean something about a hospital for the criminally insane and childish?"

The woman clapped her gloved hands together. "*Très bonne!*" she exclaimed. "Now *that* is the Monsieur Fauster I know and grudgingly tolerate!"

Milton was suddenly filled with anxiety. He clutched his chest. His Pace Taker was ticking faster and faster.

"It is time for your session with Dr. Tan," the woman said as she rolled an IV stand to Milton. She fastened the

IV tube to a stent in Milton's forearm. The bag was filled with murky black sludge.

"What is this?" Milton asked with disgust as the woman led him out of the room and into a brightly lit hallway.

"Your retox bag," she replied, her patience as thin as a baby's résumé. "Part of Dr. Tan's retox program. One of her theories about the criminally infantile is that their bodies are too pure, like a child's, and that—through the introduction of adult toxins such as nicotine, caffeine, cholesterol, and saturated fats—you can shock their systems into emotional maturity."

They stopped outside a door with a nameplate reading DR. SHARLA TAN.

"She'll be with you in a moment," the woman said as she walked away down the sterile corridor, her hard white shoes clacking earnestly.

Milton leaned against the spotless white wall, exhausted.

I feel so much older today. . . . Maybe it's this idiotic "retox" thing.

Milton, with a queasy yank, disconnected the IV from his arm. He wrapped the thin plastic tube around his wrist so that he still appeared to be connected. It was like wearing a wristband for the least frequented amusement park *ever*.

The door opened. There, staring at Milton, stood an

elderly yet timelessly beautiful Asian woman. Milton was struck by a feeling of déjà vu.

The woman smiled at Milton's odd expression—a smile so open and genuine that it burned away all doubt.

"*Sara?*" he murmured. "Sara Bardo?"

The woman held out the hem of her pink plastic smock and curtsied. "At your service," she giggled.

It can't be Sara, the girl I met in Snivel. The girl who helped me brave Arcadia's Sense-o-Rama and thwart Nikola Tesla's plan to steal souls from the Surface. The girl who, last I saw, nearly had her conjoined twin brother hacked off by Edgar Allan Poe's pendulum . . .

Sara cocked her head at Milton like a dog at the sudden tweet of a whistle. "I've been here for nearly a year and this is the first time you've ever said anything to me . . . other than 'pass the cigarette gravy.' "

"So you remember me?" Milton replied, still dazed. "I mean, before this place? Before we got old?"

Sara grinned suspiciously, like she had been told a joke that she knew *had* to be funny but didn't quite get the punch line.

"Monsieur Fauster," a voice called out from the room, bursting Milton's confused reverie like a pin to a balloon. "Don't keep me waiting. You're almost seven seconds late."

A middle-aged Filipino woman with gray-streaked hair motioned toward an unwelcoming gray metal chair.

Milton stared at Sara as she disappeared down the hall.

He sighed and sat down as the woman, Dr. Sharla Tan, eased her skinny, rigid self into her padded black recliner.

"So, how are—"

"How did I get here?" Milton blurted.

Dr. Tan gazed at Milton with disconcerted surprise as if he were a bag of just-microwaved popcorn that still had one unexpected "pop" left in it. She clasped her tiny hands together.

"*Très intéressant.* Amnesia. We'll just lower your Equi-Lib dosage," the doctor said as the ground shuddered. "You came here ten years ago after your judgment."

"Judgment?"

"After your unforgivable crimes against the state, it seemed inevitable that you would be having a swift date with the electric guillotine," the doctor said, settling back into her chair. "But your sister, Minister Fauster, ruled most uncharacteristically and spared you, declaring you *légalement fou,* which is why you've been here for"—Dr. Tan glanced down at the "year" hand of her Pace Taker and arched her dyed-gray eyebrow—"*exactly* ten years . . . for a crime committed *exactly* twenty years ago!" she said with subdued excitement.

"Twenty years?"

"If ours was a culture that believed in coincidence, I'd think this 'anniversary' quite remarkable. But we're not, so I don't."

So I've not been me for twenty *years? Why?*

Dr. Tan leaned forward, her varicose vein–stockinged

knees pressed together. "I don't see it," she said. "Apart from . . . well, *this discussion right now,* you've exhibited no overtly *fou* behavior. If it were up to me—and it *would* be if you stepped out of line for any reason—I'd send you straight to Hekla."

"Heck?" Milton gulped.

Dr. Tan rolled her pitch-black eyes. "Hek*la* . . . Iceland. The empire's military base in the Hekla volcano. Where no one is allowed except top military officials and, of course, the worst enemies of the state."

Dr. Tan quickly checked her Pace Taker, which now seemed to be ticking faster than before.

"So, before today's session concludes, do you have anything you'd care to discuss?"

Other than the fact that I'm a seventy-one-year-old eleven-year-old who has no idea why I'm in this terrible world or how I got here or what I'm supposed to do before I die of unnaturally natural causes by the end of the week?!

"Well, I *am* feeling—" Milton said before Dr. Tan rushed to her feet.

"Feelings are like rickety old bridges," she replied, ushering Milton out into the hall. "You just have to get over them as quickly as possible. *Bonjour.*"

Milton shambled into the ward's common area in his plastic sandals and smock. Fifteen or so of his fellow patients milled about the room in bored circuits. Sara looked over at Milton and, noting his defeated expression, gave him a smile that cut through the somber atmosphere of the room like a lighthouse beam through fog.

"You look like you've either just pooped a porcupine," she said, "or had a session with Dr. Tan. I'm not sure which is worse. . . ."

Milton studied Sara. She had the restless energy and unflappable optimism of a little girl, only trapped in an old woman's body. It occurred to Milton that she was flying solo, meaning she wasn't attached to her surly conjoined twin, Sam.

"So," Milton asked, feeling shy despite the fact that he was seven decades old. "Why are you here?"

Sara's smile dimmed a few watts. She rubbed her side absentmindedly, with sad sweeps of her hand.

"I don't really want to talk about it," she said in a faraway voice. "It's boring. Besides . . . there are so many more interesting people here . . . like Glasco, for instance." She pointed at a large, bald, beet-faced man in the corner.

"Glasco?" Milton replied. "What makes him so interesting?"

"Wow . . . we *are* different today," she replied playfully. "Okay, I'll bite. Well—as if you didn't know— Glasco thinks he's a vending machine, one that produces the worst candy imaginable."

Milton looked across the room at a middle-aged

blond woman holding a pocket mirror. "What's her deal? Is she really obsessed with her looks?"

"That's Katrice," Sara explained. "She's afraid to look at anyone directly in the eye. Only uses her mirror. She thinks she has a lethal gaze. I'm not quite sure why. See, we don't talk much . . . just can't seem to see eye to eye on things. Get it?"

Milton snickered. "Yup, I get it."

"And then there's Claire over there," Sara said, pointing to the far wall. "She thinks she's invisible."

"Really?" Milton said. "Where is she? I don't see anyone."

"Wow, she's worse off than I thought!" Sara said before Milton burst out laughing. The sound erupted throughout the room like a scream. Sara studied Milton with unexpected delight, as if she had just found a hundred franc bill in her sock drawer. Two orderlies dressed in stiff white uniforms stormed into the room.

"What's that awful ruckus?" shouted a thick-necked man with a bushy mustache glued above his lip.

"A ruckus?" Sara repeated with a look of mock confusion on her face. "Did you hear a *ruckus*, Monsieur Fauster?"

"I don't believe I heard a ruckus," Milton said, scratching his head. "But we'll be sure to let you know if we do."

The orderly glared at Milton, the vein on his neck

bulging with anger, before he and his associate stomped out of the room.

"*Blancs*," Sara said. "Fun spoilers supreme."

"*Blancs?*"

"You know, *blanc*: French for 'white.' Because of the uniforms."

Milton surveyed the room full of dazed men and women. "What's everyone doing just standing around?" he asked.

"Waiting for Jell-O'clock," Sara replied. "I hear today's batch is extra seaweedy."

Milton saw an overflowing metal tub next to a brick wall painted blue. He walked over to it and started sifting through the collection of junk.

"What's all this stuff?" he asked as Sara joined him.

The old woman shrugged. "Just random things they couldn't find space for," Sara replied. "It's not like anyone here is even curious enough to notice it, really."

"What's this?" Milton asked, holding up a couple of metal paddles.

"Cardiac paddles, for when people have heart attacks. Must be broken."

"Why is there duct tape on this?" Milton said, tearing the sticky tape off a small rubber ball.

"Sometimes a patient really loses it," she replied sadly, "just starts screaming, so they tape that over their mouth."

"That's horrible."

Sara shrugged. "It tastes better than the food does."

Milton pulled out someone's discarded pantyhose. He stared across the room at an empty table. "Let's liven things up around here," he said with an impish grin.

"It's called Ping-Pong," Milton said as he bounced the ball on the table. He had taken two plastic spoons and duct-taped them to the sides of the table, and stretched the pantyhose across like a net. "You hit the ball over to the other side of the table, like this. . . ."

Milton batted the ball to Glasco, who held the other paddle and watched the ball bounce away. Milton bounded after it, snatched it up, and returned to his side of the makeshift Ping-Pong table.

"Now next time, Glasco, you hit it back with your paddle," Milton said slowly.

The large bald man nodded and Milton gently served the ball. Glasco swatted it back to Milton.

"Good job!" Milton said as he and the man hit the ball back and forth. The other patients began to crowd around the table, at first following the ball's trajectory with confusion, then, slowly, smiles stretching across their faces. A dark-skinned man with frizzy gray hair started to clap with delight.

The two orderlies strode urgently back into the room with Dr. Tan close behind.

"What is going on?" the thick-necked orderly barked, his stormy gray eyes bulging out of his head.

"Game over," Sara muttered, covering her smile with her wrinkled hand. Glasco quickly swallowed the ball.

Dr. Tan clapped her hands together.

"Well, then, patients . . . it sure has been a busy day," she said in a condescending tone, as if talking to a room full of paste-eating toddlers. "How about some fresh air?"

The patients were led outside into a small grim courtyard. It was encircled by three lofty guard towers, connected to one another by lengths of tall chain-link fence with coils of barbed wire on top. The grass, so bright green that it was obviously fake, was dusted with patches of thick, dark-gray ash that fluttered down to the ground like dirty snow. Milton looked up at the Widow's Veil. The thick black mantle of soot looked like the lid of an enormous coffin, with the world laid to eternal rest beneath. A band of cloud cover seemed to "ripple," but in a flash, the sky sealed back up like a small cut.

Milton's eyes watered. His throat and lungs burned. All around him, his fellow patients coughed and wheezed.

"*Bien,* that's enough fresh air!" a nurse said through her gauze mask. "Back inside for lunch! I hear the chef has created a seriously unhealthy meal for you all today!"

As Milton turned to follow the shambling patients back into the facility, he heard something thud to the ground. There on the AstroTurf was an empty wine bottle. Milton looked quickly from side to side, but no one was around. He snatched the bottle. Inside was a curled-up sheet of paper, *actual* paper, with FROM THE DESK OF ALBERT EINSTEIN stamped on the top. Below, written in Milton's own carefully composed handwriting—not the sloppy scrawl of his alter ego—was a note.

> Escape tonight, just before midnight. Requisition as much baking soda for Hekla as possible.
> —Milton Fauster (You, later)

"A note . . . from me?" Milton murmured. "The *real* me? But how?"

Milton looked up at the sky. A rippling scar appeared across the Widow's Veil. He could see the bottom of some craft tacking across the sky, followed by what looked like—

Milton quickly rubbed his eyes.

Must be the soot, he thought.

But there it was again: the glimmering silhouette of an angel, streaking across the Widow's Veil, leaving a rainbow in its wake as it followed the craft above. The charcoal-black cloud cover sealed itself shut.

Milton stared at the note in his hand.

I wanted a sign and I got one: a big, blinking neon sign at that. I mean, angels and rainbows. *It doesn't get much more hopeful than that. It's like I have a divine stamp of approval for . . . what, exactly, I have no clue. . . .*

26 · ESCAPED CRUSADER

"MONSIEUR FAUSTER!" THE nurse called out. "What's that in your hand?"

Milton quickly wadded up the note, put it into his mouth, and kicked away the bottle. The nurse hobbled over to him, swaying as the earth wobbled beneath her white imitation-leather shoes.

"What did you just eat?" she asked, her eyes scowling above the edge of her white mask.

Milton swallowed. "Just something I found on the ground."

The edges of the woman's brown eyes crinkled. *"Très bonne!* Eating stuff you find on the ground is an excellent way of retoxifying your system!"

Milton nodded and swept past the nurse to look for Sara. He found her in the pastel blue corridor, secretively unspooling a long strand of stolen dental floss from her finger. She held both ends, then proceeded to jump rope, slowly at first, until finally she was hopping and skipping with a luminous smile. Sara started to laugh. The sound, to Milton, was like the tinkling of ice in a glass of lemonade served on a sweltering hot day.

Two "blancs" rushed at Sara and quickly confiscated her floss jump rope. Her smile dimmed, but as she saw Milton approach, she gave him a conspiratorial wink.

"Very creative," he said to the old woman with the little girl trapped inside her.

"*Merci* buckets," she said, holding the hem of her pink plastic smock out to her sides in a curtsy.

"Listen," Milton whispered, glancing furtively over his shoulder. "We need to escape. *Tonight*. See, I found a note—"

"Sure," Sara chirped.

"Really? Just like that?" Milton sputtered back.

Two orderlies walked by, glaring at Milton and Sara.

"Okay, um . . . great, then," Milton whispered once the two *blancs* turned the corner. "And—this will sound weird—but do you know anything about baking soda?"

"Baking soda?" Sara repeated. "Like, sodium bicarbonate?"

"Yeah, specifically requisitioning some for Hekla," Milton said uncertainly. "Lots of it . . . I know I sound nuts, but . . ."

Sara took Milton's wrinkled hand in hers and led him down the corridor. A strange feeling washed over

Milton. Part of him felt hot and nervous, holding hands with a girl he sort of, well, *liked. A lot.* Yet part of him—the eleven-year-old he was inside—felt like he was earning a Boy Scout merit badge, helping some old lady across the street. They stopped in front of a door marked REQUISITION THERAPY.

"Ask and ye shall receive," Sara said, flinging open the door.

Inside the dimly lit office were three rows of shabby metal desks, each occupied by a near-catatonic patient hunched over sheaves of electronic paper-foil, like the kind Milton had used twenty years ago/yesterday at the Ministry of Persuasion to clog the ARM with nonsense. One of the patients briefly looked up, his gaunt face ravaged by the harsh greenish light streaming up from the digital paper, before scratching his leg, making the shackle secured around his ankle jingle.

"What's going on?" Milton asked.

"Like it says on the door . . . requisition therapy," Sara replied. "I'm sure you've had to do this—we *all* have at some time."

"Well, humor me, then. What are they doing?"

"We could all use some more humor, that's for sure," Sara replied grimly as she noted the vacuous expression of her fellow patients. "Most every ministry prison or mental hospital has inmates do the boring stuff. Here, that's checking and entering purchase orders for basic supplies—stuff like baking soda to help calm the upset tummies of everyone who has eaten nothing but sea-weed since the Widow's Veil killed off everything else."

Milton stepped up to one of the desks. The patient—an African American woman with wide, nervous eyes—compared two digital paper-foils crowded with numbers and check boxes. The squat, bearded man behind her grunted and rolled up his digital paper-foil and fed it into a tube attached to his desk. His reward was another pair of forms arriving from a pneumatic tube.

"Why *us*?" Milton asked.

"This work is so tedious it would drive someone crazy," Sara replied with her hands on her hips. "And since we already *are*—crazy, that is—they give it all to us."

The shackle on the bearded man's ankle popped open. He slowly rose from the desk and shambled out of the room. Sara scooted into his spot and secured the ankle chain to the leg of the desk, where it snapped shut like a bear trap. A tube of digital paper-foil appeared with a pneumatic whoosh of air. Sara smoothed it out and grabbed the electronic pen.

"See, they have all the projected needs mapped out for years, based on trends and data analysis, blah blah blah," Sara explained. "If you wanted to do something as pointless as requisitioning more baking soda to Hekla, I'd suggest adding a few thousand kilograms here and there over the course of, I don't know, the next ten years: borrowing bits from other ministry institutions. It's more tedious that way, but no one should notice."

Milton crouched down next to her, grabbed an electric pen, and started poring through a form, subtracting zeroes from any baking soda request he could find and adding them to Hekla's requisition. Sara did the same, pausing to steal a quick glance at Milton.

"I keep having this dream that I used to have a brother," she blurted. "But I think maybe it's real."

"What?"

"A brother . . . attached to me. A conjoined twin," she whispered spookily while gently patting her side. "I call him—"

"Sam," Milton replied.

Sara's mouth fell open.

"How did you—"

Milton shrugged mysteriously as he continued sabotaging the requisition form. Sara stared off into space.

"No one believed me," Sara continued. "About Sam. That's what I called him, weirdly enough. There was no physical proof. In the dream, we separated just before being born. Maybe he just didn't want to be here. I don't blame him. But sometimes I can hear him talking to me—he's kind of mean but means well—and sometimes I, well, talk back."

She snorted softly.

"You probably think I'm crazy, huh?" she asked softly with a trace of fear.

"No . . . not at all," Milton replied cautiously, not wanting to freak Sara out with stories of alternative universes and comments like, "Yes, you *did* have a brother, but you both died and I met you in a place called Heck. . . ." He set his pen down and gazed into Sara's dark and glittering eyes. "But it doesn't matter what I or anyone thinks. And what does 'crazy' mean, anyway? Sometimes it's just a healthy reaction to a crazy situation. And you'd have to be crazy to *not* be crazy here, right?"

Sara laughed. The other patients craned their necks toward the sound so strange to their ears.

"Yeah . . . I guess you're right."

"You think this will work?" Milton said as he and Sara crept down the darkened corridor. Milton glanced down at his Pace Taker, which read eleven o'clock and some change.

"Who knows?" Sara replied in the dark.

"Awesome," Milton sighed sarcastically.

Sara whisper-giggled. *"Awesome?* I haven't heard that word in *decades.* Next you'll be saying, 'That's *très* Nile!'"

They turned a corner and tiptoed past the Stabilizing Room—a padded cell for patients so criminally infantile that they indulged in tantrums.

They arrived at a corner just beyond Dr. Tan's office. There, at the bend, was Katrice, peering down the hall leading to the basement with her pocket mirror. She nodded, giving Milton and Sara a reflected wink that the coast was clear. Then she backed slowly away.

"Thanks," Sara whispered as she and Milton crept

around the corner. At the end of the hall was a dark metal door.

"So you're *sure* they collect all the used plastic smocks in the basement at eleven-fifteen and take them to some recycling plant where they're melted down and remolded?" Milton whispered as they approached the door.

"That's what I heard," Sara replied.

She tried opening the door leading to the basement, but it was locked.

"Shoot."

Hard imitation-leather footsteps sounded down the hall.

"*Blancs,*" Milton whispered.

"Shoot . . . *laundry* chute!" Sara said, pointing to a gray metal square on the wall a few yards away. "But the *blancs* will see us before we can make it."

"Hey!" Katrice shouted down the hall outside of the common area. "Glasco really *is* a vending machine! He just made candy bars. Lots of them!"

The footsteps stopped, then abruptly trotted away.

"Wow, that cleared the room faster than a Q-Bomb," Sara muttered as she ran to the chute and opened the small door.

"A Q-Bomb?" Milton said as he helped Sara inside the chute.

"You know, quantum bomb? Einstein's theoretical . . . Oh, never mind," Sara said before tumbling down the shaft, with Milton climbing inside after her.

★ ★ ★

In the overflowing bin of used plastic smocks, Milton heard footsteps tromping closer. Suddenly, the bin was wheeled across the floor and dumped into the back of a large van. Milton could hear muffled voices as the van's engine sputtered to life. The vehicle bumped along for a few minutes before stopping suddenly.

"We can't be outside the gates yet," Milton muttered. He cleared away a few layers of pink and blue plastic smocks and stuck his head out of the mound.

"*Bien,*" the driver said. "Let's dump all these smocks into the pit with the others."

"Can I set fire to them this time?" the other orderly asked.

Figures that no one would actually recycle in this stupid, shortsighted world, Milton thought with dread.

"We've got to get out of here," Milton whispered to Sara as the orderlies rounded the van. "When they open the door, just spring out and—"

Milton could feel Sara trembling beside him.

"Sara?"

"I don't think I—" she murmured.

The back of the van slid open. Milton leapt out of the pile of soiled plastic smocks, tugging Sara by the arm. Startled, the orderlies fell onto the AstroTurf.

Milton ran for the fence, with Sara lagging behind.

"Sara, *run!*" Milton yelled.

But Sara hung back, twirling her graying hair with her finger like a lost little girl. Milton kicked off his sandals.

"We can scale the fence! Sure, we might get scratched up, but—"

"It's not that," she said, biting her lower lip in quiet desperation. "It's . . . running away. Even if we can, nothing will change. We'll still be tucked under the Widow's Veil . . . under the unblinking eye of the ministry, forced to keep a stiff upper lip. No laughter. No hope. Living side by side, yet"—she rubbed her side with a distracted, haunted air—"ultimately alone."

Milton stared across the courtyard at Sara. Her almond eyes gleamed like crazy black diamonds.

"But you should go," she urged softly. "I can tell there's something important you need to do. Something in your eyes that wasn't there yesterday and that I have a feeling won't be there tomorrow . . ."

Klieg lights slashed at the night like glowing swords through black velvet.

"Remember, life's a big joke," Sara said with a faint smile as guards streamed down from the towers like a river of uniforms. "So be sure you get the last laugh."

Milton nodded, swiped his wet eyes with the back of his hand, then turned to make a break for the fence. He ran across the courtyard as fast as a seventy-one-year-old man could. Orderlies in their crisp white uniforms filed out of the facility. Two of them grabbed Sara by the shoulders, pinned her to the ground, and gave her a shot.

A sharp stitch burned into Milton's side. Panting and sweating, he stopped at the bottom of the fence. It was at least twenty feet high, with jagged loops of rusted barbed wire coiling on top like deadly metal vines. Milton stepped back to make a mad, desperate leap for the top and tripped, falling onto his back.

"Argh!"

At Milton's side atop the ash-dusted artificial grass was a bottle. Milton uncorked it and out tumbled another note written by his own hand.

Turn yourself in. Demand to be taken to Hekla as a member of HAHAHA. YOU HAVE TO TELL THE MINISTRY WHERE THEIR SECRET HEADQUARTERS IS AND REVEAL THEIR IDENTITIES: SHIRLEY EUJEST, TOM FULLERY ... ALL OF THEM. SORRY ABOUT ALL THE CAPITALS BUT THIS IS IMPORTANT.
—Milton Fauster (You, later ... promise)

A group of orderlies rushed upon Milton as he sat on the ground, stunned.

"You're in *beaucoup* trouble now, Fauster!" one of the male *blancs* spat as he readied a syringe.

Why would I want to try to get out, only to betray the resistance? That will undo everything they've fought for!

Milton looked up. Across the black clouds was a

radiant glimmer—the strange rippling craft, again floating above as if on water. It left behind a dull rainbow-colored trail in its wake.

The orderly grabbed Milton's arm, preparing to jab him with some kind of sedative. If Milton fell asleep now, he wouldn't wake up as him for another ten years. He grabbed the man's forearm just as he was about to plunge the needle into Milton's shoulder.

"Wait," Milton said in a shaky voice. "I need to talk to Dr. Tan. I have some important information . . . *for the ministry.*"

The orderly considered Milton with his dull, cruel eyes before—with a trace of reluctance—putting the syringe back into his hip satchel. He nodded to the guards, who then hoisted Milton to his feet.

"No matter what you've got to say, you're still in a world of trouble," the orderly grumbled. "There's no way you're going free. *Ever.*"

As the guards dragged Milton across the courtyard, he stole another glance at the night sky. Up above was the angel, this time radiating a blazing, flickering light. The angel was waving its arms wildly in the air as if in triumph. The creature left a merry swirl of rainbow-hued light as he rippled away. Milton sighed.

I must know what I'm doing, he thought, *even if I don't.*

27 · GONE TO MEET HiS TROUBLEMAKER

"OWW!" MARLO CRIED as her head hit the inside of her sleeping cabinet. She felt around the dark metal catacomb frantically with her hands.

"I'm . . . I'm . . . ," she said, hyperventilating.

Her drawer was yanked open.

"Totally irritating," Lyon said, yawning, over the foot of Marlo's filing cabinet.

Marlo sat up on her elbows. "I was in the infirmary," she murmured. "But then I was also in this weird, depressing place where I was really old—and so were you, Lyon—and I was supposed to sentence my mother and brother to death."

"Maybe you were going to *bore* them to death," Lyon said.

Marlo climbed down the chain ladder dangling from her cabinet.

"It was like a dream . . . but it wasn't," Marlo muttered as she and the girls were prodded out into the hallway by the feisty, freshly hatched mayfly demons.

Frances smiled at Marlo through her curtain of fuchsia hair.

"What?" Marlo said, sort of smiling back but not quite sure why.

"You don't remember, do you?"

Most every girl, except for Lyon, was giving Marlo a shy, envious smile.

"I . . . kinda sort of . . . remember something about . . . *a dance* . . . ," Marlo said, absentmindedly touching her mouth as if hoping to seize a memory that had evaporated from her lips.

The girls were herded out by the sulfur water coolers to wait for the Sylla-Bus. Marlo spotted Virgil leaning against the elevator door, asleep. She walked over to him.

"Hey . . . Virgil . . . wake up."

Virgil's eyes fluttered open. "Marlo!" he said, his smile crinkling the freckles across the bridge of his nose.

"What's going on?" Marlo replied as Virgil rose to his feet.

"I was waiting for you," he mumbled. "You must have got past me when I fell asleep. I mean, I tried to get down to the infirmary after it happened, but Angelo rushed you into the elevator with Dr. Curie and he let the door close on me even though I totally know that he saw me running for it." Virgil pointed over Marlo's shoulder.

Angelo was jogging laps around the eighteenth floor. The sweat on his dark, smooth skin made him look like a well-oiled machine. Lyon sidled up to Marlo, giving Angelo a fingertip wave. Angelo replied with a brilliant blue wink.

The Sylla-Bus pulled up, with Kali waving the children aboard with her massive blue arms.

"He only kissed you to make me jealous, you know," Lyon whispered out of the side of her mouth.

That's right! Marlo thought with a gasp as the memory of Angelo's kiss left her weak in the knees. *I totally fainted at the dance! But why? I don't even really* like *Angelo . . . or do I?*

Milton awoke and, this time, there was no doubt where he was. He was in a gloomy concrete cell with a grimy foam rubber mat.

"A jail," he muttered in a voice ravaged by time. "The ministry's secret military base in Iceland." The floor rumbled beneath him in steady, rolling waves. "In the Hekla volcano . . ."

Milton clutched the Pace Taker surgically embedded in his chest. It ticked slowly and deliberately, as if it were gradually dying down, like a windup toy whose spring was getting looser and looser.

The cell had tiny scratches notched on the wall that, judging from Milton's torn fingernails, he had been clawing himself for the last decade: a long, grim, tedious decade, by the looks of it, laid out in 3,650 tally marks, give or take a leap year.

There was a tray by the thick metal door with a bowl of watery soup and a half-eaten bar of compressed seaweed. A small portal at the bottom of the door slid open and a pair of gloved hands swiftly removed the tray.

"Not too hungry, no?" a deep voice said from the other side of the door. "I wouldn't have much of an appetite on my last day either. . . ."

"Last day?" Milton replied weakly.

The guard snorted.

"*Oui,* you *misérable* traitor! The day that time stops for you and your fellow jokers: the enemies of the state!"

The cell trembled like the inside of a large, concrete Chihuahua.

"So I'm here . . . in Hekla," he muttered, trying to speak the thoughts in his head since his brain felt slow and fuzzy. "Just where that note that fell from the sky told me to be. And, since the guard mentioned some other 'jokers,' the ministry must have captured HAHAHA: thanks to me turning them in."

Milton cradled his head in his age-spotted hands and saw his reflection staring back at him in the shiny floor tiles. Though he looked like a living cadaver, his eyes sparkled inside their sockets.

"I'm still me," Milton said with a weary, bedraggled wonder. *"Inside.* Eleven years old going on eighty-one. I can *do* this . . . whatever 'this' is."

The cell door creaked open. The guard had a bushy salt-and-pepper mustache and wore blinking blinders like Dr. Einstein back in Precocia. He trained his William club at Milton's face.

"It's time for your journey to the Duat, where you will meet Osiris, the god of death," the guard said, his pupils squeezed into black pinpoints.

"The journey to the Duat?" Milton replied.

"Oui . . . that sounds a lot better than 'I'm taking you to be thrown into the volcano.' "

Milton swallowed as the guard nudged the William club into Milton's back, leading him down the hall for his date with certain death.

Lucky's pink eyes were dull and lifeless, like bubble gum after it had been chewed all day. He paced in sluggish circles in his cage.

"What's wrong with Lucky?" Marlo called out from the Sylla-Bus as it crept slowly toward Dr. Skinner.

"Lucky?" the gaunt man with the tortoiseshell glasses replied.

Marlo sighed. "Bueller," she said reluctantly.

"Oh yes," Dr. Skinner said as he peered into Lucky's cage. "An obstinate creature. Most resistant to the conditioning process . . . as are another puzzling group of subjects."

He removed the sheet covering a terrarium filled with the large, corkscrew-shaped white worms that Marlo had seen in the Undermines.

"These specimens, for instance, are also impervious to basic behavioral modification. . . ."

He scooped out one of the grater-skinned creatures from the terrarium and placed it in a bed of rock.

"They're also as scratchy as all get-out," he mumbled, rubbing his hand.

The worm began to dig an intricate spiral groove in the rock.

"The specimen, despite a constant diet of negative reinforcement, continues to plow a very specific design, unlike any of the other specimens. No matter what I do to it, the creature bores its own unique pattern with an unshakeable tenacity—"

"Now back to, um . . . *Bueller*," Marlo interrupted.

The Sylla-Bus rattled past Dr. Skinner. The doctor adjusted his thick glasses.

"As I was saying, I am trying to transform the subject into a passive, useful creature that responds to commands."

Dr. Skinner withdrew a sleek mobile device from the inside of his lab coat.

"Commands?" Marlo said with a snicker of doubt. "Lucky—*Bueller*—doesn't *do* commands."

"I admit it will take a little work," the doctor said with a nervous tick of the mouth as he pulled up his Conditioning app.

Inside Lucky's cage, a grainy image of Milton appeared while a boy's filthy sock tumbled from a chute. Lucky's eyes sparkled briefly as he sniffed the sock. The fuzzy white ferret stood on his haunches to better take in the picture of his master. Dr. Skinner tapped his Conditioning app. Lucky squealed and twitched with wrenching spasms of pain.

"Lucky!" Marlo shrieked as the Sylla-Bus turned the corner. "What are you doing to him?" She struggled to free herself from the restraining bar but it wouldn't budge.

Up ahead was Dr. Einstein standing in front of a projector screen.

"*Guten morgen,* children, and *willkommen* to Advanced PowerPoint," the most brilliant man in history said, his wide, vacant eyes glittering with the flashing red, blue, and yellow LCDs of his electric blinders.

I've got to get out of this bus thing, Marlo fumed. *Dr. Demento's torturing Lucky! Milton's either really sick or being held hostage down in the infirmary, and if something happens to his pet ferret, he'll never forgive me. . . .*

"PowerPoint is a corporate tool that lines up creative thinking before a firing squad and assassinates it vith meaningless bullet points," Dr. Einstein said as the blinking lights of his platinum blinders began to falter.

A slide of two intersecting circles appeared on the

screen behind the teacher. The left circle was marked DIS REALITY; the right circle was marked DAT REALITY, with the letter "Q" in the middle.

Napoléon, marching from the copy machine, stopped suddenly. He cocked his eyebrow at Dr. Einstein as if he were cocking the hammer of a pistol.

"Now using this Venn diagram, invented by Dr. Venn Diagram," Dr. Einstein continued, "I vill vainly attempt to illustrate the thinking behind my theoretical Q-Bomb, or Bomb-bmoB, that can transmit matter from one dimension to another. . . ."

Napoléon pulled out his silver mobile device from his inside breast pocket.

"I'll teach zhat teacher to actually teach," the liter-sized vice principal groused as he jabbed the touch screen.

"It vorks like this," Dr. Einstein said before an electrical storm of flashing lights shrunk both his pupils and his free will into tiny, dull pinpoints.

As her teacher started to sway and drool, Marlo noticed Napoléon slip his mind control gizmo back into his pocket and storm away.

It's the same kind as that psycho Skinner's. . . . That gives me an idea.

Marlo glanced over at Myung-Dae next to her, scribbling notes with his electric gyroscopic pen. Without warning, she grabbed his arm and wedged it tight beneath the restraining bar.

"Hey!" the boy exclaimed.

"Dr. Einstein!" Marlo shouted. "Myung-Dae has a question! I mean, a real doozy, don't you, Myung-Dae?"

Myung-Dae began to sweat and tremble. Suddenly, in one herculean sweep of his overdeveloped right arm, he raised his hand and broke the restraining bar.

Marlo bolted off the Sylla-Bus and ran around the corner to Dr. Skinner.

"What is going on?" the teacher shouted.

Marlo knocked over a terrarium full of dazed white mice. The mice, tasting freedom with their twitching whiskers, scurried in every direction. Marlo scooped up a handful of rodents and stumbled toward the paralyzed teacher.

"Dr. Skinner!" she shouted. "You have mice all over you!"

The doctor screamed a high-pitched lady scream. "Where?"

Marlo brushed Dr. Skinner's lab coat, stealing his mobile device and filling his pockets full of mice.

"Everywhere!" Marlo replied. "I'll go get help!"

Marlo tore across the coffee-stained carpet. Vice Principal Napoléon was marching back to his palatial boardroom in tyrannical baby steps.

"Vee-Pee-Wee!" Marlo called out.

Napoléon whizzed about angrily as Marlo staggered to him, panting. She clutched his shoulder with feigned exhaustion. "There's a situation."

"A situation?"

"Yes," Marlo said, slyly sliding her hand inside his coat, "a set of circumstances that one finds oneself—"

"I KNOW WHAT A SITUATION IS!" the vice principal said, shrugging her off.

"Then you know about all the wild lab animals," Marlo said.

"*Quoi?*" Napoléon screamed.

"Let me show you," Marlo said as she darted down the hall ahead of the vice principal. As she ran, she patted her pocket.

I switched Napoléon's evil Game Boy with Skinner's. Now I'll do the same thing in reverse.

Mice were scurrying across the floor. Dr. Skinner looked like he was dancing the Rodent Rumba.

"Your lab coat!" Marlo shrieked as she ran toward the panicked teacher. "It's covered with mice!"

"They're *on* me?"

Dr. Skinner ripped off his white lab coat and threw it to the floor. Marlo grabbed it and slipped Napoléon's mind control device inside.

She walked back to the Sylla-Bus and sat next to Frances. They watched as Dr. Skinner, Napoléon, and Kali tried to corral the mice.

Chaos, Marlo thought, panting, as the adults hopped around like squealing idiots. That's *what this place needs. And* that's *how I can get to the infirmary and spring Milton loose from whatever sicko thing these crusty old creeps have going on down there. . . .*

The seemingly endless concrete tunnel curved gently out of sight as Milton and the guard walked onward through the Hekla ministry complex. Exposed air duct pipes ran along the eight-foot-tall ceiling while, on the left-hand wall, a long rectangular window looked out across the jagged Icelandic mountainside. Just below the window protruded the petulant rim of the Hekla volcano. A great smoke-colored column pierced the center of the volcano, climbing up to meet the billowing gray Widow's Veil. The chimney-like structure rippled and swayed, as if it were composed of thick, churning soot.

They arrived at a set of closed steel doors. The guard pressed his fingertips to an access panel, and the doors opened. The emotionless man shoved Milton into an elevator, buckled himself against the wall, then punched a button. The elevator plummeted, and Milton crumpled to the floor.

It stopped suddenly. The doors opened to an enormous pointy-roofed room, cast in a sinister red glow from a glass wall, and lined with banks of high-tech equipment. The guard dragged Milton across the complex.

It's like the inside of a pyramid, Milton thought, *designed as if someone had put ancient Egyptian and Napoléonic era French decor in a blender, switched it to* frappe, *and splashed it across every surface.*

Ministry police in charcoal-gray uniforms stood

cradling William clubs by the rails of the balconies above. Milton and the guard stopped in front of a tall gilded door.

The door whooshed open, disappearing into the top of the door's ornate frame like a guillotine in reverse.

Beyond was a chamber carved out of volcanic rock, illuminated by a suspended chandelier flaunting burning wax candles. Fur rugs covered the black brick floor, leading to the back of a solid gold throne.

"You may leave," a strange voice, like two voices wrapped together with silk, ordered.

The guard bowed stiffly and left the room.

That voice, Milton thought. *It's familiar yet totally weird. Almost like two people talking at the same time.*

The throne swiveled until Milton was face to face with the reason why he was here in the first place.

An elegant, effeminate man with smooth, butterscotch skin and long dark hair studied Milton with a knowing smirk. He was small and lean, with fine white teeth, a slightly curved nose, and mismatched eyes. One was gray-blue while the other gleamed a dark, bottomless brown.

"*Bonjour,*" the man said in a voice as incongruous as his eyes. "We are Emperor Leo Patrick Napolette. So nice to see you again."

"We?" Milton croaked.

"The *royal* 'we' as in me," Emperor Leo Patrick Napolette said in a deeper, snootier voice while turning to show Milton his profile: that of a young Napoléon. "And *me*," he continued in a higher voice that tumbled off his tongue like sunbaked satin, presenting Milton with the other side of his face.

"*Cleopatra?*" Milton gasped. "And Napoléon!"

"*Oui* . . . it is we," Emperor Leo Patrick Napolette said with a cryptic smile.

The emperor pulled a gold stopwatch from his gray velvet waistcoat. A bright beam of laser light radiated from its base, settling on a tiny barcode on Milton's Pace Taker. The emperor jabbed the button with his thumb. Milton fell to the floor, clutching his chest.

"And 'we' wanted to zhank you, Monsieur Fauster. *Personally* . . ."

Milton's Pace Taker had stopped ticking, as had his heart.

"Before your time runs out . . ."

28 · FROM A WHiSPER TO A SCHEME

MILTON WRITHED ON the plush fur rug with tight, burning pain spreading rapidly from his chest.

"My . . . Pace Taker," he moaned, pounding the clock surgically attached to his heart.

The unsettling blend of Napoléon and Cleopatra pressed their shared thumb against the button of the gold stopwatch. Instantly, Milton's Pace Taker began to tick.

"*Pardonne-moi,*" the emperor replied without any true regret, "your time is not up . . . yet."

"Why keep me alive?" Milton said as he got to his shaky knees, dizzy and sick from his coronary.

"Oh, to thank you . . . and to rub your face in all of this a bit," Emperor Leo Patrick Napolette said with a petulant smirk. "We may be the most powerful ruler in all of history, but we are not immune to zhe gloating. . . ."

"Thank me? And how can you be a *we*?"

The emperor stood, playing with his chunky gold necklace.

"Thanks to *you*, we—Napoléon and Cleopatra—were able to locate zhe perfect world for us: a reality where zhe French and Egyptian empires flourished," the foppish man said, flipping back his gleaming black hair. "We returned as ourselves and hopped from heir to heir, tweaking history to our liking, until we finally arrived—quite unexpectedly—in this unique situation as roommates, if you will: occupying one body with our mingled blood coursing through its veins. *Parfait!* Saves a lot on zhe phone bills . . ."

Milton tried to stand but was too weak from his heart attack.

"It began when we found zhe broken Kronosgraph pieces," Emperor Leo Patrick Napolette said as he paced in front of his golden throne. "And etched upon them in intricate grooves were unique dimensions. An infinitude of possibilities. Maps to zhe Time Pools secreted away beneath the fabric of time itself."

The Time Pools, Milton thought. *That must have been where Marlo and I nearly drowned, down in that luminous grotto.*

"Dr. Einstein found a way to 'play' zhe Kronosgraph disks, but it required that zhe needle—or person—be exceptionally open-minded," the emperor continued. "This excluded adults. And most every child in the underworld has a mind closed up like a fist, ready for a fight! But *certain* children would do. And *did*. Especially you, Milton Fauster. The Kronosgraph that you were . . . are 'playing' is zhe world you find yourself in right now."

I'm being . . . played? Milton thought. *Of course! I was taken to the infirmary back in Precocia, had that hood put on me, and then it felt like I was being held upside down. All of this, all of my so-called life here, is just a selection of tracks on a fourth-dimensional record: the worst greatest hits compilation ever . . .*

"We transcribed most of what you sleep-mumbled, up until zhe end when your sister tried to rescue you. We got enough to know that this was indeed zhe place for us."

Milton looked the emperor in his creepy mismatched eye.

"Marlo rescues me?"

"She did . . . or *will*, to you. It's complicated," the emperor replied with an irritated nod. "But she will not truly save you. You will die here and become a helpful, manageable zombie boy back in Precocia."

"How's that?"

"When a needle—an open-minded child suspended over zhe Kronosgraph disk—dies in zhe lifetime that they are experiencing, they . . . *lose* something in zhe process. And, since you were taken down, zombified, we knew that you died here—or *will* die here. *Today.* So I couldn't execute you or your foolish friends until right now, because . . . well, zhat's how it happened! Anyhoo, we zhen sent you down deep into zhe Undermines. You and your sister caused some trouble but were quickly captured and tortured, giving us zhe information we needed to not only find zhe correct Time Pool, but also to locate zhe Fountain of Youth."

"The Fountain of Youth?" Milton replied doubtfully. "But that's just a myth."

Emperor Leo Patrick Napolette threw back his head and laughed.

"Zhe Fountain of Youth may be a myth up on zhe Surface but it is all too real in zhe afterlife, outside of time, where it springs forth and feeds into zhe Time Pools, rejuvenating zhe flow of reality." The emperor's expression soured. "It floods childhood, washing away all reason, dignity, and productivity. *Répugnant!* By plugging zhe flow, we were able to eliminate childhood altogether, so that zhe first few years of a person's life can be spent being *useful:* under our absolute rule, of course. . . ."

The emperor marched in self-satisfied circles across the fur rug.

"Next, we—Cleopatra and Napoléon—took a dip in the Time Pools, swimming through history, hopping from blood relative to blood relative just before their deaths so that we didn't suffer what *you* shall suffer—a soulful diminishment. And when zhe time was ripe, we engineered zhe Unfortunate Shower—"

"How can you *engineer* a mass meteor shower?" Milton interrupted.

"You can't. But you *can* make thousands of rock-shaped satellites plummet to the Earth and vaporize upon impact."

Emperor Leo Patrick Napolette watched Milton's shock with deep satisfaction, as if it were the emperor's favorite movie being played across the eighty-one-year-old boy's face.

So that's why none of the meteorites seemed to destroy anything, Milton thought.

"So it was all just a show? But why?"

The emperor smiled, revealing a white-picket fence of perfect teeth. The teeth of a predator.

"Come. See for yourself . . ."

Emperor Leo Patrick Napolette pressed his palm against the scanner and opened the gilded door. Milton hobbled behind the emperor as he swept across the pyramid-shaped control room, stopping at the wall of smoked glass that overlooked Hekla's molten throat. He beckoned Milton with a regal wave of his hand.

Milton looked down into the maw of the volcano. A catwalk ran along the inside of it, with walkways leading out to an immense circular machine clogging the center of the volcano. It reminded Milton of a tremendous steel-gray crown, with its tines wilted inward. A wide-mouth intake pipe hung from the bottom, disappearing down into the furious red glow below. The towering charcoal-gray column that Milton had seen earlier wasn't man-made at all. It was a monolithic outpouring of impenetrable smoke stretching up to the sky, the exact same color and composition as . . .

"The Widow's Veil," Milton murmured. "It's coming from the Hekla volcano. . . ."

A malicious smile caused Emperor Leo Patrick Napolette's cold, elegant face to cave in on itself.

"As it has been doing, without fail, for exactly seventy years, two hours, thirteen minutes, and forty-seven seconds," the emperor said, watching Milton's face with delight and expectation, as if he were a toddler winding a jack-in-the-box.

"Why?" was all that Milton could manage as he stared at the thick tornado of soot.

The emperor pointed to the dark gray sky hovering a mile above the Hekla volcano.

"The Widow's Veil blocks zhe sun, zhe sky, zhe watchful gaze of the heavens that allows us to tell night from day, winter from spring . . . even what year it is. Now there is no time beyond what we, the ministry, *say* is zhe time. With zhe world united under one time zone, everyone rises and retires together, working as one. It's *beaucoup plus* efficient that way. . . ."

Milton looked down into the volcano. The machine

seemed to be slurping up something down in the depths of the earth.

"It must take incredible amounts of energy," Milton muttered dismally.

The emperor nodded, his eyelids heavy with smug gratification.

"*Oui* . . . the machine runs on magma, or *precarium* as we've been calling it. We've nearly exhausted our supply, but in just a few years, it won't matter: there will be enough Widow's Veil in zhe atmosphere for it to sustain itself . . . *forever.*"

"But magma is the superhot fluid at the center of the planet," Milton said, gazing fretfully into Emperor Leo Patrick Napolette's mismatched eyes. "Like the filling in a Hot Pocket. Without that massive ocean of molten lava sloshing about, the Earth would be hollow. All the earthquakes . . . they're death spasms! The Earth's a big, empty, crumbling piñata that you strip-mined of candy!"

Emperor Leo Patrick Napolette clapped his hands. A pair of guards approached.

"The future of zhe Earth shouldn't be any of your concern," the emperor said as the guards grabbed Milton by the arms. The emperor's privileged mouth curled into a cruel smile. "But you can say *au revoir* to the planet's molten core *yourself.* . . ."

★ ★ ★

Marlo stuck her head into the break room freezer. It was like a subzero museum of no-fat, no-calorie, no-flavor microwaveable convenience food.

"Wow . . . a food morgue," Marlo mumbled. "Where forgotten office food goes to die . . . Ooh, *this* looks promising!"

She pulled out a few boxes of stuffed green peppers.

"Nasty . . . but perfect with *this* . . ."

Marlo wrested free a bottle of Dante's Infernal Prescription-Strength Tabasco Sauce. She elbowed the freezer door closed and arranged the boxes of stuffed Green Pepper Popperz, Kwik Ribz in Turbo Sauce, Cheezplosive Pocket Snax, and Reheat-a Fajita Fandangos on the counter.

"I've gathered you all here today because something is seriously wrong down below," Marlo said earnestly to the other Junior Executives.

Lyon cocked her eyebrow at Marlo's butt.

"You're telling me," she said with a sneer.

"My brother and the other kids have been in the infirmary *way* too long."

"Marlo's right," Angelo offered. "When I took Marlo there, Dr. Curie said that the kids were having their treatments. And she looked really nervous. More than usual."

Marlo stared at Angelo. Her feelings for the painfully gorgeous boy left her seriously conflicted, like how she felt when her favorite band Funeral Petz released their orchestral-acoustic album *Epic Frail*. Her mind didn't trust him, yet her heart skipped a beat at the sight of his sadistically blue eyes.

"So what are we supposed to do about it?" Midori asked, chewing on her fingernails. "There are guards swarming—literally—everywhere and we'd need a card key to get down to the infirmary."

Marlo smiled, a blindly confident smile that—had Milton been one of the eight children currently hovering in the break room—would have instantly turned his blood into a plasma-rich slushie.

"Did you see how clueless all of those uptight adults were today with the mice?" she said. "They are so obsessed with keeping order and having everything be all boring and grown-up that they get severiously fried when things get random. So what *I* propose is a good old-fashioned food fight. . . ."

Myung-Dae raised his hand.

Marlo smirked.

"You don't have to . . . okay, whatever . . . *yes, Myung-Dae?*" she said, leaning against the loud, rusted refrigerator.

"Will this act of civil disobedience go toward our final grade?" the boy asked.

Marlo tossed a bottle of Tabasco sauce in her hand, a condiment so old that it was eligible for Social Security several times over.

"I can almost guarantee it," she said with a faraway grin.

★　★　★

Searing vapors lashed at Milton's face as he was led out onto the catwalk lining the inside of the volcano. The stifling hot blast smelled like a nest of rotten dinosaur eggs being cooked by a jet engine. Tongues of crackling fire lapped at the sides of the volcano hundreds of feet below. The glass-walled pyramid control center protruded from the side of the volcano's throat, with an eye-shaped beacon casting light out into the shaft.

The emperor put two fingers in his mouth and let loose a surprisingly piercing whistle.

Eight doors whooshed open, leading out to the walkways suspended over the volcano's maw. Ministry guards jabbed their William clubs into the backs of nearly two dozen prisoners.

The first prisoner was an old woman with blond-gray curls and wide-set blue eyes.

Shirley Eujest, Milton thought as the woman was led to the massive circular machine, with the Widow's Veil spewing out of it like an angry, uncorked genie. *The leader of HAHAHA . . .*

Milton was filled with an intense, burning shame even hotter than the furnace-like blast gushing out of the volcano.

I'm the reason they're all here, ready to be thrown into the volcano. All because of some dumb letter that fell from the sky, a letter I probably never wrote to begin with. It's got to be some trick, some practical joke, with me and my only friends in this horrible world paying the price . . .

Shirley, who had been staring at her boots as she was led along the walkway, suddenly looked up at Milton and gave him a sly wink before, again, hanging her head down in apparent abject misery.

Emperor Leo Patrick Napolette nodded to the guards clutching Milton's arms. The guards shoved Milton forward out onto one of the walkways. The fierce, hot wind gushed upward with relentless force.

"Now we have zhe perfect society," Emperor Leo Patrick Napolette shouted over the roar of the volcano and the machine spewing out the Widow's Veil. "And no silly kids' stuff: nothing but serious, mature highly effective world domination! As you all can see, controlling the world—controlling time itself—is our destiny!"

Shirley lifted her head and glared across the sweltering abyss at the emperor. Milton could see her face, her cheeks flushed with passion, her eyes blazing with purpose.

"Destiny is supposed to be something greater than you, something you could never have imagined, not ticking off meaningless tasks on some big evil to-do list!" she shouted, and smiled a blazing, audacious smile.

"Life isn't 'to-do,' it's . . ."

She and her comrades-in-disarming behavior clicked their heels together, their shoes ballooning out to twice their original size.

". . . ta-da!"

And with that, all Heck broke loose down in the Hekla volcano.

29 · MiDNiGHT SNACK ATTACK!

MARLO PEERED OUT from behind a cluster of jammed copiers in the darkened office commons. The elevator leading down to the infirmary was blocked by three grumpy twenty-three-hours-old mayfly demons.

Virgil, Frances, Lyon, and Angelo crept along to Marlo's side, with Midori, Myung-Dae, and Paloma close behind.

"Is the coast clear?" Virgil whispered.

"As clear as a band geek's complexion," Marlo muttered.

"This food is really hot," Lyon complained as she cradled an assortment of microwaved food in a paper towel sash.

"That's what happens when you microwave food on

high," Marlo replied slowly, as if talking to her parents about the Internet.

Angelo scooted along the floor to Marlo. He trained his perfectly arranged features upon her. "So what do you propose we do?" he said.

Marlo stared intently at the elevator, feeling Angelo's gaze burn her cheek. "Well, I propose—"

"You propose?" Angelo said with a dazzling smile. "Already? We just met. . . ."

"I *propose* that we wait for some kind of diversion," Marlo said, her words steamrolling through her discomfort. "Something will happen and, when we see whatever that something is, we'll just run with it."

The children hunkered down in the dim stillness until a chaotic rush of footsteps broke the silence.

"He's dead!" screamed Dr. Curie as she ran frantically across the eighteenth floor, sobbing into her hanky. She fell to her knees and slammed the floor with her glowing green fists. "WHY?" she howled, having a full-blown nuclear meltdown.

"Huh?" Marlo whispered to Midori.

"Solomon Grundy, died on Saturday," Midori replied.

Marlo shook her head. "How have I not *heard* this rhyme before?" she said. "And why is she so upset? Her husband dies once a week. Big deal. We all have problems."

Dr. Curie shambled away, with two of the mayfly demons flitting behind her.

"And we've got our diversion," Marlo said. "Virgil, you're up."

Virgil nodded and took a swig of some old soup. He crouched down and, clutching his stomach, made his way to the Time Trapper, set right next to the elevator.

The mayfly demon buzzed with irritation. "What are you doing out of your filing cabinet?" he hissed, brandishing his small yet not-to-be-trifled-with pitchspork.

"Am . . . sick," Virgil said as he leaned against the row of Time Trapper punch cards. "Gonna . . . *puke.*"

Virgil spat semi-reheated soup onto the floor.

The mayfly demon grimaced.

"Help me . . . clean up . . . before vice principals . . . see," Virgil muttered. "Or else . . . *mad.*"

The mayfly demon sighed.

"Seriously? My last hour of life spent cleaning kiddie spew?"

Virgil grabbed a fistful of time cards. The clock mounted on top ticked angrily. Virgil fell to the ground just as the bright red boxing glove thrust out of the box, knocking the demon guard out cold. Virgil yanked the mayfly demon's card key lanyard from his neck and gave a whistle. The children joined him at the elevator.

"Great job!" Marlo said with a crooked smile.

Virgil beamed shyly. "Thanks. But it was your idea . . . a real, um . . . *knockout.*"

Angelo grabbed the card key from Virgil and swiped it through the sensor.

"Excuse me, Barfeo and Juliet, but we've gotta make tracks," he said as the elevator door whooshed open. "Five-O is on to us . . . and they called for backup."

Coming at them from across the office commons was a swarm of mayfly demons led by Kali. The giant blue goddess waved her four arms that, much to Marlo's distress, happened to be engulfed in flame.

"Yeah, and they have *firearms*," she said. "First battalion, are you ready?"

Midori and Myung-Dae nodded and stepped forward, holding scalding-hot Green Pepper Popperz in their oven-mitted hands. They bit off the stems like pins from a grenade. Marlo filled the insides with Dante's Infernal Prescription-Strength Tabasco Sauce and backed away quickly as if she had just lit the fuse from an illegal firework.

"Ready . . . aim . . . FIRE!" she yelled.

Midori and Myung-Dae lobbed their hot stuffed peppers across the commons, with Myung-Dae's hurling farther and faster due to his muscular arm. His green pepper exploded in Kali's face.

"Aaaaaaarggghhh!" she bellowed, clutching the front of her head in agony.

Meanwhile, Midori's Tabasco-infused Green Pepper Popperz took out two mayfly demons, who dropped onto the floor, squealing in pain. A new swarm of demons, followed by William the Kid and Dr. Jung, converged on the office commons.

Angelo grabbed Marlo and shoved her into the elevator.

"Hey!" she yelped. "What are you doing?"

Virgil, Frances, Paloma, and Lyon joined them inside.

"If we're going to do this, we've got to do it now," Angelo said as he hit the elevator button with his fist.

Midori and Myung-Dae looked behind them at Marlo with grim surprise as dozens of buzzing demons surged toward them.

"We can't just leave them!" Marlo yelped as she moved to stop the door from closing, but Angelo held her back.

"You can't help them," he said as the doors shut. "Casualties of . . . food fight."

The elevator descended a few yards, then stopped with a jerk. The fluorescent lights flickered off.

"They've cut the power," Marlo murmured.

"Virgil," Angelo ordered in the dim light. "Hit the deck and I'll stand on you to see if there's a way out up on top."

"Why me? Virgil said.

"C'mon, man . . . don't make me spell it out in front of the ladies."

Virgil sighed. "Fine," he said as he got down on all fours.

Angelo stepped on Virgil's back and opened the ceiling panel. He peered up the darkened shaft. "It looks like we're all—" he said before the door to the eighteenth floor was pried apart by four flaming arms. Kali glared down the shaft at Angelo. "In for some *seriously* hot curry," he continued. "Toss me up a few Cheezplosive Pocket Snax."

Frances handed Angelo the microwaved food. He hurled the scalding-hot, Tabasco-injected Hot Pockets up at the fuming Indian goddess. Two spattered against the side of the shaft, spewing hot cheese shrapnel across Kali's chest. The third hit Kali smack on her bindi between her thick black eyebrows. She fell back. Before the elevator doors closed, three mayfly demons flew through the crack. Angelo hopped off Virgil's back.

"That's a no-go," he said as Virgil, grunting, got off the floor.

"I have an idea," Virgil replied. He pried off the elevator's control panel, untangled the clump of wires, and scrutinized two wires—one red, one yellow—before, with a shrug, yanking out the red one.

"I'm pretty sure that this leads to the power supply," Virgil said.

"*Pretty* sure?" Lyon said with a sneer.

"He means 'sure' with lots of makeup on it," Marlo added.

Virgil unbuttoned his Power Suit and, after feeling around the lining, ripped out a wire.

"These suits make energy when we move: mostly to power things that shock us. But maybe we can use that energy to power up the elevator."

"Guess there are *two* Einsteins in Precocia," Marlo said as she unbuttoned her Power Suit.

Virgil grinned. He ripped the power cords from the lining of the children's suits and knotted them together into one electricity-conducting braid. Demon guards banged away at the top of the elevator.

"I think that did it," he said, connecting the wires to the elevator's power cable.

The mayfly demons began to pry open the roof panel with their pitchsporks.

"Now what?" Lyon gasped as she glommed onto Angelo's side like a bleached-blond barnacle to the hull of a hunky ship.

"We do jumping jacks like we've never done them before," Virgil replied.

For a sliver of a second, everything went so quiet that all Milton could hear was the ticktock of his Pace Taker.

Shirley Eujest and the other twenty-two members of HAHAHA inflated their plain leather boots into buoyant bright red clown shoes. They leapt into the hot, hazy air, conquering the gravity of their situation, as if the volcano were a sweltering bouncy house.

The ministry soldiers were paralyzed by the chaos. Just as one managed to train his pneumatic club upon a prisoner, the fugitive clown sprang out of range.

The clowns landed as one, crouching low on the steel walkways, and ripped off their drab hair: freeing shocking rainbows of fluorescent-hued locks beneath. They picked through the inside of their wigs for concealed gadgets, then pitched the hairpieces into the volcano.

Shirley pulled a red foam rubber clown nose from her ear and secured it on the tip of her nose.

"Stink bombs are go!" she ordered as a palm-sized disk slid out of her sleeve. Shirley hurled the bomb at the side of the volcano. The other clowns did the same, choking Hekla's throat with thick, noxious smoke.

Emperor Leo Patrick Napolette backed away from the mayhem and felt his way along the catwalk. He pulled his stopwatch from his pocket and tried, vainly, to train its laser light upon an unsuspecting target.

"*Gardes!*" he shrieked. "Clear the air, *imbéciles!*"

A soldier fired his William club, thinning a dense chunk of smoke with a mighty whoosh. A HAHAHA terrorist was exposed as he dabbed clownouflage greasepaint on his face. The emperor aimed the laser light from his stopwatch onto the clown's Pace Taker and pressed the button. The clown clutched his chest and fell to his knees, yet just as he seemed about to pass out, he started to laugh.

"Do you like our Pace *Fakers*, Emperor?" the man chuckled as he rose to his feet.

A guard came from behind, following the clown's laughter, and pulled the trigger of his William club. The clown was whisked off the walkway with a mad gush of compressed air and tumbled into the volcano.

The clown commandos reached into their mouths

and pulled out round red retainers. They charged at the stunned guards and clamped the rings to the tips of their weapons.

A ministry guard stepped toward a burly clown who Milton recognized through clear patches in the stinking smoke as Tom Fullery.

"Get ready to be blown away, traitor!" the guard hissed as he fired his William club. Instantly, a huge polka-dotted balloon inflated out the tip of his weapon. The guard floated up off the catwalk.

Tom Fullery laughed. "Helium convertor rings," he said as several other soldiers took to the air, clutching their William clubs tight in terror. The clown grabbed the guard's leg.

"Did you say *blown away*?" Tom Fullery sneered, his face a scary mask of greasepaint. "Your *whoosh* is my command!"

The guerilla jester heaved the squirming guard into the air, where he was carried up, up, and away by the coiling stream of Widow's Veil into the Icelandic sky.

A bright red dot of laser light traveled up Milton's leg.

"I trust *your* Pace Taker, Monsieur Fauster, is in perfect working order!" Emperor Leo Patrick Napolette yelled from a nearby walkway. Thinking fast, Shirley grabbed a floating guard and sent him soaring straight into the emperor.

"*Sacré* balloon!" the emperor gasped as he was

slammed to the ground. His stopwatch flew out of his hand and skidded across the walkway.

"Grab him!" Shirley shouted. "We'll need him as a hostage so that the ministry will turn off this terrible machine!"

The emperor sprang from the ground with catlike reflexes and bounded back into the glass-walled control pyramid, with a pair of elderly clowns in hot pursuit.

Milton turned and stared into Shirley's wide-set blue eyes.

"I thought I had signed your death sentence," he murmured in awe. "For finking you out and sending you here. How did you do all of this?"

Shirley smiled, an expression amplified by the shiny red face-paint smeared around her mouth.

"I remembered what you said years ago, about how— for one day every decade—you weren't quite yourself," she explained. "You were our perfect ally, yet still, we needed to prepare in case you—or the you you are when you *aren't* you—betrayed us, either on purpose or by accident. So we've been planning for something like this ever since. There's no way a ragtag team of gangster gagsters could break into the ministry's maximum-security base. But as prisoners, we could strike from the *inside*. The ultimate prank! After you turned us in, we managed to elude the ministry to make it look like we didn't want to be captured, before they finally brought us in last month. Luckily, the emperor has an extreme sense of irony and wanted us tossed into Hekla together, *now,* on this very day. He said you'd understand why. So we've been biding our time like a jack-in-the-box until— *sproing!* And sproing has indeed *sprung!*"

Milton noticed a small rainbow-colored gash in the Widow's Veil directly above. It was that same little boat, tacking across the sky, followed by a young angel with gleaming wings and a shimmering orange halo.

"*Please* tell me you see that," Milton said to Shirley, pointing to the sky.

Shirley squinted up at the thick cloud mass above. "It looks like the northern lights," she replied. "But there's no way we could see them *below* the Widow's Veil."

The sky surrounding the multicolored wound in the clouds seemed to froth and foam. Suddenly, several seemingly unrelated notions overlapped in Milton's mind, forming a startlingly vivid picture.

"Of course," he muttered to himself. "Baking soda . . . foam . . ."

A violent shudder erupted through the facility.

"Volcanoes."

Milton and Shirley gripped the rails.

"The planet is dying," Shirley said. "We've got to put the mirth back into the Earth soon."

Milton turned to the sad-eyed clown. "Do you know where they keep their supplies here?"

"Yes, in the storage depot, three floors down. Why?"

"I think I know how to blow away this whole place. For good. *For great.*"

"No joke?" Shirley said with a sly grin that was a little frightened to commit to a full-on smile.

"Not on us, hopefully," Milton said, looking up at the sky as the rainbow gash healed to nothing. "I just hope that a close friend of mine crashes the party . . . and brings along some serious vinegar."

The elevator made a slow, jerky descent as the Junior Executives provided electricity using their Power Suits.

"We're . . . *moving!*" Virgil puffed as he and the other five children did jumping jacks.

"Where is . . . the infirmary anyway?" Marlo panted.

"It was on the ninth floor," Angelo said. He seemed to be the only one who wasn't the least bit winded. "I counted the dings."

The mayfly demons dented the top of the elevator with the ceaseless stabbing of their pitchsporks. Marlo cast her wary eyes up to the ceiling.

"Man, they get . . . grumpy in their . . . old age."

The floors "dinged" past faster and faster.

"We should start . . . ," Virgil puffed, "slowing down."

The elevator settled halfway between the ninth and tenth floors. The ceiling panel fell to the floor and the angry horde of mayfly demons dropped into the elevator. Angelo kicked one unconscious against the wall and batted another away with the fallen panel. He rushed to the door and pried it open with amazing strength.

The Junior Executives "limboed" to fit through the gap between floors. One by one, they squeezed themselves through and dropped onto the ninth floor.

"Which way?" Marlo asked as she looked up and down the concrete hall. Angelo nodded to his left.

They bounded around a corner and through a pair of swinging aluminum doors.

The infirmary was quiet. Pungent fumes of antiseptic curled the children's noses. Marlo scanned the two rows of beds. Four of the beds were occupied by sleeping zombie teenagers; the rest were empty. The dim room suddenly brightened with an eerie green light.

"What is going on?" Dr. Curie said from across the room, blocking another set of double doors. She blew a whistle hanging from her neck.

The zombie teenagers bolted upright, tumbled out of their beds, and shambled forward.

"Kwik Ribz in Turbo Sauce!" Marlo yelled. Frances handed her a few of the piping hot ribs.

"Cover me with Reheat-a Fajita Fandangos," she ordered as Virgil and Frances cradled the steaming fajita bowls. "Ready . . . aim . . . FIRE!"

Marlo flung a Kwik Rib at the nearest zombie boy. It smacked him hard against the jaw before fluttering back to Marlo like a boomerang. Bowls of scalding-hot fajitas hit the chests of the other zombified teenagers. They yowled in pain and fell to their knees.

"¡Ayúdenme!" Paloma yelled with a piercing shriek from the entryway. "They got me!"

The Latino girl was covered with mayfly demons. They dragged her away, screaming, back into the hall.

Dr. Curie's silvery eyes widened with alarm. She backed away through the double doors and ran out into the other hallway. Marlo's boomerang rib bounced off the door, leaving behind a smear of barbecue sauce.

"Charge!" Marlo yelled as she, Virgil, Angelo, Lyon, and Frances bounded after Dr. Curie. They passed a large bin full of strange, hooded helmets with pointed tips and burst through another set of doors. The Junior Executives skidded to a halt.

"Flamin' monkey diapers," Marlo muttered in awe, her jaw hanging open at the sight before her. The spacious room rattled with the whine of machines. It was colossally huge, with walls that flared upward and outward. The space easily took up most of the levels beneath the eighteenth floor and was monopolized by five circular platforms as big as merry-go-rounds with large stone disks rotating slowly upon each. The groaning machines had long mechanical arms suspended over the spiral disks.

Spirals . . . like those etchings in the Undermines, Marlo thought with amazement.

The whole place looked like the Jolly Green Giant's DJ setup. And dangling at the ends of the five arms were squirming upside-down things with pointy black helmets whose tips scraped the disks like needles on old record players. The squirming things looked like . . .

"Kids!" Marlo gasped.

Dr. Einstein turned groggily to face Marlo. His blank eyes reflected the blinking lights of his blinders. Next to the absentminded professor was Dr. Curie, pointing her glowing fingers at the children. A dozen mayfly demons swarmed to attack.

"Aaarrrghhh!" Virgil roared as he charged forward. Three demons swooped down upon him. Instantly, Virgil fell onto one hand and swung his legs in a cruel arc.

"Oy . . . *vey*!" he grunted as his feet made a brutal connection with the three guards, sending them flying into one of the machines. He hopped to his feet while Marlo rushed to his side.

"Wow . . . smooth moves, Ex-Lax!" she said.

Virgil shrugged. "Just something I picked up in Hebrew-jitsu class," he explained.

Marlo saw Napoléon's demon foot servants, Armstrong and Patrick Harris, disconnecting two students from the long arms of the massive machines. The pin-headed, upside-down students were at the end of their "records," smacking against the raised center of their disks. The foot servants dragged the children off the machines, ripped off their hoods, and laid them against the wall in an inert, drooling pile. Marlo sighed with relief that neither of the now-zombified children was Milton.

"Get off me!" Lyon shrieked as two mayfly demons descended upon her. Marlo grabbed her remaining Kwik Rib and flung it at the demon guards, knocking them out cold. Lyon straightened her Power Suit and gave Marlo a faint nod.

"Stop, you filthy *enfants!*" Napoléon shouted from the doorway. "You'll ruin everything!" He was joined by Cleopatra, a literally fuming Kali, and two dozen buzzing mayfly demons.

Marlo turned back toward the remaining three machines, trying to locate her brother, when it hit her.

"Oww!" she yelped as her Kwik Rib boomerang returned, smacking her in the back of the head.

The kid with the long skinny feet, Marlo thought as she stared at the titanic turntable nearest Dr. Einstein. *I'd recognize those feet anywhere, considering I had to wear them back in Fibble.*

Marlo studied the group of demons and faculty blocking the exit. They were hopelessly outnumbered.

I've got to get Milton off that thing before he turns into a brain-dead teenage slave. But how?

30 · VOLCANIC DISRUPTION

"ROLL OUT THE barrel, we'll have a barrel of fun," sang the HAHAHA clowns as they transported hundreds of Styrofoam kegs packed tight with baking soda out to the Widow's Veil machine. They arranged the last load of barrels onto the catwalk.

"Let's pop off the lids," Milton instructed as Shirley stepped out onto the crowded catwalk, having just overseen the capture of the ministry guards.

"Now's the time to roll the barrel . . . ," the clowns sang as two more of them marched out to the Widow's Veil machine. They had Emperor Leo Patrick Napolette in handcuffs and shoved him out onto the catwalk.

"For the gang's all here!" Shirley Eujest squealed.

The emperor cast an inscrutable glance down at his stiff, motionless hands bound together at his waist. "Surprise!" he yelled while untucking his arms—his *real* arms—from behind his back. "I, too, have some tricks up my sleeves. In fact, my sleeves *are* tricks!"

Holding two William clubs in each of his now-free hands, the emperor whooshed away the clowns holding him with one-two blasts of deadly air. The HAHAHA crusaders toppled into the volcanic abyss below.

The emperor backed slowly away, tucking one of the weapons in his tight gray breeches. He seized Milton by the arm, holding the William club to his head.

"No sudden movements or Monsieur Fauster will have his brains whooshed out of his skull," Emperor Leo Patrick Napolette hissed between clenched white teeth. He cocked his eyebrows at the barrels of baking soda.

"What gives with zhe barrels?"

Shirley shrugged. "To absorb odors?" she offered.

The emperor spotted his stopwatch on the ground and slowly knelt down to retrieve it.

"Why don't you just kill me now?" Milton murmured as the emperor tucked his stopwatch into his inside pocket.

"Because it is not time. It does not happen like that," the emperor replied in his two-tone voice.

The emperor regarded Shirley with his mismatched eyes as he backed into the main control center with Milton. "No funny business, clowns. Or his brains will be on your conscience . . . not to mention your ridiculous clothes."

The emperor untied one of his guards, then ushered

Milton up a staircase to the third level. The control center quaked as the Earth began to shiver apart. The emperor prodded Milton through a hatchway leading to a small room with an eye-shaped window.

"Sit, *s'il vous plaît*," he said as he took out his stopwatch. "You still have a little time. *Very* little."

Marlo, Virgil, Lyon, Angelo, and Frances huddled together.

"What do we do, Karate Kid?" Angelo asked Virgil as the swarm of guards drew near.

Virgil looked up at the clock hanging above the doorway. It was nearly midnight, straight up.

"We wait," Virgil replied.

"We wait?" Lyon gasped. "Until when?"

The clock struck midnight. The two dozen mayfly demon guards fell to the ground, dead.

"Now!"

The Vee-Pees and Kali stared slack-jawed at the mound of expired mayflies surrounding them.

"Hurry! Before new guards hatch!" Marlo shouted.

Frances and Lyon hurled their piping-hot Reheat-a Fajita Fandangos at Kali. The goddess batted one away with her third arm, but the other exploded on her already tender face. "Aaaaaarrrgghhhh!" she bellowed.

"You guys rescue those two kids over there," Marlo said. "I'm going to grab Milton over at Einstein's machine."

"I'm helping you," Angelo said as he studied Milton's struggling body with narrowed eyes.

Marlo shrugged. "Whatever floats your dreamboat," she replied before suddenly catching herself. "I mean *boat*. A regular one. Not a dream one."

They dashed toward Dr. Einstein's turntable machine.

"Armstrong! Patrick Harris!" Napoléon roared, his snooty face flushed with rage. "Seize them!"

The canvas-wrapped creatures doddered toward Marlo and Angelo, their restrictive chains rattling. Marlo flung her Kwik rib at the nearest demon foot servant. The rib slashed across the creature's chest, breaking his chain. The demon stopped in surprise, gazing upon his unchained self with glowing red eyes. He straightened out to his full height of just over six feet.

"*Kneel*, Armstrong!" Napoléon yelled. "You are not to exceed your master's height!"

Armstrong waddled over to Patrick Harris and, with a colossal tug emboldened by freedom, unchained his companion. The newly liberated creature stretched in defiant delight.

"*Kneel*, Patrick Harris!"

The two creatures came at Napoléon. He pulled out his mobile mind controller from his coat and waved it at his mutinous servants, yet they stalked closer all the same. Dr. Einstein watched the proceedings with a flicker of curiosity. He touched his blinders with confusion, as if slowly waking from a dream.

Kali wiped the spicy fajita from her face and lunged forward, grabbing Armstrong and Patrick Harris's canvas-covered heads and slamming them together. The two demon foot servants fell to the ground.

Marlo ran to the giant machine, the stone disk spinning in groaning revolutions. Milton hung upside down like a sleeping bat in a dunce cap, almost at the end of the disk's long, spiraling groove. Angelo stepped back from the machine, slyly pulling a silver blade from the back of his suit and, hunkering down, leapt straight at Milton. Though scarcely off the ground, Kali snatched the boy from the air and threw him hard to the floor.

Marlo noticed a twitching black device about the size of a suitcase next to the rotating turntable. A megaphone jutted out of the machine, trained earnestly upon Milton, the lower part of his face exposed so that Marlo could see her brother's lips moving. A mechanical hand grasping a quill scribbled furiously upon a slow-turning drum covered with paper.

It's writing down everything that Milton is mumbling, she thought.

"Dr. Einstein . . . seize her!" Napoléon shrieked.

"Caesar?" Cleopatra replied, whipping her regal head about. "Here?"

"Grab that grubby girl before she touches the Trance-Scriber!" Napoléon bellowed. "She'll ruin everything!"

Milton peered out of the big glass eye down into the Hekla volcano. Dozens of freed ministry soldiers overtook the clown commandos.

He noticed a tiny, shimmering blur drop slowly from the sky. Milton wiped his eyes, but the blur—a small bottle, by the looks of it—continued its slow descent, as if it were sinking in a vast, invisible ocean. Whatever was happening, Milton needed to buy a little time.

"Um . . . tell me more about your brilliant plan," Milton said. "How does this all help you, *exactly*?"

Emperor Leo Patrick Napolette studied Milton intently. "Hmm . . . well, at least you are realizing genius when you see it. *Bien,* I'll bite. We—Cleopatra and Napoléon, as vice principals—had physically binding contracts with zhe Powers Zhat Be Evil. And the only way *out* of them was to eliminate childhood altogether."

"How?"

"Now, when a young person dies, they have an *adult* soul—rigid, inflexible, and jaded—and will go either all the way up or all the way down, making Heck obsolete. So with no children and no Heck, there is no contract."

Milton shivered, despite being only a glass-breadth's away from an active volcano. Every moment of his afterlife had been spent plotting ways to shut Heck down. And Napoléon and Cleopatra had figured out a way to do it—a brilliant way, actually—yet at the awful expense of childhood. There was no way he was *ever* going to let that happen.

Milton stared, glassy-eyed, out of the large glass eye. The shimmering bottle floated down, following the coiling tornado of smoke, until it landed gently at the base of the Widow's Veil machine.

The military base convulsed as if having a seizure.

"What is going on?" the emperor cried.

A mountain of rock and dirt, crowned with what seemed to be a wine cellar, materialized in the mouth of the volcano. The clowns dashed off the catwalk just as the bottles met the barrels of baking soda.

"Nothing at all," Milton replied. "Why do you ask?"

A pinpoint of laser light grazed Milton's ticking Pace Taker. Emperor Leo Patrick Napolette drew closer, taking careful, deliberate steps like a panther that didn't want to startle its next meal.

"Zhe Pace Taker . . . an incredible invention."

Milton gulped down the bitter taste of guilt.

"Now every heart beats to zhe same drummer. Everyone is aligned and in step with zhe ministry! And, by controlling a person's internal rhythm, we control a citizen's life right down to the second. *Now* a person knows when their time has run out based on their productivity ratings. The only citizens who must experience the cruel uncertainty of old-fashioned death are prisoners like you and your friends at HAHAHA. . . ."

Milton gripped his chair with his elderly hands.

"And make no mistake, Monsieur Fauster. No matter what happens here"—the emperor's thumb hovered over the deadly button of his golden stopwatch—"your time runs out."

Dr. Einstein considered Marlo with soulful brown eyes.

"Vhat am I doing?" he murmured. "Why would I hurt a little girl?"

Napoléon trained what he thought was *his* mobile mind control device on Dr. Einstein. Marlo leaned into the baffled genius.

"Hey, Doc, just play along . . . Fun-Size over there has the wrong doohickey, so he can't do anything to you. But you can't *act* like you're not under control . . . so grab me."

Dr. Einstein nodded his wild mane of hair and weakly grabbed Marlo around the wrists.

"Oh . . . no . . . please . . . stop!" Marlo protested while working the old man's arms up and down, as if he were a seriously outmoded fitness machine. Suddenly, she broke free and bounded up onto the spinning disk.

Marlo tried to balance herself on the revolving platter. Milton murmured above her.

"The laser light . . . on my Pace Taker. No matter what happens here . . . the emperor's stopwatch . . . your time runs out."

Marlo patted the pockets in her Power Suit.

I don't know what he's yammering about, but the Vee-Pees seem to think it's important, which means it's important for me to stop it. . . .

She pulled out the wool gnome doll she had stolen from St. Nicholas and, jumping, shoved it into Milton's open mouth.

That should do it until I figure out how to get him down from there, she thought. Marlo revolved away from her brother as he neared the end of his groove.

Summoning all of his strength, Milton hurled the chair through the eye-shaped window. Shards of glass rained down below. Emperor Leo Patrick Napolette pressed down hard on his stopwatch, its laser just missing its mark, as Milton leapt into the mouth of the volcano. . . .

Kali and Angelo, locked in the throes of fierce struggle, slammed hard against the side of the massive turntable. The long mechanical arm shuddered. Milton, the pendulous needle, skipped in his time groove.

Milton leapt into the mouth of the volcano. . . . Milton leapt into the mouth of the volcano. . . . Milton leapt into the mouth of the volcano. . . .

★　★　★

Kali threw a brutal punch, but Angelo swiftly ducked the blow. Her blue fists pummeled the side of the turntable and knocked Milton back into his groove.

Milton shook the weird déjà vu from his head as he tumbled into the seething, bubbling chaos below. He was blinded by a flash of white and felt a sturdy, tingling caress. When his sight returned, Milton half wished it hadn't. There he was, jostling atop a column of surging foam rising from the volcano. The walkways twisted and bent like the limbs of a contortionist until they and the Widow's Veil machine were washed away by the gush of angry froth. Seconds later, the pyramid control center was sheared off the side of the volcano's throat.

Just like in science class, Milton thought as he was buffeted about by the volatile chemical marriage of tons of baking soda saying "I do" to gallons of vinegar.

The geyser of foam propelled Milton up over Hekla's crown. A shattered Styrofoam barrel emerged a few yards away from him. He paddled through the cascading froth and clutched onto it for dear life. Up and out, great petals of foam curled around on themselves, with Milton speeding toward the hovering Widow's Veil above.

"Ooomph!" Milton gasped as he slammed into the dense, soot-dark shroud. With brute force, the eruption punched a hole into the Widow's Veil, revealing a vibrant riot of stars gleaming and flickering against the deep velvet of night. A luminous yolk-yellow moon shone with an almost salacious clarity.

"Surprise!" Shirley shouted from a flying Styrofoam barrel a hundred feet away. "We did it! Eventually the Widow's Veil will break apart and humanity can start over again! We won't be around to see it, but hey, so it goes. . . ." She spiraled farther and farther away. "You're always supposed to leave with a joke, so here I go," she yelled. "Two cannibals are eating a clown and one says to the other, 'Does this taste funny to you?'"

With that, Shirley disappeared, her barrel rolling out of sight as she succumbed to the law of gravity: the one law she couldn't manage to break in her wonderfully ludicrous life. His eyes brimming with tears, Milton looked up. A shimmering rainbow trail slowly faded away to nothing. In the distance, he saw what looked like an angel, blazing with light, tearing up the sky. Milton grew light-headed from cold and lack of oxygen until, with a smile carved deep into his leathery face, he let loose his consciousness and slipped deep inside himself, never to see this world again. . . .

★   ★   ★

Angelo grabbed on to the enormous record player and kicked Kali squarely in the chest. The blue goddess was thrown onto her back with the wind knocked out of her. Virgil helped Lyon drag Bordeaux to the wall and then, taking his last weaponized stuffed green pepper, lobbed it at Kali, where it exploded on the Hindu goddess's face.

Angelo clambered onto the turntable and swung up onto the long metal arm extending above the revolving platter. He scrambled across to Milton. "This assignment has gone on for *way* too long," Angelo muttered.

Angelo drew his blade and reached down for Milton's neck. Suddenly, the laboratory shook with a massive shock wave as one of the stone disks, spinning madly out of control, broke free of the colossal now-unbalanced turntable. It crashed onto the floor, breaking into fractured pieces. The blade fell from Angelo's hands.

"Look out!" Virgil cried as he and Frances dragged a frail boy away from one of the machines.

Another stone platter broke free of its groaning mechanical turntable and shattered onto the floor.

Marlo tried to keep her balance as the spiral-grooved disk revolved back to her brother. The glint of something shiny caught her thieving magpie eyes.

"Cool," she said, snatching up Angelo's feather-shaped blade. "I can use this to cut Milton down."

Angelo glared down at Marlo from the machine's

thick metal arm. "Throw that to me, Margot," he said testily. "I'll deal with your brother."

There was something about Angelo's tone and the coldness in his ice-blue eyes that disturbed Marlo.

"I wanna do it," she said, hopping up on the arm and scooting toward her brother. "And it's *Marlo*."

"Right . . . I was just kidding," Angelo said. "Now give it here . . . you'll hurt yourself."

As Angelo reached for the blade, the turntable shook and he tumbled off the arm and revolved away. Kali had hopped up onto the disk and was tromping closer. The disk only had a few yards of groove left, so Marlo went to work slicing through Milton's bonds.

"Gotta do it . . . quick or he's . . . zombie toast," she said between gritted teeth as she sawed through the thick cable binding his feet. Then, with only a foot of groove left before the record ended, Marlo cut her brother free. He fell onto the stone platter. Angelo stalked toward him and grabbed Milton by the neck. Marlo hopped down off the arm, the disk wobbling as it spun faster.

Angelo whispered into Milton's ear. "I'll be quick. You won't feel a—"

The disk broke apart, and they were hurled off the spinning platter and onto the laboratory floor. Marlo was flung alongside Kali, with huge shards of stone smashing to the ground around them.

Angelo rose woozily to his feet, his muscular arm still wrapped tightly around Milton's neck. Dozens of newly hatched mayfly demons swarmed into the laboratory around him and the other fugitive children.

Marlo ran up to Angelo. "Let go!" she shouted.

The brawny boy sighed as the demon guards converged.

"Milton!" Marlo shrieked as she wrested her brother from Angelo's strong grip. "Are you okay?"

Milton blinked, his sister's face plastered with that rarest of expressions—genuine concern—slowly coming into focus.

"*Mmmmrmmphrlooooog,*" he replied, his mouth stuffed with a wool gnome.

"Oh, sorry," Marlo replied as she plucked the spit-soaked dwarf from Milton's mouth.

Milton tilted his groggy head to the side, the floor soothingly cool and solid under his cheek. There, blurry yet intimidating all the same, were Napoléon and Cleopatra, studying him closely. Between the vice principals and a pile of large broken stone disks was a machine—a quill attached to a sort of extendable metal arm—writing down every word that was said. Milton returned his bleary gaze to his sister, his tongue lolling out of his mouth and his eyes rolling back into his head.

"How may I serve?" Milton said as drool trickled down his chin.

Marlo hid her tear-streaked face in her hands. "We were too late!" she sobbed. "My brother's a zombie!"

31 · ALWAYS THE CENTER OF DETENTiON

MILTON STARED BLANKLY at the blank beige walls inside the Board-Stiff-Room, where the mutinous Junior Executives were being held.

Marlo shook her brother by the shoulders.

"Milton? Can you hear me? It's me . . . your sister! *Please* don't be some drooling zombie boy. Mom will kill me!"

Lyon, her pinkie entwined with that of her reunited BFF Bordeaux as they leaned against a wall, made a faint, retching gasp.

"You don't see me, like, all worried about Bordeaux being a zombie or whatever," Lyon said.

"How would we even *know*?" Marlo replied.

The mayfly demons threw Virgil, the last of the

prisoners, to the floor and bumbled out of the room, slamming the door behind them.

Milton blinked and wiped the drool from his chin. "Are they gone?" he whispered.

Marlo smiled a smile so wide that it nearly touched her ears. "Milton! You're back!" she gasped as she crushed her brother in a hug. "What happened? You seemed blanker than a hobo's address book."

Milton scanned the faces of his fellow prisoners. "Who's he?" he asked, staring at Angelo.

Marlo's cheeks went pink. "He's Angelo. He's . . . nobody."

"Thanks," Angelo replied, tugging his black stocking cap over his ears.

"He seems familiar . . . like I've seen him someplace before," Milton replied. "Anyway, I don't want the vice principals to know I'm not some used-up zombie teen."

"Why?" Virgil asked.

Milton drew a deep, shaky breath. "That machine," he managed. "The one I was hooked up to. It connected me to another . . . *me*. Another world. A terrible place that was like the Surface but different in both little ways and really big ways."

"Like an alternate universe?" Virgil asked.

"*Exactly,*" Milton said with a nod. "It puts you inside a different you, but for only one day every decade. Then you live this other life, only really quickly. You get"— Milton shuddered—"*old*. And if the you that you are in this alternative universe dies, then you—the *real* you who's hooked up to the machine—lose a bit of your soul and turn into one of those zombie teens. But—don't ask me, it's complicated—I have to make the vice principals think that *that's* what happened to me."

Virgil leaned toward Milton, sitting cross-legged on the floor. "Okay, then, what was this other world like?"

Milton gave his fellow detainees a breathless recap of his past week: everything from the meteor shower, the Widow's Veil, the French-Egyptian alliance, the clown commandos of HAHAHA, the weird message in a bottle from himself, and the incredible events that led to the destruction of the Hekla volcano base in Iceland while saving the world from shaking itself apart. After a profound silence, Marlo blew a strand of blue hair from her forehead and broke the awkward quietude.

"Milton: I believe you. You wanna know why?"

"Why?"

"Cherry pie," Marlo said with a smirk. "And because . . . well, I think *I* was there, too. For a bit. In that awful, uptight world."

Milton scooted closer to his sister. "Really?"

"Yeah. But just for one day. The whole thing seemed like a dream, though. Or like I was having some fever-baked hallucination in the infirmary after Angelo kissed me at the dance . . ."

Milton shot Angelo a confused look. The boy was staring at Milton intently with his unnerving blue eyes.

"He kissed *you?"*

Marlo scowled. "You yammer on about some freaky French-fried world, then act like it's weird that someone would actually kiss me?"

"It's just that . . . *never mind.* Just tell me what happened."

"Well, I was old but really powerful. Some kind of judge. And Lyon here was my assistant!"

Lyon's jaw fell open. "As if!"

"Totally. I had to pass judgment on Mom and you for acts of treason against the state or whatever."

"So *that's* why I ended up in that mental hospital and wasn't executed!" Milton replied.

"They must have got us mixed up when they put me in the infirmary," Marlo speculated.

Just then, Dr. Einstein opened the door. He looked nervously behind his shoulder as he eased into the Board-Stiff-Room, shutting the door behind him. Milton immediately let his jaw go slack and stared blankly at the wall, as if his entire personality had suddenly gone out to lunch.

"Are you all right, young man?" Dr. Einstein asked as he knelt before Milton.

Milton couldn't help but catch a glimpse of the scientist's wide, soulful eyes. His pupils were large and full of compassion.

"It's okay, Milton," Marlo said. "Ein-stein-with-mein-little-ein here was being controlled by Napoléon. Not so much now thanks to me and my sticky-fingered awesomnosity."

Milton wiped his chin and sighed. "But you made those machines that stuck us into that awful alternative world," he said to Dr. Einstein, looking down at the old man's worn slippers. "They're how Napoléon and Cleopatra destroy childhood. . . ."

Dr. Einstein exhaled a dusty wheeze. "All I can say in my defense is that I vasn't myself," he replied with crumpled sadness. "Vhen I realized that an adult's closed mind made playing the disks dangerous—if not impossible— the vice principals suggested using students. I refused and threatened to disassemble the machines until one night, vhen I vas asleep in my filing cabinet, they surgically implanted *this* device into my head." The scientist tapped his electronic blinders. The red, yellow, and blue lights flashed weakly. "The rest, for me, is rather a blur. . . ."

The old man sighed.

"Right now, the vice principals are poring over the copious notes taken by the Trance-Scriber and are eager to take over the vorld it describes! Once they know the vorld's history, they will lead an expedition to the part of the Undermines vhere the disk was found and—if vhat you said is true—ultimately find its Time Pool and, apparently, destroy childhood. I fear now that it's all only a matter of time."

Time, Milton thought. It was something that he had always taken for granted when he was alive. But now, in the hands of Napoléon and Cleopatra, time was some kind of terrible weapon . . .

But wait, Milton thought. *I know one thing that they don't . . . and that's how it all ends. . . .*

"I was able to do something," Milton murmured. "I saw a boat in the sky . . . and an angel."

"Vhat vas that?" Dr. Einstein replied while Angelo sat up and scooted closer.

"What I mean is that, in this alternate universe, I was able to do something about it, right at the end," Milton explained. "I'm just not quite sure how."

Milton told Dr. Einstein everything: about the tons of baking soda, the Hekla volcano, and the Earth shaking itself apart due to its magma being drained to fuel the Widow's Veil.

"Just as I was about to die," Milton added, "something fell from the sky, and when it hit the volcano, thousands of old wine bottles materialized from nowhere. It created a massive eruption of foam, like a model volcano in science class. It filled the Earth and destroyed the base— and the emperor seemed to know everything that was going to happen *except* that!"

Marlo scrunched up her turned-up nose.

"The wool gnome," she murmured.

"Huh?" Milton replied.

"I stuck it in your mouth because I saw that Trance-Scription machine or whatever taking down everything you were saying. So I shut you up."

Dr. Einstein's bushy white mustache twitched like the whiskers of a curious cat. "You mentioned some boat floating above you in this alternate vorld?" he asked.

Milton nodded. "Yeah . . . I think it was, well . . . *me*. And I, or whoever, dropped a few messages from the sky in these odd bottles . . . like old wine bottles."

"Napoléon's private reserve in the Undermines," Marlo said. "That old wine that tastes like vinegar."

Dr. Einstein nodded. "I vas thinking the same thing . . . all of those bottles, delivered right on cue from one of the Time Pools."

Cue, Milton thought. *Q. Sara had mentioned something about a Q-Bomb back in the mental hospital. Something to do with Einstein . . . something that could clear out a room . . .*

"What's a Q-bomb?" Milton asked.

Dr. Einstein nodded with a rumpled smile. "The Q-Bomb vas a theoretical hobby of mine . . . a vay of transferring matter from one universe to another," he murmured. "Not the most practical invention, as you vould need to place a receiver in the other universe to receive the matter from *our* universe. Regardless, I *did* build a prototype, just for fun."

Dr. Einstein rubbed his chin in contemplation.

"You see, a Q-Bomb or Bomb-bmoB—the vord 'bomb' backward and forward—is like a very, very long cat. You pull his tail in *this* universe and his head is meowing in another. Understand? A quantum bomb operates exactly the same way: You send something from here; they get it there. The only difference is that there is no cat."

The mayfly demon guards buzzed with anxious attention on the other side of the Bored-Stiff-Room door.

"Where is *le docteur* Einstein?" Vice Principal Napoléon roared, like a tiny angry mouse, from outside. "I've been looking for that ingenious *imbécile* for fifty-two minutes and sixteen seconds! I've nearly drained the battery on my iRule device!"

Dr. Einstein hurried to the door. "I have an idea," he whispered. "Something I haven't had in a good long time. I will leave instructions in Dr. Skinner's laboratory. I believe he has the key to unlocking the mysteries of the Time Pools. Go there first thing in the morning. I will keep him occupied. You will know vhat to do. . . ."

Dr. Einstein closed the door and shuffled away. The Junior Executives could hear him talking to Vice Principal Napoléon.

"I wonder what he's got in mind," Virgil asked.

"Well, considering he's got a big mind, I'm sure it's a big idea," Marlo replied.

Angelo bore his blue eyes into Milton, his hands twitching as if they were restless for something to grab on to. Milton wrapped his arms around himself, suddenly uncomfortably cold in the oddly familiar boy's presence.

"What?" Milton asked, unable to endure the maddening prickle of the boy's stare.

"You sort of got us all in a big mess, huh?" Angelo said grimly. "You know, Milton, if you wanted to end it all right here, we'd *totally* understand."

"Angelo!" Marlo yelped. "What are you talking about?"

"I was just . . . kidding," the handsome boy said with a shrug of his broad shoulders. "My sense of humor runs dark. *Ha ha ha . . .*"

Vice Principal Napoléon burst into the Bored-Stiff-Room. "What is zhat horrible sound?" he cried, a scowl plastered across his sickly white face. "Ugh . . . there's nothing worse than zhe sound of a child's laughter. Anyway, I came to tell you *enfants horribles* zhat your punishment has been decided. Tomorrow morning you will go down into the Undermines and locate zhe Fountain of Youth zhat feeds zhe Time Pools, and you will *stay* down zhere until you find it."

"Unsupervised?" Angelo asked, arching his eyebrow in Milton's direction.

"Of course not . . . I will dispatch a team of guards to accompany you and to prevent any . . . *mischief.*"

Marlo squared her jaw in defiance. "Listen, you French-fried lawn gnome—"

Milton clapped his hand over his sister's furious mouth. He could feel her lips forming a number of less-than-civil words. The vice principal glared at Milton down his curved nose.

"The girl should not disrespect the great Napoléon,"

Milton replied in a dull monotone, a trickle of drool running down his chin.

Napoléon's gray-blue eyes rolled as if they were playing Russian roulette. *"Children! Zhe* underworld will be much better off without them!" the vice principal shouted as he slammed the door.

Marlo whipped toward her brother, her eyes sizzling dangerously like just-lit fuses. "Why did you—"

"Don't you see?" Milton said. "Dr. Einstein tricked Napoléon into sending us down there."

"But why?" Virgil asked.

"So we can do what we already did," Milton replied in a spooky murmur. "So we can prevent what has already happened . . ."

Milton and Marlo stole out of their respective Room-and-Boardrooms as the other groggy children were prodded out of filing cabinets by the day's newly hatched demon guards.

"Any idea where Dr. Skinner's laboratory is?" Milton asked. "We've got to get there before the Vee-Pees round us up for our field trip—maybe our last field trip *ever.*"

Marlo stretched. "Well, you said we already *did it,* right? Saved this other world?"

"I guess." Milton shrugged. "But if we don't do it *exactly* the same way, it could ruin everything."

"First things first, Lesser Fauster . . . I think Skinner's lab must be over there somewhere," Marlo said, pointing past some abandoned workstations. "That's where he came from when we took his awful behavior class."

As they walked toward the laboratory, Milton and Marlo heard voices up ahead. They snuck behind a smoldering copy machine that seemed to have choked to death on a paper jam and peered around the corner.

"Solomon . . . or Sol, as I called him, was a man nobody can replace . . . at least not in my heart," Dr. Curie was saying, dabbing away bright green tears.

Doctors Curie and Einstein and another teacher were huddled around a black casket. Soon, a bald, skinny preacher joined them.

"That's Skinner," Marlo said. "The guy with the fivehead."

"Fivehead?"

"You know . . . a really big *fore*head."

"Oh . . . so what's going on?" asked Milton.

"You know, 'Solomon Grundy, buried on Sunday. This is the end, of Solomon Grundy.' C'mon, *everybody* knows that rhyme," Marlo replied with a smirk.

Dr. Einstein spotted the Fausters and quickly put his arms around Doctors Skinner and Curie, positioning them so that their backs were to Milton and Marlo.

"Now, now, Dr. Curie," Dr. Einstein said, glancing over his shoulder at the Fausters and pointing to a nearby boardroom with his eyes. "I'm sure you will find love again . . . first thing tomorrow, actually. . . ."

"Now's our chance," Milton whispered as he and his sister hunkered down and trotted toward the laboratory.

Dr. Skinner's laboratory was nothing more than a messy boardroom that reeked of poorly-cared-for animals forced into cramped cages.

"What are we looking for?" Marlo said.

"I'm not sure," Milton said as he flipped through papers strewn across the boardroom table. "He said we'd know it when we see it. But this place is such a mess. To find what we need in time will take a serious stroke of . . . *Lucky!*"

Milton pulled out a small cage from beneath a chair. He opened the door, but Lucky—his white fur nappy with stress and neglect—reared back and hissed.

"What's wrong, little guy?" Milton murmured. "He usually makes that cute *dook* sound when I reach into his cage, telling me to pick him up. But it's like he doesn't want anything to do with me."

Milton stared into his pet's tiny red eyes. They bubbled with rage like a pair of hot cinnamon Red Hots melting in a microwave.

Marlo put her hand on her brother's shoulder. "You can start by calling him Bueller."

"*Bueller?*"

"Yeah . . . Dr. Psycho changed Lucky's behavior and started with a new name."

Milton noticed a shredded photograph of himself on the bottom of Lucky's cage. It looked as if it had been ripped apart with needle-sharp teeth. Milton noticed something else on the bottom of Lucky's cage, words and numbers written on a freshly soiled piece of paper: 23-15-18-13 EAB.

"A code," Milton said. "Numbers and letters . . . numbers and . . . I got it! The numbers correspond to letters, and the letters correspond to numbers."

"*Obviously,*" Marlo said, her eyes rolling like violet marbles.

"So that would mean it says . . . W-O-R-M. *Worm.* Five-one-two." Milton scratched his brown mop of hair. "That didn't help much," he sighed.

Marlo noticed a stack of jars in the corner. "The worms from the Undermines," she said as she walked over to the two dozen jars of odd, rainbow-tinted liquid, each containing one of the corkscrew worms. "There must be, like, twenty-three squidoos here. . . ."

The jars had strips of white tape stuck to their lids with numbers scrawled across them in black marker.

"This one," Marlo said, carefully removing one of the small jars from the stack. "Five-one-two. And there's a weird little thingie at the bottom."

In a Baggie at the bottom of the jar was a slender device, like an infinity symbol cast of gleaming black metal. Etched on the side was the letter "Q." Marlo tucked the jar into her Power Suit.

"We'd better bolt," she said as Milton headed back to Lucky's cage. Lucky hissed and nipped at Milton's hands as he reached inside the smelly cage. Milton quickly scooped up his brainwashed pet, wincing as Lucky's claws scratched at his forearms. He stuck the wriggling ferret inside his suit, where the animal slowly began to settle down.

"Hopefully you'll remember me, Lucky," Milton muttered sadly as he turned to leave. *"Bueller."*

Milton noticed a small handheld tape recorder on a chair by the door. Compelled to pick it up, he quickly rewound the cassette and played the recording.

"Specimens are numbered based on the areas in which they were discovered," Dr. Skinner droned. *"The specimens, upon capture, were nearly a foot long. Now they are just over eight inches in length. It's as if they—and this is hard to swallow— are aging backward. And the liquid they secrete . . . it's as if it doesn't fully exist in this dimension . . . as if it lives in between dimensions. My experiments putting one specimen into the liquid of another have proved most frustrating, with either the subjects dissolving outright or the specimen—upon its return to its native jar of liquid—becoming seemingly overwhelmed by amnesia, unable to produce its unique spiral pattern. Perhaps this is a way for the specimens to keep to their own temporal territory. . . ."*

Marlo smacked her brother on the arm. "C'mon, we've got to go," she said. "Or else Short Stuff and Queenie walk away with everything."

32 · YOUTH OR CONSEQUENCES

MILTON AND MARLO inched along the lava tunnel on their elbows and knees. The rock looked like burnt chocolate cake. Unfortunately for their legs and arms, it felt more like broken glass.

"You're sure this is the way?" Milton whispered so that the mayfly demons wouldn't overhear.

"Nappy's old vino-to-vinegar vault should be around that corner," Marlo said as they crawled past a cluster of spirals etched into the rock wall.

Lyon's irritating giggle echoed throughout the tunnel.

"Oh, Angelo, *thank you* for helping me over that boulder! You're, like, so strong!"

Marlo rolled her eyes. "Everything she says is just so . . . *hurl*," she muttered, vaguely irritated and confused. The only boy she ever *really* liked was Zane Covington, whom she had first met in Rapacia and later in Fibble, except Marlo had been Milton then. But Angelo had been her first kiss, and there was no redoing your first kiss. She sighed.

Up ahead was a crack in the rock wall. Milton looked inside. His headlamp shone across rows of dusty old wine bottles.

Just like the ones back in the Hekla volcano, Milton thought. *Right before it foamed over like a fizzy Mount Vesuvius.*

"Why are we stopping?" one of the demon guards hissed, jabbing Virgil in the butt with his pitchspork.

"Oww! What did *I* do?" Virgil yelped.

"Bathroom break," Marlo said as she climbed through the fissure in the rock.

"Yeah, we've got to go," Milton said as he followed Marlo into the cavern. "Real bad."

Milton leaned into his sister. "We've got to hide the Q-Bomb somewhere and grab three of these bottles to use for later," he whispered. "I'll stash the bomb while you get the bottles and stow them away."

Marlo nodded. Angelo was carrying a sack of equipment that Dr. Einstein had left in the stagecoach. Marlo helped him tug it through the crack.

"Thanks," he said.

"I didn't want you to accidentally tear it apart as you tried to 'rescue it' from the crack in the wall," Marlo replied.

"There was so much going on," Angelo said. "I was just trying to help your brother. . . ."

Angelo's eyes caught Marlo like a deer in headlights. It was as if he were a big piece of mouthwatering candy, making a convincing argument that he was, in fact, good for you. She broke free of his mesmerizing gaze and looked over at Milton, who was creeping away toward the back of the cave.

Milton stopped and reached inside his pocket for the Q-Bomb. The Baggie was still wet with iridescent goo from the worm jar that Marlo had tucked away in her Power Suit. He removed the slender, surprisingly heavy device. It was shaped like the number eight lying on its side: the symbol for infinity.

Part of this is supposed to be the receiver and the other part the transmitter, but which—

"What have you got there?" hissed the mayfly demon nearest Milton.

"Hey!" Marlo shouted from across the cellar. "One of these bottles is full of honey!" she said, waving a dusty bottle in the air. "And *poo!*"

The mayfly demons swarmed around her. Milton nodded in his sister's direction, then examined the Q-Bomb as he snuck to the back of the cellar. He noticed the word "Bomb-bmoB" written in tiny letters along the slim stem of the device.

bmoB . . . "Bomb" backward. The opposite of a bomb. That must be the receiver.

Milton twisted the Q-Bomb. It came apart in two equal teardrop-shaped pieces. The "bmoB" piece blinked green from a light at the tip of its stem, while the "Bomb" piece flashed red. Milton walked across a patch of silvery sand and placed the "bmoB" piece, the transmitter, into an empty pothole carved into the porous lava wall.

He turned to leave but found that he was now up to his shins in the soft, silvery sand. Milton struggled to step out of the dusty swamp, but the more he tried, the faster he sank.

Quicksand! he yelled in his mind, still not wanting to attract attention to where he'd placed the transmitter but also not wanting to sink any deeper into the Underworld. Now up to his chest, Milton scratched at the chalky dust surrounding him.

"Help," Milton muttered weakly, the sand now up to his shoulders.

Marlo whipped around, her hands full of bottles.

Milton tried to fill his sand-compressed chest full of air for one last yelp, but the sandy grit stifled his cry, as if the sinkhole were trying to kidnap him.

Milton shook the sand from his hair as he rose from the small mountain of twinkling dust. He gazed out at a subterranean plain of silvery mounds that were growing slowly fatter from steady trickles of finely pulverized stone falling from the craggy ceiling a hundred feet above. The cascading grit reminded him of sand falling from an hourglass—*hundreds* of hourglasses—and he felt trapped at the bottom, about to be buried by the passage of time. . . .

"Ooomph!" he gasped as Marlo and the equipment bag fell onto his shoulders, knocking him onto his stomach.

Marlo looked out across the underground valley of silver sandfalls. "Sorry," she said, shaking her blue hair. "Hey, what's that?"

At the bottom of the mound was a round black hat adorned with a scarlet feather. A pair of footprints trailed away from the hat, meandering for several hundred yards before disappearing behind a sparkling hill in the distance.

"Ponce de León was here," Marlo said. "We saw him sink into the quicksand while Napoléon just looked on and laughed."

"Thanks for warning me," Milton replied.

"It seemed to work out okay," Marlo whispered, looking up to the ceiling she fell through. "Maybe he found the Time Pools, and all we have to do is—"

"Follow his tracks," Milton said, rising shakily to his feet atop the mound of sand. "He didn't discover the Fountain of Youth when he was alive. But maybe he did now, in death. Let's find out before the others drop in. . . ."

★ ★ ★

The tracks led them across the sparkling floor of dust and up a gradually swelling hillock. Marlo studied the multicolored grit that crunched beneath her shoes.

"It's like ground-up Rainbow Pony bones," she said.

A sweet-smelling mist tickled Milton's nose. He looked at the top of the glittering mound. Hundreds of tributaries spiraled down the hill, spilling along what looked like Slip 'N Slides. The radiant gushes, surging down like merry streams of melted crayon, disappeared into widemouthed lava tubes perforating the mound of rock. Atop the hill was a gigantic, inflatable fountain cast of bright yellow, blue, and red plastic, where a trio of monstrous fiberglass cupids relieved themselves in strong, steady streams of iridescent water that splashed along the side in arcs of brilliant color.

"*¡Lo encontré!*" squealed a tiny voice in the distance. "I found it!"

Milton squinted up through the kaleidoscopic spray. A light-brown baby splashed in the fountain. The trail of footprints grew more and more chaotic as they wound to the top of the hill, ending in a riot of scuffs and a pile of hastily doffed period clothes.

"Ponce de León," Marlo muttered. "Or *Pipsqueak* León now, by the looks of it. He really did it."

"So *that's* the Fountain of Youth," Milton murmured. "And it seems to be working. . . ."

The explorer's tiny head disappeared behind the inflatable wall of the fountain.

"I *deed* it!" the man-boy cried out, his tiny voice nearly lost in the roar of cascading water. "I am the most famous explorer who ever—" Ponce de León disappeared into nothing.

"Lived, then died, then became younger and younger until he was unborn . . . ," Marlo continued.

Milton and Marlo tromped up the hillock to the fountain. The air was damp, electric, and smelled vaguely of Jolly Rancher candies. Despite the cheery, playful structure ahead, Milton was filled with sadness.

"We can't let them find this," Milton said to his sister.

Muffled voices sounded in the distance.

"It's too late," Marlo replied, glancing quickly over her shoulder. "It's only a matter of—"

"Time . . . yeah, I know. . . ." Milton noticed the gaping lava tube holes in the ground ahead, where the giddy waters coursing from the Fountain of Youth spilled down to rejuvenate the Time Pools.

"But they don't know exactly where *their* Time Pool is," Milton replied with determination, "and what we do to stop all of this from happening. . . ."

"But we don't know either," Marlo replied.

"Maybe . . . not yet. But we have something they don't. . . ."

Milton reached inside Marlo's equipment bag. He pulled out a stick, a string, and the jar holding the corkscrew worm. Tying the string to the stick, he made a little noose. He plucked the wriggling worm from the jar and fit the loop of string around its slimy mid-section. It dangled for a few seconds before suddenly stiffening, as if pointing to a specific lava tube several yards away.

"That way," he said, stowing the worm back into the bag.

Milton and Marlo raced for the tube as the voices grew louder, accompanied by the telltale buzz of mayfly demons. The Fausters hunkered down, then flopped onto their stomachs, plunging into the slick chute, racing faster and faster.

Milton and Marlo climbed atop the equipment bag as they shot down the tube. The sizzle of the bag slicing through the water hissed like fire.

"Here comes a turn," Milton said. "Lean into it."

They skidded up the sides of the lava tube, riding the equipment bag like a toboggan. Milton and Marlo dipped for a few hundred feet, then hit a small, bulbous hump of rock before the lava tube straightened out. They swept along faster.

"Hold . . . on," Milton said between gritted teeth.

Milton and Marlo shot out of one tube—slicing through an arcing fall of water—and hurtled into another lava tube, sloshing along with the surging water rapids. Their knees and palms were scraped raw.

"There's . . . a light," Milton sputtered through the foaming water. "At the end of the—"

Milton and Marlo spilled out onto a marshy bed of

gravel and sand. The buzz of mayfly demons echoed from the other end of the lava tube.

Milton groaned as he rose from the ground. Marlo dumped the contents of the bag onto the oozing loam.

"What are you doing?" Milton asked.

"Just grab the other end," Marlo replied as she stretched the empty bag snugly against the mouth of the lava tube.

With a mighty *whoomp*, the bag was now squirming with angry mayfly demons, buzzing curses that would make a larva blush. Marlo quickly zipped the bag as the demons prodded at the inside with their pitchsporks.

"This should quiet them down," she said as she spun the bag around and around. She abruptly let go, and the bag slammed against the side of the volcanic rock wall.

Marlo walked back to the pile of equipment. "What a load of junk . . ."

Milton knelt down. There were a couple of long, deflated balloons; a piece of mesh with a wide slit in the middle and Velcro on the ends; a couple of collapsible paddles; a long piece of twine; a metal stake; a pad of paper; a pen; three old wine bottles (thanks to Marlo); and the long stick with the wriggling worm tied to the end. Milton saw a scrap of paper that he had nearly missed, partially buried by the sparkling sand. It was a note written in small, perfectly shaped letters on Dr. Einstein's stationery. Marlo leaned over Milton's shoulder as they read the letter.

Mister and Miss Fauster,

It is so _wunderbar_ not to have the blinders on
so I can see and think again with clarity! It is very
important for you not to fall in the Time Pool when
you are dropping the bottles. To fall into the world you
are paddling across would be to allow the memory of
one world to intermingle with the reality of another.
This disturbance will create something new, something
different, and change _everything_. If my theory is
correct, doing so would force the sudden creation
of new timelines, new pools. Remember: focus on the
task at hand!

Glück!
AE

Milton ripped up the note and buried the pieces deep
in the sand. Marlo sighed as she gazed out at magnifi-
cent stalagmites, glittering in all the colors of the rainbow, protruding from a floor of silvery sand.

"There are so many pools," she said weakly. "It's like
trying to find a needle . . . in a grotto full of swirling
Time Pools. I don't even know where we'd begin."

Milton held the stick out toward the pools. The
squirming white worm dangling on the string stiffened
sharply. It pointed resolutely to the left like a long coiling
finger, quivering with what seemed like intense longing.

"How about . . . _that way_?"

33 · A GLiTCH iN TiME SAVES MANKiND?

MILTON AND MARLO kicked off the shore into the shallows. It was like gliding across a blurry liquid television. The two balloons that Dr. Einstein had left them were actually inflatable pontoons that—when lashed together with the Velcro and mesh—formed a small catamaran. Milton had pounded the stake onto the shore and tied the line to it to keep the boat from being dragged away by conflicting currents as they headed out into the pool.

Fresh time sprang forth from the lava tubes, spilling out in radiant surges from the Fountain of Youth, whose gush fed near-infinite tributaries leading out to near-infinite Time Pools.

The corkscrew worm—resembling a long squirming

piece of undercooked pasta—spun in delirious circles as it dangled from the stick.

"It pointed the way here, and now it seems to want to be let go," Milton said. "To swim back home."

Milton freed the worm and flung it into the multi-colored pool. The vast expanse of water, the size of a small inland lake, spread before Milton and Marlo until it was lost in the distance. On all sides were enormous cliffs visible through fleecy wisps of mist.

The catamaran bobbed about playfully in the shallow edge of the curling current. Milton looked down through the wide slit in the mesh. A dash of prickly spray blew into his face, tickling his cheeks.

Through the crest of a ripple, Milton could see a brown-haired toddler trying to make sense of a copy of *Moby-Dick* beneath the shade of a tree.

"It's *me*," Milton mumbled.

Marlo gradually let the line out. Perhaps it was the spray from the Fountain of Youth, but she felt foolishly brave inside, enough to think that two kids could prevent a world from being adulted out of existence.

"This must be the child's end of the Time Pool," Marlo said as she gazed out across the colorful water. "Guess we don't need our floaties here, huh?"

The lagoon became cloudy with gray soot that grew progressively darker as Milton and Marlo drifted out.

"The Widow's Veil," Milton said. "It started when I was eleven."

The catamaran rocked back and forth as choppy waves slapped against the pontoons. Milton lay on his stomach and peered through the slit. Looking down at his alternative self was like gazing into a mirror and seeing what you looked like with your eyes closed. The other-Milton was older than Milton was now but not by much, picking at a pimple on his chin in the bathroom, then flexing his muscles in the mirror.

"We've reached adolescence," Milton said.

"Ooh . . . what am I doing?" Marlo said. "Am I a raging drop-dead gorgeous storm of unchecked hormones?"

Milton stared down at a serious, teenage Marlo wearing a drab gray uniform and studying in a grim library.

"Not exactly."

The flow of time deepened and coursed with a sort of hectic purpose. Milton stuck his face in the Time Pool. Through the dreary gray smear of the Widow's Veil, he could see himself in the Senegal desert, quickly rebuilding the homes that his fellow Habitat for Inhumanity volunteers had dismantled.

"We're in adulthood now," Milton said.

"Then you'd better get busy writing your first note," Marlo said as the rope grew taut, the Time Pool gaining power and strength.

My first note, Milton thought desperately as he reached inside the inner pocket of his Power Suit for a pen. *What if I can't remember what I—*

Lucky bit his hand.

"Oww!" Milton cried as he snatched back his hand. "Bad . . . *Bueller*. At least you're safe," Milton whispered, leaning in to kiss the restless lump in his coat.

He tore a page from Dr. Einstein's notepad and tried to remember, exactly, what he had first written himself. He closed his eyes and pictured the note.

Escape tonight, just before midnight. Requisition as much baking soda for Hekla as possible.
—Milton Fauster (You, later)

Milton dashed down the words before the image faded.

"Quick, write the other one, too!" Marlo said as she struggled against the pull of the line. "I can barely keep us put!"

Milton closed his eyes and tried to envision the second note that fell from the sky. Suddenly, it appeared in his mind, fully formed. Milton furiously jotted down the note before it fled from his memory.

He grabbed Napoléon's old wine bottles, uncorked them, and let the spoiled wine spill over the side of the catamaran. He rolled up the notes and tucked them inside the bottles.

"Time Torpedo One," he muttered as he set the first bottle on the mesh.

Milton plunged his head into the Time Pool. He could see his alternative self being dragged out of an ambulance and through the Hôpital pour les Malades Mentaux Criminels et Enfantin courtyard.

"It should be coming up soon," Milton said as he grabbed the first bottle. "One . . . two . . ."

Suddenly, the catamaran lurched to a violent stop. Marlo fell to her knees as the line was tugged from her grasp.

"My hands!" she shrieked. The thin rope unspooled swiftly on the deck of the makeshift boat. Marlo quickly grabbed the end and tied it around her waist. Milton's message in a bottle rolled across the mesh and smacked alongside the other two bottles.

Marlo looked out across the swirling Time Pool. There, heaving the catamaran to shore, was Angelo.

"What's he doing?" Milton asked with mounting alarm.

"Hey, Angelo!" Marlo yelled. "Let go of the rope!"

Angelo continued to reel them in, his intense gaze locked on the boat like twin blue lighthouse beams.

"Um . . . he must not be able to hear me yelling," Marlo said. "There's only one thing to do then: untie me."

Milton nodded and quickly untied the knot around Marlo's waist. Angelo gave one last yank and, with the catamaran now unbound, fell onto his back. The boat abruptly sped toward the center of the Time Pool, fishtailing as it skipped across the currents. Marlo squealed.

"We're free"—the Fausters hurtled toward a round

abyss at the center of the pool where the flow of time spilled down into deep, dark nothingness—"king *doomed*," Marlo continued.

The catamaran shimmied from side to side as it was caught in the unstoppable surge.

"Our time isn't up yet," Marlo said as she grabbed an oar. "Quick, *paddle!*"

Milton grabbed the other oar and rowed furiously. Their oars whipped the liquid time around them into a sparkling rainbow froth. "Okay . . . we're creeping back to where we were. Are you ready?"

Milton grabbed the first bottle and nodded. He plunged his head down into the Time Pool and could see himself entering the mental hospital's courtyard for the first time.

"Just about there," he said. "Try to keep us in this spot for as long as you can."

"Um, Milton?" Marlo said uncertainly. "I . . . I think I might have been touched by an angel at the dance."

"*What?* C'mon . . . this isn't a joke. Just try to—"

"Angelo," Marlo said with a quaver in her voice. "He's coming. And he's either got wings or really freaky shoulder blades. . . ."

"What are you talking—" Milton said as he pulled himself out of the Time Pool, wiped the tingling Technicolor goo off his face, and gasped.

Angelo glided toward them with great silver wings— gently beating pinions feathered with sharp, savage blades—extended proudly from the back of his shredded Power Suit. His face was set tight with determination and pain, as if the act of taking to the air was labored agony. Angelo's eyes, trained intently on Milton, left no question as to whom he wished to transfer that agony.

"He's the angel," Milton finally managed once he remembered how to breathe. "The one I saw floating above when I was down there. I saw . . . *this*. From the ground, he seemed hopeful. I mean, what's more encouraging and uplifting than the sight of an angel?"

Marlo swallowed. "He doesn't look like something you'd put on the top of a Christmas tree."

Marlo stabbed the Time Pool with her paddle, using it as a rudder to steer them back to where they had been.

"Focus, Fauster, focus!" Marlo said. "Drop the first bottle. *Now*. Before flyboy clips us with those nasty wings of his."

Milton plunged his head back under the surface. He saw himself outside in the hospital courtyard, with the nurse yelling something that made the patients shuffle back inside. Milton flung the bottle as hard as he could. It looped softly downward until it landed just behind Milton's alternative self.

Milton gasped for air.

"One . . . down," he sputtered, choking on the stinging, almost gelatinous fluid. "Two more . . . to go . . ."

He snatched the second bottle. Marlo leaned into her oar and fought against the rush of the current.

Milton could see smudges of bright, nervous light crisscrossing the darkness below.

Klieg lights from the guard towers, Milton thought. *I'm escaping. Right now!*

But they were drifting away. *Fast.*

"Stay on target," Milton ordered.

"He's too close!"

"Stay on target!"

Milton sucked in so much air that he thought his lungs would burst and plunged his head back under. He could see an old man racing toward a tall fence garnished with gleaming barbed-wire. The old man leapt into the air . . .

Now! Milton thought as he hurled the bottle downward. His alter ego, readying his desperate jump over the fence, tripped backward over the bottle.

Milton yanked his head out of the Time Pool, choking on the electric glitter sludge.

"Milton," Marlo said spookily, her blue hair flapping like a flag for some creepy Goth-girl country. "We've got company. . . ."

Angelo hovered a few yards away from the catamaran, the beating of his wings ruffling Milton's goopy hair. His blade-feathers scraped against each other, sounding like an army of knights casually sharpening their swords.

"So, um . . . are you a good angel?" Marlo asked.

Angelo smiled, casting a cold, radiant light that left

Marlo feeling dazed and empty inside, as if she were a cobra mesmerized by a particularly charming snake charmer.

"What do *you* think?" he said with a smirk.

"Mom told me about boys like you, though she never mentioned the whole 'knives for wings' part," Marlo replied.

"Most bad boys keep their knives on the *inside*," Angelo said. "As an angel, or *fallen* angel to be more precise, I have the decency to spread my heavy metal wings for all to see . . . usually the *last* thing they see."

The catamaran revolved slowly in the surge. The boat was caught in a dotty eddy addling the gray murky water toward the end of the tightly coiling current.

We're caught in old age, Milton thought, looking over his shoulder. The Time Pool disappeared a hundred feet away and emptied into the gulping, pitch-black maw, spraying the air with its last breath.

"Why?" Milton said simply, against the roar.

Angelo trained his sharp, predatory gaze upon Milton. "I'm not at liberty to disclose such information to a target," he replied.

"Target?" Milton and Marlo said in unison.

"Jinx," Angelo said as he reached back over his shoulder and, with a wince, plucked a long, gleaming blade from his wing. "Yes, you, Milton Fauster, are my target. And *finally,* there are no witnesses. . . ."

"Um . . . what about me?" Marlo said.

"Okay . . . there *won't* be any witnesses," Angelo clarified, twirling the razor-sharp feather in his hand.

"Why not just let us disappear down here in the Undermines?" Marlo asked. "It's not like we're ever going to find our way out of here."

"That's how a human might do things," Angelo said with disdain. "Sloppy . . . open-ended. But not me. After an assignment, I trap the target's last breath in a vial as proof of completion." Angelo removed a small glass container from his pocket.

"Trust me: all of my brother's breaths are vile," Marlo said. "Can't he just breathe in it and you let us go?"

Angelo beat his wings, rising in the air, casting a dark shadow over Milton. Milton felt like prey that didn't have a prayer.

"Cheaters never prosper," Angelo said as he raised the blade over his shoulder.

Suddenly, a lasso wrapped around the boy's massive wings and was tugged tight. Angelo fell into the water.

"Yee-to-the-haw!" Virgil yelled from the shore, pulling the rope that he had fashioned into a makeshift lariat.

Marlo squealed with delight. "How did you *do* that?" she shouted.

Virgil shrugged his rounded shoulders as Lyon and Bordeaux staggered behind him.

"I'm from Texas," he yelled with a slight drawl. "Guess it's in my blood."

Angelo struggled in the Time Pool and dragged Virgil into the shallows.

"Help!" he cried as Bordeaux, then, reluctantly, Lyon joined him at the edge of the water and pulled.

Marlo slashed at the pool with her paddle.

"We've got to leave Angelo to them. Is the Q-Bomb ready?"

Milton checked the half-infinity-shaped receiver in his pocket. "Yeah, I just need another bottle," he said.

"Okay, I'll grab it. You see where we are."

Milton plunged his head into the surging, prickling liquid. Down below, he could see his alter ego wasting away in his prison cell at the Hekla volcano military base. Milton came back up and gasped for breath, wiping away the rainbow goop from his face.

"We've got to get closer to the edge," he said to Marlo. "Right to the edge of death . . ."

"Cheery," Marlo said as she paddled furiously. She noticed the last wine bottle rolling on the mesh. "Let me get the bottle. . . ."

Angelo shredded the lasso tied around him with his razor-edged wings. He flapped with furious beats and closed in on Milton and Marlo.

Milton peered through the slit at the bottom of the catamaran. He could see his ancient, alternate self being led onto the catwalk lining the mouth of the Hekla volcano.

So close, he thought.

Marlo grabbed the bottle of spoiled wine as Angelo fluttered closer. The fallen angel took off his black stocking cap and tossed it aside. Marlo winced and gasped. Hovering over the boy's head was a flaming halo.

Angelo grabbed hold of the sizzling ring. He drew his arm back across his chest, cocked his wrist, and flung the hoop of fire at Milton's neck.

"No!" Marlo shrieked as she reached across the catamaran and snatched the flaming halo from the air. She screamed in pain as the fire burned her hand.

"No one steals a kiss from me!" she yelled before uncorking the wine bottle with her mouth. "*I'm the one who steals things!*"

She took a huge mouthful of Napoléon's wine and spat it out at Angelo. "And here's your ring back!" she yelled as she tossed the burning halo back at Angelo. He grabbed it, confused, as fire spread out across his chest. Marlo took another deep swig of wine and sprayed it at the hovering angel.

"*We're breaking up!*"

The blast of alcohol fed the fire and Angelo was soon engulfed in flame.

"Aaaaarrrggghh!" he screamed, flailing in the air.

Marlo tossed the empty bottle to her brother. Milton pressed the flashing green button on the "bmoB" receiver piece of the Q-Bomb and dropped it into the bottle.

"It's now or forever," Marlo said, kneeling and sticking her smoldering hand in the Time Pool.

Milton stuck his head underneath the surface, which, thankfully, drowned out Angelo's screaming. Shirley Eujest and the rest of HAHAHA were out on the catwalk, along with the hundreds of barrels of baking soda.

I must be in the eye of the pyramid with the emperor, Milton thought as he spied the ministry's control center protruding from inside the volcano. He positioned the bottle over the volcano's soot-belching vent and let it drop.

Milton pulled his head out of the pool and gasped for air.

"I did it!" he yelled as the catamaran rushed toward the empty black center of the Time Pool. Marlo whipped the water into a froth with her oar.

"We can't . . . outpaddle time," she gasped, sweat plastering her blue bangs to her forehead.

Milton grabbed the other oar and paddled as hard as he could.

Below, Milton's quantum-message-in-a-bottle-tossed-into-an-ocean-of-time hit its mark. The Q-Bomb detonated with an odd, muffled boom, followed by a great whooshing *moob.* The tremendous vault of rock around them trembled. In the distance, beyond the shore, behind Virgil, Lyon, Bordeaux, and the lava tubes, the volcanic rock shimmied and swayed like a humongous hula dancer made of dark, sparkling stone. The glittering rock wall fell in on itself, cascading down in jagged shears, with huge patches of stone in the distance disappearing in rippling waves.

Suddenly, a great swell of time liquid bulged at the inner rim of the Time Pool. The surface of the small whirling ocean turned white with foam.

"The bomb!" Milton yelled. "The sudden change in mass displaced the time liquid, creating a heavy surge—"

"English, please, Brainiac," Marlo replied.

"The big boom made a wave," he replied as the catamaran was lifted up by the enormous, cresting swell. "Hopefully it will wash us away from—"

Angelo, still flaming in patches, darted toward them. "—danger."

As the screaming and smoldering angel sped closer, another sound gurgled from the churning depths. The surface of the water grew brighter until, like a glistening white leviathan, out shot a gargantuan corkscrew squid, blinking its angry floodlight eye. The sound it made was so horrible that Milton couldn't possibly imagine how it was created: an infuriated, mewling noise that seemed to come from everywhere at once.

The creature snatched up Angelo with one of its sawtooth tentacles and dove back into the Time Pool.

A shower of stalactites fell from the rock ceiling as Milton and Marlo straddled their inflatable pontoons, held tight to one another's hands, and were hurled out upon a tidal wave of time.

34 · THE KiDS
AREN'T ALL RiGHT

THEIR HANDS BLOODIED, their lungs burning, Milton and Marlo climbed the sheer, treacherous fracture cleaved into the rock by the sudden quantum transport of thousands of tons of dirt and stone, ejected from the bowels of one dimension and thrust into another.

Geysers of time shot into the air. The rock cliff was slick with it. The orange-brown smog of Precocia loomed overhead.

"We're almost there," Milton grunted. "Once we're back up at the entrance of the Undermines, we can make a break for it."

Milton ached as he pulled himself up and over the lip of the newly formed volcanic bluff.

"Phew . . . we're"—Milton found himself sitting on

the overly manicured path winding toward the oppressive upside-down pyramid—"right back in Precocia," he said with a hopeless, weary sigh.

He helped Marlo up, tugging on her non-flaming-halo-burned hand. Thick rainbow jelly from the Time Pools sloshed all over the grounds. A hundred feet away, a manhole cover shot into the air like a spit wad out of a straw. Virgil, Bordeaux, and Lyon clambered out, gasping for breath.

The elevator at the base of the upside-down pyramid dinged.

Out poured a fresh swarm of mayfly demons, followed by Dr. Skinner, William the Kid, and Dr. Curie, cradling the newly reborn Solomon Grundy in her arms.

The ground trembled as the soil shifted unsteadily beneath Precocia, its volcanic foundation suddenly hollowed out for miles beneath. Vice Principals Napoléon and Cleopatra strutted purposefully out of the elevator, surveying the situation with a mixture of disgust, alarm, and a knowing satisfaction, as if they were witnessing a tragedy that they had somehow seen coming.

Milton broke out in a cold sweat.

"We've got to make a break for Childhood," Milton said, tilting his head toward the WELCOME TO CHILDHOOD sign written in Lite-Brite pegs in the distance. "Pretend you're taking me there because, you know, I'm supposed to be a zombie."

Marlo nodded and quickly shot to her feet, dragging

her brother with her. They rushed toward the cul-de-sac, blocked off by a cheerful, primary-colored gate. Milton and Marlo crossed an awkward, buckling bridge of rope and planks marked ADOLESCENT ARCHWAY and clambered up and over the gate, hopping onto the flooded streets of Childhood with a double splash.

Through the gate's colorful bars, Milton and Marlo watched Virgil, Bordeaux, and Lyon run toward them. A team of mayfly demons quickly overcame Lyon and Bordeaux and dragged them both, squealing and kicking, back to the vice principals. Virgil, halfway across the squeaky, unsteady Adolescent Archway, turned and stared at Precocia. The ugly upside-down pyramid of concrete and steel quivered precariously. Soon he, too, was besieged by demon drones and hauled away across the synthetic grass.

Milton and Marlo turned and sloshed through the puddles past houses and structures that became more haphazard, more colorful, and somehow more childlike with every step.

Kali stormed out of the elevator and strode across the AstroTurf toward Childhood. She flexed her four strong blue hands.

"We'd better run faster," Marlo said, looking over her shoulder.

"From what?"

"From super-Kali's tragic grip on kids who are precocious."

Milton eyed the angry Hindu goddess. "Yeah, you're right . . . even though the sound of it is something quite atrocious. . . ."

They were soon up to their waists in glittering, multicolored sludge. The tingling liquid sloshed against the play structures.

Just then, great geysers of high-pressure time burst through Childhood. Patches of ground gave way. The pool around them drained to a wide, shallow puddle. Kali and the demon guards marched on, drawing nearer.

The grim, upturned pyramid of Precocia creaked and quivered and, with a weary sigh of strained steel, listed to one side.

Marlo squealed with delight.

"It's going to—"

Suddenly, small jets protruding from the hindquarters of four gargoyles stationed at the corners of the building's immense roof flared to life and, with a brusque roar, righted the structure. A squeal of feedback slashed through the brief, stunned silence.

"There is no way you grubby, insolent children can win," Cleopatra growled through a megaphone. "Time is a snake consuming its own tail . . . an endlessly turning wheel. With each revolution, the fortunes reverse, and the world will, once again, know the supreme authority of Cleopatra and Napoléon!"

The ground buckled, fracturing in a honeycomb of cracks. Milton could see Napoléon remove his mobile mind control device from inside his military coat. Dr. Einstein robotically shambled to his side. Napoléon took the megaphone from Cleopatra.

"Did you think we would not find out about Dr. Einstein?" He chuckled as he headed across the grounds. "Now, enough with zhis foolishness: it's time for your interrogation, where we will know all zhere is to know about zhe mysterious Undermines!"

Marlo swatted Milton's shoulder. "C'mon . . . we've gotta bolt for the wall!" she shrieked as she hopscotched across the fractured ground toward the cul-de-sac of cribs at the beginning of Childhood.

Dr. Skinner took the megaphone from Vice Principal Napoléon. "Bueller!" the man shouted in his flat, emotionless voice. *"Attack!"*

Lucky squirmed violently inside Milton's Power Suit. With a fierce scrabble of claws and teeth, he tore through the mustard-colored fabric.

"Lucky!" Milton gasped as he stared at his panting ferret. Lucky's eyes blazed hot pink and shiny with blind rage.

Lucky was deeply confused. He wanted to nuzzle the boy's warm, salty neck. But he also wanted to sink his fangs into that neck until he punctured it clean through.

"Attack!"

Lucky convulsed and reared back, as if to strike. Suddenly, the ferret went limp in Milton's arms.

"Lucky!" Milton cried as he cradled his lifeless pet. "No! You can't be—"

Marlo grabbed Milton by the shoulders. "Zombies don't cry," Marlo said.

Shaken, Milton handed Lucky's inert body to Marlo. She tucked him inside her Power Suit while another manhole cover popped from the ground. Out climbed Angelo, his blue eyes brimming with fury as he wiped steaming white entrails from his filthy suit.

Milton and Marlo ran toward the soaring brick wall enclosing Precocia, with the brightly colored play structures becoming playpens, then cribs. With each step, they found it harder and harder to walk, until finally they were forced to crawl on their hands and knees like babies. Milton gazed up at the top of the wall. He had no idea how they would scale it, but they had to try. Milton tried to call out to his sister, but all that came out was . . .

"Goo-goo."

Suddenly, two ladders fell onto the top of the imposing brick wall from the other side. A snarling demon beast with a pushed-in mastiff face poked its head from one ladder while Principal Bubb reared her rearlike head from the other.

"I should have known," she sneered with a twist of her thin gash of a mouth. The principal looked out across the devastation.

"And I *did* know, obviously, which is why I'm here, catching you red-handed trying to destroy Precocia!"

But Napoléon and Cleopatra are plotting to destroy childhood and make Heck obsolete! Milton screamed in his mind, but all that came out through his numb, clumsy lips was "goo-goo," followed by a gush of warm drool.

"Baby talk will not get you out of this mess, Mr. Fauster," the principal said as more of her demon guards joined her atop the wall. "In no uncertain terms, you are surrounded. I'm mad as Heck and I'm not going to take it anymore! Whatever is left after Vice Principals Napoléon and Cleopatra punish you is *all mine.*"

The ground shook apart around Milton and Marlo, the fissures growing wider and deeper, until they found themselves perched atop a precarious column of rock as tall as an office building. Thousands of feet below, Milton could see the black center of a Time Pool just beneath them, the surge of life cascading down into the depths of death.

He and his sister were surrounded on all sides, without any tricks up their polyester sleeves. Milton and Marlo stared down, sighed, and held hands in sympathy before making an Olympics-worthy leap of faith into the angry gush below. . . .

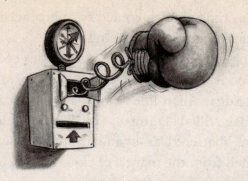

35 · TiLL DEPTHS
DO US PART

MILTON'S LUNGS FELT like they were stuffed tight with jellyfish. He choked in the darkness, until the cool liquid caress became a hot sticky clench that smelled of copper, sweat, and fear. A muffled explosion . . . a shimmering crash . . . a sudden chaotic gush of noise flooded his consciousness. Milton's eyes shot open.

Beneath him he could see . . . *himself.* Covered in blood. His hand clasped tight on Sara—not the dotty old mental patient, but the preteen girl, screaming and bleeding, as Milton held her dangling above the Dumps. Snivel trembled beyond, welling like a glass teardrop, hanging morosely from its cloak of clouds.

It's me, Milton thought as he bobbed in the murky liquid, watching the monks of the Moanastery drag him, Sara, and Sara's conjoined twin brother Sam up to the balcony. *Back outside of Snivel . . .*

Gaping wounds puckered out the sides of Sam's and Sara's bloody Arcadia Gr8 G4m3rz uniforms, slashed open by Edgar Allan Poe's runaway pendulum. Across the garbage-filled Dumps, Snivel's pendulous glass enclosure shattered as it and its manic, secret twin Arcadia fell from the mantle of cloud.

I must have fallen through the center of a Time Pool, down into someplace even deeper . . . down into an afterlife pool. . . .

A team of leathery, bat-faced goat demons marched onto the balcony. Rising up onto his hind legs, the team commander trotted to a halt before the Fausters.

This is where we get the subpoena . . . the order to appear at the Trial of the Millennium: The State vs. Satan. . . .

Suddenly, Milton was swept away by the current of events. He tumbled head over heels in the thick, prickly liquid as people and places streaked past him, ultimately settling in the Provincial Court of Res Judicata where Judge Judas presided.

"Milton and Marlo Fauster!" a tall, festering demon bailiff with an eagleish head clamped down onto his shoulders bellowed. "You're the next contestants on *Holding Court with Judge Judas!*"

"No further questions," Johnny Cockroach, the prosecuting attorney, said as he skittered back to the plaintiff's table.

Satan was escorted from the stands by two burly demon guards.

Algernon Cole, the recently-dead-but-knee-deep-in-denial lawyer, approached the bench in his khaki shorts and Birkenstocks.

"Algernon Cole?" the other Milton below said.

The ponytailed lawyer grinned and held open the tiny door to the witness stand. "Milton! So nice to see you again—alive and well—even if all of this is just a crazy, crazy dream!"

Milton hovered above the courtroom as Marlo and his other self gave their testimony. It was like watching a plasma-screen television installed at the bottom of a swimming pool filled with Vaseline, with someone sitting on the remote, making the image fast-forward in fits and starts.

"It says here, Miss Fauster, that you worked for Satan as a production assistant. . . . Actually, that was me. . . . Annubis—the dog god—switched my soul with my sister's back in h-e-double-hockey-sticks . . . but Annubis switched us back after Fibble was flooded with liquid truth . . . as a production assistant, it was one of my jobs to review submissions to the network. One show I reviewed was called *The Man Who Soldeth the World* . . . about someone selling the Earth to aliens and evicting all of humanity. . . ."

Wow, it sounds even crazier looking down on it all now than it did then, Milton thought as he floated in the multi-colored goo of time. *And that's really saying something.*

"And I saw a napkin on his desk in one of the episodes. It had 'Revelation twelve-seven' written on it, which mentions a war in heaven, led by . . ."

The Milton down below in the witness stand stood up, pointing at the archangel Michael. "Him!"

Judge Judas, a hawk-nosed man with a coiling beard, rubbed his hands together. "Just when I thought our ratings had flatlined, here comes someone with paddles shouting, 'Clear!'" the jaded judge exclaimed.

Milton sighed with a gurgle as he floated above the courtroom. He saw the arrogant archangel Michael take the stand and confess to the heretofore unspeakable crime of attempting to incite the Apocalypse and selling the world to extraterrestrials and banishing all of humanity to a miserable planetoid in the Sirius Lelayme system. Milton felt trapped, watching a movie that he had seen before, rushing toward a totally irritating ending.

The lights dimmed and Judge Judas was bathed in a spotlight. Syrupy violins poured out of the court's speaker system.

"I hereby decree that Satan be removed from his post and serve, instead, at the holy side of the Big Guy Upstairs," the judge declared, speaking directly to the camera. "That leaves a gaping hole in the gaping hole that is down here. So, I can think of no better, oddly poetic punishment than to have Michael rule in your stead."

He smacked his gavel hard, sending a shot put disk

up a small pole on his bench to the very top, cleaving the bell in two.

"Justice is served!" Judge Judas roared.

The other Milton and Marlo were led out of the courtroom, with Principal Bubb clacking beside them.

"You Fausters are *far* too big for your britches," the principal said.

"Britches?" Marlo mumbled below. "What are—"

"Which is why I'm sending you insufferably precocious brats to—"

"Precocia!" Judge Judas ruled with a bang of his gavel.

Milton sighed as he floated just above the ceiling.

Precocia. *And me, stuck here, forced to watch it play out all over again like a summer rerun. Injustice after injustice . . . with no way of switching the channel . . .*

Milton, floating in the glittering goo, felt himself almost magnetically drawn to his alter ego. He was yanked along in the other Milton's wake, like a balloon sucked into a draft.

Dr. Einstein said it was dangerous for me to be here . . . for there to be two Miltons in one reality. That I would create something new, something different . . .

Milton's other self was now being led with Marlo into a marble-floored lobby. He paddled hard to keep his distance.

"I want to see my lawyer!" the other Milton shouted below as the bat-faced goat demon gripped him by his wrists.

My lawyer, Milton thought as he was pulled closer to himself. *That reminds me of something . . .*

"It's interesting, this . . . place," Algernon Cole said with a wobble of his graying ponytail. "It seems that everything here is governed with rules, more so than in the land of the living. It's like they actually, physically hold it all together. Which reminded me of your case and a little loophole I believe I found that could—"

Milton stopped paddling and looked down upon Algernon Cole.

That's right! It's all coming back to me! The first time I was here, Algernon Cole mentioned a loophole, but I didn't get the chance to pursue it. Now I can!

Although he was starting to run out of breath, Milton paddled closer . . . closer . . . *too* close. Suddenly, he felt himself caught in the undertow of his other self. He kicked hard but was no match for the magnetic pull. In one great gush of noise and light, he popped into the other Milton's body.

I'll just get my information, then break free, Milton thought, his borrowed body coursing with overwhelming sensations.

"Mr. Cole!" Milton gasped breathlessly as he swayed in the hall, fighting the urge to swim. "The loophole! Is there something we can exploit to get out of here?"

A team of security demons grabbed Algernon Cole by the shoulders.

"Quick, before they take us to Precocia!" Milton yelped. "Is there—"

"Precocia," Algernon Cole replied, shrugging off the demon guard's talons. "I remember reading about that place. I don't think it really holds up, legality-wise."

"What do you mean?"

"Well, it's a facility that treats minors—i.e., children—like adults for the supposed 'crime' of children merely *acting* as adults: something that society *itself* is pressuring these poor children to do. This crime of normal adulthood is not, in itself, a crime, though. As Precocia would have it, adulthood is a crime if it is perpetrated by a child, which is exactly what these children are not permitted to be during the course of their punishment—"

Milton began to grow dizzy.

I'm running out of air. I don't have much time. . . .

"Are you saying there's a way out of Precocia . . . legally, I mean?"

The pair of brawny, molting demons—with their hooked bills and scowling yellow eyes—dragged Algernon Cole away.

"Oww!" he squealed. "Easy, legal eagles . . ."

Algernon Cole's Birkenstocks squeaked along the floor.

"Wait, Mr. Cole!" Milton shouted. "About Precocia!"

The wiry middle-aged man struggled in the eagle demons' unrelenting grasp. "Yes . . . a minor could disaffirm or renounce that kind of contract," he grunted.

"But it's more than that. Precocia in itself *shouldn't exist at all here*. It doesn't make sense. . . ."

The guards heaved Algernon Cole around the corner.

"Can you get us an appeal?" Milton shouted. "Or make a case for Precocia being legally shut down?"

"I will try!" the lawyer said, his voice a gauzy echo in the distance. "They used to call me the 'worm' back in community law school . . . always able to *worm* my way through some legal obstruction. . . ."

The goat-bat demons shoved Milton and Marlo toward the exit. Principal Bubb was outside by the stagecoach, fuming as she clutched her smoldering ear.

Worm, Milton thought. *That seems familiar. . . . I remember something about memory . . . and worms . . . about how the worms came down with amnesia when they went from one Time Pool to another. . . . Each one of them must hold the memory of its own unique time. . . .*

Growing dizzier, Milton fought to leave his borrowed body. He imagined—as hard as he could—himself floating upward. After a few seconds, he began to tingle and feel slightly out of phase with himself. It was similar to how he had felt upon his return to the Surface after his first death when his soul, robbed of its etheric energy, lost its grip on his body.

Finally, he rose up and out of his other self, just before the other Milton was thrown into the carriage. Below, Milton saw the angel Gabriel stare at him as he floated above the stagecoach, his gray-blue eyes wide and unnerved, his mouth hanging slightly open in incomprehension.

Uh-oh, Milton thought, kicking as hard as he could. *It's like he can see me.*

Milton swam upward, the courthouse disappearing beneath him. He saw a shape floating a few hundred feet away. Milton swam hard toward the figure as his mind went blurry around the edges from oxygen deprivation.

Marlo . . . must grab her . . . must . . .

Milton's consciousness was emptying faster than a leaky water balloon.

We'll forget what happened once we leave this Time Pool. Like we did back in that grotto, where I used sign language . . . telling us we had to do it again . . .

A white worm wriggled past Milton. It was almost two feet long. After considering Milton with its tiny headlamp eye, it swam upward. The creature flicked its tail, beckoning Milton to follow.

. . . and they age backward *in time! That's it! When they're young and big, they swim in the Time Pools and memorize every current. . . . I know what we've got to do . . . to make sure we don't forget . . .*

Milton's mind went as blank as a freshly scrubbed chalkboard.

36 · OUT THROUGH THE iN DOOR

THE ONLY THOUGHT in Milton Fauster's baffled head that seemed to make any sense at all was that nothing around him made any sense at all. He had a sinking feeling that he was floating . . . or a floating feeling that he was sinking . . . and that something terrible had just happened, something that he couldn't prevent but had *tried* to prevent, right up to the very end until it had proved unpreventable.

Milton was dizzy, nauseous, and utterly confused.

He also happened to be drowning.

Milton was thoroughly submerged in goopy, luminescent water that glimmered with ghostly faces and the shimmering blur of moments. He kicked against the gurgling images and up toward a softly glowing constellation of green lights hovering above.

Milton shot to the surface of a vast lagoon. It flowed inward like a coiling river. The sky was an expansive ceiling of volcanic rock coated with clumps of bright, phosphorescent moss. Milton coughed up a gush of Technicolor goo, as if he had inhaled an electric rainbow trout that had choked to death on crayons.

He paddled to the shore against the surging undertow, his hands oddly stiff, and heaved himself up onto the sparkling sand.

Milton gazed with dumb wonder at his remarkable surroundings. He was inside a spacious underground grotto—at least a half mile across—with twinkling cascades of liquid tumbling from the rock roof feeding the massive, churning pool. Milton noticed that his hands were rigid. His right hand was cupped toward him and seemed to want to connect with his mouth.

Sign language for "eat"? Milton thought as he noticed his left hand, flattened, like it was caught in a handshake. The index finger on his right hand started to wriggle, as if wanting to squirm across his left palm.

"Sign language for 'worm'?" Milton muttered. "Eat . . . *worm*? What could that possibly—"

A splash and a gasp grabbed Milton's attention. A mop of damp blue hair appeared in the whirlpool like a wet cotton-candy lily pad.

"Marlo!" Milton yelped as he dove into the pool, forcing his oddly rigid hands to paddle until he reached his sister. Marlo was bobbing in the water like a remote Goth island. Milton grabbed her by the wrist and towed her to shore.

Marlo's eyes fluttered. Milton pumped the center of his sister's chest until a torrent of rainbow jelly gushed out of her mouth. He tilted Marlo's head back, lifted her chin, and—after pinching her nose—fought against crashing waves of revulsion to administer mouth-to-mouth to his—*please don't hurl*—sister.

Suddenly, Marlo's hand reached for Milton's throat.

"Not gonna happen," Marlo gurgled as more multicolored marmalade trickled down her chin. "This isn't how my first kiss goes down. . . ." She bolted upright, regaining sudden consciousness.

"Or is it my *second* kiss?" Marlo murmured vaguely. *"Très fou."* She let go of Milton's throat. "Were we able to do it?" The twinkling pool flashed in her violently violet eyes.

"I . . . don't know what you mean . . . but, then again, I kind of do," Milton coughed.

"That's really helpful; then again, it totally isn't," Marlo said with a derisive snort.

Milton noticed some weird-looking white worms swimming to shore. He rubbed his still-stiff hands.

"When I came out of the pool, my hands were sort of twisted," Milton said uncertainly, "like sign language."

"What did your hands say . . . and don't say 'hands don't talk' or I'll punch you," Marlo said.

"I was making the signs for 'eat' and 'worm,'" he said as they both watched the slimy corkscrew-shaped worms wriggle across the shore, etching spiraling grooves into the volcanic rock.

"Um . . . *right* . . . nice try," Marlo replied with a smirk. "I give that an eight-point-five, but your dismount was a little off. . . ."

"No, seriously," Milton said. "It felt like I was trying to tell myself something with my hands, because I knew I wouldn't remember it."

A warm, humid wind tinged with electricity—like a dragon burping after eating a power station—ruffled Marlo's blue hair. She rose to her feet and straightened the drab floral-print dress she'd been given back in Snivel.

"Okay, but we do it at the same time," Marlo said.

Milton walked over to the pool's edge, knelt down, and—with a grimace of disgust—grabbed two of the wriggling worms. He handed one to Marlo.

"All right, on the count of three," Marlo said, tilting back her head and holding the nearly foot-long worm over her mouth. "One . . . two . . . ick . . . *three!*"

They choked down the worms, being careful to avoid contact with both tongue and teeth.

Marlo scowled. "I think it's trying to crawl back up." She coughed. "It's not bad, though. Sort of rich and spicy . . ."

"Yeah, it tastes kind of like thyme," Milton said before his mind suddenly caught fire. Searing agony clutched his skull as if it were seized in the barbed talons of a flaming hawk. He dropped to his knees and screamed, his shrieks slashing alongside those of his sister's, like two knives sharpening one another.

The grotto quaked and shimmered around them. Memories filled his feverish brain like microwaved popcorn until he just couldn't contain them anymore. The memories of every life lived in this particular Time Pool. Milton cradled his head in his hands. He feared his brain would break suddenly, wrenched open by the pressure, with all of these memories spilling out and washing away who he really was. Decades . . . years . . . months . . . weeks . . . days . . . hours . . . minutes . . . seconds . . . stretching so far and tight that they couldn't possibly stretch any further without snapping.

"Oww!" Milton yelped, wincing.

Suddenly, with a swift twinge of excruciating pain, the memories were gone, leaving Milton only with his last trip down into the Time Pools—to Precocia, drugged and hooked to the Kronosgraph machine, thrust into the alternate French-Egyptian Earth, the showdown in Childhood; then he was leaping down into some deeper Nether-Pool and finally emerging back here again in this grotto, where it all began. The volcanic rock walls of the subterranean chamber quivered and shimmered, as if they had just been replaced by exact replicas.

"I was a prom queen . . . I was a jock . . . I was a brainiac . . . ," Marlo murmured as she sat down across from Milton. "You were a thug . . . you were a freak. . . ."

"Sounds like we were *The Breakfast Club*," Milton replied.

Flashing lights zigzagged across Milton's vision, gradually disappearing to nothing.

"The worms must be born big somehow and spend their lives swimming in the Time Pools," Milton said. "They grow smaller and smaller and then, instinctively, scratch the time currents into the rock. It's like how salmon can swim upstream for hundreds of miles and find the exact point where they were born . . . a way of keeping track of their migrations."

Marlo tried to rub away the pins-and-needles sensation on her scalp. "And we just ate up its memory," she said, the weird lemon-pepper-thyme taste still in her mouth. "*Real* brain food. But our brains couldn't take it. It was like the top of my head blew off . . . it even looked like everything around me got all shimmery."

Milton rode out the squirmy feeling in his belly. "Yeah, me too . . . Maybe we're like cups that can only contain so much liquid," he speculated, pushing his broken glasses up his nose. "Perhaps our brains are designed to accommodate only one lifetime. *Our* lifetime. Anything more and it spills out over the brim."

"Well, my head feels like a piñata on the day after Cinco de Mayo."

"That would be *Seis* de Mayo. . . ."

Milton and Marlo sighed, feeling old beyond their years. Sure, they were back in the grotto where they began, but why? They could remember their last dip in the Time Pools, but how would that help prevent Napoléon and Cleopatra from conquering time, from finding them and extracting the information they needed to plug the Fountain of Youth and poison untold Time Pools with their unquenchable thirst for power?

Suddenly, Milton's kerchief pouch wriggled.

"Lucky?" Milton gasped as he untied the kerchief with his clumsy hands.

Out popped Lucky's fuzzy white head. He sniffed at Milton, then lunged at him, but instead of going for his throat, Lucky nipped lovingly at his master. He curled up in Milton's lap, rolling over to make his belly available for scritches.

"Lucky is how he was," Milton said through his almost painfully wide grin. "Before Dr. Skinner turned him against me . . ."

"Or maybe the shock of almost drowning washed the brainwash out of his brain," Marlo said as she crawled to Lucky to give him a pat. Milton noticed that they weren't wearing their Power Suits. He was in his bloodied Arcadia uniform, while his sister was in her dreary Snivel dress.

Something has changed, Milton thought. *And maybe when something changes, you create something new . . . a* surprise.

Suddenly, the quiet was shattered by a wince-inducing scrape followed by a monstrous splash. A beam of light, like an incandescent torpedo, sped toward the shore. A barbed tentacle thrust through the surface of the pool and thrashed in the air as if it were preparing to give Milton and Marlo a fatal high five to the head.

Marlo shot to her feet while Milton tucked Lucky back into his kerchief pouch and cinched it to his belt.

"We actually swallowed its *parents*," Milton said. "No wonder it's mad."

They jogged away from the Time Pool, looking for the crack in the limestone ceiling where they had escaped once . . . *twice* . . . who knows how many times before.

A purple-orange light drizzled down from above. Marlo hoisted herself up through the large, jagged crack in the rock ceiling as the grotto echoed with monstrous yowls, scrapes, and splashes.

"Sounds like Satan's Halloween mix CD," Marlo grunted as she wedged herself into the cleft of stone. Milton, though exhausted, managed to summon the strength to lift himself up and into the fissure. After scaling the smooth limestone walls foot by excruciating foot, Marlo flung herself out of the long cleft in the rock and reached down to grab Milton's wrist, hoisting him up to the floor of a shallow cave.

"The sky is weird," Marlo said as she walked to the mouth of the small rock hollow, her deep violet eyes gazing upward. "It's not like it was."

Milton joined her. There was no thick brown smog above, only a soft orange haze.

"There's no excavation site either," Milton said as he surveyed the barren landscape of volcanic rock and sparkling black dust. "Something is different. It's not like it was before we came to Precocia *or* when we left."

"Maybe they just cleaned up the site and moved on," Marlo said. "The smog could have drifted away, too. When Childhood collapsed, it could have messed up Precocia somehow."

"Whatever happened, maybe we have a chance for a redo."

Milton's stomach suddenly dropped as if he had missed a step on a staircase. Poking out from behind a large, gnarled lump of volcanic rock was a gleaming black stagecoach. Time seemed strangely thick, as if it were waiting for the Fausters to make a crucial move. Milton could hear his sister swallow beside him.

"There you are!" a festering demon shrieked from several yards away, its skin peeling off its raw red body.

A rope net spilled over Milton and Marlo before they could make a break for it. They fell to the ground in a tangle of shock and fear.

"I don't know how they got out, but we got them now!" the demon's feather-fringed partner said as they tugged the Fausters across the dirt. Two black Night Mares pawed the ground as the demons heaved Milton and Marlo into the stagecoach, slamming the door and latching it closed.

"I guess this is it," Milton said. "When Napoléon and Cleopatra said we were captured, they must have meant *right now*."

Hoofbeats filled the air like a swelling drum roll. The stagecoach lurched around a rocky crag.

Marlo leaned forward toward the two scaly, decomposing demons. "Hey, we'll tell you about this cool, secret place we found if you don't take us back to Precocia," she whispered.

The blue-feathered demon scratched his sparsely plumed head. *"Precocia?"* the creature clucked. "What the heck is a Precocia?"

"It's a . . . ," Milton replied before stopping short. "It's nothing," he continued cautiously. "So where are we headed, then?"

"Wise Acres, of course!" the red demon hissed.

"Wise Acres?" Milton replied. "What's that?"

"The circle of Heck for mouthy, impertinent little twerps like yourself!"

Marlo furrowed her brows.

"Don't you mean Lipptor?"

"Lipptor?" The scabby bluebird demon grimaced. "What is that? A circle for children with unfortunate mouth piercings?"

Marlo leaned back in her seat, shaking her head.

"Well, I'll be darned," she muttered. "More than I already am, that is . . ."

"And none of your sass!" the red, raw demon barked as it shoved a pair of old socks into Milton's and Marlo's mouths, then sealed them in place with two strips of duct tape. "You'll have plenty of time for that later on."

Milton and Marlo traded shocked glances as the stagecoach teetered along the bleak landscape.

Something has shifted, Milton thought. He had somehow made a ripple in the afterlife, back in the Provincial Court of Res Judicata, and it sloshed over that timeline to create a whole new one. *This* one. When Algernon Cole had mentioned that Precocia shouldn't be, Milton and Marlo had taken that notion and brought it back *here,* and it was strong enough to alter the illogical logic of Heck. Strong enough to erase an entire circle, with a little something left over to change the name of another.

Milton and Marlo had actually done it: they had stopped Napoléon and Cleopatra from strangling childhood and enslaving the world by preventing them from finding the Time Pools in the first place. Milton's brief feeling of elation was, however, snuffed out by a horrible, smothering feeling of responsibility.

As Algernon Cole said, Heck was held together with rules. And by breaking or questioning those rules, Milton had made things start to unravel. Now the only thing left of Precocia—and everything that had happened to Milton and Marlo—was a memory.

Maybe that's what growing up is all about, Milton thought. *It's not about being bigger or better or busier, but about having the courage to bear all of those memories, both the bad ones that never really scab over, and even the good ones of moments that slipped away. More than just growing up, but also growing* down: *into who you really are and what you're truly capable of . . .*

While Milton's mind grappled with the intricacies of growing up, his fingers twitched like restless toddlers. They craved nervous action, some playful release, like the strangely satisfying act of kneading a roll of bubble wrap. *Bubble wrap . . .* a boring adult invention made totally fun through a kid's ingeniously immature perspective.

As the roar of wheels rolling across gravel slowly evolved to the sound of crinkling paper, the only thing clear to Milton now was that grown-ups had made a nightmare of things—both in the real world and in the afterlife—and had clear-cut wonder like a grove of young trees felled by chainsaws.

Milton stared out the window through the smears of snot and dust clouding the glass.

Maybe it's up to a kid to make things right. And who knows? Perhaps Marlo and I are just the kids to twist this twisted wad of bubble wrap and make the whole place "pop."

BACKWORD

Humanity is just like any human, only much more so. It crawled out of the Cradle of Civilization, then— stooped, drooling, and grunting—began to finger-paint on the walls of caves (sort of the prehistoric family refrigerator); got busy with its LEGOs in the Bronze and Iron ages; locked itself in its room for a preteen sulk during the Dark Ages; had a Middle Ages crisis before getting its groove back in the Renaissance; grew curiouser and curiouser in the Age of Discovery; ignored Mother Earth's plea to "Go play outside! It's lovely!" in the Industrial Age; gained knowledge in the twentieth century, before running out of ideas altogether in the early twenty-first century: the age of mere fine-tuning, making gadgets finger-foilingly small, or simply adding a lower-case "i" in front of everything. . . .

And if humanity has any interest in remaining

human, then it is high time for a little time off. All work and no play makes Jack a dull proverb. We need time to play in the sandbox (not the cat box, mind you: that's where pinworms play) to reconnect with what it really means to be human. Progress is all fine and good, yet now that the world has officially been declared round, all of this flying forward will one day have us catching up with ourselves, risking one doozy of a rear-end collision.

Childhood helps put the vivid "hue" in human . . . the "kind" in humankind. Childhood is a time before toy soldiers become real soldiers and broken dollies suffer from crippling esteem issues. It's a no-backs-touching-black safety zone that allows imagination to blossom, endowing humanity with the rare ability to creatively problem-solve. Without this ability, life is like fishing for eighty-something years only to find out that it wasn't fish you were really after, after all.

Speaking of after, even in the afterlife there are those who feel far too grown up to leave things to the greasy kids' stuff of chance and faith. These addled post-adults are under the delusion that existence is about power. About control. About maturity at any price.

But in the rarefied realms of eternity, everything is about to be turned on its otherworldy head. And it's not about power. It's not about control.

It's about time.

And humanity may well be caught between the cradle and a grave situation indeed. . . .

ACKNOWLEDGMENTS

THE BOOK THAT you are either squinting at and sort of reading-ish on your e-reader/phone/music player/digital overlord while doing thirteen other things at once or are thoroughly engaged with because you're actually holding it in your hands, inhaling its sweet pulpy scent, the book itself the last dying wish of a tree, was made possible through the efforts of a great many talented professionals, as well as a couple of complete loons who are just sort of along for the ride.

Specifically, I'd like to thank the valiant booksellers of the world, those in the trenches or who wear trench coats or who are afflicted with trench mouth or—sadly—all three. Modern-day booksellers must sometimes feel like liquid-paper salesmen, peddling the outmoded while the world whizzes past them toward the next big thing invented solely to justify the loss of the *last* big thing. But they're much more than that.

If you were to blindfold a bookseller . . . well, they might get mad. But they could still help you find the perfect story to lose yourself in regardless. Booksellers are living, breathing search engines that exude infectious enthusiasm for the written word. And no matter how books evolve, there will always be stories and—luckily—their obliging champions, taking us by the hand so that we may find our tale.

ABOUT THE AUTHOR

DALE E. BASYE is an author inhabiting the deep waters off the coasts of Australia and Tasmania. His flesh is a gelatinous mass, and he is rarely seen by humans. Oh, wait—that's the Tasmanian blobfish.

Here's what the *real* Dale E. Basye has to say about his sixth book: "There is a precarious stage of life when everything becomes a hectic blur. You're so busy with classes, recitals, sports, and studying that—before you know it—sand castles become skyscrapers. Chasing butterflies becomes chasing deadlines. And playing hide-and-seek becomes working nine-to-five. Heck is like that. And no matter what anyone tells you, Heck is real. This story is real. Or as real as anything like this can be."

Dale E. Basye lives in Portland, Oregon, where he dances like no one is watching—which is too bad, as he is on the bus, and everyone is watching yet trying not to.

DON'T MISS THE NEXT BOOK ABOUT MILTON AND MARLO'S ADVENTURES IN HECK!

AVAILABLE NOW!

1 · TO GRAMMAR'S HOUSE WE GO

ELEVEN-YEAR-OLD MILTON FAUSTER and his thirteen-year-old sister, Marlo, were not so different from your average children making a grudging trek to their first day at a new school. Only instead of having been dropped off by distracted parents on their way to work, Milton and Marlo had been dragged kicking and screaming out of a stagecoach by decomposing demons and thrown roughly to the unhallowed ground. Instead of carrying backpacks stuffed with new notebooks and sharpened pencils, Milton cradled his pet ferret, Lucky, in a filthy kerchief while Marlo sulked along holding nothing but a grudge against the snarled web of supremely sucky events that conspired against her. And instead of making their way to a new school wearing the latest fall fashions, Milton and Marlo were headed for Wise Acres—the circle of Heck for kids who sass back—dressed in shabby hand-me-downs splotched with dried blood.

Oh, and there was the whole "being stone-cold dead way before your time" thing, too.

The sleek black stagecoach, drawn by two hideous, snorting Night Mares, sped away behind the Fauster children in a tight crescent, its wooden wheels slicing across the rumpled, reddish-brown hills. The freakish whinnies of the festering horses faded away into nothing.

The only sound Milton and Marlo made as they trudged along was the crinkle of footfalls. The rolling hills seemed to be coated with a vast carpet of paper so ancient that it shredded beneath the Fausters' filthy boots. It was as if their shoes were having a secret conversation composed of dry crumples and scrunches.

A wind picked up, whipping itself into a squall. Milton coughed at the wind's gagging, sickly sweet stench. His face and arms were speckled with dark, pricking droplets of what looked like ink. Milton glanced over at his sister. Marlo was slogging through the shredded paper just behind him, her head hung low and brooding.

Marlo sighed softly to herself and rubbed her violet, red-rimmed eyes, wiping away a tear that left a smear of black ink-rain on her cheek. Being dead was starting to get her down. Even her first kiss had been tainted by the fact that the boy on the other side of those perfect, pouty lips had been a fallen hit-angel who was simply using her to find Milton and slit his throat with a gleaming razor-feather.

"Oww!" Milton cried out, touching his now-bleeding

cheek. He pulled out what looked like a big splinter. A few hundred feet away was a gnarled grove of nasty-looking trees. Angry blasts of wind sheared swarms of needles from the trees and sent them whizzing into the air like clouds of tiny wooden daggers.

"Seriously, li'l *bother*," Marlo said with a croak, her voice craggy from lack of use, "how much can a splinter possibly— *Oww!*"

Marlo yanked a small needle, sort of like a pine needle, from her forearm. After examining it, though, she discovered it was really a tiny, tightly rolled parchment. Marlo unrolled it and squinted at the itsy-bitsy letters formed in the pulpy, leaflike paper:

What are yew looking at?!

Milton glanced over Marlo's shoulder at the note, then surveyed the grove of sinister trees up ahead. The trees sported ropes of mottled, flaking bark coiling up their trunks.

"They spelled 'you' wrong," Marlo said.

"No, they didn't . . . or *it* didn't," Milton said, pointing to a nearby tree. "It's like a weird hybrid of a sycamore and a yew tree."

"A *Syca-Yew*, of course," Marlo said as she crumpled up the parchment and tossed it at the tree. "Well, I'm sick of you, *too*, you dumb tree!"